JUDAS CHILD

JUDAS CHILD

Carol O'Connell

HUTCHINSON
LONDON

This edition first published in 1999 by Hutchinson

Random House (UK) Limited
20 Vauxhall Bridge Road, London SW1V 2SA

Random House Australia (Pty) Limited
20 Alfred Street, Milsons Point, Sydney,
New South Wales 2061, Australia

Random House New Zealand Limited
18 Poland Road, Glenfield, Auckland 10, New Zealand

Random House South Africa (Pty) Limited
Endulini, 5A Jubilee Road, Parktown 2193, South Africa

A CIP record for this book is available from the British Library

Papers used by Random House UK Limited are natural,
recyclable products made from wood grown in sustainable forests.
The manufacturing processes conform to the environmental
regulations of the country of origin.

ISBN 0 09 180194 X

Phototypeset in Galliard by Intype London Ltd

Printed and bound in Great Britain
by Mackays of Chatham PLC

This book is dedicated to the memory of Michael Abney, a talented Arizona photographer and a good friend from my student days. Over many a beer, I gave him useful insights on women. However, Mike's reciprocal information about men turned out to be pure gender bragging, for the true prince was not a common occurrence in nature, but a rare one – and I miss him.

PROLOGUE

Up and down the lane ran two bright ribbons of grass, still green so deep in December. Long, flanking rows of pine trees ended where the modern public road met this private one of ancient cobblestones. Though there was no proper name on any map, the townspeople called it the Christmas tree lane.

Hidden beyond the west bank of evergreens lay all the brown dead leaves of a bare-branched forest. The dry carcass of an eyeless sparrow was crushed under the man's shoe as he shifted his weight from one foot to the other. The day had turned chilly and mean. Wisps of fog hung low where the denuded woodland was protected by the windbreak of tall pines. The highest boughs of a nearby oak disappeared in the haze, and the trees behind it were only ghosts of birch and elm.

The man glanced at his watch.

Any moment now.

His fingers splayed wide and then balled into fists. The surrounding air was dead still; the brittle leaves and low-lying clouds of the woods never stirred as a clean breeze whipped down the Christmas tree lane.

He took great pride in this art of selecting the time and the place. Soon, a solitary child would come riding by on her bicycle, as she did every Saturday afternoon at this same time. The little girl would be fearless, for the cobblestoned roadway of trimmed grass and majestic pine trees was so different from

1

the atmosphere of the forest, it might have been carved out of another world, a better one, where this man could not exist.

CHAPTER 1

She slowed the purple bicycle and turned around to look directly at him with the full force of big brown eyes and a wicked grin.

The boy's front wheel wobbled at the exact moment he braked to a dead stop. And then the child resigned himself to the short flight over the handlebars, all but shrugging in midair. The hard landing on the road was all the pain and punishment he had expected it to be.

Why did she do these things to him?

Though Sadie Green had never laid a hand on him outside of dancing class, one day at school she had caused him to step off a second-floor landing, to fall down the stairs and cut his head – but only because the sudden sight of her had blinded him to science – more precisely, the law of gravity. For one fraction of a second, he had believed he could step out into thin air and not pay for that.

Now David Shore sat cross-legged on the cold ground near his fallen bicycle. He pulled off a torn woolen glove to pick the gravel out of his hand. Sadie's bike was describing lazy circles in the road, and by her wide smile, he could tell she was enjoying this enormously. As he plucked out one sharp bit of stone, the indent of his skin filled with a red droplet. He looked up at her.

How much blood is enough, Sadie?

Even from the distance of several yards, he could see all two hundred of her freckles jump as she laughed at him. He could still hear her laughing – like the maniac she was – as she sped around the clot of shrubs, turning off the road and into the Christmas tree lane. He was on his bike again and in motion, when her laughter stopped abruptly, not trailing away with distance, but ending, as though she had been turned off.

For the first time, he stopped his bike at the foot of the lane. On every other Saturday, he had pedaled on by in the pretense that he had some business of his own farther along the public road. Now he stared down that long empty space between the two rows of evergreen trees.

Where was she? The lane was a straightaway to Gwen Hubble's house, and Sadie could not have covered all that ground so fast.

David stood with one foot planted on the road, rocking his bike from side to side. He didn't want to look into the woods beyond the pine trees, for fear of seeing her there, writhing on the ground and holding her bloody intestines in her hands.

She had done that to him before.

Sadie went to entirely too much trouble to frighten him. If she only knew how much fear she inspired whenever he thought about actually talking to her – as opposed to merely stalking her on Saturday afternoons.

He rode on down the lane, but stopped halfway to Gwen's house, a stately white Georgian mansion locked behind intimidating iron gates. The profile of a security guard and his newspaper was silhouetted in the window of the gatehouse. But the guard might as well be posted on the moon, for David rarely spoke to people – or girls. Anxiety and hysteria froze his vocal cords each time he tried.

The boy cocked his head toward the left bank of pine trees. He heard a faint and garbled slew of sounds coming from the woods on the other side. Of course it was Sadie – baiting him. If she were carrying a spare set of pig's intestines from the biology lab, she would not want to waste them.

Well, he would play the fool for her if that made her happy.

He got off his bike and wheeled it through the tight brace

of evergreens. One bough of prickly needles scratched his face in yet another blood sacrifice, and then he was standing in the woods, looking at the stark trees bereft of leaves, shrouded in mist and feathering out to hazy and indistinct forms in the distance.

Oh, this was Sadie country, prime for horror. She must be loving this, wherever she was hiding.

He stood very still, tensing every muscle in his body. At any moment, she would come flying around the trunk of an oak tree, perhaps with some new weapon, another trick to cleave his poor startled brain into equal parts of terror and delight.

Two small animals ran across his path. A gray cat crackled leaves and snapped dry twigs in pursuit of a squirrel. But this was not the noise he had heard from the lane. He listened for the sound of something female, ten years old and nearly human. He rolled his bike farther into the woods, and now he saw the small metallic swatch of purple.

Everything Sadie owned was purple, even her running shoes exactly matched her purple parka.

Her bike was partially covered by a gunnysack, dirt-encrusted and blending well with the dead leaves. She was probably in a hurry and making better time through the woods on foot. He could guess where she was heading, and that would explain why she had not gone all the way to Gwen's. If they were meeting at the old boathouse, then Sadie must be in fresh trouble. The girls had not gone there since the last time Gwen's father had forbidden them to play together.

Confident that Sadie was not planning an ambush, he relaxed and took his time walking his bike around the tree trunks and fallen branches. At the edge of the woods, his vista opened to the wide lawn of St Ursula's Academy. Grass rolled downhill to the lake, a calm mirror of the gray winter sky. The near shoreline was obscured by rock formations and foliage. He laid down his bicycle and drew closer to the boathouse. Now he could see part of the long wharf spanning the other side of the building and reaching far out on the lake. Its boards were worn smooth by the barefoot steps of generations of children.

St Ursula's Academy was very old, and over the past century, the students had marked every bit of it. The vast green lawn spreading upward from the lake was scarred with ancient rough trails where boys and girls had worn away the grass as they departed from the normal paths. And this departure was at the heart of the boarding school for not quite normal, and some said quite unnatural, children.

He drew back when he heard the sound of a door being pulled shut. Now a single loud bark came from inside the boathouse.

Had Gwen brought her dog along this time? She had never done that before.

David didn't take up his regular post beneath the window; that might set the dog to barking again. He walked back toward the woods and sat down on a patch of ground behind the cover of shrubs. Here he resolved to wait until Sadie came out, so he could follow her home.

The dog barked again and kept it up for a long time. Then it stopped suddenly, the same way that Sadie's laughter had ended in the lane – the dog had been switched off. Over the next hour, this was repeated three more times.

What were Gwen and Sadie doing to that animal?

Now there was another noise behind him. He shrank back behind the massive trunk of a centurion oak. A small blond girl was running through the woods. Gwen?

But how could that be?

Gwen Hubble puffed white clouds of breath, and her legs churned faster. The child–pink locomotive with the flapping red scarf and blue jeans ran a weaving path, skirting the trees. Her running shoes, laces undone, smashed brittle leaves to powder. Dry twigs snapped with sharp cracks in sync with her heartbeat.

The printed message on her pager had been an odd one. 'Urgent – boathouse – tell no one.' But that was Sadie's style, the cliffhanger.

Gwen broke through a tight line of speckled trees at the edge of the wood. Her flushed face was scratched, and her socks fell in loose woolen rolls around her ankles. Breath came with ragged tears at her throat, and the bones of her shins were going to splinters with every hard-pounding footfall. She rounded the side of the old boathouse, her thick blond braid thumping at the back of a red parka.

She stepped onto the wharf, and as she walked toward the boathouse door, her steps slowed. A rock lay on the boards amid the debris of splintered century-old wood, a rusted padlock and its crusty hasp. Well, perhaps the groundskeeper had changed the lock since Sadie mastered the combination.

Or maybe not.

The crude breakage would be an improvement on Sadie's usual method of operations. *Yes, that must be it.* And Gwen approved. Now this was really scary.

She pushed through the door and walked into the dark.

No candles?

She braced herself for the assault. Would Sadie be waiting behind the door?

No – not this time.

Gwen's eyes had adjusted to the light streaming in the door behind her. And now she made out the small body, the familiar head of light brown hair and the purple down jacket. Sadie was lying at the center of the floor. Gwen was disappointed. After the big production of the broken lock, she had expected something more imaginative. She knelt down beside her friend and shook her.

'Hey, I'm not buying it. Get up.'

The child lying on the floor made no response. Gwen looked up to see the lock on the boathouse phone box had also been broken.

'Sadie, it's not funny. Sadie?'

*

David stood up and stamped his feet. They had gone numb while he sat hunched and hidden in the bushes. Now his toes tingled as they came back to life. The air was growing colder. He pulled up the collar of his jacket against a sudden rush of wind off the lake.

Sadie should have come out long before now if she expected to get home by dark. He walked out onto open ground, emboldened by curiosity.

He hadn't heard the dog bark for a very long time. If Gwen had not brought her own dog, then where had the animal come from?

David moved closer to the boathouse, the better to eavesdrop. The window facing the shore was the source of all his Sadie trivia. He pressed one ear against the rough wood of the shutters, but there was no sound of barks, no giggles, nothing.

The grass and the trees were all melding into the same gray hue, and the sky was darkening. The boy walked around the side of the building and stepped onto the wharf. He popped off the balls of his feet and hung there in the air for a moment, hesitating. If they caught him spying on them, what story could he give?

Oh, sure. Like he could actually get the words out. Well, he didn't need a story. He had the strongest right to be here as a boarder at the school. The girls were only day students, townies.

David guessed it was close to dinnertime, and soon his housemother would be standing in the door of the cottage, calling out his name the way the real mothers did in the neighborhoods of Makers Village. But he couldn't leave yet. He had to know what was going on in there, though he strongly suspected it was another one of Sadie's traps set to scare him to death. He spotted the padlock and hasp on the wharf beside the door.

That was odd.

Sadie's plotting had never been so elaborate. She always went for the swift shock. A slow build to terror, and now this violence upon private property – well, this was entirely too subtle.

He pushed the door open and went inside. Though the interior was black, but for a few feet of bad light from the open doorway, he knew immediately that the boathouse was empty. But the girls could not have gotten past him. No way.

David walked deeper into the darkness, memory leading him safely around the tarpaulined canoes, a sailboat and stacks of boxes. His two classmates were only impressions on the air. He sniffed the musty space to separate the smell of the lake water from the smell of dog hair and traces of girl in the faint residue of spearmint gum and talcum powder.

The boy's head snapped to one side.

What was that?

A queer, rude finger of ice stroked his spine. There it was again – a furtive shadow within shadows and the quick scratching of small feet. On some level, he knew it was a rat, but he would not believe in it. Although he owed his scholarship to a festering rat bite as much as to his IQ score, his brain was blind to vermin. They could not follow him here. They were all back there in the foster home. He had seen that place for the last time when a social worker had carted him off to the hospital. There were no more rats in the world. He would not believe in them.

The wind banged the door shut behind him, and his world went black. David stopped breathing for all the time it took to cross the wide room, to bang his legs against a wooden box and find the knob for the door. And then the boy was swinging into the air, holding onto the door handle and dangling over freezing water. He had opened the wrong door, and his long legs had overstepped the shallow stairs leading down to the sheltered boat slip. The wider door beyond this one was standing open to the remains of daylight.

David used his body, swinging his weight to bring the door close to its wood frame again. His feet, pedaling in midair, found purchase on the ladder, and he climbed back into the

9

boathouse. With the dim light from the slip, he found the right door and stepped onto the solid planks of the wharf. He walked to the end of the building and stared at the lakeside doors. This was the only other exit – by water.

That must be how they had gotten past him, paddling behind the rocks and foliage along the shore. He could count the canoes to see if one was missing. But no – he was not going back in there, not for anything.

He walked out to the far end of the long wharf where it hung on stilts over the water. The lake had become a choppy agitation of white caps; wind-driven waves licked and slapped the pilings. There was no boat in sight along the shoreline. David turned back toward the massive red-brick building at the top of the hill, looming there like a great authoritarian parent, five stories tall counting the two narrow rows of dormer windows set in black shingles. His own cottage was left of the main building and farther back in the woods. He longed to go there; he was aching from the cold and very hungry.

The girls were probably home by now. It was almost dinnertime. But still he hated to leave this riddle undone. He headed back through the woods to look for Sadie's bike. She would not have left it behind.

He found the gunnysack, but the bike was gone. So they had at least not drowned in the lake.

Of course not, idiot.

They were probably at Gwen's house having a hot dinner.

Passing through the wall of pine trees, he entered the Christmas tree lane near the public road. Sadie's purple bike was parked by the bus stop, propped up against a signpost, and this made no sense at all – nothing did. First a canoe and now a bus? Why would they take the bus so close to dinnertime? What new game was this?

David looked toward Gwen Hubble's home at the top of the long cobblestone driveway. The lights were going on, one by one, as though someone were racing from room to room in a great panic, in absolute terror of the dark, turning on all the lamps in the house.

The purple bicycle lay in the middle of Miss Fowler's broken picket fence. She stood on the front lawn, shivering in a coat she had pulled over her nightgown at the obscene hour of two o'clock in the morning. She frowned at the damaged fence slats while three men screamed in a hellish concert. The uniformed policeman was loudest, almost hysterically childlike when he reached a high C on the musical scale. And now the other two men had ceased to shout foul words at one another. They stared at him with something close to awe, and so did Miss Fowler. This young policeman might be one of very few Americans who could sing the more difficult notes in the national anthem.

The officer was holding each man by one arm, keeping them apart. He was calmer now, saying, 'I want you guys to cool off, or I'm gonna start writing tickets.'

'Tickets?' Miss Fowler's voice had the effect of a gunshot. Three heads turned in unison to face the imperious seventy-two-year-old woman, five-ten in her fluffy pink slippers. Not for nothing had she spent the last forty years terrorizing the young.

'I don't have any use for tickets, Officer. I want them arrested.' She looked from one culprit to the other. 'Unless one of you pays for the damage to my fence – and right this minute. Do I make myself clear?' She turned to the young patrolman who had surely begun to shave only last week, and then only nicking a few whiskers his first time out with a razor.

'It was his fault!' yelled the smaller of the young policeman's captives, pointing one bony finger at the larger man, who squirmed out of the policeman's grasp and ran down the sidewalk. The officer sprinted after the escapee and tackled him. Miss Fowler grasped the smaller man firmly by the arm, lest he also tried to escape. And now she caught sight of a familiar car rolling slowly past them. One fogged window was half open, the better to see what was going on.

It was Rouge Kendall, and he was out of uniform. No doubt he had just come out of Dame's Tavern at the end of the street. He was probably planning to drive right by, to roll on home and into a nice warm bed and a long sweet sleep.

Well, she would fix that.

She called out to him, 'Rouge, you *better* stop!' Her tone of voice implied that she could still make his life a living hell of extended piano practice, though he had not been her student since he was nine years old.

He did bring the car to a guilty stop. Old habits died hard; he had always been a polite child, respectful to his elders. The car glided to the curb as the other policeman was marching his prisoner back to the broken fence. The uniformed officer turned to Rouge and waved him off. 'I can handle it.'

Miss Fowler thought not. She turned a stony eye on Rouge. He grinned at her and shrugged. Behind a long fringe of auburn hair, his slow-roving hazel eyes took in the damage to her fence. He might be over six feet tall, but otherwise Rouge had not changed so much since the days when he had been her worst student. The general features of the boy hung on in the man – but for the eyes. She thought his eyes were too old for a youngster of twenty-five, almost a breach of natural law.

Well, all of St Ursula's students had been a bit odd in one way or another.

While the other policeman was flipping through the pages of his notebook, Rouge's gaze was fixed on the purple bicycle. 'Which one of them was riding it, Phil?'

'Butt out,' said the officer in uniform, puffing up his chest like a blowfish imitating a larger fish. He spoke to the two men. 'I'm going to issue tickets for disturbing the—'

Tickets again?

'It was that one,' said Miss Fowler, pointing at the larger of the two men. 'I saw him fall off the bicycle.'

She had seen his type before, a shabby dresser, an unshaven, wandering man. And by the smell of him, she knew the derelict was in dire need of a change of underwear. So she was hoping to pin fault on the smaller man, who seemed a more solvent prospect to pay for the broken fence.

Rouge turned to the man in uniform. 'It's a girl's bike, Phil. Top-of-the-line racer – maybe three, four hundred dollars.' And now he turned back to the unshaven man with the secondhand clothes and the bad smell. 'So what's wrong with this picture?'

Phil turned on the man squirming under his grip. 'You *stole* that bike,' he said as though this were his own sudden flash of insight.

The derelict broke loose again and would have run, but Rouge extended one long, lazy leg to trip the man and bring him down.

The uniformed officer sat down on top of the thief and handcuffed him. 'Rouge, I can handle this myself.'

Rouge was amiable, despite the rebuff. 'The bike won't fit in your trunk, not unless you throw out all the roadblock gear.'

'What?' said the officer.

Miss Fowler looked at the back end of the patrol car. The trunk latch was tied down with wire, and through the partial opening, she could see the blue wood of a barricade and the tips of orange cones used to divert traffic from an accident scene.

'Phil, you can have all the credit for the great bike caper, okay? But now you've got two disorderly drunks and a bike to transport. And your witness, Miss Fowler? She doesn't drive.'

Phil was staring at his patrol car and working on the logistics of who would fit where. He nodded in defeat.

Five minutes later, Rouge pulled his car away from the curb. The purple bike was in his back seat, and Miss Fowler sat beside him. She thought he took her criticism quite well, responding with a 'Yes, ma'am' at every suggestion for turn signals. She graced him with a rare smile. Rouge was a strange one, and she believed he spent entirely too much time in Dame's Tavern, but he was fundamentally a good boy.

Rouge's car turned left into the station house driveway, following the only patrol car in Makers Village. Once, the town had sported two cruisers, but the second one had disappeared into Green's Auto Shop last summer and was never seen again. Some had believed the vehicle might be saved; others said no. The mayor had finally settled this debate, claiming the patrol car had gone to heaven to live with Jesus. Miss Fowler suspected that the mayor also drank.

When they pulled into the police station parking lot, which was actually the library parking lot, it was hard to miss the bright lights of the camera crews and all the vans with major news-show logos printed on their sides. As she stepped out of the car, she also noted four New York State Police vehicles, one long black limousine and two riderless motorcycles.

Miss Fowler was first to reach the top of the stairs. She held the door open for Rouge as he carried the bicycle into the station house. The reception area was not much bigger than her own front parlor and crowded with so many people, it was certainly in violation of the fire codes. Before the door had swung shut behind them, a woman's voice yelled out, 'The bike!'

A portly figure in a shapeless blue dress was walking toward them, a woman of average height and average features, even to the limp mouse-brown hair. She yelled again, 'That's my daughter's bike!' A photographer blinded Rouge with flashes, and another man with a microphone was bearing down on him.

What a lot of fuss over a stolen bicycle.

Or maybe there was more to this, for the yelling woman had clearly been crying, and now she was caressing her child's purple bicycle. Well, this person was obviously a professional mother. Miss Fowler knew the breed: the soft plump arms and ample bosom could comfort three children at once on a bad

14

day, and the thick waist spoke well for her cooking. The woman's face was full of mother terror, and there was a siren in her voice, teetering on the screaming pitch of a three-alarm fire.

Miss Fowler was nodding in general approval of traditional motherhood when another woman stepped forward. This one was slender and smartly tailored, with suspicious highlights in her upswept ash-blond hair. No yelling from this one – only cool composure and élan.

And doesn't she seem familiar?

This blonde had the classic good looks of a television personality, but when she spoke, her voice was laced with acid. 'Well, at least someone on the force is awake and earning his salary.' The blond woman turned on the prisoners, looking from one to the other, as though deciding which man she would have boiled alive for her late supper.

Miss Fowler made a moue of distaste as she recalled this woman's face from a recent photograph in the Sunday newspaper. The blonde was Marsha Hubble, estranged wife of the reclusive Peter Hubble, whose family had lived in the same house since 1875. Oh, and she was also the lieutenant governor of New York State.

And now Miss Fowler realized she had overestimated the lady politician's composure, for Mrs Hubble's eyes were struck with fear. On the inside, this woman was screaming – silently, madly.

Another mother.

CHAPTER 2

In the late afternoon, Rouge Kendall had ended his longest tour of duty, and now he sat on a barstool in Dame's Tavern. His eyes were red and sore; he had not seen his bed since yesterday morning. Finding that purple bicycle had changed his plans to sleep off last night's liquor.

A television set was mounted high on the wall behind the bar, and photographs of the missing children appeared on the screen in a pastiche of home videos and still shots. Mercifully, the bartender had turned off the volume. The silent pictures changed to coverage on the young boy who had spotted Sadie Green's abandoned bicycle at a bus stop. Young David Shore had neatly backed up the bike thief's story. The camera framed the thief with a jacket pulled up over his head to hide his face from the press as he was led away by state troopers.

In the next shot, a camera zoomed in on ten-year-old David exiting the building with his guardian, Mrs Hofstra, a willowy woman with iron-gray hair. The boy was tall for his age, handsome and graceful. There was much about him to inspire self-confidence, yet throughout the police interview, shy David had never said one word which was not whispered into Mrs Hofstra's ear and relayed by her larger voice.

Now the television screen showed Rouge an event he had not witnessed from his post inside the building. The reporters were converging on the boy, their winter coats flapping in the wind like the wings of crows as they screamed out their questions and thrust microphones in the child's face. David's blue eyes rounded out with extreme fear as both hands rose high to fend off the assault. His guardian put one protective arm around the ten-year-old and guided him into the waiting car. Rouge couldn't tell what Mrs Hofstra was saying to the reporters, but he hoped it was obscene.

A camera panned back to the door of the police station. Lieutenant Governor Marsha Hubble was standing at the top of the steps, an imperious blonde in a black leather trench coat. She was not as pretty as her daughter Gwen, but she did hold a man's attention. She was flanked by the two male FBI agents who had questioned David at the station. These men might be taller than Marsha Hubble, but there was no mistaking where the power lay in this trio. The lieutenant governor was raising one fist in the air, and Rouge could guess what that was about. The bicycle at the bus stop supported the theory of runaways. But the lady politician preferred her own game plan of wall-to-wall federal agents, troopers, roadblocks and a tristate manhunt for a kidnapper. Her face was an angry hot flush.

Gwen's mother was a strong woman, pushy as hell, and Rouge admired that. This politician would do anything to get her child back, and she didn't care if the voters took her for a world-class bitch.

Rouge lifted his glass to the screen. *Go, Marsha, go.*

The images changed, and Sadie's mother, Becca Green, was eliciting more sympathy with her simple cloth coat and her plain broad face. The camera cut to a shot of this crying woman, clutching a microphone and imploring everyone to help find her little girl.

It was just as well the television's volume had been turned off. Rouge didn't need to hear those words ever again. His own mother had said them all, fifteen years ago, in a futile public begging for his sister's life.

The moment he thought of Susan, something moved in the mirror on the other side of the mahogany bar. He caught

17

sight of his dead twin's hazel eyes peeking out from behind a line of bottles.

Fool. Of course they were his own eyes and not Susan's – only a reflection, nothing more. Yet he moved to a stool farther down the bar and away from the mirror. Now, between Rouge and the back wall of dark wood, a large pyramid of stacked wineglasses replicated his pale face in a honeycomb of small distorted images; his short hair elongated around the curving bulb of every glass. And so, twenty little girls with shoulder-length auburn tresses moved their faces in tandem with Rouge as he swiveled his stool around to scan the room.

Most of the tables were empty. Two women sat near the front window. One was a blonde, and the other was blonder. They both played catch-eyes with him, looking up and then dropping veils of thick mascara.

Another woman interested him more, but this one had no face yet. As she moved across the floor, her slender hips rolled to a soft rock tune from the jukebox. Sleek chestnut hair hung down to her shoulders, making a straight line across the back of a creamy silk blouse. Her long black skirt ended a few inches above a pair of high heels.

All the heads of the Susans in the wineglasses were nodding in appreciation. Rouge loved high heels.

The woman sat down at a nearby table and showed him the curve of her left cheek, but no more. The slit of her skirt fell open to expose a long leg, a knee and a bit of thigh.

Thank you, God.

And she was wearing her own skin – no tinted stretch of nylon between his eyes and the white flesh – an ocular feast in winter. One high heel dangled at the end of her foot. The shoe fell to the floor, exposing unpolished, naked toes.

Well, that's it.

He planned to give himself up without the customary token resistance. She could come and get him anytime she liked.

The woman turned around to stare at him, and he couldn't

look away. Only two things could fascinate so; extreme beauty was one. But he was looking at the most grotesque face he had ever seen a woman wear in public. A jagged line ran down her right cheek in an angry red scar, twisting her lips up on one side and forcing her to smile with half her mouth.

As she took in his reaction, the other side of her mouth also tilted up. Her pale-gray eyes were unnaturally far apart, and the eyebrows were thick and dark, nearly meeting above a small, straight nose, her only perfect feature.

She rose gracefully and walked to the bar. 'Hello, Vanity,' she said, sliding onto the stool next to his.

'Pardon?'

'Well, you *are* vain, aren't you?' She leaned toward him. 'You're a beautiful man, and you know it.'

He liked the soft voice, but her eyes unnerved him. A neat trick of eye shadow made them seem even farther apart, set off to each side of her head, with a bird's peripheral vision to encompass the whole room. Yet now she was focussed on him; it was hypnotic and disorienting.

When she spoke, the scar elongated and contracted. She leaned closer, forcing him to look only at her eyes, and he found some humor there.

'It must be comforting', she said, 'to be in love with yourself. No fear of rejection – ever. You might be a coward. Who would know?' She sat well back on her stool, and now her lips were pulled up on only one side.

At first, he didn't know which end of her mouth to believe, and then he decided she must be laughing at him. 'Can I buy you a drink?'

She only nodded, and that was just a formality. He knew she had been expecting this as her due. He gathered that the scar had not interfered with the basic relationship of man to woman – the man still had to pay.

'I'll have what you're having.' She passed his glass under her nose, testing the bouquet. 'Cheap scotch and tap water.'

Well, she was getting more interesting by the minute. He

19

put up one hand to the bartender, pointed to his own drink and then to the woman beside him. While they waited for her glass to arrive, he never even tried to avoid looking at her scar. She seemed not to mind this, only smiling, indulging him, as if she were allowing a free peep show of her nude body.

The woman had clearly mastered the art of makeup. Above the high collar of her blouse, the skin was colored with glowing good health from bottles of flesh and tubes of roses. But she had done nothing to minimize the mutilation of her face – quite the opposite; she wore fire-engine-red lipstick on her twisted mouth. When he understood this as defiance, he liked her better.

He was staring at the scar when he asked, 'How did you get that?'

Her eyebrows arched and a small, delicate laugh came out in a surprised puff of air. Now she was as patronizing as any woman confronted by a small child, a dog, or a man. 'That nasty wound on your ring finger? You got that when you were nine years old.' She lightly touched the back of his hand. 'You had an accident during a skating party for the children's choir. But I'll never tell anyone. The history belongs to you.'

His own scar was not visible beneath the heavy gold ring, a legacy from his late father. 'We've never met. So how—'

'Are you sure about that, Rouge? I remember *you*.' She sipped her drink slowly and drove him crazy for all the seconds that slipped by before she said, 'You broke a lot of hearts when you went away. Did you like the military school better than St Ursula's?'

She couldn't have attended St Ursula's Academy. He shook his head. 'I would have remembered you.'

'I don't think so,' she said, with the vague implication that he was only half bright, and thus she did not expect much from him.

Women were so good at this.

She touched her damaged right cheek. 'You never saw

20

this.' When she turned to look up at the television set, the scar was hidden on the other side of her profile.

Rouge's own photograph was framed in the bright screen above the bar. The woman and her scar turned back to him. 'So you're the crack cop who broke the case of the purple bicycle.'

Was there sarcasm in her voice? Definitely. 'No, that was another cop.' He might be falling in love, and perhaps the feeling would last for another round of drinks. 'I only happened by in time to carry the bike back to the station.'

'A coincidence? You were just in the right place at the right time?'

He shrugged. It was hardly a coincidence. He always checked Miss Fowler's place on his way home from Dame's Tavern – every night of the week. Since his ex-piano teacher lived on the main street, he could go nowhere in Makers Village without passing her house.

'Well, Rouge, I guess the cameras liked you best. Oh, there you are again.' She pointed at the screen. 'I saw that piece of film this morning. You do the stoic silent routine very well.'

Yeah, he might be falling in love with the left side of her.

'Still – quite a coincidence,' she said. 'Your sister was killed by a kidnapper, and now you catch one.'

He pulled back as though she had pointed a gun at his face. 'He's not a kidnapper – he's a bike thief. And the kids are runaways.' Or that was the State Police Department's line to the press. Was this woman—

'Gwen's mother doesn't seem to agree,' she said, pointing to a shot of the lieutenant governor descending the stairs and bearing down on the spokesman for the Bureau of Criminal Investigation. 'And your sister was snatched right before Christmas vacation, too. That would have been a few months after you were sent away to military school.'

He turned to the pyramid of wineglasses and the twenty small portraits of Susan, each one a study in shock. 'The man who killed my sister is in jail. Are you a reporter?' The State

Police investigators had made a point of telling the village cops not to talk to the press.

'And all three kids went to the same private school.' She drained her glass.

Please stop.

'There's no connection between my sister and those runaways. Are you a—'

'No, I'm not a reporter.' She held her glass up to the bartender and raised one eyebrow to ask him for a refill. She was watching the television when she said, 'But I do read the papers. Those two little girls were the same age as Susan.'

'What's your name?'

'You wouldn't remember it, Rouge. My family moved out of town when I was in the fifth grade.' Gwen Hubble's photograph filled the television screen. 'That kid is from a family as rich as yours used to be.'

'Are you with the feds?'

'Your sister was pretty too. Just like Gwen – a little princess. One more coincidence and we may have the makings of a damn miracle.' She turned to face him now. 'No, I'm not FBI. Just spending the holidays with my uncle. Interesting old man – a devout atheist. His only religious ideation is the growing suspicion that there are no random events. Are you sure the priest killed your sister?'

That last bomb of hers was almost thrown away as an afterthought.

'The bastard did it.' There was no acrimony in this, only the dry recitation of information he had memorized along with tables of weights and measures. He simply preferred 'bastard' to 'priest'.

'All the evidence was circumstantial,' she said, as if she were merely speculating on whether it would rain or snow. 'No ransom money was ever found.'

'He killed her.' Rouge's voice was calm as he reiterated this simple fact of life – of death. 'Now who are you?'

She only looked at him with grave disappointment, as

22

though she had found him wanting. 'I have to go to the ladies' room.'

He watched her walk off toward the rest rooms at the back of the bar. The small Susans in the wineglasses expressed vague confusion, heads moving slowly from side to side. How could he have met this woman and not remembered her? He played a waiting game, calling up images of all his old classmates, and she was not among them.

The military school had been a short-lived experiment in separating him from his twin. After Susan died and he had been reinstated at St Ursula's Academy, the same faces had greeted him and passed through the years with him. His return to the school had been yet another experiment, offering the comfort of familiar surroundings to offset the novelty of a dead sister.

When twenty minutes had passed by, he was still waiting for the woman to return from the ladies' room.

Now how bright is that?

He stayed long enough to down another drink, not wanting to believe that he had been dumped.

More stupidity.

Rouge put his money on the bar and went outside. The sky had grown dark in the past few hours. Winking colored lights were strung in the bare branches of the trees along the curb, and every shop window was cluttered with garish decorations and pricey gifts. The architecture of the village storefronts had not been altered in this century. However, the holiday season had changed: two of the town's children were missing – but commerce stopped for no one. The street was clogged by slow-moving traffic, and the sidewalks were alive with the hustle of Christmas shoppers, trotting from store to store with bulky packages, with determination, resolve and speed.

Only Rouge Kendall was standing still. Though he knew the brunette was long gone, he looked into the passing faces of every female with long dark hair.

Fool.

He decided to go home and speak to no more women. His mother was always on his side, and so he did not count her in their camp.

Her daughter's dead body had been found on December 25th, and there had not been another Christmas tree in Ellen Kendall's house for fifteen years. This evening, she stared at the television set and watched the two frantic mothers of missing children. Her own text was overriding the announcer's words:

Merry Christmas, ladies – only six more shopping days for the ultimate gift. Just a little something from hell to kill your holiday forever, a little body, cold and still – one for each of you.

Ellen had a bottle of pills that would kill these dark ideas, but she didn't care for the side effects: the feeling of walking through a morass and struggling only to frame a thought of what she would have for dinner.

She switched off the television set, and her own reflected image filled the darkened glass – portrait of a lean woman with good bone structure and badly in need of a drink. With a better mirror, she knew she would look a decade older than her fifty-six years, with hair more gray than brown. Drink had done that for her, though now she kept no alcohol in the house.

But that had not been her own idea. Rouge had taken all the bottles away when he was only sixteen years old and practicing to be the man of the house – a full three years before his father died.

How prescient. But then, he had been an unusual boy at every age.

When she heard the car pull into the circular driveway, she crossed the wide room to the front window and parted the drapes. The old Volvo sat in front of the house. The engine had been turned off, but Rouge gave no sign of leaving the car. He was sitting behind the wheel and staring up toward the gables. Was he looking at his sister's dark window? They never spoke of her anymore, but the dead child was always a stronger presence this close to Christmas. It was the season of the trinity: mother, son and Susan's ghost.

Ellen Kendall had spent the entire morning steeped in memories of that endless wait for her daughter's ransom note. All this afternoon had been spent imagining Susan's small body in the snowbank, where she had been thrown away when there was no more life in her. And just now, Ellen was reliving the funeral.

Rouge had been so quiet on the day they had lain his sister in the ground. Ellen had admired her solid little man, only ten years old, yet so poised, so calm. And then she had noticed that one of the boy's arms was held out from his body at an odd angle. She was seeing it all over again – the small cupped hand, his fingers curled around another hand that was not there. As his sister's coffin was lowered into the ground, he had turned to the empty space beside him. His face registered shock for the first time that day, and Ellen knew her small son had expected to see someone standing next to him, someone with his young eyes and hair the color of his own. The boy had pitched forward in a faint. He would have fallen on the coffin if his father had not reached out one hand to snatch their only remaining child away from the open grave.

Back in the present again, Ellen stared out the window. Her son was still sitting behind the wheel of the car.

And a merry Christmas to you, Rouge. Are you thinking of murder?

He might have something more mundane on his mind. Perhaps he was wondering how to pay the property taxes and the upkeep on this huge house. It was miles too big for the two remaining Kendalls. They had closed off the upper floors to save on utility bills, but still the maintenance was costly. Once, she had suggested moving to a smaller home. This had made Rouge angry. In the days following that discussion, the silence between them had been hurtful, for she knew how hard her son worked to keep this place for her. But it was only for his sake that she remained here and lived through each new day of sad reminders. Painful endurance was the twisted gift they gave to one another, each with the best intentions.

The art collection and most of the antiques had been sold. She liked the house better now that it was less cluttered. The psychiatric care and his father's heart transplant, the ransom and more money for the detective – all had taken their toll on the publishing fortune her late husband's family had amassed over many generations.

Ellen listened to the opening and closing of the front door, and then her son's footsteps crossing the marble tiles. The foyer, obscene in its size, ate up monstrous amounts of heat. She had wanted to use the back door of the house so they could seal it off, but her son had told her they would not camp out in their own home.

When had Rouge become the head of the household?

Long ago.

She and her late husband had made him into a little man before he was full grown – an unwitting piece of cruelty. They had not been any comfort to their surviving child, only passing by his room, walking through the mechanics of a life, speaking automatic phrases of 'good morning' and 'good night'.

'Hi, Mom.'

She turned to see Rouge stroll into the parlor, and in a trick of the lamplight, his shadow seemed to walk beside him as an independent creature.

'Hello, dear.' Did that sound too cheerful? Was it forced and artificial? *Yes.* 'I can have dinner ready in twenty minutes.'

'Fine,' he said, kissing her cheek.

And wasn't that small act a bit too perfunctory? Did Rouge seem more distracted than usual?

Ellen sensed his pain or something akin to it. A sickness? She felt an impulse, some vestige of the mother she used to be in the days when she had two living children. Her hand was rising to touch his forehead, to test for a fever, when he turned away from her.

He walked into the foyer, and then climbed the grand

staircase toward the floors they no longer used. She trailed him as far as the balustrade, and shook her head in disbelief as she watched him on the landing. He was pulling the weather stripping away from Susan's door.

Gwen Hubble was not quite awake, but fighting her way to a conscious thought. She struggled to rise, then fell back on the cot, exhausted, as though her small body were made of far heavier stuff than a ten-year-old's flesh and bone. She lay still for a moment, gathering strength to try again. Her eyes focussed on the dim illumination of a plastic night-light in the wall plug.

When her mind had cleared a bit, she found it easier to sit up.

There was another tray on the small table by her cot. The last time, it had held a glass of orange juice and an egg. *Not enough food.* Now she was looking at half a cup of cocoa and a tiny roll. *Not enough.*

With dull fixation, she stared at the glow of light on the ceramic tiles. The surrounding space was as large as her father's master bathroom. And the tub in this room was also an antique with four clawed lion's paws for feet. The toilet seemed a long way off; the night-light was only a tiny spark of reflection on its porcelain.

The urge to urinate was stronger than hunger. She pushed back the bedding and touched a rough wool surface with her bare feet.

Where were her socks?

On the first day, she had only missed her red parka, and the next morning – this morning? – her shoes were gone. Her hand went to the chain around her neck and closed on the amulet that Sadie Green had given her, a good-luck charm with the engraved image of an all-seeing eye. So she still had that. Ah, but her braid had come undone in the night.

Is it night?

She tried to stand too quickly and her head ached. Slowly,

she stood up and walked toward the toilet, unsteady on her legs. As she passed close to the door, she tried the knob, not really expecting it to open this time either.

Why is this happening?

That thought was too hard to hold on to, and she let it slide away as she went through the automatic actions of raising the toilet lid, tearing paper sheets from the roller and carefully setting the squares around the rim of the wooden seat, her ingrained protocol for strange bathrooms, and last, the flush.

Now that her eyes had adjusted to the poor light, she could see more detail in the room. There was no mirror above the sink. She hadn't noticed that the last time. She did remember the massive piece of furniture against the far wall. *An armoire in a bathroom?*

The hamper was new to her, wasn't it? She stared at it now. It was like the pull-out hampers in her own house, built into the wall. But this one had a long chain looping once through its handle and twice around the towel bar mounted next to it. The chain was padlocked.

Why? What's in the hamper? The question died away almost as soon as she had formed it.

She was so hungry.

Returning to the narrow cot, she stared down at the tray on the table. This morning when she ate the egg, she had fallen asleep immediately. At least she *thought* the first meal had been in the morning – if she could only rely on the formula of juice and an egg as breakfast food. Now she was looking at the miserly dinner roll and the cocoa. Gwen was starting to form another concept, a connection of food and sleep. But then she drifted on to thoughts of her best friend. Where was Sadie, and *how* was she?

Gwen ate the small roll. *Not enough food.* Her stomach growled. It was work to hold on to a single idea. She stared at the cocoa in her cup. Again, she made the connection of food and sleep. *Food? Or drink?* She walked back to the sink and poured the cocoa down the drain, running water in the basin to clean away the dark splatters.

When Gwen came back to the cot, she was facing the hamper and its padlocked chain. She walked toward it, moving very slowly – so drowsy. It was like having the flu – or her brain might be filled with cotton wadding; the child gave equal weight to both possibilities. She touched the handle of the hamper, then her legs failed her and she was sinking to her knees.

So it was not the cocoa that made her sleep; she had guessed wrong. Her face pressed into the rough wool of a small oval rug. And though she lay sprawled on the floor, there was one moment of fright that came with the sensation of falling, the idea that the tiled surface might not be solid, that the rules of the universe no longer applied to her.

Her eyes closed.

Late on the night of her daughter's death, all those years ago, Ellen Kendall had opened the door of Rouge's bedroom and found her small son rolled into a ball studded with auburn cowlicks, tiny fingers and pajama feet. His eyes had snapped open. Uncurling swiftly, he had flung out his arms and legs, a child unfurled, as though opening his breast to make an easy target for whatever had come for him in the dark. Realizing that it was only his frightened mother on the threshold, his face had flooded with disappointment. And Ellen knew her ten-year-old son wanted to die, to go with his sister – into the ground. On the following day, she had placed her surviving child in the care of a psychiatrist, not believing that she could keep Rouge alive by herself. What good had she been to Susan?

And then she had poured herself into a bottle – no meager feat; Ellen had not become a drunk in one day.

Now, years of sobriety later, she stood at Susan's door and stared at the walls for a moment, mildly startled by what time had done to her daughter's bedroom. Over the past fifteen years, the once bright wall paint had settled down to a calm, pale pink.

Rouge sat tailor-fashion on a dusty braided rug woven with threads of every color, all of them muted now. Ghosty white sheets draped the furniture, and a gray film lay over every inch of the exposed floorboards. He was digging through a large cardboard box of Susan's personal effects.

Ellen crept silently into the room. Her son paid no attention to her, he was so engrossed in an old yearbook from St Ursula's Academy.

Why must he do this to himself – to her?

She wanted to cry, but her voice was surprisingly normal when she spoke to him. 'Need some help? Are you looking for something of—?'

'I met a woman tonight.' He set one book down and opened a volume for another year. 'She knew us when we were nine or ten. But I don't remember her name. I thought there might be a picture in here.'

Ellen was on guard now, and worried. The *us* and *we* had lingered in Rouge's sentences for more than a year after his twin's death. And now the words were back again, like ghosts in his mouth.

'Could you describe the woman, Rouge?'

He selected another volume from the stack of school annuals. All of them dated back to the years before Susan was murdered. 'She has wide-set eyes and a—' Suddenly, he slammed one of the books. 'She's not here. She didn't go to St Ursula's.' He pushed the books to one side and raked both hands through his hair.

Ellen knelt down on the rug beside him. 'Do you know anything about her people? What her father did for a living – her mother?'

'No.' He threw up his hands, defeated. 'She said her family left town when she was in the fifth grade.' And now one fist pounded the floor, and the stack of yearbooks toppled over.

She knew he hadn't slept since yesterday, but this was more

than fatigue. His frustration helped her to gauge how much he'd had to drink. This tone only entered his voice when he wasn't thinking clearly, when intoxication was an obstacle to an idea. Normally, his mind worked much faster than hers, and better. Perhaps this was why he stopped at Dame's Tavern every night, to slow down that beautiful fleet brain.

'At least you know she didn't go to St Ursula's. That's something.' In her younger days as a reporter, she had chased people down without much more information. So the child had moved away when she was a fifth-grader. There was only one public elementary school in town, and there would be group portraits on record. Ah, but wait – she had her own photographs.

Ellen reached out and opened the lower drawer of Susan's bureau. She rested one hand on her daughter's scrapbook. 'Rouge? This woman you met? Maybe she was in the children's choir. That was a mix of kids from both schools.' She pulled out the scrapbook and flipped through the pages, looking for the yearly snapshots of the choir field trips.

'The choir – right. She remembered my scar.' Now he was shoulder to shoulder with her. He put out his hand to stop the falling pages at one large photograph. 'That one. Was it taken the year I cut my finger?'

'Cut? You almost cut it *off*, Rouge.' She looked down at the three rows of children, kneeling and standing, all holding their ice skates and grinning for the camera. She pointed to the first girl in the front row. 'Now that's Meg Tomlin, the fire chief's daughter. She moved to Cooperstown when she got married three years ago. And that's Jenny Adler. You remember her from St Ursula's? She graduated from MIT and went to work for a company in Tokyo.'

He was staring at her face – all curiosity now. She understood. Rouge was wondering how a housebound recluse like herself would know of these events in the world outside.

'Well, babe, the family may not own any of the newspapers anymore, but I do read them. You'd be surprised what I know.'

31

'You still have any of your old sources?'

'Oh, I'm sure I do.' And apparently, all the old friends had turned out for her. There were a number of similarities between her daughter's kidnapping and the recent theft of two more children from St Ursula's, yet there was no mention of Susan in the newspapers or the television coverage. But that protection wouldn't last if these girls turned up dead on Christmas morning.

Her son was staring at her, momentarily distracted from the scrapbook. 'Mom, what do you know about the lieutenant governor?'

'Marsha Hubble? She comes from a long line of politicians, but I'd swear she's clean. That's despite proximity to a mobbed-up senator.'

'And the puppet governor?'

'*Alleged* puppet, dear. He's been trying to unload Hubble for the past year. My theory is that she doesn't play nicely with major campaign contributors of the cockroach persuasion.'

Rouge bowed his head over the scrapbook, but his eyes were looking inward. Ellen knew she was losing him again. She pointed to a child in the middle row of the photograph. 'Look here. This girl has wide-set eyes, but I have no idea who she is. Damn, after all my showboating.'

She turned the photograph over to read the names of all the children. The list, penned in her own hand, was one name short. The child with the wide-set eyes was the only member of the choir she could not account for. 'Sorry, Rouge. I can't remember her.'

'She has a scar. Here.' He ran one finger down his right cheek in a jagged line. 'Do you remember any other accidents with kids?'

'No, and something like that would've been a standout.' She flipped the page. 'Now you're not in this photo. It was taken after you went off to military school. And there she is again, just behind Susan, see? No scars on her face. So the accident probably happened after she left town.'

She knew her son was drifting away again, sailing off on that familiar sea that fit so neatly in a whiskey glass. Ellen could smell it, almost taste it. But she could hardly lecture Rouge on booze. She had only stopped drinking after the crowning humiliation of her teenage son finding her dead drunk on the bathroom floor. 'Rouge? You said she left town when she was in the fifth grade?'

He stared at the page and nodded.

'The schools are closed for Christmas vacation, but you could try the church. Father Domina might have kept the old attendance books. Could be worth a shot.' She ruffled his hair to get his attention. 'I could help you. Tomorrow morning?'

'Can't. I have to work the first shift tomorrow.' Rouge stood up and dusted off his jeans. 'They're putting me on a plainclothes detail.' He was scanning the titles on the small bookshelf by the bed. 'What happened to Susan's diary?'

'The police took it away. I don't know if they ever returned it or not. We could check the other boxes in the attic if you like?' She turned back to the photograph of the choir. 'It's odd I can't place this child.'

Or perhaps it wasn't. Apart from the eyes there was nothing remarkable about the little girl. She was in the middle range of everything – not the smallest or even the most plain.

Rouge pulled a dust sheet away from the desk. A silver bracelet was lying on the faded green blotter. This was Susan's last birthday gift from her father. Rouge picked it up. 'I thought Dad said she lost this?'

Lost it? Perhaps they should talk more about Susan's death. What else might he have misunderstood in those days when his father was locked away in the study, when his mother lived in a bottle seven days out of seven. Or maybe the bracelet *had* been lost instead of stolen – and later *found*, not *seized* as evidence.

'Those last few months, your sister was always losing something at choir practice.' And Ellen had found that strange. The children had always been so careful with their possessions. At the time, she had blamed the separation of the twins for the odd changes in her daughter's behavior.

Sometimes, late at night, Ellen played a morbid game of 'what if'. What if she had stood up to her husband and kept the twins in the same school? Then Rouge would have been with Susan on the day she was stolen. The twins had gone everywhere together, needing no one else's company or conversation. Would Susan have lived, or would both of them have perished?

She stared at the silver bracelet as Rouge slipped it into her hand. When had she seen it last? At the trial? Yes, the bracelet had been used as evidence. The police must have returned it to her husband. She imagined Bradly Kendall quietly walking into this room and carefully setting the small bit of jewelry on his daughter's desk. And perhaps Brad had sat down on the bed and cried because the bracelet's circle was so tiny it broke his heart.

Ellen closed her hand over the piece of silver. 'The police said this was found in the priest's room.'

'You mean Paul Marie's room.' Rouge's correction was unemotional, but pointed. Considering her son's quiet ways, this was almost an argument. She had forgotten how much it irritated him when she referred to the child killer as a priest.

But each time she thought of Paul Marie, she saw the trappings of the church, cassock and collar. The man had been so young when she last saw him, barely into his twenties when he stood beside the elder priest at Communion. Nothing interesting had been written on his face yet, no lines of character or personality. Some people had thought him very handsome, she remembered that much, but there had been nothing else to distinguish him. He had been such an ordinary man, uninspired in his sermons and merely adequate as a choirmaster.

But the children loved him.

Ellen's hands flew up to cover her burning face, as if this

34

thought had been spoken aloud – as though she had just told an obscene joke in church.

CHAPTER 3

'I like it.' The appreciation seemed genuine as he admired her jagged scar and the twisted mouth of bright red.

Ali Cray remembered this priest as a tall man, but slight, almost delicate. The aesthetic's face had been paler then, ethereal, framed by dark hair and black vestment. When she was ten years old and Paul Marie was in his early twenties, his large, lustrous brown eyes had peered out from a portrait of Lord Byron on a dog-eared page of her poetry text.

Fifteen years older now, the bound man on the other side of the table was well muscled; broad shoulders strained at the seams of his blue denim shirt; and there was a hardness to his face. The chains on his hands and feet did nothing to diminish him, but made him seem even more powerful, held in check only by his manacles. He filled the whole room with his presence.

Ali Cray felt her own personality being crowded up against the wall when he looked at her. Gone were the poet's eyes; *Good night, Byron.*

Lowering her head, she stared at the pages on her clipboard, though she knew each line of print by heart. Her gaze drifted across the table to the jailhouse tattoos on his hands. It was a common trait of the convict, this mutilation of the flesh with pin pricks and ink to while away the days. But his were not typical markings. On the back of the right hand was an *S*, and on his left was an *E*; both were wrought in the style of ornate capitals from illuminated manuscripts.

She looked up at his face, his faint smile.

'The letters stand for *sin eater*,' he said. 'A euphemism for sucking on penises. I was forced to do a lot of that while I was in the general prison population.'

'In this prison, all sex offenders are segregated,' she said, as though she had caught him in a lie.

'A clerical error – according to the warden. My paperwork was fouled up.'

Not likely. She knew that someone would have to use influence or quite a bit of money for a mistake of that magnitude; it was nearly a death sentence for a child molester. Susan's father could have arranged it. When Bradly Kendall was alive, he had had the necessary political connections and wealth. 'But your lawyer would have—'

'He never believed I was innocent. That's why the little bastard dragged his feet for two years.' Paul Marie shrugged, as though this gross betrayal really mattered very little to him. 'The lawyer knew what was being done to me. I think it fit his own sense of rough justice.'

'I gather the Church believed in you. You were never defrocked.'

The prisoner leaned forward, and Ali leaned back.

'The Church has a shortage of priests. I wouldn't be released from my vows for murdering a little girl. It's not as if I advocated birth control.'

Ali looked down at her clipboard again and made a quick note at the bottom of one sheet. She didn't look at him when she asked, 'Did you go on functioning as a priest?'

'Yes – those first two years. I heard confessions and meted out penance.'

Paul Marie's voice had lost all the gentle tones. She couldn't take much more of this changeling phenomenon. It was like a little death.

He went on in this voice of a stranger, 'There was a man who made a point of saying, "Father, forgive me", each time I was raped. One day, I beat the crap out of him with a lead pipe. And *then* I forgave him. The pipe scrambled his brains,

37

so he no longer remembers what I forgave him for. But I did keep the sacraments. Though I had to improvise on the penance. One *Hail Mary* equals a broken nose. Three *Our Fathers* is a smashed testicle.'

Nothing remained of her old choirmaster.

'I wish they'd left me in the general population. On this cell block, I only hear the confessions of insects. The perverts share everything with me, all the things they won't even tell their lawyers.'

'Do they ever talk about the local case? The two girls?'

'Sometimes. But they prefer to reminisce about their own crimes against women and children. They lie in their beds when the lights go out, and they jerk off their cocks while they confess to me in the dark. And then the corridor fills up with the stink of semen.' He pushed back from the table. 'But I don't think you need to hear any of that. Confession isn't a perk of the priesthood. It's a kind of hell.'

'Father, I know you won't remember me. I was—'

'I remember you missed choir practice the week before I was arrested.' He sat back and regarded her with greater attention, making more assessments of her hair, her clothes, the scar. 'Father Domina said your family moved out of town.'

So at least a few people had noticed her passing by, taking up space in the world, and she marveled over that for a moment. 'My parents never told me about Susan Kendall's death.' She had been eighteen years old before she learned of the murder.

An uneasy silence prevailed between them. Other noises intruded on the room, sounds from the prison yard outside the window, voices of men and the rhythm of a ball bouncing off the exterior wall. She noted the thrum of heavy machinery. The prison laundry must be close by; she could see the steam escaping past the side of the barred window.

At last, he said, 'I used to worry about you, Sally. You were the only child I ever knew who aspired to blend into the walls.'

She understood this perception. As a little girl, she had

been neither pretty nor homely, tall nor short, only finding her voice when she sang in the choir.

'My name is Ali now,' she reminded him. Her open wallet of credentials still lay on the table between them, and her altered name was punctuated with a Ph.D. She wondered if he didn't find that advanced degree quite odd, given the bland child she had been.

He nodded in approval. 'Ali suits you better. As I recall, you were in danger of an ordinary life. I'm glad mediocrity passed you by. I imagine the scar had a lot to do with that.'

The choirmaster from her childhood came back to visit with her for a few moments. Father Paul's eyes were penetrating, gently probing the soft places, silently asking where the hurt was – just like old times. Oh, but now he saw something new in her expression. Had she unwittingly given herself away? Whatever it was, it jarred him. He physically pulled back and cast his eyes down, perhaps in time to rescue himself from discovery.

This morning, a state trooper manned the front desk, displacing the village police sergeant who usually sat behind the glass window with his newspaper and a cup of coffee.

Rouge thought Chief Croft had been a good sport about handing his station house over to the BCI investigators. But then, Charlie Croft had always maintained that he could run the village's six-man police force from a telephone booth. The chief's small private office was on the floor above, but the remaining space had been used only for town council meetings once a month, and as a voting place in an election year. Now there were footsteps from many pairs of shoes walking across the ceiling. The ground floor of the station house was almost eerie in the absence of yesterday's circus of noise and raucous energy. One man sat on a plastic chair in the reception area. A press pass was clipped to the lapel of his suit.

Where had all the other newspeople gone?

Rouge pinned his new identification tag to his jacket and

signed the state trooper's logbook. Then he climbed one flight of the narrow staircase and opened the door to a wide front room and a steady din of conversations punctuated by the ring of telephones. FBI agents and state investigators sat at tables and desks raided from the public library next door. They were taking statements from civilians, while the uniformed officers were hauling reams of paper from one end of the room to the other. A portable radio unit spat out a burst of static and garbled words from the state troopers' cars out on the road.

The old landmark building had retained its fifteen-foot ceilings, but long tubes of fluorescent lights marred this one remaining detail. The exposed brick of the walls had been painted over to disguise the building material as something more plastic, less sturdy. According to Chief Croft, the new color of the walls was 'puke green' and *not* 'essence of willow', as the painter had asserted. Movable partitions of padded fabric had been brought in by the Bureau of Criminal Investigation to divide the fringe space into cubicles, and computers sat on every surface as more solid reminders that the world had changed overnight.

Rouge was surprised to see Marge Jonas at her desk this morning. The civilian secretary was the only other survivor of the State Police takeover. She was wearing her platinum-blond hair this morning. Marge had wigs in every color except her own natural iron-gray.

He would have said hello, but the secretary was immersed in a technical manual. By her muttered obscenities, he knew she was deep into the latest computer glitch to plague the new system installed by the BCI task force. Beneath her chin, three rolls of flesh jiggled to the rhythm of her bobbing head as she looked down to the manual and then up to the lighted screen of scrambled text.

He walked on by, and she called after him, 'Not so fast, Rouge Kendall!' Marge only used his full name if she was irritated.

He stopped dead and turned to face her. 'Hey, Marge.'

One pudgy finger marked her place in the closed manual as she leaned over her desk to stare at his legs. 'When I told you to come in wearing street clothes, I meant a *suit*. Are those your Sunday-go-to-meeting jeans? I notice they're still sort of blue.'

'It's all I had.' His late father's tweed jacket had fit perfectly, but his mother could do nothing with the old man's trousers, tailored for legs two inches shorter than his own.

'You need work.' Marge stood up to display two hundred and twenty-five imposing pounds of authority as she rolled one hand to motion him closer. 'Honey, come here. Let me fix that.' Her dexterous fingers quickly undid the sloppy knot below the collar of his shirt. 'We don't want Captain Costello to know you've never worn a tie in your life.'

This was close to the truth. He had always worn a uniform to work and lived a blue jeans existence after hours. And so he stood by her chair, in docile surrender, while she properly knotted his father's silk tie. A brown suede jacket lined with sheepskin was slung over one arm. This was his own, but purchased in his college days and showing some wear and shine.

Marge stepped back to admire her handiwork. 'Now you look like a BCI investigator.'

'Hey, I'm just reporting for a plainclothes detail.'

'Don't contradict me, hon. I typed up your press release this morning.'

'My what?'

She shot him a warning glance and nodded toward the private office appropriated by the BCI commander. The man standing in the open doorway had been a familiar sight in Makers Village for more than a decade. Captain Costello kept a summer house on the lake, but he frequented the shops and restaurants in every season. Many villagers had come to regard him as a local man, one of their own, though they found him somewhat aloof. Over the past ten years, the captain had never set foot in this local police station – and now he ruled it.

Costello was walking toward them. The man did not look happy, and neither did he look like anyone's idea of a top cop in the BCI. The captain might have stood five feet ten on his tallest day, but the permanent slouch had made him inches shorter in middle age. Small in the bones and introspective in demeanor, he seemed better suited to academic work.

Yet when Costello addressed his troops *en masse*, his voice took on a working man's character, a rough and colorful vocabulary so at odds with his physique and the bow tie. In more personal conferences, rumor had it that he could cut off a larger man's balls in ten words or less.

Rouge wondered if this came naturally, or was it art?

Captain Costello slapped a newspaper down on the secretary's desk with the crack of a rifle shot. Marge jumped, Rouge didn't; he was staring down at a five-year-old photograph of himself in the baseball uniform of the Yankees rookie league. The headline said, LOCAL HERO. A companion photograph showed him carrying Sadie Green's bicycle.

Now Costello held up the arrest report with Phil Chapel's signature at the bottom. 'Why didn't *you* make out this report, Kendall?' The captain's words were vaguely threatening.

'It was Phil Chapel's arrest. I just carried the bike for him.'

Costello shook his head. 'Miss Fowler set the reporters straight on who did what and why.' The threatening tone was not vague anymore. 'I really *hate* this, Kendall. From now on, you report directly to me, and you report every damn thing you do. You can start with an *accurate* arrest report. Then I wanna talk to you.'

When the door to the private office had slammed shut, Marge put one hand on Rouge's shoulder. 'It's not as bad as you think.' She opened her appointment calendar. 'See this? I got you down for an applicant interview. That's what he wants to see you about. It's a transfer to the State Police *and* a promotion.' Now she waved his mouth shut. 'It doesn't matter if you never filed the application. It wouldn't be on his desk unless he asked for it. So you're going to be a baby BCI investigator. Okay?'

She handed him a sheaf of papers. 'That's your report. I got all the facts from Miss Fowler's interview. Just sign it and wait ten minutes before you hand it in. If you don't pretend you typed it yourself, you'll jerk him out of shape again.'

'Thanks, Marge.'

'Anything else I can do for you?'

'I need to find a woman.'

'I'm not easy, Rouge. I have to be seduced. I want flowers.'

'She's tall, brunette—'

'I can do brunette. But I look better as a blonde.'

'The trooper at the desk said she was in here yesterday, but he didn't get her name on the logbook. She's got a scar on the right cheek. It runs down to her mouth. Looks like she's always smiling on one side.'

'I've seen her.' Marge shook her head in mock wonder. 'God, did she turn heads in this place. I don't know what got the most attention, the face or that skirt. It's slit up to—'

'Where can I find her?'

'You'll see her tomorrow at the briefing.' Marge looked down at her appointment calendar. 'She's giving a lecture to the task force at ten o'clock. But you should think this through, Rouge. In my experience, nice girls wear panty hose.'

'So what do you think of our Ali now?' The prisoner addressed the shadow lying underneath his bed. He found great peace in merely sitting on the floor, leaning back against the cool wall and staring into that patch of darkness.

It was insane to regard a shadow as a sentient being. Or perhaps the young were on to something when they suspected their own beds of harboring entities; the children all knew they were not alone in the dark. And now Paul Marie knew it, too.

The shadow understood things about children, and little girls in particular. The thing under the bed had absorbed all the guilt of the prisoners in neighboring cells as well as their extensive knowledge. It was always awake to their confessions, so the priest might sleep through the long nights of whispered atrocities.

In the early days of confinement, when he had suffered the rapists, the shadow had emanated sorrow for him – and forgiveness for them. When Paul Marie had increased his size and beaten an assailant nearly to death, the shadow had absorbed the blows of the beaten man, felt all the pain, and thus allowed the priest to wield pipe and fist, to break the bones of faces and limbs without remorse, untroubled by empathy.

In exchange for services rendered, the prisoner gave sanctuary to the thing under the bed. He sometimes suspected it of being a flawed and somewhat shopworn deity in search of redemption, and doing hard time as the surrogate soul of a priest. He knew he had either lost his mind or found his faith. One of these things must be true.

But which?

No matter. He would not take the thing back inside himself. It could die under the bed for all he cared. Yet he did nothing to harm it, made no attempt to kill it, though it would have been as simple as lifting up the mattress and exposing the shadow to the overhead light.

Now Father Marie inclined his head in a prelude to conversation with the dark thing. 'Are you hungry? What would you like best? Shall I throw you a bone – or a little girl?'

He stood up and made a square tour of his small, austere cell, ten feet by ten, trailing one hand along the bare wall and then the bars.

So two more children are missing.

Had something new been added to his delusion? He could hear the buzzing of flies, but there were none about. *No flights of angels' wings – only the buzz of fat black insects?* A brain tumor perhaps. He would welcome that. Yes, perhaps the flies were inside him.

But now one flew past him, and then another brushed his skin, and he recoiled.

One more turn around the cell. He came to rest in front of the bed and knelt down to speak more intimately with the shadow. 'About those little girls – you know how this will all turn out, don't you?'

The flies had stopped their buzzing. They had gone away and left him in deep silence where the real madness was. Now the priest could hear his own heart beating, and then another heartbeat layered over this one, light and tripping, skipping beats, struck with fear – the wild heart of a child.

Only Captain Costello was aware of David Shore. The small boy was not simply timid or nervous; he was clearly frightened, all but hugging the wall as he shrank back from the heavy foot traffic in the wide, noisy room of adults. Costello watched the youngster through a crack in the blinds covering the glass on his door. The child seemed fixated on the red-haired cop seated just outside the office.

Shy David was springing off the toes of his running shoes, set to fly, anchored only by fascination for Officer Rouge Kendall. Now David ventured away from the wall with short, halting steps, and Costello was reminded of that first endless trek across a ballroom, heading for the sure rejection of an invitation to a dance.

The child came to rest in front of the young cop, who was engrossed in a handful of papers. David bit down on his lower lip. His running shoes were undecided, stepping one foot forward and one foot back. A baseball card was clutched in his small hand. Captain Costello had to squint to make out the New York Yankees logo and a portrait of Rouge Kendall with his pitcher's glove.

Well, the trading card was hardly valuable, since the pitcher had washed out in his first season on the rookie league.

The young cop looked up, surprised to see David hovering over him. Kendall stared at the boy's card bearing the picture of himself as a twenty-year-old baseball player with his whole life in front of him.

Captain Costello sucked in his breath.

Please, Kendall, don't blow this chance.

So far, the little boy from St Ursula's Academy had spoken to no one but Mrs Hofstra, his school housemother. Costello was convinced that David would have more to say if he could only speak for himself.

Kendall took the proffered card from the boy's hand, and while the cop searched his pockets for a pen to sign it, David melded into the crisscrossing patterns of uniformed officers, BCI investigators and feds. The child disappeared so quietly the cop had not yet noticed. His head was bent over the card as he signed his autograph for the ten-year-old fan.

Costello winced. The new trainee had blown it.

Rouge Kendall looked up to see the empty space where David had been standing.

Too late now. The captain opened his office door. 'In here, Kendall.'

The policeman entered the office with no sense of fear that Costello could immediately detect. But then, this was the first time he had been alone with the younger man. In the past four years, Kendall's undistinguished career in a one-car town had made him invisible to the New York State Police. If not for the open file on his desk, Costello would have known nothing about him.

Though the captain had only moved to this state ten years ago, every county resident knew the name of child killer Paul Marie. The victim, Susan Kendall, had become less famous over time, and her sibling was totally anonymous. Until last night, when Costello had called for the background material, he never made the connection between this ordinary village cop and a formerly powerful publishing family.

As Rouge Kendall sat down in the chair by his desk, Captain Costello had an uneasy feeling. He was looking at a perfect specimen of youth, only twenty-five years old, yet bearing the calm demeanor of a more mature man and the weary eyes of a very old soul. Perhaps damage could account for that, and a murdered sister was a lot of damage. Certainly nothing else about this officer was outstanding. The captain had already decided that Rouge Kendall did not belong with the State Police – not as an investigator, and not even as a trooper.

Costello turned his attention to the hastily assembled file on his desk, too thick for such a mediocre cop. 'This is all about you, kid.' He tapped the folder. 'The Internal Affairs idiots see you paying property taxes on a fifteen-room mansion, and sirens go off in their pointy heads. They don't know that even the white trash in this town have nice houses. So one of them ran a check on your source of income, and now he thinks a Manhattan auction house is fencing your stolen goods.'

Costello crumpled these papers into a ball. 'We transfer all the shooflies to IA. Keeps them from playing with their guns and shooting themselves in the foot.' He separated out the bulk of the file and pushed it to one side. 'I know you were born in that house. I guess you've been selling off heirlooms to make the taxes and upkeep?'

Rouge Kendall nodded.

'So we throw out the IA crap – except for this.' He held up two sheets of paper. 'They took a statement from your bartender at Dame's Tavern. And that's how I happen to know you drink too much, and you drink alone.'

No response. Evidently the new recruit didn't mind that his captain thought he was a lush. Or maybe this statement was also crap. Costello put it in the bogus pile at the edge of his desk.

'Now what's left, Kendall? For the rest of your life, I only need one page, maybe half a page. When you were a kid, you washed out of a military academy after less than four months. You played ball in prep school, and the Yankees won you in a first-round draft. Instead, you went on to Princeton University and quit school at nineteen. You went back to the Yankees and signed for a hefty bonus. Again, you washed out. One of the

47

coaches on the rookie league remembered you. The guy said you had the talent, but you never had any heart for the game. You blew every chance to dazzle the managers and never made the cut. Your coach wondered why you even gave it a shot.'

And now Costello leaned back in his chair and waited, but Rouge Kendall did not rush in to fill the silence with excuses and explanations.

The captain made his own best guess. 'I figure you were after the money. Your old man left a lot of debts, didn't he? That contract bonus was your only chance to make some real cash. Am I right?'

The young policeman only stared at him. There was nothing in Kendall's face to suggest insubordination; evidently, he simply didn't care if Costello got it right.

'Kendall, I don't think you've got the heart for this job either – not the makings of a good investigator. You're a twenty-five-year-old man who doesn't know what he wants to be when he grows up. I don't think you'll last a month.'

'Then why am I here?' There was no sarcasm. Kendall seemed only curious.

Costello picked up the BCI application and flipped through to the last page, a form required for separation from the Makers Village Police. *No signature?* Apparently, no one had even asked if this cop wanted a transfer. *Now whose screwup was that?* He set the application forms to one side.

'Fair question, Kendall. You're here because you made us look good when you brought in that girl's bike.' And this was the truth, or part of it. 'Thanks to you, we got a leg-up on the feds, and right out of the chute, too.' God, he had loved that. 'And I can make use of you for a while.'

The captain waited for some response. He had no idea what the younger man was thinking, and he was feeling oddly manipulated by the continuing silence.

Costello looked back at the slender biography. 'So you went to St Ursula's Academy. Good. Marge Jonas got you an appointment with the school's director. After you talk to him,

I want you to get cozy with David Shore. I think the kid's holding something back, probably nothing important. Maybe he's just feeble. David was abandoned in a department store when he was three, lived in foster homes till he was six – that's all we know about him. See what you can add to that.'

He had meant that Kendall should get out of his office and get on with the information gathering, but the younger man took him more literally.

'He's not feeble,' said Kendall. 'If David's not from money then he has a full scholarship at St Ursula's. That means his IQ goes right off the charts. The cutoff number is lower for paying students, but all the scholarship kids are high in the genius range.'

The new recruit was holding up the boy's trading card, and now Costello could read the false prophecy, 'Tomorrow's Star,' printed at the bottom of the special issue.

Kendall slipped it into the pocket of his jacket. 'And David is so crazy about baseball, he kept a five-year-old card on a player who never made the cut. He can't say two words out loud, not to a stranger, but he talks to Mary Hofstra. So he's—'

'Mary? You know the housemother?'

'I remember her, and she probably remembers me. If David's holding back, it's not because he can't communicate. Either he doesn't want to rat out the girls for something *they* did, or he's ashamed of something *he* did.'

Costello nodded as he leaned far back in his chair. *So this cop can think. So?* Rouge Kendall's brains had never been in question, but his history worked against him. 'Okay, you be David's new best friend. Nail down a case for runaways. Any questions?'

'You leaked the runaway theory to the press *before* I brought in Sadie Green's bike.' This was not an accusation, only a dry delivery of fact. 'Why?'

'Gwen Hubble's father is a security fanatic. Pathetic, isn't it? The poor bastard sets up this elaborate alarm system to keep the bogeyman out. Never occurred him that it was useless for keeping a kid *inside*. We found Gwen's prints on the number pad for the door alarm. So she slipped out to meet her little friend Sadie, and they left town on the bus.'

'You've had time to interview all the drivers on that route.'

'Very good, kid. And we came up dry. Interesting, huh?' In the next moment, Costello wondered when – precisely *when* he had become Rouge Kendall's interrogation subject.

'So I'm the only one working the runaway angle,' said the younger man, 'because you really think they were snatched.'

Costello smiled. Kendall obviously understood his place in the world. While the real BCI investigators were working the case, he was to be the fetcher of minor facts and loose threads, the task-force janitor, and most important, the press decoy.

Rouge Kendall rose from his chair. 'You don't seriously think a ten-year-old went out to meet this pervert in secret – like a lover. You figure it was someone who knew Gwen would see Sadie that day. But you don't know if it was a relative, a friend of the family or a stalker.'

All right, so Kendall has the raw makings. But there was still the matter of a heart for the job.

The young cop turned his back and walked to the door, saying, 'You think David Shore is hiding something, maybe he saw something – important.' His hand was pulling on the knob. 'Are you sure you don't want a *real* investigator to cozy up to the kid?' Kendall passed through the open door, and his voice trailed into the next room. 'Oh, sorry. You probably tried that, and it didn't work.'

Costello sighed. Perhaps the heart was overrated.

And tell me, Dr Mortimer Cray, how does your garden grow? With guilty secrets and children's graves laid out all in a row.

The air of the conservatory was dense and moist, rich in aromas of flowering plants and earth. A small pony motor hummed with the work of running the plant mister, and his spade scraped out the grittier noises of metal, soil and a clay pot. Outside the glass walls, living leaves still clung to his hardiest hybrids, but the ceiling of the pearl-gray sky was low and menacing. Nature was threatening to kill his garden with the first snow.

Always in thoughts of death these days. Mortimer Cray knew when he would die and how, just as he knew the times and particulars of all his appointments.

His right hand, thick with veins and dappled with liver spots, dropped the spade and began to tremble. A side effect of ending the new medication, he supposed. This little self-deceit was short lived; he knew what the tremors meant.

At age sixty-nine, he was semiretired from the practice of psychiatry, removed from all but a few of the really dangerous minds. Still, he thought of death six times in an hour. It rankled him that he should spend his last days troubled by a Sunday school God Whom he had tossed out in childhood, but Who had lately come back to him with such great wrath. New atrocities bloomed in the doctor's brain and would not leave him be.

These past few days since the girls had disappeared, he had tended to put off going to his bed. Fully clothed, he would fall asleep at the desk in his study and wake up at odd hours. All his habits of regimentation had dissipated, and he was without any order which servants did not create for him. The meals were still served and eaten at the same hours, but the man who ate them was unshaved, unwashed. And he always brought something to the table with him, something in his eyes which made his valet Dodd avoid looking directly at him.

His niece Ali had planned a small cocktail party today, and for this occasion, he had allowed Dodd to make him presentable with a razor and a clean shirt. Also thanks to the valet, his suit had been recently tailored to fit the ever decreasing dimensions of his thin body. Now he was disguised as merely slender, not sick and wasting.

The gravel in the driveway crunched under a slow and ponderous weight. He wiped one hand across his apron and adjusted the frames of his gold-rimmed glasses, the better

51

to see the black Porsche pull into formation with his own vintage Mercedes. Standing behind a camouflage of dangling vines and a mosaic of flowers, Mortimer peered through the glass wall as Dr Myles Penny unfolded his lanky body from the passenger's side.

Ali had only requested William's presence, but of course Myles would come along. The Penny brothers lived together, ate together and practiced medicine in the same clinic.

Myles moved a few steps closer to the conservatory. Pure-white thinning hair and poor posture made the general practitioner seem a decade older than his fifty-eight years. And because he had never learned how to sit down in a suit, his pants bagged out at the knees, and his jacket wrinkled at the mid-section.

The elder brother, Dr William Penny, stepped out from behind the wheel of his sports car. This doctor's hair was still a luxuriant brown, not a single strand of gray. His jowls and all the deepest wrinkles had been removed, but the surgically shortened nose had been a grave mistake. It was too pug, like a canine breeding error, giving William the carnival aspect of an aged dog-faced boy. And though this glaring flaw sat in the middle of his face, the heart surgeon seemed unaware of it as he preened before his own reflection in the greenhouse panes.

Mortimer left the cover of his plants, moved closer to the wall of glass and waved at his visitors. Proper William – never Bill or Will – elegantly lifted one hand in slow salutation as he stood beside his rumpled brother.

Mortimer pressed the intercom button.

'Yes, sir,' said Dodd's mechanized voice.

'Tell my niece our guests have arrived.'

The slanted glass roof afforded a partial view of the main house; four stories of stucco facing and wooden beams joined the conservatory in a common wall. The greenhouse was large, even by commercial standards, yet an intimate space had been carved out amid the plant life to accommodate the small grouping of chairs and a table.

'So Ali has her Ph.D.' Myles Penny did not wait on ceremony, but poured his own wine from the decanter and then made two more splashes into Mortimer's glass and William's. 'Bet you never figured she'd go that far at twenty-five.'

'Actually, she was twenty-three when she completed her dissertation.' And in truth, Mortimer Cray had never believed his niece would ever attempt any advanced degrees.

William sipped his wine and nodded with approval, as if he had the palate to know a bad burgundy from a good one. 'You must be very proud of her, Mortimer.'

Shocked would be a better word. Mortimer remembered Ali when she was small and barely there in every respect, a quiet, plain little girl with no distinguishing marks or characteristics.

'Has she had anything done about the scar yet?'

'No, Myles.' *She isn't done with the bloody thing yet.*

'I know a plastic surgeon in Manhattan – good man,' said William. 'When he's done with her, she can cover the damage with makeup.'

Mortimer shook his head, but not because William's nose was such a poor advertisement for a cosmetic surgeon. He knew his niece would never give up her mutilation. Perverse young woman – she was miles more interesting now, wasn't she? 'I'm afraid Ali didn't ask you here for a referral, William.'

'She's not worried about your heart condition, is she?'

'No, but it *is* a consultation of sorts. Sorry – I know you're officially on vacation.' And William was fanatical about his free time. Patients could drop like ninepins and not interfere with the heart surgeon's holiday plans.

'But Ali's field is pedophilia,' said William. 'Not my territory.' He looked toward the door at the far end of the room and raised his hand in greeting. 'Well, hello there, young lady.'

Ali Cray slowly walked down the corridor of orchid tables, and Mortimer noted that the long skirt had no slit. No doubt, this was her concession to the company of genteel William. Yet there was a sensuous freedom in the artless swing of Ali's arms and the sway of her hips. She carried herself with such confidence. As a small child, she had walked close to the walls of every room, eyes cast down with the humility of a tiny nun.

'Ali, you look wonderful,' said courtly William, holding out her chair. 'Academia must suit you. My belated congratulations on the Ph.D. Bright girl.'

Myles Penny lifted his wineglass. 'I'll second that, Ali. Now why didn't you go to St Ursula's when you were a kid? You've certainly got the brains. And I know your old uncle here would have kicked in the obscene tuition.'

'Ali's parents would never take money from me,' said Mortimer, in a hurry to get the words out before Ali could admit, unabashed, that she had failed the entrance exam.

In light of how far she had come, and how fast, he sometimes wondered if Ali had deliberately scored low on St Ursula's intelligence test. In early childhood, she had avoided calling any attention to herself. But that was years before her face had been marred, making her the focal point of every room she entered. He suspected the secret of Ali's academic success was a bit darker; that she had worked harder than more gifted students – so that she might live up to the scar.

His niece went against everything he knew of human behavior and logic. The mutilation of her face should have crushed her ego. In no reasonable scenario could Ali have blossomed in this way.

'Allow me, young lady.' William poured her a glass of wine. 'I was just telling Mortimer, I don't know how I could possibly help you. You probably know more about pedophiles than anyone on the Eastern Seaboard. I don't even dabble in the subject.'

'But fifteen years ago you did,' said Ali. 'When you were the acting county medical examiner? You worked on the body of a victim – Susan Kendall.'

William leaned close to her, his voice conspiratorial, almost prissy. 'Now why would you want to dredge up that sad business of the little Kendall girl?'

'I wondered why you didn't collect any forensic evidence.'

'Well, it was obvious she died by a broken neck. No need to go any further. I gave testimony in—'

'No rape kit?'

'No!' William's face flushed to a high red color. 'Ali, it wasn't necessary. The priest was charged with murder, not molestation.'

'One year after the murder', said Ali, 'you published a paper on a genetic abnormality.'

'Genetics?' Mortimer was surprised, for this was far outside the surgeon's field. Most of William Penny's papers had been related to procedures, hardware and chemicals for the heart. Ah, but publishing in another area would fit well with the inflated image of himself as a Renaissance man of modern medicine.

Ali continued, 'It was a postmortem on a little girl. Her surviving identical twin was a boy – a case in a billion.'

'Identical?' Mortimer spilled red drops of wine on the white tablecloth. 'Ali, surely you don't mean monozygotic twins?' When she nodded, he turned to William. 'Of different genders? That's *possible*?'

'That's the problem with shrinks,' said Myles Penny, addressing Ali with a wink. 'They don't keep up on the medical literature.' And now he smiled at his host. 'But you're *way* behind. The first case was reported back in the sixties.'

The psychiatrist dabbed at the wine spill and made it worse. 'A hermaphrodite perhaps? The testicles never descended?'

'No, Mortimer, a *real* girl,' said Myles, despite his brother's attempt at signaling him to shut up. 'Susan Kendall only had female genitalia. 'Course the ovaries were just fibrous knots.'

William slumped back in his chair, lips pressed together in a thin, tight line as he glared unkindly at his brother.

Ali was smiling, and now Mortimer realized she had been on a fishing expedition. Any physician would have taken great care to disguise the identity of his subject, changing the age of the girl and the date of the postmortem.

'Thank you so much, Myles,' said William. 'Old fool. Ali, you can't disclose that information to anyone.'

'I read your autopsy report,' she said. 'There's no mention of the organ abnormalities or the monozygotic aspect. Did you leave out those details so you could be first to publish?'

'Certainly not!' William seemed appalled by Ali's suggestion.

But to Mortimer's thinking, that didn't mean it wasn't true. 'Surely William wasn't the *first* to do a paper on the Kendall twins.'

'I was the *only* one,' said William, somewhat offended. 'Apparently the twins' obstetrician never even considered the possibility. He probably delivered them with separate placentas – that sometimes happens. Any *common* doctor would have assumed they were fraternal.'

Ali was leaning in for another shot at William. Mortimer headed her off, saying, 'So except for the genitalia, the twins were exactly the same?'

'Not exactly.' William happily settled into the lecture mode. 'There would have been a notable increase in chromosomal differences as they aged. But they were much closer than fraternal twins.'

Ali was about to speak, but Mortimer was faster, asking, 'What about the brother? Did he have any problems?'

'Physical problems? No,' said William. 'Perfectly normal. He was the boy Susan should have become – but for some accident of chemistry in the womb. There's a theory that the zygote only divides because it's detected a flaw and wants to slough off the damaged—'

Ali tinged her fork against a glass. A bit gauche in Mortimer's view, but effective. 'Could we get back to the autopsy report?'

'Initially,' said William, 'I withheld the most bizarre aspects out of compassion for the family.'

Ali seemed unconvinced. 'And the father was powerful – influential.'

'That was never a factor.' The surgeon's tone was scolding.

And Mortimer thought William was right to admonish her, for there was quite a distinction between taking graft and the lesser crimes of pomposity and a ruthless rush to publish. He sipped his wine without really tasting it, hardly listening to William anymore.

'Why should I have made the Kendall twins into a freak show for the tabloids?'

'You didn't need a full autopsy,' said Ali. 'A rape kit might have cleared Paul Marie. A surviving sample for DNA—'

'We didn't do DNA tests. They weren't admissible evidence in those days. And the semen was from a nonsecretor, so why bother to keep—' And now William realized he had just confirmed the molestation, and he slowly closed his mouth.

Myles picked up the conversation. 'Ali, you can't type blood from a nonsecretor, but the priest was also a nonsecretor. His own lawyer went along with all of this. Less hostile pretrial publicity if they left out the rape.'

'There was full disclosure.' William had recovered his composure. 'Nothing was done under the table.'

'But none of the autopsy evidence survived, did it?' She had her answer in the ensuing silence.

Mortimer wound one thin hand around the neck of the wine decanter, debating whether or not he could pour with a steady hand. 'They also found Paul Marie's fingerprints on the child's bracelet. That was rather damning.'

'Not necessarily.' Ali stared at her uncle over the rim of her wineglass. 'Susan used to hide things under the cushions of the choir pews. I think it gave her an excuse to go back to the church after choir practice. She probably had a crush on the priest. Every girl in the choir did. He had the most beautiful eyes.'

Mortimer Cray longed to fill his glass again, to surpass a

sick man's allotment of alcohol. But the vessel was made of fine crystal. If his hand should tremble—

Myles Penny reached out and took the decanter. He held it carelessly for a moment, almost as a hostage in an attempt to engage Mortimer's eyes, but the psychiatrist only stared at his empty glass. Myles relented and filled the wineglass almost to the brim.

'I can well believe the child was in love with the priest.' William was on the defensive again. 'You're the expert, Ali. Pedophilia is a disease of seduction, is it not?'

'Sometimes.' Though Ali spoke to William, her eyes were on her uncle. 'But it's a one-sided affair. The child is revolted by the molestation. Isn't that right, Uncle Mortimer?'

He wondered what his niece was playing at, and what was the precise meaning of her unspoken subtext. He chose his words with care. 'Sometimes young children exhibit seductive behavior, most often quite innocent. But I suppose one might speculate on the child's awareness of this behavior.'

'Maybe your patients are coloring your logic, Uncle Mortimer. One patient in particular?'

Mortimer ignored her question and sipped his wine with real thirst. 'William is right. The priest had a fair trial.'

William Penny edged his chair closer to Ali's. 'Tell me you're not on some fanciful mission. You don't want to get that animal out of jail, do you?'

'I don't believe the animal ever went to jail,' she said.

Two more red drops fell from Mortimer's glass to stain the white linen, and he regarded them with a little terror, as though they had come from his own body, and he had been caught in the distasteful act of dying in public.

'I think the monster is still out there, still killing.' She delivered this line with just a shade of anger. 'I've got data on a lot of children. It always happens just before the holidays.' And now she stared at the wine stains on the white cloth, as though they had just reminded her of another matter. 'Uncle

Mortimer? I have to lecture the task force tomorrow. Any theories on the missing girls?'

The psychiatrist only shook his head, and she went on. 'No? Well, I'm guessing this pedophile doesn't have a police record. Too smart and too knowledgeable to get caught.'

'Most of them are never caught. Even the ones with quite ordinary brains get away with it for years – forever.' He now recalled that this had been the main thrust of Ali's Ph.D. dissertation, and she was hardly going to forget it. Was she setting him up for—

'True,' she said. 'But this one's far from the ordinary pervert. There's a strong element of sadism extending beyond the victims. And he doesn't go for the most vulnerable child – that's another departure. He goes for the challenge – takes the girls in broad daylight. I think he likes the risk, or maybe there's more to it. Uncle Mortimer, wouldn't you say he was almost begging to get caught? Sound like any local man you know? Perhaps in a professional—'

'You know better than to ask about my patients, Ali.'

'So you *are* treating a pedophile.'

'I'm not so easy to entrap.' He hastily smiled an apology to William, who had been entirely *too* easy.

'Well, she made a good guess.' Myles turned to Ali. 'So your man is sadistic? He'd never miss an opportunity for torture, would he? Imagine what his confession would do to the shrink he unloaded on. What fun for a sadist.'

'A priest would be safer,' said Mortimer. 'Under certain circumstances, the law can compel a psychiatrist to testify.'

Myles shook his head. 'Only a psychiatrist could really appreciate the details.'

Mortimer kept his silence, disinclined to engage Myles, the more clever of the brothers, though less successful in his medical practice. And this was yet another bit of evidence that the world had come loose from its rational moorings. The ordinary minds excelled, and the extraordinary lagged behind. The Kendall boy once had the promise of a brilliant future, but he had become a common policeman. Ali should have been an anonymous file clerk, not a college professor with a Ph.D. And that damned priest should have grown old in obscurity. Mortimer wondered if he might spend his remaining days writing a paper on the universe pulled inside out, the reversal of reason, the death of logical progression.

And where is the winter? He turned to the glass wall and the green plants just beyond it. There should be two feet of snow in his garden. What was the Lady Nature thinking of to be so late? What else might be wrong with the world?

Myles picked up the dragging end of the conversation. 'What if you were a child killer's confessor, Mortimer? Would you shield a bastard like that?'

Mortimer only stared at the last drops of wine in his glass, but he could feel Myles's eyes on him. In peripheral vision, he caught the quizzical tilt of the doctor's white head.

By the time Dodd appeared, all real conversation had ended, dying off to banal small talk. While the servant cleared away the debris of decanter and wineglasses, Ali walked William out to the car, and Myles Penny lingered awhile to stand by the glass wall with his host.

Mortimer was preoccupied by the dregs of his burgundy and one drop of red on the cuff of his white shirt. And now Myles also fixed upon this spot, pointing to it.

'So what does that remind you of, Mortimer?'

The psychiatrist averted his eyes from the stain and from the man who hovered close by – too close. Mortimer could sense the intense scrutiny of every gesture and perhaps even his thoughts, for Myles was a canny observer.

'I know why you'll never tell.' Myles's voice had the tone of a tentative foray. 'It's not the threat of ruin for exposing a patient. It's pride, isn't it? Your ethics, your rigid laws and rules for a life. The heart is my brother's territory, but I'd say you're practicing the religion of a man who's about to have a massive coronary.'

Mortimer gave no sign that he had heard any of this,

though every word was true. Since he had ceased to take his medication, he could even roughly figure the timing of his final heart attack.

Rouge parked his old Volvo at the main entrance to St Ursula's Academy. The front of the immense red-brick institution was even more imposing than the lakeside view. Four white columns supporting the portico marked it as a serious temple, and atop the black shingles was a cupola of wood and glass, the architect's idea of a formal hat. The only light and gentle elements were taped to the second-floor classroom windows: bright paper silhouettes of Christmas angels, snowflakes and bells.

Rouge glanced at his watch. He was fifteen minutes early for his appointment with Eliot Caruthers, the school's director.

He walked around the side of the building and up the gravel path to Mrs Hofstra's cottage. This week, each of the small group homes would hold only one scholarship child and a housemother. All the students with real families would be gone over the holidays. Though it was early afternoon, the sky was overcast and dark. Warm yellow house lamps and multicolored Christmas tree lights glowed in the cottage window. David was standing on the front stoop, bundled up in a parka that bulged with layers of sweaters. One gloved hand rested on the brass doorknob.

'David!'

The boy jerked his hand away from the knob, as if caught in the attempt to steal it. And now he gaped at the policeman.

'Sorry,' said Rouge, drawing closer. 'I didn't mean to startle you.' He reached into his jacket pocket and pulled out the baseball card. 'I thought you might want this back.'

David reached out and accepted the card. He looked down at it, admiring his new autograph.

'So you like baseball?' A stupid question, but where else to make a beginning?

David nodded, his eyes still cast down on the card in his hand.

'What position do you play?' Ah, now they had a problem. This question required words. But at least David was looking at him. That was progress.

The door opened, and Mrs Hofstra stood in a warm, cheery rectangle of light. 'Well, Rouge Kendall. What a nice surprise.'

By her voice and her smile, he knew she was pleased but *not* surprised to see him again. In his student days, he had lived at home with his parents. Only the boarding students had been charges of the housemothers. But over the years at St Ursula's, these women had all become more than mere acquaintances. When Susan's death had driven his own mother to the solitude of her locked bedroom, Mary Hofstra had rocked him for hours while he cried for his twin. Every one of the housemothers had been kind to him, sensing his needs, knowing when to hold him and when to leave him be. Each of them had nourished him with endless amounts of honey and peppermint tea. He knew all the kitchen tables of all the cottages, and to this day, the scent of peppermint called up memories of love and pain.

'Hi, Mrs Hofstra. I was just asking David what position he played on the baseball team.'

David put one cupped hand to his mouth, and the woman bent down to him so he could whisper in her ear. She smiled at Rouge. 'He wants to be a pitcher – like you.'

'Wants to?' He looked down at David. 'What position do you play now?'

'None,' said Mrs Hofstra, answering for the boy. 'Right now, he plays alone. He's wonderful at bat. They still have the same old machine in the gym, the one you used for batting practice.'

David was walking backward into the cottage, his eyes on Rouge until he disappeared behind Mrs Hofstra's dress.

'Nippy weather, isn't it, Rouge? Come in for a cup of tea.' She turned her head to see David climbing the stairs. In a lower voice, she said, 'Don't be discouraged. It took a month before he'd talk to me. I hope you'll keep trying.' And now she was drawing him inside with the light pressure of her hand on his arm. 'Now don't you worry. I know all about your appointment with Eliot Caruthers. I'll just call and tell him you're with me.'

He knew the school's director would wait with endless patience until Mrs Hofstra was done with her visitor. Rouge remembered the power of the housemothers. They had the last word on the treatment of children, boarders and townies alike. Many a punishment had been averted by being on the good side of this particular woman. The faculty always deferred to Mrs Hofstra, a consummate artist in the mothering trade.

When he was seated at the kitchen table, he noted that nothing had changed but the brand names on the cereal boxes. It might be the same old copper kettle on the stove, and he imagined the flame burning beneath it as eternal. Teas with fruit and candy names filled the cupboard shelves, for this was Mary Hofstra's secret ingredient for healing all wounds. One long, thin hand grazed the tins, as though she might be reading the contents with her fingertips.

She had her back to him when he asked, 'What's wrong with David?'

'He's very shy,' she said, without turning around.

'It's more serious than that.'

'If you need the medical jargon, Rouge, it's called Selective Mutism.'

'And that means—'

'That he's very shy.' She plucked a tin from the shelf and opened it. 'A psychiatrist recommended drug therapy. But I don't much care for the idea of drugging a little boy, so I had Mr Caruthers fire that woman.'

The teakettle's whistle beckoned her to the stove. 'Now David and I work on it the old-fashioned way. He's encouraged to speak, even rewarded for it, but there is absolutely no pressure. If he feels threatened, he withdraws and his therapy is set back.' She looked at Rouge over one shoulder, smiling sweetly as she poured scalding water into the tea mugs. 'So, if you have something like that in mind, my dear – I won't allow it.'

The implied threat hovered between them, though her voice was eminently civil. Even now, as an adult, he knew better than to get on the bad side of a housemother. He reverted to the childhood practice of enlisting her in his cause. 'So, how do I get him to open up with me?'

'Don't worry, Rouge. I'll be encouraging that. I know how much he wants to talk to you. I drove him to the police station this morning. I gathered your meeting with him was unsuccessful.'

They spent the next few minutes basking in the peace of the cottage, dunking their tea bags in companionable silence. Even before he smelled the aroma from the mug, he knew it would be peppermint heavily laced with honey.

'David is making good progress,' Mrs Hofstra confided. 'He makes more eye contact now, and he talks to most of the boys who board with me. But he won't speak to any of his teachers, and he never talks in class. On the bright side, he seems highly motivated to talk to you, dear.' And this pleased her. 'It's going to take some time and patience is all.'

'I don't have time, Mrs Hofstra. Do you know any shortcuts?'

She leaned forward, and with only a trace of suspicion, she studied his face, perhaps looking for deviations from the child she had known. 'There is a way.' And now she smiled. So she must have found him unchanged – still her own Rouge.

'It's a matter of trust, my dear. You have to imagine what it's like to be David, and then create a comfort zone for him. Listen carefully.' Her wrinkled hand lay over his, warm but feather-light and dry as a covering of paper. 'If you take a more direct approach he'll retreat so far inside himself, you'll never reach him again – you'll get nothing.'

Rouge was not surprised that St Ursula's director remembered him so well. Twins tended to linger in the mind, particularly when one of them was found murdered.

'How have you been, Rouge?'

So it was to be 'Rouge', not 'officer' nor any other grown-up title. And of course, he would address the elder man as *Mister* or *sir*; some things never changed.

Eliot Caruthers was the same inscrutable Santa Claus in a three-piece suit. And like the doctor's mythic double, one would say his bearded face was timeless rather than old. The hair had gone from gray to snow white, but it was still a basic bird's nest of lost pencils sticking out at dangerous angles. Now Mr Caruthers recalled where he had left one of them, and he plucked it out from behind his ear to tap it on the desk as a prompt for Rouge. School was still in session between them. The director had asked a test question, and he was waiting on a response.

How have I been?

Well, he had been treading water for most of his life – life after Susan – and he was very tired. 'Oh, I've been just fine, Mr Caruthers. And you?' He looked at his watch, hoping this would convey that a policeman's time was slightly more important. And now he came straight to the business at hand. 'What can you tell me about Gwen Hubble?'

'Only what's in her file.' Mr Caruthers' attitude said he took no offense at Rouge's brusque manner. In fact, he took no notice of it at all.

'So Gwen wasn't a standout in any way?'

The director opened the bulky manila folder on his desk blotter and looked down on the glossy color photograph clipped to the paperwork. 'She's certainly one of the prettiest children I've ever seen. Sometimes I think beauty is a sufficient gift. An intellect in a beautiful child seems almost ostentatious, don't you think?'

Rouge sensed the invitation to another level of dialogue.

He elected to ignore it. 'Other than that pretty face, you're saying Gwen Hubble is ordinary?'

'We don't have ordinary students here.' The director betrayed only the lightest sign of impatience with this former pupil. 'Don't you remember your own entrance exam?'

'You just don't feel like cooperating?'

Now the director smiled. 'Under certain conditions, I have every intention of exchanging confidences with you.'

So nothing said is to leave this room. Rouge continued to stare at the man in silence.

Mr Caruthers broadened his smile in approval of this gambit. 'I can also put valuable resources at your disposal.'

Okay, I'll play. 'Is there something I can do for you, sir?'

The old man inclined his head, almost imperceptibly, and a deal had been struck. 'I have a present for you – one of our teachers.' He opened his desk drawer and pulled out another folder. 'Though he's probably not the man you're looking for. This one only likes little boys. However, I want you to take him with you when our discussion is over. You only have to parade him past a few reporters. And if you can manage it, drop a few unfortunate slips to the press – mention NAMBLA a few times. You're familiar with the initials?'

'Grown-ups who want to date little boys.'

'Close enough.'

'You have proof?'

'No, my boy. If I had proof, I wouldn't need you. I've done a thorough background check and come up with nothing but glowing references. That's not unusual – one school passing the problem along to another. If they can't prove a charge of pedophilia, they want to avoid the lawsuit. And so does St Ursula's.'

He pushed a résumé across the desk. A photograph was clipped to the sheets, a portrait of a pasty white, slack-faced man. 'But this school doesn't intend to pass Gerald Beckerman along. Of course I'd like to have him put away. But if you can't pull that off, I'll settle for a public crucifixion.'

66

'Wouldn't it be easier to fire him?'

'But not nearly as satisfying. And Beckerman has a powerful protector on the board of trustees. I believe that protection will be withdrawn after the press has a turn at the little pervert.'

Rouge scanned the top lines of the résumé.

'You will note,' said Mr Caruthers, 'that he's thirty-eight years old. A predatory interest in children doesn't start so late in life.'

'And you figure, somewhere there must be a history on him.'

'I know you'll find it, Rouge. Then you'll be sure to tell Beckerman's attorney that you uncovered the pedophilia in the course of your kidnap investigation.'

So the director didn't buy the story of runaways, either. 'Sir, how did you find out about this man?'

Caruthers hesitated, perhaps wondering how far to trust this former student. Tentatively, he said, 'I wouldn't like the school to be sued for reading his private mail. However, I will admit to reading his E-mail. The software to eavesdrop came with our computer network. Things have changed a bit since you were with us, Rouge. Every student has a personal computer, even the five-year-olds, so we monitor the children's chat rooms on the Internet. An interesting thing about computer communication – people tend to write the way they talk. Formal structure falls away. It's not like writing a letter when they're typing dialogue in real time. There was a pedophile in one of those chat rooms. He wrote the way Gerald Beckerman talked. You could say I recognized his voice, and it made my flesh crawl.'

'If you can't find any history on him, what makes you think I can?'

'I know you can, Rouge. I know more about you than your mother does.' With a casual hand gesture, he waved these ominous words aside. 'Now what can I do for *you*? You have only to ask.'

Rouge faced the casement window near his chair. Beyond

the glass pane, a small moving figure captured his attention. David was walking down the sloping grass and heading toward the lake. 'I understand David Shore has a scholarship.'

Mr Caruthers nodded. 'I've heard the rumors in town. They think all the scholarship children were sold to us for science experiments. And of course, that's true.'

Rouge smiled, though it wasn't always easy to tell when Mr Caruthers was joking. He kept his eyes on the window, following David's progress toward the boathouse. The foot of the wharf and all but the roof and the far edge of the building were hidden by a stand of evergreen trees. David disappeared behind this cover.

The director continued, 'Sadie Green is also a scholarship child, but she's an exception. Her parents are rather attached to her, so it never occurred to us to make a cash offer.'

Rouge's smile was edging off. David had reappeared on the wharf beyond the point where it was obscured by trees, and he was slowly walking toward the end of the planks extending far into the lake. The boy stopped and turned to look back at the boathouse.

'Most of our scholarship children are harvested from foster homes. The absentee parents are tracked down and paid off. Our attorneys nail down absolute custody for—'

'Stop,' said Rouge. Now Mr Caruthers had his complete attention again. 'Backup. You really do this? You *buy* the scholarship kids?'

'Oh, yes. Though, technically, the housemothers are the legal guardians. We can't have the biological parents coming back and messing up the child's future with poverty.'

And what about the children? Did Mr Caruthers think they didn't miss their parents, that—

'This is hardly a cold, impersonal orphanage, Rouge,' said the mind-reading director. 'Each of the housemothers has one scholarship child in her care all year round. A very stable environment.'

Rouge turned back to the window. David was gone again.

The end of the wharf was deserted. Now the boy re-emerged on the other side of the dense clot of pines, all but standing at attention and staring at the boathouse. Then he turned abruptly to look back toward the school. David was too far away for Rouge to guess the focus point of the boy's eyes, but there was an unsettling feeling of communion.

Without turning away from the window, Rouge said, 'David's high in the genius range, right? Are you planning to make him into a little scientist, sir?'

'We don't do that, Rouge. We never interfere with the child's ambition. It wasn't done to you or Susan, was it? No, of course not. That would be counter to our interests. We're in the prediction business.' Mr Caruthers swiveled his chair around to look out the window, and together they watched the child walk back up the hill toward the school.

Rouge pulled out his notebook and pen. 'What do you predict for David?'

'I'd say he has a future in baseball. That's based on his passion and physical aptitude. We never made that prediction for you, Rouge. Even though your case was marred by the loss of wealth, I believe our original prophecy will play out.'

Mr Caruthers moved his chair around to face his visitor, and there was a vague disappointment in the man's eyes, perhaps because Rouge seemed not to care about this portent of his own future. The director went on in a drier recital. 'Later in life, David will be drawn to a second career in physics. That's based on his intellectual gifts.'

Now the boy was standing on the grass under the window. Rouge looked past the child to the lake and wondered what that little scene had been about. David was also staring at the lake and nodding his head.

Something was going on here. David turned his small face up to the window. Their eyes met, and Rouge was hardly paying attention to the school's director anymore.

What am I missing, David?

'The personality profiles tell us much more interesting

things,' said Mr Caruthers. 'And very early on. You and your sister, for instance. By the time you and Susan were eight, we knew you were both destined for formidable careers in law.'

David walked away in the direction of the cottage. Rouge looked down at his notebook and made a crude map of the wharf and the boathouse.

Mr Caruthers droned on. 'Your own profile was matched with distinguished graduates over the past hundred years. But you were unique for the way you processed information. We always had a keen interest in your future.'

'And my father's money.' Rouge made a note on the stand of pine trees between the window and the boathouse.

'The high tuition favors the student with money to exploit his full potential. Without that backing, the child might not reach the projected goal, and that would ruin our statistics.'

'Like I did?'

'Did you, Rouge? It was regrettable that you had to leave Princeton, but understandable with your father's death, all the family debts – and your mother's *health* problems. Now that year in baseball was a fascinating quirk. But I found it more interesting that you became a policeman. And now with your recent promotion to BCI investigator, you seem to have found your calling. You were quite literally born to do this work.'

Rouge shifted in his chair. He was feeling naked and not liking it at all. Though the director persisted in his Santa Claus persona, the doppelgänger seemed darker now.

'Surprised, Rouge? Did you think we'd lost interest in you? Oh, no. We're always collecting data.'

'I need to know more about the girls.' He turned to a new page in his notebook. 'Could they outsmart the average adult?'

'Don't count on it. Gwen Hubble has the higher IQ – close to yours. However, she's very literal – no good at subter- fuge.' He sorted through the papers in her file. 'Based on extensive psychological profiles, I predict that she will physi- cally and emotionally shut down in any fearful situation. I'd say her prospects of finding her own way home are rather bleak.'

'And Sadie Green?'

'Completely different story. Sadie once managed to outwit the school nurse *and* the village police. She faked her own death with an arrow.'

'That was her?' Rouge remembered the day, only three weeks ago. Two of the village cops had come back to the station at the end of their shift; one was laughing, and the other man's face was red with humiliation. Chief Croft still tormented the poor rookie who had called for the county meat wagon. The town's youngest officer, Billy Poor, had never suspected that the arrow in the child's chest might be a prop decorated with fake blood – not until the little girl jumped up and ran away laughing. Patrolman Poor had sworn that the child's eyes never blinked, and this had been his criterion for a corpse.

Rouge made a drawing of an arrow at the top of a clean page in his notebook. 'Is Sadie a good student?'

'The worst. She daydreams in class, and she's late with all her assignments. The child has a grisly imagination and absolutely adores bloody violence. But we'd still like to have her back.'

'Could Sadie have engineered the disappearance? She seems to have a—'

'Not her style, though she *is* a bad influence on Gwen Hubble. No, I'd say faking a kidnapping is much too subtle. Sadie only goes for the gold – the death scene. I think she needs the immediate gratification of scaring the shit out of people.'

The word 'shit' was not in this man's vocabulary, and Rouge wondered if Sadie had also been a bad influence on Mr Caruthers. 'Exactly how smart is this kid?'

'I'd say we were evenly matched. When Sadie and I lock horns over some disciplinary problem, she only beats me half the time.'

'Didn't you say she had a scholarship? That puts her in David's IQ range, right?'

'Not even close. Sadie won her tuition waiver with a comic book.' Mr Caruthers reached out to the corner of his desk and opened another file. He handed Rouge a small homemade magazine of crayon drawings and little paragraphs carefully penned inside white balloon shapes. 'I hope you had an early lunch. It's gross. She was seven years old when she made it.'

Rouge thumbed through the comic book of brilliant colors and outrageous pictures. All the bizarre cartoon characters had rather interesting ideas on how to kill one another with the maximum amount of mutilation.

'I don't know what goes on inside that child,' said Mr Caruthers. 'There's no test for it.'

Rouge closed the comic book and held it up to the director. 'Are you saying *this* was her entrance exam?'

Caruthers shook his head. 'Sadie failed the exam. She's very bright, but she missed the cutoff score by more than just a few points. Even if her parents could've managed the full tuition, we would've denied her a place in the school. However, Sadie's mother doesn't take rejection very well. The woman insisted on an appointment.'

'Mrs Green talked you into—'

'No. I expected histrionics, but Mrs Green outsmarted me. Never even said hello when she walked in. She stood Sadie in front of my desk, handed me that comic book and left the room. *Neglected* to collect her child on the way out. Interesting woman.'

He slapped one hand down on the desk. 'I read every single page of that incredibly gory, bloody – *thing*. And then I looked up at Sadie. It's hard to describe her smile – I'd swear she was daring me to let her in.' Mr Caruthers took back the comic book, handling it with great care, almost tenderness. 'Now three years have gone by, and Sadie still takes prisoners – but that sweet stage won't last long.'

*

There was no window in the room, and she knew there was something odd about that, but the idea slipped away from her as she stared at the tray.

Never enough food.

Gwen Hubble had awakened to cocoa and a buttered roll this time. The juice and egg had been her last meal, so another day must have gone by.

How many days now? Three?

She had intended to flush her last meal down the toilet, knowing it must be tainted with the potion that made her sleep all the time. Though her dog's medications were always put into his water bowl, she had eliminated the liquid possibilities by drinking her morning orange juice with no ill effects. Then weakness had won out, and she had eaten the drugged breakfast egg. With a clearer mind, she might have reasoned it out sooner, for liquid could be had from the water tap, and solid food would be the strongest lure.

Now, with greater resolve, she crumbled her dinner roll into small pieces that wouldn't clog the toilet. Her stomach was knotting up with hunger pains, and she was feeling another wave of nausea.

Gwen worked by the dim glow of the night-light. It was not bright enough to see clearly, and it was by touch that she detected the soft, moist center of the roll. Perhaps the drug was injected into the middle of the bread.

So hungry.

She tested one of the dry crumbs of the outer crust, resting it on her tongue. There was nothing unusual in the taste, and so she swallowed it.

Perhaps she wouldn't have to flush away the entire roll.

The child separated the suspicious center from the rest of the roll and set it off to one side of the plate. She continued to shred the dry section to make the tiny meal last longer. She ate another dry crumb and stared at the chained wall hamper. Then she stood up and walked across the oval rug to pull on its door. The hamper opened a crack, but there was not enough light to see what was inside, and her hand would not fit through the narrow opening. Gwen went back to the cot and sat down again, eyes fixed on the locked chain strung between the hamper's handle and the towel rack.

She was trying to remember something important about padlocks, but then her eye wandered back to the large armoire, so out of place in this bathroom. She tried to recall a train of thought that revolved around this massive piece of furniture, but like a dream, the harder she worked to remember it, the more it receded into the dark and fuzzy recesses of her mind.

She ate another crumb.

Now she moved slowly across the rug and onto the bare tiles, hands reaching out to the armoire. The doors were locked. She speculated on what it might be holding – or concealing.

That's it.

There should be a window in this room, for it was not a closet, not a boxroom. And this was no modern building like Sadie's house with electric fans for ventilation. By the high ceiling and the molding around the tiles, she guessed it was as old as her own house where each one of the numerous bathrooms had a window.

One small hand squeezed between the back of the armoire and the wall. Her fingers found the wooden frame, and then the sill – a window. She pushed against the furniture with all her might, but it would not move. She went back to the tray on the table by her cot and ate more crumbs for energy.

Oh, how dumb. She needed leverage, not muscle.

Gwen picked at the remaining crumbs as she looked around the room for something she could use as a prybar. The cot was a trove of levers in its legs and slats. And now her eyes were riveted to the tray. She could see more clearly – too clearly.

She had eaten the entire roll, including the dangerous moist center.

Oh, stupid Gwen! Stupid, stupid!

74

Tears streamed down her face as her legs folded, and her small body fell to the floor. Her eyes were closing. And only now it occurred to her that someone might be starving Sadie too, and drugging her best friend's eggs and rolls.

Her hand went to the amulet with the magic engraving of the all-seeing eye, a gift from Sadie, a comfort in the dark.

It was gone.

Gwen sat up, resisting, fighting sleep. She spread her hands along the floor, searching with her fingertips, exploring all the ridges of the rug and the grout between the tiles.

It was not here. She had lost her eye. The amulet was gone.

And now her body was made of lead. She spread out flat on the tiles, and her soft, rounded cheek pressed into the hard floor.

First she whispered it as a question, and then with great effort, she lifted her face and screamed, 'Sadie! Where are you!'

The reporters were back in full force this evening, filling the short flight of stone steps leading up to the station house. Most of them were feeding on sandwiches and coffee. Some were stamping their feet to shake off the cold night air.

Rouge opened the passenger door and roughly pulled out his gift from Mr Caruthers. Gerald Beckerman was startled, mouth hanging open as he was dragged from the front seat. The English teacher had been lured into the car with the pretense of polite questions about his missing students. Beckerman had made amiable conversation all the way to the police station. But now he was being treated like a criminal. And then he began to act like one, eyes full of fear as he tried to pull away from Rouge's firm grasp.

One reporter's nose went up. And then the rest of them were turning on the car, heads swiveling to watch the cop and his prisoner. The men and women were slowly moving down the steps. Some had already crossed to the parking lot, heading toward Rouge and the teacher, circling around them, watching, waiting.

When the media people were all together in one encompassing mob, Rouge made the promised announcement. 'Gerald Beckerman is only here to assist the police in the investigation. This has nothing to do with any connections he might have to NAMBLA.'

One reporter stood out in the lead. 'So, you're saying he only does little boys?'

First blood.

Two reporters converged in a flanking maneuver. 'Hey, Beckerman, is that right? Or do you swing both ways?'

And now they were on the man, the whole pack, elbowing and crowding one another, jockeying for position, yelling questions, coming at Beckerman from every side and backing him up against the car – no escape now, nowhere to run.

Rouge stood at the edge of the fray and watched the teacher go down, figuratively and literally, for Beckerman was sliding along the side of the Volvo, tucking in his head as he sank to the ground. His hands were outstretched, flailing wildly in an attempt to stave off the cameras.

Behind him Rouge heard one of the reporters talking to Marge Jonas, addressing her as *doctor*. The secretary had just passed herself off as a cophouse shrink, and Rouge supposed this was closer to her true job description. He looked back over one shoulder to see Marge primping her blond wig in the reflection of a wide camera lens.

The reporter was saying, 'Isn't that the same cop who caught the guy with the purple bike?'

'Yes,' said Marge, winking at Rouge. 'He's as good as it gets. Real star quality, don't you think?'

'So, Dr Jonas, that's two suspects for the State Police in two days. And what contribution has the FBI made?'

'None,' said Marge. 'But the feds are real nice guys. They bought the doughnuts yesterday *and* today.'

A dour Captain Costello stood at the top of the stairs,

hands jammed in his pockets and watching the carnage in the parking lot. A woman with a microphone was climbing toward the captain in company with a cameraman. And once again, it was a reporter who delivered the rookie investigator's arrest report.

The last thing Rouge had expected was Captain Costello's broad grin.

CHAPTER 4

The daily routine of St Ursula's had been altered for the scholarship students who remained at school over Christmas vacation. The adults' soft lies of 'lost classmates' had percolated through the children's conversations and were distilled into truth.

So the girls had been kidnapped, their lives interrupted – but boyhood was an ongoing thing. Defying the new rules confining them to the campus, two students had voyaged across the lake to conduct an experiment unobserved. They had taken a canoe, but not the requisite adult – another broken rule.

One twelve-year-old was fair and the other was dark, but beneath the cosmetic differences of skin and hair, they had been up to no good when they started out after breakfast; they were indistinguishable in this. And so it was predictable that they would be in deep trouble within half an hour of landing on the far shore.

Adding to the misery of guilt and impending doom, their shoes and socks were wet. The canoe had not been pulled far enough onto the rocky beach, and the constant lap of water had coaxed it back into the lake. The boys watched the craft glide away until it disappeared around an outcrop of rocks. They turned to face the sprawling old house. It had seemed so normal when they arrived, but now the building took on a sinister character. They read the weathered paint as disease, and the dark windows with drawn curtains were taken for deception and secrecy. A stiff, cold wind rushed off the lake and drove them to shelter on the shadow side of the structure.

Here, they took a closer look at their own recent violence of a broken window. A foul odor wafted through the shards of glass. Vomit was rising in the children's throats, a second visit from this morning's sausages and eggs – a taste of things to come. Wait till the adults found out about their science experiment, which had more power, greater velocity, and – best of all – it made more noise than the average child's toy gun.

'We're gonna catch it this time.' Jesse hid the modified pistol behind his back, as though they had already been caught in the act. 'He'll find out, whether we tell him or not. Sometimes I think Mr Caruthers knows what we're going to do before we do it.'

Mark lightly punched him on the arm. 'You know why, you dork? When he said hello this morning, your face turned bright red. You think that didn't tip him off?'

They looked across the lake to the red-brick institution atop the hill. Might the old man be watching them now? Over the years at St Ursula's Academy, they had forgotten the unlimited freedom of neglect in old environs, and they had become accustomed to the ever watchful housemothers and the faculty's deep interest in all their affairs, rule-abiding or illicit.

They turned back to the broken window. A curtain covered the hole, and neither boy wanted to see what lay beyond the cloth.

'What *is* that smell?' Jesse thought it was very like the odor of old people – his own grandmother rotting away in the state nursing home.

But Mark had come from an urban rat maze of a thousand anonymous doors along thirty flights of corridors, and he knew exactly what it was. 'That's what death smells like.'

'Oh, Jesus.' Jesse dropped the gun. 'We killed somebody?'

'No, jerkoff. It's *old* death.' Like the odorous deaths that had seeped under the doorsills of the tenement house that was once his home. Bodies, waiting on discovery, had sent stinking invitations along the hallways to their undertakers. Mark sought a reference point that his more rural classmate might understand. 'It's like old roadkill – something that got run over *days* ago.'

Though the briefing was limited to members of the task force, reporters and politicians outnumbered and outshouted the FBI agents and BCI investigators. The armed presence of state troopers had no effect on the feeding frenzy of television crews and journalists. A crush of bodies closed around Rouge Kendall as he backed up to the wall of the ground-floor reception area.

Captain Costello appeared at the bottom of the stairs, and the crowd shifted toward him, creating a momentary parting in the screaming sea of bobbing heads and camera equipment. It was no surprise to see Senator Berman, tall, reedy and cadaver white. Wherever there was human misery and a photo opportunity, the state's most mobbed-up senator would be there, doing nothing useful, yet maintaining the illusion of being in charge. But now the reporters were in love with Costello and turned their backs on the Senator. In the absence of focussed cameras, Berman wore no expression as he moved toward the door. The lifeless, dull brown eyes seemed blind to the press of living flesh all around him.

Standing only a few feet away was the familiar and more repulsive figure of a former BCI investigator. Oz Almo was swaddled in a winter coat and a sick-sweet cloud of cologne. Rouge remembered the excess of scent from his childhood, though it was a cheaper brand the first time they had met. As a ten-year-old he had wondered if the perfume was slathered on to mask another odor, for the intuition of something hidden was strong and persistent. The ex-BCI man was slowly turning around as he pulled a fur hat from his sweating bald

80

head. And now the detail of reddened eyes completed the image of a pudgy, wrinkled baby who drank too much.

Before Oz Almo could make eye contact, Rouge moved away quickly. He was about to climb the stairs to the task-force room when Marge Jonas appeared in front of him, decked out like a fire engine in a bright-red sweater dress. All her chins jiggled as she shook her head in dismay. 'Sweetie, tell me you're not wearing the same thing you had on yesterday.'

He flashed his best smile. 'I changed my shirt and under-wear, just for you.'

'You devil.' She dropped a veil of false eyelashes and put a warm cup in his hand. The coffee was black, and he knew it would contain exactly three sugars, as it always did when Marge was about to make a strong suggestion.

Oz Almo was looking at him now, raising one hand in a friendly wave. There was no escape for Rouge; Marge's fingers had a death grip on his arm. 'Hon, I saw all the paperwork for your pay raise. You can afford another sports coat, okay? Maybe some trousers? A new tie?'

He had lost track of Almo by sight, but he could smell the man's cologne. And now a thick hand weighed down his shoulder.

'Rouge, boy,' said Almo as if they were old friends. They were not. 'How the hell are you, kid? You know, we don't see enough of each other these days.'

'Almo,' said Rouge, nodding curtly to the older, shorter man, though his mother had taught him better manners; he knew well enough to address a person of sixty-five with more respect.

Oz Almo grabbed up Rouge's right hand and pumped it between two sweaty palms. 'Great to see you again, boy. Hey, Marge, how ya doin'?'

'Hello, Oz.' Marge's nostrils were delicately flared and obviously offended. She left them quickly, stepping lightly into the crowd, and it closed behind her like a door.

Rouge pulled his hand free of Almo's and wiped it on his

jacket, as though he had touched something unclean. And he had.

The old man appeared not to notice the insult. His mouth was a wide, fake smile of yellow teeth. 'You have to stop by my place sometime, kid. You never saw my lake house, did you? Say, why not come over for dinner tonight?'

Rouge only stared at him, making no response. The older man's face fell, but then he recovered his smile. 'Hey, I read about your task-force assignment. Congratulations. I never made investigator till I was close to forty.' He nodded toward the double doors at the end of the hall. 'Can you get me into the briefing?'

'What for?'

'Well, I like to keep my hand in, kid. I really do miss the action.'

By the expensive winter coat, Rouge guessed the trade of private detective had been far more lucrative. And he had to wonder about that in a town six inches wide.

'Say, you're doing great, Rouge. Saw you on TV last night, bringing in that pervert schoolteacher. Oh, and the bike thief – that was fuckin' fantastic. How'd you find the kid's bike so fast?'

'Dumb luck – same way you found my sister's body.'

Almo's jaw went slack. 'Now that's no way to talk. Your old man wouldn't a liked that. You know, since your dad died, I think of you as my own—'

'Push off, Oz!' Captain Costello's voice cut through the surrounding babble. He was almost on top of Almo when the old man, quick as a thief, ducked back into the crowd. The captain turned to Rouge. 'You can pass on the briefing, Kendall.'

'I'm on the task force. Oz read that in the morning newspaper, so it must be true.'

Captain Costello elected to pass on the light sarcasm. He nodded toward the staircase leading up to the briefing room.

'There's crime scene shots of old cases all over the walls. Lots of little girls – all dead.'

'So?'

County Medical Examiner Howard Chainy was a man of average height in middle age. A meticulously trimmed moustache gave his bushy eyebrows the comparative look of unkempt hedges. And because he had fallen in love with his ratty old athletic shoes and would not part with them, one might believe he had stolen the well-made topcoat and the black fedora. Under his winter wrapping, he was dressed for a game of racquetball. He glanced at his watch and worried about losing his court reservation.

Well, how complicated could this be?

Dr Chainy had stepped out of his private car just in time to settle the disputed ownership of the dead body. The van from the county morgue was parked close to the lake, and its gray metal doors hung open, awaiting the corpse. Only a few yards away, a closed black body bag lay on a gurney.

As the doctor examined his assistant's hasty notes, he lifted one hand in a greeting for Eliot Caruthers, of St Ursula's Academy. Then he glanced at the two boys, identified as Mark and Jesse. Both children had the look of pained expectations. Apparently, Caruthers was saving his lecture for a more private moment when he had the errant students alone in his office. This was a minor bit of sadism practiced by every good parent or guardian: let the child's imagination do all the hard work, conjuring up the worst possible penalties for possessing a pellet gun and breaking a window. Later there would be a punishment, but first, the real torture – anticipation.

The medical examiner looked over the rest of the assembled company. Two men in dark suits stood by the black hearse from the Makers Village Funeral Parlor. They were engaged in a heated argument with a local police officer, Phil Chapel, who was saying – yelling – that the corpse on the gurney belonged to him.

Dr Chainy had no idea why the young policeman might want a dead body.

The chief of the village police stood off to one side of the battle. Chief Croft's hair had gone gray, and his weathered face was gathering more wrinkles by the minute, but the blue eyes were young and gleeful. The director of the funeral home was exasperated; the young cop was livid; another uniformed officer was studying the clouds overhead and pretending that he did not know Phil Chapel; and Charlie Croft was obviously enjoying the show as a pure spectator.

Dr Chainy caught the chief's eye and nodded in Phil Chapel's direction. 'I gather he's the one who called out my meat wagon?'

Chief Croft smiled. 'How'd you guess?'

'Oh, shot in the dark.'

In recent years, the local funeral parlor had passed into the hands of an idiot renowned for grinning corpses; fixing features of the deceased in expressions more appropriate to a winter vacation in the tropics. The faces of happy, albeit dead, customers communicated postcard sentiments of, 'Having a wonderful time, wish you were here'. In any fair comparison, Officer Chapel was not a complete fool. He had merely gone a little strange today.

The medical examiner looked at his watch again. He might still make his date for racquetball. He pointed to the zippered body bag on the gurney. 'My assistant says it's a natural death.'

'I should hope so. The old lady must have been ninety years old. Take a look for yourself.'

'No thanks, Charlie. I understand her own doctor examined her a few days ago?'

'Right again, Doc. I found a bottle of pills with Dr Penny's name on it and called his office. The nurse was a little put out. Said she already gave that information to the funeral parlor.'

Officer Chapel and the funeral director were engaged in a swordplay of pointing fingers. The other uniformed cop was

84

walking away from the gurney, perhaps not wanting to be on the winning side of a contest for a corpse.

Sensible young man.

Dr Chainy turned back to the chief, who was still maintaining neutrality. 'What am I doing here, Charlie? Her own doctor can sign the death certificate.'

'Well, Phil tends to get a little excited sometimes. Part of the ceiling came down in the old lady's bedroom. Phil thinks it might be a sign of foul play. He's hoping it's a gigantic bullet hole.'

Dr Chainy looked back at the small pellet gun Eliot Caruthers was holding, and he shook his head. 'But no holes in the body? We still got a natural death here?'

'Yeah, your guy called it right. I'd say she died in her sleep. Looked real peaceful when we found her. Dr Penny's on the way over now.'

'So, Charlie, did you get a good look at the *alleged* bullet hole in the ceiling?'

'Yeah. It's a real mess. I suppose a large military cannon could've done it. But whoever aimed it was a real poor shot. Missed the old woman by a mile. Her bed was clear on the other side of—'

'And in the *absence* of a cannon?'

'You're taking all the fun out of this, Howard. Well, there was a lot of water pouring out of the hole. I had to turn off the feed line for a toilet tank on the second floor. Stank some. I figure it was stopped up awhile before it broke. That's probably what brought down the ceiling plaster. That or the cannonball nicked a pipe. Phil thought there was a whiff of gunpowder between the stink of the corpse and the toilet. Couldn't smell it myself. Say, maybe you could stick your nose in the door and give me a professional—'

'I like the leaky pipe theory.' Dr Chainy called out to the excited young officer, who was still arguing with the funeral director. 'Phil? We're gonna let them have the damn body.'

The men in dark suits were moving toward the gurney, but

the policeman wrapped both hands around the chrome rail and held fast.

Chief Croft stepped forward and yelled, 'I think they really want that body more than you do, Phil. Be a good sport, okay?' He turned to Dr Chainy. 'I don't like to thwart Phil's enthusiasm.'

A deflated young officer stood to one side as the men in the dark suits captured the gurney and wheeled it toward the black hearse.

They would need the death certificate before they could take the body away. The medical examiner reluctantly pulled a block of printed forms from his briefcase and resigned himself to losing the racquetball court. It was unlikely that the old woman's personal physician would show up in time to take the paperwork off his hands.

'Charlie, you got a statement from the little boys?'

'You mean the salt and pepper gang?'

Dr Chainy was suppressing a smile when he joined Eliot Caruthers and the guilt-ridden duo, Mark and Jesse. 'You're not in any trouble, kids. In fact, it's a good thing you found her. She was a very old lady – probably didn't have any local family to check in on her.'

He glanced at the homemade gun in Eliot Caruthers' hand. It had the look of a clumsy plastic toy. 'So that's the *weapon*. I guess you could mess up a good-sized flea with a pellet from a thing like that. I had one of those guns when I was a kid.'

Mark and Jesse were looking up at him, and their eyes said, no, they didn't think so – not a gun quite like this one.

Well, he reasoned, kids could never imagine adults as young people. To Caruthers he said, 'Eliot, you can take them on back to the school. How many kids have you got over the holidays?'

'Eleven.' The school's director gave no outward sign of his feelings. The boys stole guilty glances at him in a futile attempt to assess their damages.

'Well, I'd keep them close to home till we find out what happened to those girls.'

'Thank you, Howard, I will.' Eliot Caruthers shook hands with the medical examiner. As he was marching his young charges toward the vintage Rolls-Royce, he turned back with an afterthought. 'Oh, Howard? There won't be any news of this incident in the—'

'The newspapers? No, not if I can help it.' There were already enough rumors circulating about the school for the rich and the strange. No need to feed the townspeople ideas about the children being dangerous. He watched the school's director load the boys into his car and drive back toward the dirt road connecting all the lakefront houses.

Charlie Croft shrugged, saying, 'Kids.' In that one word he summed up all the world's pranks, rude noises and now a dead body.

Another car came down the road, announcing itself with a coughing engine and churning dust. The station wagon pulled up next to the black hearse. The driver, Dr Myles Penny, seemed mildly pissed off as he opened the car door. The general practitioner's hair was ruffled, and he had not yet shaved this morning.

'Hey, Myles,' said Charlie Croft. 'Sorry about your patient.'

'She's William's patient, not mine. But he's on vacation this week.' Myles slammed the car door a bit harder than necessary. 'You know William and his damn vacation time.'

Indeed. However, Dr Chainy knew for a fact that William was still in town. He had seen the man skulking about in the village tobacco store that stocked his personal blend. But God forbid a dead patient should intrude on the heart surgeon's personal time.

Myles Penny pulled back the zipper on the body bag and looked down on the ivory-white face of an elderly woman. 'Yeah, she's dead all right.' The general practitioner glared at the county medical examiner. 'So, Howard, you guys called me all the way out here for a second opinion? How many gradations of dead are there? *Very* dead, *really* dead, *completely* dead—'

'I understand she had a thorough exam four days ago. Is that right, Myles?'

'Three or four days. William wanted to put her in the hospital and crack her chest open again. The old lady told him to stick that entire hospital where the sun never shines. Her very words.'

And now it was Dr Chainy's turn to be angry. 'So that SOB *knew* she was in bad shape, and he never bothered to check on—'

'Settle down, Howard.' Myles put one hand on the medical examiner's shoulder to remind him of his high blood pressure. 'She wasn't all alone out here. There's a hired girl comes in every day to cook and clean.' He rubbed one hand over the stubble on his chin. 'I can't recall her name.'

'Well, this is a waste of time.' Dr Chainy ripped a sheet of paper from his pad. 'Here, Myles. You can take care of the paperwork.'

Myles Penny frowned as he accepted the printed form for the death certificate. 'Am I supposed to thank you for this, Howard?'

'No need. You know if there's a family lawyer?'

'Nope.' Myles spread the form on the hood of his station wagon and began to fill in the blank lines. 'William will know. She's been his patient for about ten, eleven years now.' He looked at the broken window and shook his head. 'Damn kids. Was it a rock, or what? My nurse said—'

'Oh, it's lucky the boys happened by and found her,' said Dr Chainy, ignoring the question. He turned to Charlie Croft. 'I think we can leave the kids out of the police report. Nobody's gonna be pressing charges for that window. Oh, and somebody ought to have a word with that hired girl. Find out why she didn't report the death.'

Chief Croft nodded. 'I'll put Phil on it. You think the girl might have run off with something valuable?'

'Now did I say that?' A crime would complicate things, but he could deal with that later. Just now he had a racquetball game awaiting him. 'Maybe you and Myles could have a look around. See if there's any *obvious* signs of theft.' *And please don't find any.* He was enjoying the lull, the unusual lack of business in his morgue. A robbery would put this old woman's corpse on his table.

Myles looked up from his paperwork. 'And since you're so busy, you figure all my patients can wait while I take care of that little chore?'

'Thanks, Myles. And maybe you can get a man out here to board up that window.'

'Right. And then later, I could just tidy up the dishes in the kitchen sink?'

Howard Chainy slapped him on the back. 'You're a real sport, Myles.'

Rouge Kendall only recognized a few faces among the FBI contingent. More agents had come to town in the past twenty-four hours, and now they accounted for nearly half this gathering of over fifty people.

At the back of the task-force room, a few men and women dangled cigarettes out an open window and exhaled blue clouds of smoke into the wind. Other BCI investigators sat on the tables and desks pushed against the walls. Most of the federal agents were clustered in standing groups of low conversations. The rest sat on folding chairs arranged in rows before a black metal lectern, which looked suspiciously like the sheet music holder from the local elementary school. The men outnumbered the women by at least six to one. No one but Rouge was under thirty-five, and most were at least ten years older.

The only man close to his own age was the uniformed state trooper posted at the door to keep out all but the invited. Rouge walked past the rows of chairs to stand by the windows of the rear wall. Turning his back on the assembly, he looked out over the vacant lot next to the station house. The grass was worn away in the configuration of a baseball diamond. This had been the home of the Makers Village Athletic League, where cops and firemen had donated their time to teach generations of kids the art of the all-American game. Now the lot was surrounded by an unfriendly chainlink fence, and the far corner was a collection of bricks and building materials. Come spring, the old baseball field would be the home of a discount furniture store, a new source of tax revenue for the town. Rouge thought the town council had made a bad trade.

When he turned around, his view of the front wall was partially obscured by the stocky build of Buddy Sorrel, a senior BCI investigator. Over the top of Sorrel's graying crew cut, Rouge could see a collage of dead children pinned to the wall in eight-by-ten color glossies and newsprint shots of black and white. Five of the photographs were poster size and set on freestanding easels. The first in this row of large portraits was hidden from him, blocked by Captain Costello's body. Rouge could make out the strands of auburn hair, a bit of pale skin – Susan?

Of course it was.

Two men passed in front of him, and when he could see this easel again, the photograph of his sister was gone, and Captain Costello was standing behind the lectern.

'Ladies and gentlemen?' The captain looked once around the room. Every head turned toward him. Paper coffee cups settled to laps and all conversation ceased. 'First, I want to give you an update on the case. Please refer to your diagrams for the bus route.'

Everyone but Rouge pulled out a sheet of paper with red and blue map lines.

'One of the troopers found a child's down jacket near the highway.' Costello held up his own map for the gathering to see, and his pencil pointed to a spot in the upper right-hand corner. 'Mark the exit for Herkimer. That's not far off the route of the bus that stops near the Hubble place. So we could still have a case of runaways. We're not giving up on that theory. I don't want to find out later that those two kids died of exposure while we were waiting on a ransom note.' He was staring at Rouge as he said this, and then his eyes traveled over all the heads in the room.

'The jacket we found is purple, and it matches the description of Sadie Green's clothing. It's torn up pretty bad. The techs say it looks like a dog's been at it. We're waiting for Sadie's mother to come in and make a positive identification.'

The captain turned to the group of men and women near the wall of windows. 'The second line of investigation is the ransom motive. Special Agent Arnie Pyle will brief us on that scenario.'

The cluster of federal agents fanned out along the bank of windows, putting some distance between themselves and a man who sat on the broad sill, legs dangling. He might be in his late thirties, and he was not Rouge's idea of a typical FBI man. Special Agent Pyle lacked the ramrod posture, and his body type was more to lean wire than the solid muscle of his companions. Even the female feds seemed to be made of more solid stuff. But it was the man's large brown eyes that captured Rouge's attention. He knew those eyes, though nothing else about the angular face was at all familiar.

The door opened, and a state trooper stood to one side to admit the woman Rouge had encountered at Dame's Tavern, the one who smiled with only half her face. Captain Costello seemed relieved to see her.

'But our first speaker', said the captain, 'will be Dr Ali Cray.' All eyes were fixed on the dark-haired woman with the long skirt and the twisted red mouth. When she turned to face them, the room was quiet. Then began the asides of low voices, and several whispered words for ugly could be discerned over the general babble of males at the back of the room.

'Dr Cray is joining the task force as a volunteer,' said Costello. 'She'll be advising us as a forensic psychologist with expertise in pedophilia. That's the third line of investigation.'

He beckoned her to the front of the room, 'Dr Cray?' He backed away to stand by the wall of photographs.

As Ali Cray walked across the wide floor, the slit in her skirt opened and closed, flashing a slice of white leg with each step, and all the men ceased to stare at her scarred face. When she came to rest behind the lectern, the pipe-thin pedestal afforded an open view of her long skirt, and though the curtain was closed, the men continued to watch the slit.

No one made a sound, not a cough, not a whisper. The lady owned the entire room. Yet she seemed so vulnerable, the only civilian among this battalion of law enforcement officers. That was the first mark against her – Ali Cray was not one of them. Then she would fall to the bottom of the scale on a male's grading system for women; the scar had cost her that many points. And last, the female investigators and feds would not forgive her for the brief but wildly inappropriate display of bare leg – another crime.

Suddenly, Rouge found her very brave, standing up there alone, hanging out in the harsh light of judgment with her scar and her slit skirt.

'Good morning,' she said, poised between two of the giant easel portraits of dead children. 'Last night on the Internet, I visited a chat room full of pedophiles. They were having a rational discussion on the *ethical* practice of child molestation – how to determine nonverbal sexual consent from a five-year-old. You see, when the child is crying and saying *no*, they believe the child might mean *yes*. And they generally refer to the child as *it*.'

Investigator Buddy Sorrel shifted his stance to block the lectern, and now Rouge's eyes were free to roam the photos on the easels. Two of the children were badly beaten and showing signs of exposure where the woodland scavengers had been at them. Two other bodies were in pristine condition. They had the appearance of having been posed for the camera.

'Every child molester is convinced that if you people only tried it once, *you* would *understand*,' said Dr Cray. 'They don't see themselves as radically different from you, and in some respects they're right. So forget your preconceptions. You won't find this one if you're looking under rocks. He could be the man sitting next to you, someone you've known for ten or twenty years.'

Rouge stared at the empty easel where Susan's portrait had been. He filled the blank space with a photograph from his imagination, a picture made from the conversations of adults when he was a child of ten. His sister was lying on the snow, arms by her side, eyes open to the sky, a study of white on white, frost crystals sparkling among the strands of auburn hair. And he could see the police officers gathering around her small body, staring down at her.

Susan.

'Most child molesters are never caught,' said Ali Cray, calling his attention back to her. 'And they know that. They consider capture and prosecution to have the same odds as a freak accident. When you do catch them, only one in five does a single day in jail.'

The older investigator moved out of his way, giving Rouge a clear view of Ali Cray. At that same moment, she discovered his face in the crowd. Perhaps she hadn't read the morning papers, for she seemed startled to see him in this company.

In a somewhat smaller voice, she said, 'You can't fit human behavior into convenient slots. It's a very wide spectrum of shadings. But I can give you the broad categories of predators. First, the situational molester – the opportunist, sometimes called a regressed pedophile. He averages eighty incidents with forty child victims, but he doesn't have a preference for children over grown women. Sometimes the kid is just more convenient for him. He's not sick. He's just short of the moral character God gave a cockroach. But in this case, he's not the one you want.'

And now she was looking at Arnie Pyle, the FBI agent. Once again, she was disconcerted. Rouge wondered if she recognized Pyle's large, sad eyes. The agent wore a faint smile as he nodded hello to her, and Rouge realized that these two had met before.

'The next group', she said, 'is the preferential pedophile. Some of these people are so introverted they never act out their fantasies. But even the extroverted seducer doesn't generally abduct the child. He may have a job that puts him in touching distance. He averages three hundred incidents of molestation with a hundred and fifty victims. He does a lot of damage, but he usually leaves them alive.'

One hand went back, gesturing to the pictures on the easels without turning to look at them. 'The one you're looking for is the sadist, the child stealer – a serial killer. He knows he's going to murder the child from the moment he takes her. Sometimes it's just the cold-blooded elimination of the only witness, and sometimes it's ritualistic. He's the least common of the pack, and he has the fewest victims.'

She paused just a beat too long in a room full of cops with urgent business.

'Have you—' An edgy BCI man in the front row suddenly remembered his briefing protocol and raised his hand. When she nodded to him, he asked, 'Have you got a more specific profile on this type? Anything useful?'

'You can't rely on profiles. In previous cases, the killers ranged from dimwit drifters to rocket scientists. Most have never married, but you can't count on that. You have to look at the crime pattern to glean anything useful about the individual. Your man is probably Caucasian – victims are usually the same race. He has a heterosexual's preference for ten-year-old girls. I believe he's been killing them for fifteen years.'

The captain raised his hand to her, and a wordless agreement between them was acknowledged by a nod of her head.

She turned back to her audience. 'Captain Costello would like you to know that this is only a theory. But *if* my theory is correct, I can tell you more about this particular man, based on details of prior crimes. He's not on the dimwit end of the spectrum – he likes a challenge. The primary target is the least accessible victim, a child of extreme wealth. And he's found a way to defeat every security system a parent can devise to protect her.'

Another BCI investigator shot up her hand. 'But the Hubble kid left the house on her own. We found her prints on the—'

'I know. He uses the child's best friend to call her out. His pattern is very convoluted. That's how I matched him to previous kidnappings. At the end of the briefing, I'll be distributing the other case summaries. It's a long list of children. Some were found dead, but most were never found. The best friend of his primary target is usually well-to-do, but never from a wealthy family. The friend is less protected, more vulnerable to attack. In the beginning—'

She turned to look at the easel where Susan's portrait had been. Finding it empty, she appeared to be revising her speech, casting about for words. She gestured to the next easel, to the portrait of a child who had been battered. 'In the beginning, he would throw away the body of the target child's friend. The corpses of these girls were found close to where they were killed. This one was tossed in an irrigation ditch. Note the careless arrangement of the limbs. All the exposed skin shows the marks of a beating inflicted before death, but she wasn't sexually molested. This is the child he used for bait.'

She moved on to the next portrait, and this girl appeared to be only sleeping, undamaged. 'He left the primary victim out in plain sight on a heavily trafficked highway – so the parents would find her quickly.'

Ali found Rouge's eyes, and she seemed almost apologetic in her next words. 'The first child – the bait – was killed the day he took her, probably within the hour. The wealthy child was kept alive until the morning her body was found. This pattern was repeated in the next pair of children on your right. It points up the element of sadism. It destroyed the holidays for the family of his primary target – knowing that the girl died on Christmas Day.'

A few of the grayer heads in the audience were turning around, and Rouge knew they were making connections to the kidnapping of an auburn-haired ten-year-old named Susan Kendall, also found on Christmas Day. Only now were the older investigators tying her to the young cop by the same name – with the same auburn hair. They scanned the room, finding him in the crowd and searching his face for Susan's likeness – and there they found it. Startled and uncomfortable, their eyes shot away from him.

'When DNA evidence achieved credibility in the courts,' said Dr Cray, 'your man stopped leaving the bodies to be found. Now that's interesting. I think the forensic possibilities worried him. So he has a pattern, but he's flexible – he improves on it. And there was a bonus to the pattern change. The children who were never found remained on the books as runaways. No one was looking for a killer anymore. The rest of the pattern remains intact. The children are always taken in pairs, they're always—'

One detective in the middle row raised his hand and she nodded to him.

'Pretty good organization skills for a psycho.' His tone of voice was dubious, distrustful.

'He's not crazy,' she said. 'Don't underestimate him. Even prominent psychiatrists are changing the language to read *evil* instead of *ill*. This man functions as a normal person. He has a job, some tie to the community. I know he understands the difference between right and wrong, because he takes steps to avoid being captured. And I believe he's a local man.'

She stood to one side of the center easel displaying a map of the tristate area. 'Most of the children were from surrounding states, but their photographs appeared in national magazines and major newspapers. But *not* Gwen Hubble. He's seen this little girl close to home – close to *his* home.'

Neither Rouge's photograph nor his sister's had ever

appeared in public either. The Kendall twins had been very protected children. He wondered if Ali Cray knew this. He suspected she did.

'There's more.' She turned to the map. 'These red flags mark the homes of the children who lived across the state line. Every location is a day trip from this town. A full tank of gas, bought locally, will get him there and back. No credit card purchases, no gas station attendant to remember a stranger in town. There's no signature on a motel registration. He's just another motorist passing through. As I said, the bodies are never found anymore. I think the other children are all close together – a mass grave in a secure location. This may support the idea that he owns property.'

She nodded to another raised hand in the crowd.

'These other cases – did they call in the feds?'

'Yes.' She gestured to the easels. 'In these two kidnappings they were called in after the bodies were found.' She pointed to the first portrait on the left. 'In this case, the FBI determined that the battered child was the main victim because of the rage in the beating that killed her. But I believe this child was the bait. He used her to call out the other girl – and he had to hurt her to make her do that.'

Another hand shot up, and a woman's voice asked, 'What's the frequency of the attacks?'

'Sometimes a few years go by between incidents. It doesn't take much time to locate the private school of the wealthy child. The newspaper articles usually solved that problem. But it does take time to find the right bait, a close friend from a less protected environment – less money, no professional security. This is important to him – everything must fit. The elaborate pattern is what identified him. All my case summaries share the same basic elements.'

She was staring down at the papers on the lectern, not meeting anyone's eyes. 'And last – all the children were taken when the schools closed for the holidays. The family's guard was down. It was perfect timing. He's sadistic, but he'll show some patience with Gwen Hubble. He's made an investment in her. He'll keep Gwen alive until Christmas morning.'

'Gwen?' A woman FBI agent stood up, not waiting to be recognized. 'What about the other girl?'

'Sadie Green is dead.' Ali Cray's tone implied that she thought this was understood. 'That's the pattern. He probably killed that child an hour after he stole her.'

In the dead silence of the room, there was a ripple of movement throughout the crowd. Younger heads were shaking from side to side in denial, and older people were nodding to say, *Yes, of course she's dead. It all fits.*

As Ali Cray moved away from the lectern, her eyes locked with those of Special Agent Arnie Pyle. A conversation took place between them in this brief exchange of passing glances, and Rouge decided there was more to this relationship than the business of criminal acts.

Wiry Agent Pyle seemed almost cocky as he walked toward the lectern. He moved with the attitude of an elegant pool hustler in clothes that hung well on his lean body. In a further departure from FBI cloning, he loosened his tie until the knot hung inches below the undone collar button. As he moved farther away from the company of federal agents, he seemed to cross over to the ranks of the state investigators, with a knowing nod and a tough smile for the troops. And they smiled back at this man's man, a cop's cop. Pyle had become one of them, even before he took his place behind the lectern. And because of this masterful illusion of defection, Rouge deeply distrusted him.

Agent Pyle stood before them without notes or props, for this was not a speech to strangers, but a conversation with old friends whom he was meeting for the first time in his life.

'Dr Cray only picked out the facts that supported her case. You *know* nationwide stats on runaways are staggering. We've got more than ninety thousand kids on the road every day of the year, right?' His expression conveyed that this was a given, that they all knew the lady's theory was crap.

Rouge looked around the room and heads were nodding, already agreeing that Ali Cray was a civilian, an outsider – an amateur.

'In an overview of any hundred cases, I can use stats to develop lots of patterns that don't exist.'

And now, judging by the expressions of the other investigators, Rouge knew that Ali's case was nearly a dead issue; the FBI man had killed her off that quickly.

Agent Pyle turned to look at the easels and pointed to a child's photograph on the far right. 'That little girl's name is Sarah. There was a ransom demand. Dr Cray never mentioned that.' His tone condemned her for that. And then, in a slight elevation of volume, he bordered on evangelistic zeal with his next words. 'We *caught* the perp who sent that ransom note, and we got a *conviction* on the bastard.' Unspoken were the words, *Praise God and the FBI, my brothers and sisters.*

There was a sprinkling of applause which died quickly, as each man and woman realized that this was not a revival meeting. But it was a contest of sorts, a game of one-upmanship. However, the agent was playing by himself. Ali Cray was only a passive observer now. If Rouge could read anything in her face, it was disappointment in Agent Pyle and no animosity whatever.

Curious.

'I can't speak for the cases where we weren't called in,' said Pyle. 'Some of the kids might've had good reason to run – abuse in the home, beatings, incest – I've seen it all. About the statistics in Dr Cray's group of ten-year-olds. Sometimes you see stats clustering in one area for no good reason. And this tristate region has a dense population.'

Rouge thought this had the ring of covering ass, or getting even. Something in Pyle's delivery made his assaults on Ali Cray's theory all too personal.

'I don't believe we're dealing with a pedophile,' said Agent Pyle. 'The logic is pretty clear. This is a crime for profit. The fact that there are no public photographs of Gwen Hubble supports this theory. The kidnapping of Sadie Green was a screwup, an accidental departure from a plan to kidnap the Hubble girl for ransom. The perp was in the right place, but he snatched the wrong kid. The only thing Dr Cray and I can agree on is that Sadie Green is probably dead. Sadie was just an error in his—'

'I heard that!'

All eyes turned to the door, where Sadie Green's mother was struggling with a state trooper. The captain waved the uniformed officer back. The woman entered the room, tightly wrapping her brown cloth coat closer about her body, perhaps feeling a sudden coldness. Costello walked toward her, moving quickly to head her off before she could see the photographs on the front wall. 'Mrs Green? The purple jacket – was it your daughter's?'

'Yes, it's Sadie's!' she screamed at the captain, but her eyes were on the FBI man at the lectern. She stretched out one arm and pointed a damning finger at Pyle, yelling, 'She is *not* dead.' Her hand closed into a fist. 'And she's not a mistake! Not an *error*!' Her voice trailed off with her next words, not from lack of anger, but from exhaustion. 'She's a little girl, and I want her back.' The angry fist was still raised high, and she paused to stare at it now, surprised to see it growing there at the end of one plump arm.

'Oh, I'm sorry.' Her hand dropped limp to her side. Four federal agents were moving in tandem to block the easels with their bodies so she would not see the giant photographs of dead children.

'I'm so sorry,' she said to all of them. 'Please don't hate me.' She was smiling as she peered into the faces of the men and women surrounding her, seeking their reassurance.

Rouge ached for her. That smile must have been bought at an enormous cost. Her shoulders sagged, and it seemed to drain her, trying to maintain this more friendly expression.

'I'm in trouble, I know that.' She turned to the captain.

'But you said if I remembered anything important – well, I did.'

She avoided Costello's attempt to take her arm. In a burst of renewed energy, she stepped to the center of the room, like a dancer hitting the chalk marks on a stage. 'But first, I want to thank you guys for turning out that time my daughter did her arrow-in-the-heart routine.' She grinned, playing to every pair of eyes in her audience. 'Sadie still looks back on that as her best day.'

Rouge didn't see what happened next. He was too far back in the crowd. Perhaps the woman had tripped on something, or maybe her legs simply gave out from the shock of identifying her daughter's purple jacket. Mrs Green fell to the floor. All the cops in the room were on their feet, moving toward her with outstretched hands.

'No, don't help me. I don't want to be any trouble.' She smiled wide and open-hearted, and then she shrugged. 'So pratfalls are not my best thing.'

Captain Costello knelt beside her, not touching her but wanting to, hovering in the manner of a parent supervising a child's first steps. Becca Green found her legs and slowly stood up.

Costello's voice was surprisingly gentle. 'Mrs Green, you said you remembered something.'

'Something important – yes.' She opened her purse and fished around inside with one hand. 'My Sadie is an artist.' And now she had found what she was looking for and brought it out. 'Here, look! This is Sadie's eye.'

The agents and the investigators stared in horror as Mrs Green held up an oozing, bloody eyeball speared on a fork. No one moved. No one breathed.

'She has lots of others,' said Becca Green. 'But this is the good one for special occasions. Like when we have company for dinner? And they don't know Sadie all that well? She palms it like this.' Mrs Green pulled the eye off the fork. It made a small sucking noise.

Though it was obvious now that the eyeball was a rubber mock-up, a veteran BCI man shuddered, spilling coffee on his pants as he settled down to a chair. Spellbound, he didn't notice the spreading stains.

Becca Green cupped the fake eye in her palm and covered her own blue eye with this same hand. 'Then she pokes the fork through her fingers, like so.'

Rouge didn't want to watch the woman stabbing the fork between her fingers and into her eye socket, but he couldn't look away.

'And *voilà*,' said Becca Green, pulling the fork out again, still covering her socket with one hand to maintain the illusion that she was now half blind. She thrust the fork high in the air, so all could see. The rubber eyeball was once again stuck to the silver prongs. 'Now *that's* entertainment.'

She lowered her arm and looked down at the bloody, slimy thing on the fork. 'Of course, you're not getting the full effect,' she said, in a somewhat offhand tone. 'When Sadie does it, she puts the eyeball in her mouth and chews on it – that's her big finale. But I can't do that.' She wagged the speared eyeball for emphasis. 'I draw lines, you know?'

The nervous laughter began with an agent in the back of the room, and then it rippled forward, and Becca Green chimed in with her own heartier laugh as she dipped back into her little purse of terrors. 'What a kid, huh?'

This time she produced a small red gargoyle. It crouched in the palm of her hand. Agent Pyle had come out from behind the lectern to stand beside her. She held the toy up to his face, and then she hurled it to the floor at his feet. The bounce of the rubber hind legs made the tiny monster appear to jump as though it were alive.

'So this is what I remembered,' she said, turning to look into all their anxious faces as one hand rose in the air, commanding their silence. 'Listen.'

And they did. They were all listening, straining so hard it

created a palpable tension in the room, a network of electric expectation.

'My kid spent her whole life in training to meet the bogeyman. She's *alive*! You got that? But she's so little. You've got to find her fast and bring her home.'

Arnie Pyle was nodding, staring at her with his great dark eyes, which conveyed compassion and sorrow with no effort at all, for they were shaped that way – just an accident of genes.

'You keep that!' Becca Green pointed to the toy at the agent's feet. 'A memento of Sadie – so you don't forget her. Don't you give up on my daughter. I won't believe she's dead until I see the body. And then I'd probably stick her with a pin – just to be on the safe side.' Sadie's mother began to laugh again. And it was echoed here and there, spreading like a contagious, nervous cough.

She moved perilously close to the backdrop of smaller photos tacked to the front wall, images of dead little girls, eyes and flesh damaged by elements and animals. Rouge pushed and elbowed his way to the front of the crowd. 'Mrs Green.' He gently grasped her shoulders to prevent her from turning around, from seeing the wall. 'Let me call your husband. He'll come and—'

'No, not yet – *please*.' She danced away from him, back to the middle of the room, to the center of the stage. 'You've got to see my Sadie the way she really is. She's not just a short, unfinished person. I swear to God, you're gonna love this kid.'

And now Captain Costello was ripping the brutal pictures off the wall and the easels, lest the mother should turn and see the decomposing bodies of small children. The photographs flew through the air, and investigators crawled on hands and knees as they collected the pictures and hid them away. Some were crying, and Becca Green was laughing high and shrill. Anyone entering the room at that moment might have believed they had all gone mad together, Sadie's mother and the cops.

CHAPTER 5

Rouge Kendall checked the rearview mirror. There were no reporters pursuing his old tan Volvo, and that made him curious. The news crews were entirely too well behaved this morning.

Becca Green slumped against the passenger door, watching the storefronts and sidewalks slip past the side window. The woman was trying very hard not to cry, and he believed she tried for his sake. Today, all her energy had gone into fashioning an etiquette for dealing with the police. How many times had she apologized for some imagined transgression in the odd society of people with guns.

'Mrs Green?'

'I'm sorry. You were asking about the boy – Sadie's shadow?' She made a poor attempt at a smile. 'My daughter calls him David the Alien – because he never speaks or consumes food.' And now the smile was more natural. 'Every time he sees Sadie in the school cafeteria, he spills his lunch in his lap, turns bright red and walks away without a word.'

Rouge nodded, recognizing the symptoms. Captain Costello might have misread David's anxiety. The boy was probably not holding anything back; he was simply in love. 'So David Shore *never* talked to your daughter? They wouldn't share secrets, anything like that?'

Becca Green shook her head. 'Sadie's not the most approachable kid for somebody as shy as David. One time, maybe a year ago, the school counselor told Sadie to stop torturing the boy. Two days later, David's housemother shows up at my door.'

'Mary Hofstra?'

'That's the one. Said she'd like to have a cup of tea with me. Well, we're coffee drinkers in my house, right? So this woman pulls a little tin box out of her purse. Next thing I know, we're sitting in the kitchen, drinking herbal tea. Not bad stuff – a little sweet maybe, but I buy it for Sadie now. Anyway, this woman is apologizing for what the counselor said. She told me David was depressed. He thought Sadie wouldn't go near him anymore because she hated him. So Mrs Hofstra actually *wanted* me to *sic* my kid on David. If Sadie promised never to pressure the boy into talking, she could torture him all she liked – that was the deal. You know, Sadie did her arrow trick just for David. He screamed out loud for the first time ever.'

'Why does Sadie do things like that?'

'Oh, I don't know. You think it might be a ploy for attention?'

Her sarcasm was light, and Rouge smiled. 'She got a lot of attention when the cops turned out for the archery trick.'

'Oh, Sadie even fooled the school nurse,' said Becca. 'Consider the genius of putting the arrow over her heart so no one could check it for beats.'

Rouge pulled up to the curb. This end of the cul-de-sac offered a panoramic view of the lake. Though the surrounding structures were more than forty years old, this elegant street of gracious homes, green lawns and grown trees was still called the new housing development. The large gray-brick colonial was not what he had expected from the owners of a gas station.

Mrs Green read his expression. 'It's a barn,' she said, apologetically, as they walked up the flagstone path. 'You won't believe how long it takes to clean the place. Harry wants me to have a cleaning woman come in, but housework is practically the only exercise I get. And I'd feel strange having some other woman touching my things. You know what I mean?'

'Yes,' he lied. Far into his teens, a staff of women had cleaned up after his own small family, cooked their meals, washed their clothes and run their errands. A personal secretary had handled the condolences on the death of his sister.

Mrs Green opened the door and motioned him inside. He walked into a wall of warm air and the ripe, fruity smell of furniture polish and fresh floor wax. He followed her through a generous foyer and into a wide room where warmth was built into the environs with the leather bindings of books, the rich print of an Oriental carpet and the glow of honey-colored walls. This space was filled with good solid furniture, built for comfort, but expensive in its quality. And he knew at least one of the paintings on the wall was not a reproduction, for the Kendall family had once owned it.

He had never appreciated the art in his own house, except for its cash value. Piece by piece, he had sold all of it. And now he was staring at the old familiar painting by Arthur Dove. It was a small work by a minor artist, but it had brought thousands at auction. He looked at every frame on a neighboring wall of photographs. Each image of a renowned person had been taken by an equally famed photographer, and one of them was a Stieglitz portrait of Georgia O'Keeffe.

'Who's the art collector in the family?'

'My husband.' She turned slowly, surveying her own living room, as if seeing it through the eyes of a stranger. 'Doesn't fit with pumping gas and fixing cars, does it? When we were students, Harry had aspirations of becoming a starving artist – a photographer. Then his uncle died and left him a chain of gas stations and a big wad of money. That pretty much killed the idea of starving.' She shrugged. 'Life can be cruel.'

Rouge didn't smile. He had a nodding acquaintance with cruelty and irony. None of the photographs in this room had been taken by Harry Green.

The house was so quiet. He had expected to see a federal agent camped out in the living room with wiretap equipment. Who was screening the crank calls? Where were the hordes of

106

reporters who filled up every local bed-and-breakfast? Why were these people so alone?

'There's a tap on your phone, right?'

She nodded. 'I signed the forms. The FBI came out and rigged up some equipment in the basement. I hope they're not too pissed off. All that trouble for a phone that never rings.' Her voice had gone listless as she drifted over to the staircase.

'It might take a few days before the newspeople get your unlisted number. Then your telephone won't stop ringing.' He offered this as an excuse, as though giving a false compliment to a homely girl at the school dance.

How had the reporters been sidetracked? The lawn should be crawling with camera crews.

Mrs Green was walking toward the staircase. 'You want the tour? It only takes a few minutes. That's how long it took the other cops. Sadie's room is this way.'

She led him up the steps and down a hallway lined with photographs from another century, family groupings and portraits of properly laced-up women and starched-collar men. All civility and gentility ended at the door where Mrs Green was waiting for him. It was decorated with a gory poster for a vintage horror movie titled *Freaks*.

He turned to the woman beside him, who seemed so normal.

'You were expecting a poster for *Little Women*?' She opened the door. 'Maybe *Snow White*?'

She stepped to one side, and he walked into a bright collage of Halloween masks, fake vomit and bottles of liquid the color of blood. Monsters stared at him from picture frames ganged on every wall. The only nonviolent bit of space was directly over the child's bed. Here was a carelessly tacked-up array of champion blue ribbons.

'Those are for gymnastics,' said Sadie's mother.

Pride was absent from her voice, and Rouge found that

odd, for there was not one second-place prize in the collection. 'Your daughter must be quite an athlete.'

'I don't know,' she said, genuinely dubious. 'Sometimes I think the blue ribbons are just a side effect of being fearless. You should see her on the parallel bars. She pushes off, flies through the air and never looks down. Cartwheels and back flips – she goes spinning across a room, and I keep thinking every second she's gonna break her neck. Her father loves it. Harry goes to every single competition. Me? I can't watch anymore.'

He moved on to the next wall with its large bulletin board and an amazing selection of long-legged rubber bugs perched on pins. Half a dozen fake eyeballs stared up at him from an open egg carton on the desk. He perused a bookcase stocked with film cassettes. Most of them were in the horror genre of the thirties and forties, almost quaint, and a few were familiar children's classics.

Becca Green plucked out a tape which had one label pasted over another to read, '*Heidi*, original screenplay by Richard Hughes'. She peeled back the top label so he could read the screenwriter's true title.

'*Eyeball Eaters From Hell*?'

'She marked it as a children's film for my sake. My Sadie is not without compassion.'

'You let her watch that stuff?'

'*Let* her? Sadie is a full-blown person. She came that way – right out of the damn egg.' Becca Green was smiling again, obviously taking pride in this. 'Seen enough?'

She made it sound like a challenge for him to brave a look into the dark of the closet, or, if he had the stomach for it, perhaps a peek under the bed.

'I've got the general idea.' He followed her out of the room and back down the stairs. The silence of the house still troubled him. 'Mrs Green, have you had any problems with the reporters?'

She shook her head as she walked into the living room.

'Just the opposite.' She pulled back the pale green drapes of the front window. 'You see that guy sleeping in the car across the street? He's the pool reporter. If Harry and I suddenly go nuts and run around the lawn naked, this guy has to share that with the other reporters. All the rest of them are over at the Hubbles' place. He tells me they have their own pressroom with a bank of telephones, free booze and food.'

Becca Green shrugged out of her coat and tossed it on the couch. She continued to stare out the window, this little round woman who probably cut her own hair. Rouge noticed the ends of her brown tresses were uneven at the back, and he found this endearing. He wished he could tell her that.

'I feel kinda sorry for that little guy,' she said, nodding at the sleeping reporter in the parked car. 'He's missing all the big press conferences and the FBI bulletins. Maybe after lunch, I'll run over there and flash my breasts for him. Just a quick one to give him a little thrill. What do you think?'

'I think it's a damn shame you're already married.'

She turned to face him with a wide grin. 'You lying bastard, I really like your style.'

He heard the front door open and close, and now a man's deep voice called out from the hall, 'Becca?'

'In here, Harry,' she yelled. In a lower tone, she said, 'Don't expect too much from my husband, all right?'

A large, barrel-chested man filled up the doorway. Wind-whipped strands of light brown hair grazed the collar of an expensive bomber jacket. The multicolored scarf was obviously homemade and impossibly long; its fringed ends hung well below the knees of his blue jeans. Rouge wondered if Becca Green had knitted this scarf on the theory that longer was warmer. With only the evidence of this silly looking garment, he knew that she deeply loved her husband, and volumes more were said by the fact that Harry Green actually wore it.

The man's dark eyes were vacuous and staring straight ahead in the manner of a ghost haunting rooms, seeing no one, only passing through. He padded slowly and silently

109

across the thick carpet, heading in the general direction of his wife.

'It's not as bad as you think, Harry,' said Mrs Green. 'We kept our clothes on the whole time.'

The man came awake to the sight of a tall policeman standing in his living room. And now he came all the way back to life with a faint smile for his wife. Gently, he passed one loving hand over her hair. He nodded to Rouge, and then his eyes went strange again as he ambled off to haunt some other room.

Becca Green turned to the fireplace and picked up a sheet of paper from a stack on the mantel. She handed it to Rouge. 'Harry made this flyer himself. He spent hours going over our scrapbooks – wanted to find just the right picture. Then he pasted it up for the copy shop. He took that photo of the kids on parents' day at summer camp.'

Rouge stared at the black-and-white image that filled half the sheet. Two little girls sat on a bench, arms wound around each other, Gwen's head leaning on Sadie's shoulder. They were staring off in different directions, each thinking their own thoughts. Long shadows slanted across the grass in the background. The camera had captured a quiet moment at the end of a busy day, when the children were tired but content just to be with one another. Beneath this photograph was the one word 'PLEASE', hand-lettered with the bold, broad strokes of a marker.

It touched him in a way he could not explain, for this was a work of art, and thus beyond his vocabulary; he only knew the price of art.

Rouge handed it back to her.

'No, you keep it. I've got hundreds of them. This morning, Harry took them all downtown to put them up in the stores, but every window was already plastered with these professional jobs.' She held up another sheet for his inspection. This one was made of more expensive glossy paper. 'Nice, huh? Gwen's mother had these done by a real printer.'

Well, Gwen's mother had screwed up royally.

There was too much information given: the children's height, weight, and every identifying mark on their small bodies – enough material to keep the sick crank calls going indefinitely. In the middle of the night, a whispery voice on the phone would tell the Greens the location of the mole on Sadie's shoulder, and then the pervert would go on to describe things that would leave the parents screaming in pain. Rouge didn't approve of the photographs either. They were candid shots, but selected to show the girls in frontal and profile views, like mug shots of tiny criminals.

He folded Harry Green's flyer into the inside pocket of his jacket. 'I like your husband's work better. Can I take a few more?'

'You just made my day – and Harry's too. Take 'em all.'

When Rouge left the Greens' house, he was startled to see Ali Cray sitting on the front seat of his old Volvo. There was no other car in sight that might belong to her. Except for the pool reporter's rental, the only vehicles along the road were parked in private driveways.

Did she mean to continue the conversation begun in Dame's Tavern?

He opened the door, and without a word or a look to say she didn't belong there, he slid in behind the wheel and set the stack of flyers on the dashboard. She plucked one sheet off the top of the pile and stared at it.

'What a heartbreaker,' she said, in lieu of hello.

'Sadie's father made them.' As Rouge put the key in the ignition, his eyes traveled over the quiet lawns of the cul-de-sac. Toys and bicycles lay abandoned on the grass of almost every house. Absent was the sound of Rollerblades and the slap of running feet on the sidewalk. There was no yelling, not one insulting simile to boogers, nor the high-pitched screams which did double duty for joy and outrage. Today, the boys and girls and all their noise had been hidden away indoors.

111

Perhaps the neighbors didn't want to taunt the Greens with an ostentatious display of precious children.

He wondered if Becca Green had noticed this.

Of course she had.

'God, this is brilliant.' Ali Cray was still admiring Harry Green's flyer. 'You know he didn't intend this for the public. It's a direct communication to the pervert. Get enough of them up, and the monster will see them every day. It's just a shame he isn't human – no heart. Anyway, it's too late for Green's child.'

'I'm not so sure about that.' Rouge put the car in gear and pulled away from the curb, assuming that she intended to stay with him awhile. 'You may be the only one who's given up on Sadie.'

'Well, the mother did an amazing public relations job on the task-force. Smart woman. She said you were all going to love her kid – and now you do. But that little girl has been dead for days, Rouge. Believe me.'

'I can't.' He smiled.

Ali leaned over and touched the sleeve of his jacket. He saw a warning in her face. Her tone was very serious, but also gentle, aiming only to protect him. 'Don't fall in love with this kid. She's dead.'

The Christmas tree lane was lined with vans and cars. More vehicles filled the circular driveway. Rouge waved to the state trooper standing by the gate. Just beyond the ornate iron bars, a dog was being choked back on a leash, and this was enough to make Rouge dislike the animal's handler, a middle-aged man with sparse blond hair, tiny darting eyes and the soft mouth of a girl.

John Stuben? Yes, that was the name. Two dogs in the State Police Canine Corps had been purchased from this man's kennel. According to newspaper accounts, both animals had been vicious attackers, going beyond the call of duty to maim every bit of flesh they touched. Four years later, New York

State was still paying off lawsuits, and the kennel had gone bankrupt. Apparently Stuben had gone to work for the Hubble estate, for his jacket was well cut, expensive, but much too large, an obvious hand-me-down from his tall and wealthy employer.

Perhaps Peter Hubble, the security fanatic, had hired the man because of his bad reputation and not despite it. So far, no one had ever walked away from an altercation with an animal trained by John Stuben.

Rouge and Ali showed their identification again at the door. An FBI agent checked Ali's name off a list of expected guests, then pointed them toward the ballroom, where the lieutenant governor was preparing for a press conference. They walked down the long gallery of marble floors and priceless paintings on paneled walls, passing the open door to a room where two women in blue jeans were feeding sheets of paper to a copier. Rouge pegged them for volunteers. Through the next doorway, he recognized an FBI man in a loosened tie, seated on a couch and speaking into the microphone of his head set. An array of wiretap equipment covered the coffee table. Another agent worked at her laptop computer. The volunteers and the agents all had the dragged-out look of a night without sleep. Rouge identified the people in the next room as reporters. His best clues were the cacophony of ringing phones, clinking glasses and the smell of food, booze and smoke.

They were near the end of the gallery and closing on the main event, the governor's press conference. A hundred independent conversations were growing in volume. A tall pair of handsomely carved wooden doors hung open, giving them a generous view of the grand ballroom. Folding chairs filled half the space, and a makeshift wooden platform was set against the back wall. Cameramen milled around with the glare of mobile strobes. More brilliant beams fell from stationary pole lights. Technicians and reporters were everywhere.

A group of five men in dark suits stood to one side of the

platform. They all wore earphones, and their gazes continually swept the room, roving from face to face in the crowd. Now all five pairs of eyes were trained on Rouge and his companion. He stopped at the door and held out his State Police identification for a trooper, who then nodded to the men on the other side of the room. They resumed their sweep, faces slowly turning left, then right with chorus-girl precision. Behind a nest of microphones on the podium stood the governor, flanked by the taller figures of Senator Berman and the lieutenant governor – better known as Gwen's mother. Makeup people moved from one to the other, powder puffing and lipsticking the political stars.

Rouge turned to Ali. 'Why don't you stick around for the show. I'm going to look for Peter Hubble.'

She nodded, and he walked back toward the ballroom door. The trooper on duty directed him down a narrow hallway leading to the back of the house, where Peter Hubble had last been seen.

This corridor opened onto a spacious warm room with exposed brick and cherrywood cabinets. A collection of pans hung from a circular rack over a large butcher-block island, and the wash of sunlight from a row of tall windows made the copper gleam. A woman in blue jeans manned a coffee urn as her colleague stacked paper cups on a tray.

Another woman, large and husky in her white uniform, appeared to stand guard over Gwen's father. Peter Hubble sat at the table, eyes closed, face pillowed on his arms. An untouched platter of food had been pushed to one side.

As Rouge moved closer to the sleeping man, the woman in white moved between them. He guessed she was a cook or a housekeeper, for this room was clearly her domain, and he was an intruder here. Everything in her face and stance said, *Back off while you can, boy.*

'Hey, Rouge.'

He turned around to see the familiar face of a state trooper.

This man had long been in the habit of stopping by the village police station once a week for coffee.

'How's it going?'

'Lousy.' Rouge nodded toward Peter Hubble. 'I guess the guy didn't sleep last night.'

'He stays out all night,' said the trooper. 'Every night.'

'Doing what?'

'That's what Captain Costello wanted to know. My partner and I had to tail him a couple of times. He drives around the back roads – just drives and drives. He's looking for his kid. Ain't that a bitch?'

Peter Hubble raised his head, awaking with confusion in his eyes. When he looked at Rouge and the trooper, his face was full of hope, quickly followed by extreme fear. Rouge shrugged to tell him there was nothing to report, and Peter Hubble laid his head down again. His face was hidden, and he made no sound, but his shoulders heaved, his breath came in sputters, and they knew the man was crying.

Hubble's protector, the woman in white, was unfazed. Apparently, she had seen him do this before. But the man's weeping drove the two police officers to backward steps. Then they turned in awkward silence and quit the room.

Special Agent Arnie Pyle stood squarely in the path of the young psychologist, halting her progress toward the platform at the back of the ballroom. For a moment, he thought Ali Cray was going to walk around him – or over him. He flirted with the idea of little round puncture wounds in his back from her stiletto heels; some scars were more romantic than others.

'Hello, Ali. No hard feelings?'

'Arnie.' Her voice was light, almost sweet. 'I'd kick you in the balls if I thought you had any.'

'But you've seen them, Ali. You even know what my cock tastes like.'

Her face was quizzical, as if this might be a difficult

memory to retrieve. 'Oh, right. Tiny shriveled thing? It was horribly deformed, wasn't it? You'd think a good surgeon—'

'You should talk.' He touched her face gently, as if they were still lovers, one finger tracing the jagged line of her scar. It was such a familiar act, seconds passed before she thought to brush his hand away.

He looked toward the ballroom doors, but Rouge Kendall was gone. 'That cop you're so tight with – the one with the red hair? I wonder what he'd think if he knew the story behind that scar.'

'Like you *do*?'

He grinned. 'Worth a try.'

'What are you doing here, Arnie? Did you get demoted from the task force on organized crime?'

'The lieutenant governor is calling in all the big guns to find her daughter. When I worked the kiddie detail, I was the best there ever was. You should remember that.'

Though she would recall that period best for all the booze he managed to consume, on and off duty. His next assignment did not require weeping with the parents of dead children, and his drinking had lessened dramatically. But by the time he had sobered up, Ali Cray was gone. She had walked away in the early days when he was too stupefied to prevent her from leaving him.

'Did you find all my files useful, Ali? I noticed you quoted some of my figures in your handout sheets. And now you're getting cozy with that BCI investigator. Still turning tricks for stats?'

Oh, what a cheap shot. And he was searching his brain for another one, a better one – even cheaper.

'Are you stalking me again, Arnie?'

'Let's say you're never out of my thoughts, and you never will be.'

She was staring over his shoulder.

Arnie turned around to face the stage. 'Well if it isn't Senator Berman's best boy – the governor.' New York State's highest-ranking politician was standing behind the podium, fussing with his notes. The natural shape of the little man's eyebrows made him appear perpetually frightened, an accident of nature and nothing to do with the close proximity of his creator and master, Senator Berman.

'Look to the right, Ali. You see that old guy walking up the steps?' He pointed to the back of a well-dressed man with silver hair and a walking cane of carved rosewood. 'You remember Julie, don't you?'

She strained to see over the heads of reporters. 'That's Julie Garret?'

'Yeah. Now watch.'

Julian Garret handed a glass of water to Senator Berman. The senator drank from the glass at the moment the governor began his opening remarks. A ripple effect of snorts and stifled laughter spread through the press corps, though the governor had said nothing funny. Senator Berman hastily handed the water glass back to Julian Garret, and then looked out over the sea of grinning reporters. He was not amused.

Now Julian Garret was striding toward them, grandly swinging his walking stick. Some regarded the rosewood cane as an affectation of style, and they were right about that. The journalist wore the sober expression of a distinguished senior citizen, but when he flashed a broad grin for Ali Cray, he seemed more like a young boy with old hair. He held out one hand to Arnie Pyle, palm up, so the gesture would not be confused with the offer of a handshake. 'Pay me.'

The FBI agent handed the reporter a twenty-dollar bill. 'I didn't think you'd really do it, Julie.'

In an aside to Ali, the elder man said, 'Arnie said the governor couldn't talk if—'

'If the senator was drinking water.' Ali nodded, only wincing a little at the bad joke. 'But you knew the senator was a world-class ventriloquist.' Ali linked her arm with the reporter's, and he seemed charmed by this, but then he was always her biggest fan. 'So, Julie, how come a political columnist turns out for a kidnapping?'

'Politically, it's a slow news week, love. But I can always depend on Senator Berman to make an ass of himself in three personal appearances out of three. Just a tidbit for the column.'

'So you're only here for the day?'

'Well, Ali, that was the original plan.' Now Garret glanced at Arnie Pyle. 'But things just got a wee bit more interesting. I might be in town for a while.' He handed her a card for the Makers Village Inn. 'Call me. We'll do lunch.'

'Goodbye, Julie.' She never even glanced at Arnie Pyle as she walked away toward the great doors where the young red-haired cop was standing in conversation with Marsha Hubble.

The journalist was watching Ali's retreat with a keen appreciation for a beautiful backside. 'I see you're still on the lady's shit list. Well good for Ali. She can do a lot better. And what're *you* doing here, Arnie? Hoping that idiot on the stage will accidentally confess to assisting mob interests?'

'Could happen. But I had no idea those pinheads were coming.'

'Oh, *right*.'

'Off the record, Julie?'

'Why not.'

'The kid's mother invited them – the biggest death penalty advocates in the country. I guess Mrs Hubble didn't think the perp had enough incentive to kill her kid.'

'Can't you control the mother?'

'No, Julie. The amateurs are running the show today.'

'So where's the mob angle?'

'Haven't got one. I'm here to find the kid.'

'Of course you are.' And by his amiable tone, the reporter seemed quite at home with base lies, perhaps regarding them as social pleasantries – preludes to dirtier acts and better news stories. 'Let me guess, Arnie. If I get it right, I get the exclusive. Deal?'

'Shoot.'

'Everybody knows the lady politician's in deep trouble with Berman. He told the governor to unload her, but she hangs on. When you consider how dirty this state is, how vicious the political machinery can be – her career should be dead by now. Obviously, she's got a bargaining chip – maybe a solid tie to mob campaign contributions?'

'So you figure this for a mob snatch? Give me a break, old man.'

'Too risky, Arnie? Or too Hollywood? For your purposes, it only matters what *Marsha* thinks. So she's cracking open a little more every day, grieving for her only child – all that pressure. And all along the way, you're right next to her, dropping hints, whispering in her ear. The mob connection is burned into her brain by the time her daughter turns up dead. And they usually die, don't they, Arnie? You can almost count on it, can't you? Then you bend over the child's corpse and ask the mother, very politely, if she wants to turn state's evidence to get even.'

'Ah, Julie, you must think I'm one evil son of a bitch.'

'And consequently, the best man for the job. I expect a phone call when you pull it off.'

Rouge held up the glossy poster Marsha Hubble had designed. 'But, ma'am, it's too much information. Here, take a look at this one.' He handed her the flyer Becca Green had given him. 'Sadie's father made it.'

The lieutenant governor stared at it for a moment, and then she smiled. 'You're absolutely right. It's better – it's wonderful. Harry Green's a damn poet, and he only had the one word to work with.'

A small, nervous woman in a severe gray suit stood beside the lieutenant governor, her pen suspended in midair, awaiting the politician's next words. Marsha Hubble placed the sheet of paper on the aide's clipboard, as if this person were a living table. 'Have someone run off a thousand of these. I want every single flyer replaced by three o'clock.'

The nervous woman's head was still bobbing like a windup toy as she hurried off down the hall, disappearing into a side room.

Marsha Hubble turned back to Rouge. 'Anything else?'

He had been prepared for an argument. Now it occurred to him that the lieutenant governor was as gullible as the general public. She believed what she read in the papers and accepted him as a State Police wunderkind.

'Yes, ma'am. I'd like to see Gwen's room. I realize it's already been—'

'Of course.' She spoke to Rouge, but she was staring at Ali, who had just joined them at the foot of the staircase.

'I'm sorry,' Rouge said. 'This is—'

'I'm Ali Cray, Mrs Hubble.' She put her hand out to the lieutenant governor. 'I'm sorry if that's not the correct form of address for—'

'Call me Marsha. I know who you are, Dr Cray. But you're certainly not what I expected. So young for a Ph.D.'

Yet, by the look on Marsha Hubble's face, this was far from a disappointment. She obviously set great store by prodigies. Rouge was not surprised that she didn't seem to notice Ali's scar, for the lieutenant governor managed to block out entire human beings, like the FBI man standing next to her, politely waiting for his turn to speak.

'Gwen's room is this way,' she said, shepherding Rouge and Ali up the stairs and leaving the waiting man to stand alone looking foolish.

'So, Dr Cray, do you make those fascinating criminal pro-files? Can you really tell the color of the bastard's eyes from the details of the crime?'

'No, ma'am. No crystal balls.'

'Not like the FBI, you mean? Good.'

So the lady was disappointed in her federal lapdogs. How long would it be before Gwen's mother became disenchanted with himself and Ali?

As Mrs Hubble neared the top of the stairs, she missed a

step and Rouge caught her arm to break the fall. She was startled when she lifted her eyes to his – so close he could feel her breath on his cheek.

'How clumsy of me. Thank you.'

Now he saw her in the unguarded, unpublic moment, and he was revisiting his own mother in the early days of Susan's disappearance – those same screaming eyes. So he had erred. Marsha Hubble was not rudely oblivious to those around her; she was simply very focussed. It was all she could do to get sanely through the next minute, the next second.

The politician's professional smile was back in place as they followed her along the second-floor landing and into a large corner room flooded with light. The walls of Gwen Hubble's bedroom held framed posters of rock groups and photographs of dogs. A standard black poodle lay across a down quilt on the four-poster bed. The dog wore a light blue ribbon on his head, and in a further humiliation, the coat was styled in traditional fuzzy balls of fur. Marsha Hubble must have read Rouge's disdain of the breed by his expression, which said, *It's not a real dog.*

'Look past the poodle cut, Rouge. May I call you Rouge? He's a very smart animal. Here, watch this.' She snapped her fingers, and the dog raised his head. 'Harpo, bring me *English.*'

The dog jumped off the bed and ran across the room toward two bright-colored notebooks lying flat on the desk and extending over the edge by a few inches. The dog grasped the green notebook and brought it to Gwen's mother. A label for English class was pasted in the middle of the cover.

'Good boy. Now, Harpo, bring me *geography.*'

The dog returned to her with the yellow notebook in his teeth.

'He only knows two subjects. My daughter won't let him bite the science notebook. Gwen loves science. She wants to be a biologist.'

A man's voice came from the hall. 'You're supposed to give Harpo a treat when he does a trick.'

121

John Stuben was standing in the doorway. The dog handler crossed over to a blue ceramic jar by the bed. He lifted the lid, pulled out a biscuit in the shape of a bone and threw it to the poodle.

Rouge wondered if this man was not entirely too familiar with a little girl's bedroom.

As Gwen's mother and Ali walked back into the hall, they passed by Agent Arnie Pyle. He was casually leaning against the doorframe and staring at John Stuben. 'Did you help the little girl train her dog?'

'Yeah, I gave her pointers.' Stuben's voice was angry. He had already been through hours of questioning, and apparently his hard feelings for the State Police extended to the FBI.

'Must take awhile to teach an animal tricks like that,' said Pyle.

'Not if you know what you're doing.' Stuben seemed somewhat mollified by a question in his area of expertise. 'It only took twenty minutes to teach Harpo to fetch notebooks. Gwen's really good with dogs. She taught him a lot of—'

'*She* taught him? According to the rest of the staff—' Pyle took out a notebook and made a show of flipping through the pages. 'Yeah, here it is. They tell me you spent a lot of time with Gwen – a *lot* of time. So you didn't spend all those *hours* training the poodle?'

'The kid likes to watch me work with the security dogs. What of it?' Stuben's attitude was meant to be surly, but the girlish mouth was pouting now, defeating his attempt at male macho.

Pyle was writing in the notebook, not looking up when he spoke to the man. 'Giving her pointers – is that part of your job? Or maybe you did that on the side?'

'On my own time. I like Gwen.'

'I'll bet you do.' Pyle looked up with a slow smile. 'How *much* do you like her, Stuben? Pretty little kid. Is she a turn-on?'

Stuben went after the fed, as though he meant to do some

damage. Pyle seemed not to care, and he held his ground, appearing only mildly interested in the man speeding toward him. The dog trainer stopped short of his target, the immovable, unblinking FBI agent, and backed off a few steps.

Stuben had already told the agent everything he wanted to know. Arnie Pyle was nodding, and Rouge could guess his thoughts.

So John Stuben has no physical courage – not with men. Perhaps with ten-year-old girls?

But Rouge could think of other scenarios. John Stuben had already lost everything once. His savings had gone for lawsuits, and his kennel had been shut down. He was not a young man. While it might be very satisfying to deck a fed, there was a price. He would lose everything; he would have to begin all over again.

This man might only be tired.

The room smelled of antiseptic layered over the earthier smell of death. A body lay on a stainless-steel table near the far wall. Half the skull was missing, neatly sawed off with the carpenter's tools of County Medical Examiner Howard Chainy. But Rouge's attention was fixed on the item in the doctor's hand.

The medical examiner seemed in good humor. 'I don't mind, Rouge.' He held up the firm dark fungus so like a large, misshapen mushroom in its texture. 'It's certainly fresher than the average customer, and one might even call it fragrant.' Dr Chainy placed the fungus on a small steel tray on his desk. He sat down and perused a selection of scalpels. After slicing off a thin section, he set it on a slide under the microscope and looked into the eyepiece for a moment. 'Well, I can see a few critters moving around, and a lot of dead ones. That might fix the time and temperature. But I can't tell you anything about the dirt particles.'

'We don't need that,' said Rouge. 'The dirt samples went to a soil expert at the university.'

'And they don't have a botanist on the faculty?'

'The captain says he has a local man coming in. He doesn't want any press leaks on this.'

'So he told me – *three* times.' Chainy adjusted his lens as he peered through the eyepiece. 'Wouldn't it be simpler to just hand everything over to the FBI? They have the world's best forensic lab – one-stop shopping.'

'It's not their case *yet*,' said Captain Costello's voice as he walked up behind them.

Dr Chainy jumped. 'Jesus, Leonard. Give a man some warning.' He bent over his scope again. 'So I hear you're playing keepaway with the feds.'

'I don't remember inviting them to the party.' Costello handed a sheaf of faxes to Rouge. 'That's the analysis from the university. The soil in the lining—'

He broke off as the door swung open, and a thin old man with gold-rimmed glasses appeared beside a uniformed escort. Costello nodded a dismissal to the state trooper, and now the white-haired civilian stood alone on the threshold, hesitating, unsure of his coming or going. Rouge was shocked to recognize Dr Mortimer Cray. The reclusive psychiatrist was not a common sight around town, and years had passed since they had seen one another. The changes in the old man were great. He was still well dressed, but not well fed, too slender to be in good health. Rouge remembered him with more authority in the way he carried himself. Just now, the old man moved like a thief, taking tentative steps into the room, testing the atmosphere.

'Dr Cray?' Costello moved toward him.

The psychiatrist nodded as the captain extended his hand in a greeting. Mortimer Cray shook the hand gingerly, as though it might conceal a weapon.

'I'm Captain Costello. This is one of my investigators, Rouge Kendall.'

The old man nodded to Rouge, as though meeting him for the first time.

'Thanks for coming over so quickly,' said Costello. 'I have

a problem, Dr Cray. You're a psychiatrist, right? No problems with keeping secrets?'

Did Dr Cray seem a little paler now? He did, and wary too, for the man's eyes were darting from face to face in hopes of discovering something. Rouge looked at his captain and realized that Costello had also picked up on this and found it interesting.

The captain's attitude altered slightly, eyes narrowing, smile broadening. 'It's about the missing girls, sir. I think you can give us information.'

A good shot by Costello. Mortimer Cray's arms were limp at his side, but his hands were not still; they opened and closed like the mouths of air-stranded fish. And the psychiatrist's stance was just a hair off balance.

Rouge knew the police made some people a little shaky under the best of circumstances; it might be only that. But the rich walked about with lawyers in their pockets, and they never seemed so rattled as the poor. This man was stiffening now. Bracing for a blow?

Costello held out the plastic bag bearing the remains of the dark fungus clotted with soil. 'We found a jacket that belonged to one of the kids, and this was in the torn lining. Your niece tells me you're a closet botanist.'

Dr Cray stared at the bag, and Rouge wondered if the man held his breath. He seemed confused, and Rouge decided that this confrontation with a fungus was far from what he had expected.

'What can you tell me about it, sir?' Costello held the bag up, and his eyes were suddenly very bright. The captain's grin was inappropriate and unnerving.

Medical Examiner Howard Chainy looked up from his microscope and rolled his eyes to heaven. 'What's the world come to, Leonard? You got me doing an autopsy on a damn fungus, and now you want a psychiatrist to analyze it?'

'A macrofungus, actually,' said Mortimer Cray, peering at the bag through thick bifocals. 'It's a truffle.'

Did the man seem relieved? The stiffening of his body passed off like premature rigor mortis, and his stance was more relaxed.

'I need to know where this came from,' said Costello. Ambiguity suggested the truffle might belong to the psychiatrist.

'May I taste it?' Mortimer Cray was not picking up on the captain's implication. He was only scrutinizing the fungus. 'It looks like a Black Diamond, but the Chinese have a similar species. The taste would tell me where it came from.'

Costello nodded to Chainy. The medical examiner sliced off a small section of the truffle and handed it to the psychiatrist, saying, '*Fine*. Now I'm serving fast food.'

Mortimer Cray placed the slice on his tongue, as if it were a communion wafer, and savored it for a moment. 'It's the real article, a Black Diamond. Tuber melanosporin. It comes from the Quercy and Périgord regions of France. Also the Umbria—'

'Any local growers?'

'Commercial cultivation? Here? Not likely, Captain. They only grow in the wild, usually in the vicinity—'

'Oh, really?' Captain Costello took the faxes from Rouge's hand. 'I got a report here that says there's fertilizer in the soil sample we scraped off that truffle. And we got another sample from the lining of the jacket.'

Dr Cray gave no indication that he had been trapped in a lie. 'There *are* experiments going on in states with more compatible soil and climate – Texas, Oregon, Washington. But nothing local, and it's only experimental – nothing on a commercial scale.'

Costello turned to the medical examiner. 'The kid's jacket was found early this morning. Last night temperatures dropped to below freezing. Now that thing was in the lining. Can you tell me if it's been frozen?'

'Oh, hell, Leonard,' said Dr Chainy, slightly annoyed. 'I don't need a microscope to see that it's never been frozen.

It's still firm, just like a fresh mushroom. Ever see a frozen one? All squishy and brown?'

'I agree.' Mortimer Cray picked up the specimen bag and probed the truffle through the plastic. 'Very firm, very fresh. And you see this marbling? That would have disappeared if it had been frozen.'

Costello moved toward Mortimer Cray. Rouge decided the game was still on as the captain crowded the other man's personal space. 'Now what kind of operation do you need to grow truffles indoors?' This was not a polite question; it was a demand.

'It can't be done.' The psychiatrist backed away from Costello and pushed his glasses back up the length of his nose. Small beads of sweat had made the frames slippery. 'Not unless you want to grow a tree in the house. You need a symbiotic relationship to—'

'See this report?' Costello waved the faxes and raised his voice, almost combative. 'I've got a slew of bacteria here that thrive at high temperatures. That puts the truffle in a green-house, or at least indoors. And I've got a long list of crap under the heading "unique to local soil". So it's a good bet the kid's jacket hasn't been traveling west of the Mississippi. That and the fertilizer tells me I've got a truffle factory in the neighborhood.'

'Very unlikely,' said the psychiatrist, less sure of himself, more defensive now. 'The truffles only grow with the roots of oak trees. You have to grow the tree specifically for that purpose, so the roots won't be contaminated. It takes seven years to develop a symbiotic relationship between the tree root and the truffle.'

'It was grown indoors,' said the captain.

'Because of the bacteria and the fertilizer? No, the most likely scenario is that the truffle was dropped in a greenhouse or a potted plant. You might check with mushroom importers and—'

Costello took back the plastic evidence bag and held it up

to the psychiatrist's face. 'When this goes to the FBI lab, I'll tell them to look into the greenhouse theory.' His words had a mildly threatening quality. 'You have quite a greenhouse, don't you, sir? Your niece tells me it's better equipped than the average commercial outfit.'

And this sounded like an accusation.

'I assure you I am not growing truffles in—'

'Oh, did I suggest that? I'm sorry.'

Rouge thought the captain's apology sounded pointedly insincere.

'I want to know if you have any connections to people who do this kind of thing,' said Costello. 'This *experimenting*. Has anyone, anywhere, *ever* grown truffles indoors?'

'Only the North American strains. They're ghastly. You never want to taste one. Any experiments on the Black Diamond would be proprietary information – not available to the public.'

'So somewhere, it *is* going on.'

'I've only heard of one experiment under greenhouse conditions. The fungus produced *without* the oak root had the DNA of a truffle, but not the taste. I assure you, this one was not grown indoors. It has the full-bodied taste of a Black Diamond. It was most certainly grown in symbiosis with the roots of an oak tree.' The doctor was regaining his authority now, almost indignant. 'And you can't grow a full-sized oak tree indoors.'

Dr Chainy pushed his chair back from the desk, apparently deciding that he was wasting his time at the microscope. 'Well, I have an atrium in the house – right in the middle of the damn house. With that twenty-foot skylight, I guess I could plant a tree if I wanted to.'

Mortimer Cray shook his head, as though Howard Chainy were an insane patient. 'The root system would tear up the foundation of your house. And you can't produce a truffle in less than seven years. Even a twenty-foot ceiling is not sufficient for a full-grown oak. Do you know how big that tree would be?'

Captain Costello turned to Rouge. 'I want photographs from the tax assessor's office. We might be able to find an atrium in the aerial shots.'

He turned on Mortimer Cray. 'Doctor, if you had a very sick patient with an atrium in his house, would you tell me?'

Costello let that remark waft around for a while, but it produced no effect on Mortimer Cray. The response was an unspoken *no*.

Now there was a trace of contempt in Costello's voice. 'How deep in the ground do truffles grow, Dr Cray?'

The old man stared at the bagged fungus which had been found in a little girl's jacket. In his face was the sudden realization that Costello was asking him to determine the possible depth of a child's grave.

'Six to eight inches below the surface.'

A shallow grave.

The captain's voice changed gears into light diplomacy as he said, 'Well, thank you for coming in, sir.' With an air of dismissal, he turned his back on the old man and spoke to Rouge. 'I got the paperwork back on the pervert. I know it's late, but I wanna go over it with you before you leave.'

Rouge noted a stretch to Mortimer Cray's neck, attenuating to a cocked ear. But Captain Costello did not elaborate to satisfy the man's curiosity. When the captain turned back to Dr Cray, he pretended surprise to see the psychiatrist still standing there. He extended his hand, saying, 'Thank you again, sir. Would you like me to call someone to escort you back to—'

'I can find the way, thank you.' But it was clearly with some regret that the doctor was leaving the room and passing into the hallway.

Through the open door, Costello called out, 'Oh, Dr Cray? Those little kids are in deep trouble, sir. So you're not gonna warn this bastard, are you?'

129

Mortimer Cray turned to stare at the captain, and then the door swung shut, blotting out the old man's startled face.

There was very little traffic in the squad room. The best-trusted investigators were chasing down importers of truffles and mushrooms, and others were visiting sites from the aerial photographs. Two of his people were watching the psychiatrist's house, noting who came to visit. Captain Costello had wanted a wiretap on Mortimer Cray's phone, but two judges had turned him down cold, forbidding him to violate the doctor–patient confidentiality of telephone consultations.

The captain stood in the open doorway of the private office and looked out over the wide expanse of empty chairs and blank computers. Only Marge Jonas's screen was alive with blue light and scrolling text. As she sat typing at the keyboard, she looked up for a moment to smile at him, a reward for playing nicely with her pet cop. Rouge Kendall was seated by the office window, engrossed in a file on Gerald Beckerman, the teacher from St Ursula's Academy.

Costello returned to his desk and lowered his tired body into a well-padded leather chair. He pulled a brown paper bag from the lower desk drawer and opened it to set out a recently purchased bottle and two small paper cups the size of shot glasses. Did he need to ask if Rouge wanted a drink, or could he put that much faith in the IA reports from Dame's Tavern? He wasn't sure. So this little exercise with the whiskey bottle was more in the nature of a science experiment than a social gesture.

The rookie investigator put up no fight, no protest, but neither did he act like a lush in need of a drink at the end of a long shift. He picked up his paper cup and sipped the golden vintage liquid, which might as well have been water for all this young cop cared.

The captain decided that the boy drank because he wanted to, and not because of a physical craving. He well understood the anesthetic effects of alcohol.

130

'I'll save you some time,' said Costello, interrupting Rouge's reading. 'There's no record on Beckerman in the States. But the Canadians want a few words with him.' The captain leaned over to tap the file Rouge was holding. 'Check out the back sheet. Smart little bastard was working his shit in a summer camp over the border. Screening services don't usually check outside the country. That's why the school had nothing on him.'

Rouge scanned this final sheet. 'A rich Ivy League graduate working as a summer camp counselor? That's minimum wage. Why didn't they—'

'He didn't put that down when he applied for the job, and that was smart. That's when the bells go off. The camp was a little mom and pop operation – no screening, and they paid him in cash. They didn't even know he was a US citizen.'

Rouge set the papers on the edge of the desk. 'But Beckerman's only interested in little boys. That doesn't help much.'

'Well, he won't get any more boys. We're gonna hold him for the Canadians. The extradition is in the hopper. That was good work, kid. Any ideas on the truffle?'

'If we're looking for a mushroom fanatic with an interest in truffles, why not tell the troopers and the town cops?'

'I want absolute containment, Rouge.'

'But the cops and troopers know the area and the people.'

'If this guy knows we're close, those kids are dead. Not a single word goes over to the uniforms.'

'Captain, one of the kids is already dead. You know that parka was in the ground. She was buried. So I can forget the runaway angle, right?'

'No. I gave you a line of investigation, and you're gonna stay on it, even if it's just for show. As long as we're searching for runaways, I got no problem with the homeowners. But if the press finds out we're looking for evidence of murder, the summer people might revoke consent for the vacant houses. Then I need probable cause and specific warrants. Got the picture, kid? So you stay with the program, or I put you back in uniform. Any questions?'

'If you're gonna bust me down to—'

'Okay, I lied.' Costello sat back and regarded the younger cop. 'That's not gonna happen, Rouge. I know this assignment was hard on you – two little girls the same age as your sister. When they found Susan's body, you must have died. You've got to be reliving that.' And he knew what it was costing this young man. '*Officially*, I need to keep you on the runaway angle as long as the press loves your face. As for what you turn up on the side – you bring that to me. I'm always here, kid. If you need help, if you got questions.'

Rouge finished his shot of whiskey and crumpled the cup as he leaned forward in a pose for confidential words. Before he said anything more, it was understood that this was just between the two of them. 'I know Susan's photograph was part of Ali Cray's briefing. She must have seen a connection, but you took it off the easel.'

'That never made any sense to me. It didn't follow the pattern. It would have confused the—'

'She said the bastard was flexible, changeable. Suppose Paul Marie didn't kill my sister?'

'The priest? Oh, for the—' One hand covered Costello's face for a moment, and then it fell away. He shook his head slowly from side to side. When he spoke, his voice was close to a whisper.

'Don't.'

It was a single-syllable instruction for Rouge to leave that idea alone – just the one word, dropped gently in the air between them, and said with the greatest kindness. It was a caution against opening old wounds, bleeding from them, and dying all over again.

The windows of every house along the shoreline had gone dark, and the clear night sky was pocked with starlight. This part of the hill was clear of trees, and unchecked breezes swept upward from the lake to rush around the stones. A racket of dead leaves spiraled in a wind devil's funnel and ran a dusty circle around his legs.

Rouge Kendall closed the iron gate behind him, as though he had entered a proper residence. He knew the legends on every marker between the gate and his sister's grave. The corner stone in the family plot bore the year 1805. Next to this reserved section lay older remains of the postman's progenitors.

Among the elaborate pieces of marble adorned with lengthy scripts, scrolls and cherubs, his sister's stone was a thing apart, austere and pure white. Only her name was engraved above the dates of her birth and her murder. Some people found it curious that there was no carved sentiment, no line of poetry. But after Susan's corpse had been found, her parents had nothing left to say. Their silence had lasted for years.

This was the first time Rouge had come to the cemetery without flowers.

As a small child in grief therapy, he had wandered the greenhouse with Dr Mortimer Cray and learned the ancient Persian art of flower talking, studying the meanings of floral shape and essence as a second language. After these sessions, he would visit the graveyard with white carnations, a child's message of ardent love. In the spring he had brought bluebells to remind Susan of his constancy. He could speak to her, but they could never again be more than half alive. Twin had not been cleaved from twin; he was forever in two places, above and below ground.

Rouge looked up into the darkness of the firmament. Instead of the stars, he saw an open rectangle of light blue sky rimmed with mourners in dark clothing. And then the first shovel of dirt flew into their eyes – his and Susan's.

He turned his face down to the simple monument, as if, after all this time, he might find some overlooked, unread line written there. And there it was. Another visitor had been here before him – and recently. He crouched down by the base of the stone and picked up two flowers, an unsigned message of hue and form. The purple hyacinth stood for sorrow, and the peony for shame.

Who gave them to you, Susan?

Not our mother. She never comes here anymore.

The base of each stem was cut at a slant, the mark of a florist shop. But they might have grown in a private greenhouse. The one who left these flowers knew something about his sister's death; Rouge was certain of that. And the involvement went deeper than guilty knowledge, for the sentiments also spoke of complicity.

Angry now, he roamed among the stones until he found wreaths and bouquets from a recent funeral. He stole a red rose and brought it back to Susan's grave, stripping off the leaves as he walked, but leaving every thorn. In the poetic art of the Persians, this told his sister's visitor, *You have everything to fear.*

The two cars were the only vehicles on Lakeshore Drive at three o'clock in the morning. The air was bitter cold, and exhaust was ghosting from the tailpipes as the Bentley and the Ford converged from opposite directions. It was a chance encounter, and each driver had surprised the other.

Instead of passing, going on in their separate directions, the cars stopped. The drivers acted in unison, each clearing a face-wide circle in the fogged window glass. They only stared at one another, with no words or gestures, and then they moved on – Gwen's father heading east, and Sadie's father heading west. The cars moved slowly, for one might easily miss a lost child in the dark.

The dog stood on two legs, choking himself on the chain with each attempt to lunge. The man smiled at every whimper, every whine and bark, knowing that the starving animal was enraged because he could smell the meat but not get at it.

The man worked by the eerie glow of the cellar lights, cutting a shallow rectangle as the dirt softly ploffed on the ground beside the second hole. The air was moist and warm; the earth gave way with ease. And now he paused to lean on his shovel and look down at his work, two tiny graves side by side – one full and one waiting.

CHAPTER 6

Investigators and agents ate their dinners from brown paper bags, take-out containers and microwave packages. Soda cans and coffee cups littered every surface in the squad room. Ali Cray jumped in her skin as one of the cans crashed into a metal wastebasket behind her chair. She looked around to see the offender three desks away. The FBI man who had made the long shot gave her an apologetic smile as he resumed feeding from a plastic dinner tray.

Only one cop seemed to have no appetite this evening, and Ali knew that was her fault, for she had given him Father Marie's trial transcript. Rouge Kendall sat at his corner desk, solemn as a schoolboy, slogging through a volume two inches thick. He was so absorbed in his reading, he took no notice of Mr Frund, the file clerk *cum* psychic.

Ali turned her attention on this small gray-suited man from Connecticut. He was standing only a few yards away in conversation with Captain Costello. Martin Frund's weak watery eyes were enlarged by thick lenses. His shoes alternately touched down and lifted again in a light tap dance, as though the floorboards might be hot. Urged by a wave of Costello's hand, the man gingerly sat down on a chair at the center of the room, but his feet went on dancing. Though Ali could barely hear his small strained voice, she understood the gist of what he was saying to Costello. Frund was claiming to be a virgin in the psychic trade.

Close to Ali's chair, two BCI men sat on either side of a desk which doubled as their dinner table.

'This is a waste of time,' said the younger man, dipping his fork into a plastic container of salad, apparently finding it much more alluring than the psychic file clerk.

'That depends on what the little guy knows – maybe something he shouldn't know,' said Buddy Sorrel, a senior investigator with an iron-gray crew cut.

Sorrel wore a suit, but whenever Ali thought of him, she saw him in an army officer's uniform, perhaps because his pants were sharply creased, and his suit jacket was not. But the real giveaway to his history was the footwear; his shoes had the high luster of a military spit-shine polish. He peeled back the top layer of rye bread and directed a look of deep suspicion at the mound of pastrami on his sandwich. But then, Ali had noticed that suspicion was Sorrel's only expression. His gray eyebrows were always arched, as if frozen that way after decades of police work. It was a good trait for a law enforcement officer. One always felt a little off balance with him, and disbelieved from the first word of the most casual conversation.

'How does the perp do it, Buddy?' The younger of the two men was perhaps thirty-five and genuinely perplexed. 'How can anybody control a kid? I can't control my five-year-old. I told my wife I don't do baths anymore.'

'Well, nobody can control *wet* kids,' said Sorrel, somewhat philosophically, as he bit into his sandwich.

A smaller voice drifted back to her from the center of the room. 'I've never told anyone about my visions before,' said Mr Frund. 'But this time, I knew I had to come forward – for the children's sake.' His tone was full of apology and humility.

'We appreciate all the help we can get, Mr Frund.' Captain Costello was very amiable today – not his natural state. Like Sorrel, he usually exhibited a deep distrust of everything that moved and everything that didn't. Yet now he was almost charming, radiating warmth and good fellowship.

'It's *Martin* Frund, isn't it? Do your friends call you Marty?'

137

'Uh, no, sir. Just plain old Martin.'

Costello put one hand on the file clerk's shoulder. 'Are you a married man, Martin? Any kids of your own?'

'No, sir, no wife, no children.' Martin Frund colored as he said this, and Ali guessed that he had not had much luck with women.

What about small children?

Was Costello wondering the same thing? Perpetrators sometimes insinuated themselves into police investigations. Some went so far as to join the search parties hunting for their victims. However, in Ali's own experience, the psychics usually had other agendas.

For his performance this evening, Martin Frund had dressed up in a brand-new cheap suit, and the opening in his jacket revealed the fold line of a white shirt fresh from a discount-store box. But the footwear was not a recent purchase. When he crossed one leg over his knee, the shoe displayed a sole with wear that threatened to become a hole with every step, and the heel was run down on one side.

The little man might be in it for all the money the tabloids would pay, or he could have a craving for public notoriety. It was also possible that Frund was a true believer, sincerely deluded in the dream that he was gifted. The need to feel special would be very strong; Ali could see his entire life, past and future, in the nervous darting of his myopic eyes, the constant tapping of one foot and the exposed sole.

All around the wide room, armed men and women were stealing glances at the little file clerk, appraising him between bites of dinner, chewing and watching.

Disgust was clear in Buddy Sorrel's eyes. The senior investigator had probably seen this man's ilk before, when other children had gone missing, when the parents had gone over the moon, all the way crazy with fear, eager for a fake to tell them lies and get them through the days of waiting.

But Sadie Green's mother didn't seem crazy, though both the fathers appeared to be catatonic. Ali looked for Gwen's mother in the crowd. She spotted Marsha Hubble standing by the rear wall and away from the show, her arms folded against the charade. This woman was definitely not a believer. Ali guessed the lieutenant governor had no faith outside herself and no god but politics. The estranged husband, Peter Hubble, was sitting quietly by a bank of tall windows, his face turned skyward, perhaps looking for omens in the clouds scudding by. Harry Green sat beside him, perusing a map and occasionally drawing lines with a red marker.

Buddy Sorrel was bent over an open notebook on his desk, making rapid pen strokes, writing disconnected words and phrases. Ali had no difficulty reading them: 'water, trees, phone lines, power cables, random letters, numbers, lone man, non-descript car, ambiguous road, purple and other flyer stats'. And now Sorrel put away his pen and pulled out a pocket tape-recorder.

So she had guessed right. This BCI man was definitely familiar with the psychic's game.

Captain Costello shouted, 'Heads up, people', and now he had the attention of every law enforcement officer but Rouge. 'Let's get this show on the road. Mr Frund? Martin? If you would please tell us about your visions?' Captain Costello withdrew to the door and stood there with his arms folded, blocking the only exit from the room.

'Could I hold something that belonged to one of the children?' Frund wore a weak smile as he addressed the captain, silently apologizing again. 'It would help me to focus.'

Becca Green was dipping into her purse when Buddy Sorrel caught her eye. He shook his head to warn her off. She withdrew her empty hand and snapped the purse shut. Sorrel reached out to one corner of his desk and picked up a sealed manila envelope. Not bothering to stand, he tossed it to the little man. Frund missed the catch and went down on one knee to retrieve it.

'That belongs to one of the kids.' Sorrel's words were

barked, and Mr Frund flinched. 'Don't break the evidence seal.' This was an order.

Frund dusted off his pant leg and returned to his chair.

Clutching the envelope to his chest, he looked up to the ceiling of bright lights and removed his glasses. The lenses were so thick Ali wondered if he was legally blind without them.

'I only see one child. Her hair is short and light brown.'

Becca Green leaned forward, for Gwen's hair was long and blond, so this must be a vision of Sadie.

'I see a name – or part of one – not the child's name. All that's clear is the letter *S*.' Frund was rising from his chair. 'The letter *S*.' He was pausing, waiting.

Though Buddy Sorrel was seated on the other side of the room he was holding Becca Green silent with one raised hand and another slow shake of his head, preventing her from feeding the man information. Then he bent down to his list, and Ali watched him make a check mark by his notation for random letters.

Frund slowly stood up, and he continued to rise on the balls of his feet. He held the pose, creating an uneasy tension in his audience. 'The letter *S*,' he said, and now it was an unmistakable prompt. Frund turned toward the mother in a mute appeal, looking to her for his missing letters. But she was looking at Sorrel.

The little psychic sank back to his chair, breathing deeply as he restored his glasses and rallied for another go at Becca Green. This time he stared at her until she turned her face to his. 'I see another letter.' Frund's eyes were squinting, as if the image might be floating out of his sight. One hand rose high over his head, fingers opening and closing, as if to pinch its meaning from the air. 'The letter is *B*.'

Becca Green kept her silence.

The psychic lowered his gaze to a patch of the floor beside his chair. 'There's something close by – crawling – so dark, only a shadow in—' A look of fear crossed his face, fleeting, then gone. His eyes were glistening now, and his voice altered slightly, more confident. 'I can smell the earth and feel the moisture.'

He stood up again, this time with a grace of movement that Ali would not have suspected from him. Behind Frund, the wall of windows made a dramatic backdrop of white clouds sailing across the dark blue sky. Across the road, a streetlamp came on, refracting off his lenses, and for a moment, his eyes seemed lit from within.

Ali turned to Becca Green. The woman's eyes were fixed on Frund, and she was ignoring Sorrel.

'A man is nearby, and she knows this.' Frund's hands began to spin in frantic circles. He turned to his left, eyes cast to the floor and focussed on some middle ground of vision. 'Her eyes are closed – she isn't moving.'

'She's playing dead,' said Becca Green with great enthusiasm. 'Good girl!' The woman stood up, unable to contain herself in the chair any longer. She stepped lightly at the fringes of the wide circle of chairs and desks surrounding the psychic.

Frund paced back and forth in short steps, as though he had lost his way in the circle, and then he stopped abruptly, and so did Becca Green.

'I can see it now!' One hand shot straight out, his pointing finger directed at no one, at nothing but the blank wall over a filing cabinet. 'There! I see the water. It's so dark.' His eyes were squinting. 'It might be a lake.' His fingertips went out to touch the air surrounding him. 'I can feel the moisture.'

This time Sorrel made several check marks beside the words on his list.

Becca Green was staring at the wall, as though she too could see through the psychic's window. The energy level in the room was humming as Frund resumed his walking to and fro. At the rim of the circle, Sadie's mother was matching his pace to keep up with him on this journey of four steps right and four steps left.

Frund stopped again, and the mother froze. His head went back, his eyes closed as one finger wrote upon the air, describing a curving line. 'There's a side road with no sign.' Both hands went up to his eyes, perhaps to shield them from the yawn of a detective seated at a nearby desk. 'And there are wires in the sky. I see a building – maybe a house. I can smell the water now.' Frund sank down to the chair and draped himself over it, giving the appearance of sudden pain and exhaustion.

Becca Green settled into a chair next to Sorrel's, but she sat on the edge of it, as though waiting on a starter's gun, set to run a race in the next moment. Sorrel was making more marks in his notebook.

'The little girl is crying. She wants her mother. That feeling is very strong.' Frund curled his body inward, making it smaller.

Child size? Yes.

And now Ali heard the sound of a small strangled cry coming from his throat – a child's cry.

You son of a bitch.

Ali quickly turned to the mother to gauge the effect on her; it was cruel. The woman's right hand was clawing at the front of her dress, and beneath that hand, the heart would be quickening. With deep empathy, Ali sensed a thickening in the woman's throat, something welling up from within, from the silent, slow-motion destruction of Becca Green.

Frund was perspiring, and Ali noted wet stains where his fingers touched the envelope.

'The little girl is very weak.'

She's dead, you bastard.

'I see something else. I can't make out the color. It might—' His hand waved about in frustration. He lifted his head, and Mrs Green did too. She was leaving her chair as Frund stood up; she was on her toes, reaching upward as Frund's hand rose higher and higher.

'The color – it's gone now,' he said. 'Too many trees.'

142

No one rushed to make notes on this, perhaps because the county was dense with trees of every species. Only Sorrel's pencil moved. Unknown to the senior investigator, Becca Green was looking down at the page in his open notebook, watching with a trace of horror as he made another check mark beside a word on his list. So far, except for the color Sadie loved best, the BCI investigator had predicted most of the items described by the psychic.

Becca Green looked up from the notebook page, utterly destroyed. She turned back to Frund, who might have mistaken her devastation for his own personal handiwork.

'The color – could it be powder-blue, like my daughter's sweatshirt?'

'Yes, I see it now,' said Frund. 'She's wearing a light-blue garment.'

Blue? Not purple? Evidently, none of the first batch of flyers had crossed the border into Mr Frund's home state of Connecticut. Well, they had only appeared in the store windows for a few hours. *A bad gaffe, little man.*

Mrs Green was calmer now, but there were tears in her voice. 'And those letters you mentioned? *S* and *B*? Could you have them backwards? Is that possible?'

Now Frund seemed pleased. At last, he was getting some cooperation. He rewarded her with his widest smile. 'Yes, that sometimes happens.'

'Maybe it's not a name, like a person's name – but a thing?'

'Yes,' said Frund. 'It's not a person, but something – something—' His eyes closed tightly with deep concentration, waiting for her to finish his sentence.

'Something warm and moist?' she offered, helpfully.

He was nodding his head with great enthusiasm. 'I definitely feel those things.' One hand covered his face. 'It's clearer now, more like—'

'Bullshit?'

Frund's hand dropped to his side, and his lips parted as he stared at the mother. He could see that she was angry now, that he had erred, but it was too late to backtrack to that place where things had gone wrong. He looked around him, seeking friendly faces in the crowd.

There were none.

Becca Green had a terrible determination in her steps as she walked to the psychic's chair and hovered in front of him. Investigator Sorrel began to rise, no doubt in the belief that she was about to strike Frund, and she would need some help with that.

All the other men and women sat motionless, unblinking, utterly fascinated by this softly rounded little mother who now controlled Frund, making him flinch as she bent down to his face and forced him to look at her. And though she whispered, the room was so quiet no one failed to hear the words, 'Cheap trick.'

Sadie's mother walked away, heading for the door in pin-drop silence. The faces all around the room no longer showed disinterest in the little man at the center of the circle. They were done feeding from their paper bags and plastic trays. They turned their eyes to him.

Ali left the door ajar as she followed the distraught mother into the next room and found her sitting in the stairwell. She sat down on the top step and put one arm around Mrs Green's shoulders. It seemed only right and fair to caution this woman against all hope, to warn her of what lay ahead. Becca was living for the moment when the police would find Sadie, never considering the possibility that they might bring her a dead child. She must consider it. Someone had to prepare her. How to begin?

Sadie is at rest. She's not in any pain, not frightened anymore. She's been gone a long time now, days and days. But Ali's throat went dry. She lost her voice, her professional distance – all her defenses. Becca Green was facing her with an openhearted smile, so vulnerable to Ali's good intention – this ugly act of kindness, the truth telling.

'I know, I know,' said Mrs Green. 'You thought I was so

desperate I'd believe anything. I suppose it's nuts to listen to that crap, but you've gotta try everything, right?'

Through the open doorway, Ali could see Sorrel walking toward the defrocked psychic at the center of the room. The investigator was smiling, and Frund smiled back, apparently taking the man's expression for sympathy.

He was wrong about that.

Becca was saying, 'Well, it wasn't a complete waste of time. At least they won't forget Sadie, will they?'

And now Ali understood the true purpose of today's exhibition. Thanks to Arnie Pyle, Becca had the fixed and frantic idea that her child would be written off as an extraneous error in a larger plan. So this woman had used the only tool that came her way, a phone call from a fake psychic; she had used him and all the men and women in that room, leaving every cop and fed crazed and bleeding from the heart. The focus had changed. *Brilliant woman, desperate woman.*

People were rising from their desks as Costello led Marsha Hubble and the fathers into his private office.

Ali turned back to Becca Green. Behind the mother's eyes was a mind at work, not disassembling, but weighing her losses and speaking in a disturbingly practical manner.

'They're little girls – and it's cold outside. You have to try *everything.*'

Ali watched the FBI agents quitting the room *en masse*, not wanting to witness what came next, nor to stop it. The remaining BCI investigators circled Frund, and some of them were removing their jackets. No one was smiling anymore. Frund was trying to run backwards while seated in his chair, feet working furiously. The chair legs only retreated by inches. He opened his mouth, and beyond the bank of windows, a siren screamed.

Rouge swiveled his chair around, paying no attention to what was going on a few yards away from him. He faced the windows and watched the clouds ganging into a pearly gray overcast, promising the first snow of winter. The old transcript of Paul Marie's trial lay open on his desk, and he was wondering how the prosecution had obtained a conviction.

'It was a vision.' The voice from the center of the room was hysterical. Frund's words were said in a high-pitched whine. The louder voices of larger men rained down questions like fistfalls.

'Anyone ever call you short-eyes?' asked Sorrel. And another voice asked if the little girls were still alive. 'And where are they?'

'I had a vision,' said the little man, crying now. 'I saw the little girl in—'

'In your *vision*. Right.' Sorrel's tone was pure acid. All the voices dropped to a lower level that was somehow more threatening.

When Rouge turned his chair back to the desk, the bodies of encircling cops had blocked Martin Frund from his view. He looked down at the transcript of the old murder trial. He was undisturbed by the rising volume of the little psychic's plaintive bleating, hardly aware of the sound of a chair hitting the floor, and then the soft crying.

Rouge scanned the property list inserted at the back of the transcript. The only physical evidence against Paul Marie was the silver bracelet. On the witness stand, BCI Investigator Oz Almo had insisted that bracelet was found in the priest's bedroom. Paul Marie had admitted to finding it, but said he had placed it in the parish lost-and-found box.

The only defense witness, Father Domina, had been vague in his recollection of 'a shining ring of silver' in the box among the more mundane lost items. The district attorney had destroyed the elderly priest's credibility with indirect attacks on the man's failing eyesight and his memory. But nothing could destroy Father Domina's faith in the young priest's innocence.

At last Rouge understood why Father Domina had remained in the church well past retirement age. He wondered if the frail old man had not overstayed his life as well, hanging on, waiting for a miracle: the parole of a child killer, so Paul Marie might take his place as the head of the parish.

Rouge skimmed the testimony of Jane Norris, the young woman who claimed Paul Marie had assaulted her when she was only fifteen. Under the most listless cross-examination by the defense counsel, it had come out, almost by accident, that Paul Marie was only fourteen years old at the time, and that the relationship had lasted four more years, culminating in a broken engagement.

When Rouge looked up from this page, he saw Sorrel handing Martin Frund his coat. The psychic's eyes roamed from face to face, perhaps wondering if this was a trick. Then he edged toward the door, tripping on the tails of the coat slung over his arm, and knocking his head into the wall with a bang.

Good. Rouge turned back to his reading, undistracted by the sound of Frund's running feet in the stairwell.

Inserted into the following page was a folded summary of police reports filed by this same witness. Aided by an enthusiastic therapist, Jane Norris had recalled early memories of incest and other sexual assaults by policemen, teachers, doctors, and the school bus driver. Rare was the man she had not accused of rape. At the bottom of the page, a handwritten footnote told him that the district attorney had read the same report before putting the bogus witness on the stand. More incredible than this, the defense attorney had received full disclosure and signed a receipt for the police reports.

But there were no appeals filed for the defendant. Other convicted felons had walked away from jail time despite more solid testimony and fewer trial errors.

Lesser offerings into evidence were signs of Susan's struggle in the snow near the church. But she had been at the church for choir practice only a few hours earlier. The attorney for the defense had not contested the rather loose description of child and adult footprints, and there were no photographs taken. Rouge wondered if this was tainted evidence as well.

He closed the transcript. There was nothing to say that Paul Marie was innocent, nor was there any proof of murder.

When he opened his desk drawer, he was startled by the rolling motion of an old baseball bearing his own signature. This had not been in the drawer twenty minutes ago when he left for the men's room.

Even before he looked out the window, he knew what he would see in the parking lot below. David Shore's small white face was floating in the gathering dusk of the dinner hour. The child was rubbing his red mittens together and stamping the cold from his feet. How long had David been standing there, patiently waiting to be noticed?

Rouge stared at the baseball's autograph. There was only one season when he could have signed it. Had David been a face in the crowd on one of those summer days after a game? He only remembered a hundred tiny hands thrusting out cards and balls and bits of paper for their heroes to sign. And now he recalled one particular day when he had spotted Mary Hofstra, miles taller than the mob of little fans at the gate. He had waved to her, thinking she had come to see him play, to cheer him on. But the housemother had disappeared by the time all the autographs were done and the last child was satisfied. And now he realized that she must have come that day for David's sake, the little boy with real heart for the game.

So they had met before – for the few seconds it took to scrawl a signature on the child's baseball. David could only have been five or six years old.

Mary Hofstra had told him to create a comfort zone to ease the boy's shyness, but he had done nothing toward that end, and David could not wait any longer; he was making a mighty effort to get past the fear of talking to an adult, a cop.

There were no civilian cars in the front lot. Where was Mary Hofstra now?

The phone rang. He never took his eyes off David as he picked up the receiver. 'Kendall here.'

'Hey, Rouge?' The state trooper's voice sounded tired and

harried. 'You gotta phone call from St Ursula's Academy. It's a lady – a Mrs Hofstra? You wanna take it?'

'Sure, put her through.' Rouge wondered if Mrs Hofstra could still read his mind, and from such a distance.

'Rouge?'

'Yes, ma'am.' He was haunted by the scent of peppermint tea, as though he could smell it through the telephone wires.

'Is David with you?'

'Yes, ma'am, he's here. I'll bring him home.'

'Thank you, Rouge.' Then Mary Hofstra was gone, and the peppermint connection was broken.

He threw up the sash and leaned out into the cold air. 'Hey, David?' The boy raised one red-mittened hand, and his breath came out in white puffs on the cold night air. 'You wait there, all right? Mrs Hofstra wants me to drive you back to school. I'll be down in a few minutes.'

Rouge closed the window, donned his jacket and put the baseball into his pocket. He didn't take the hallway to the parking lot, but went down the back stairs to the basement. He flicked on the light near the door, and it bounced off the row of new metal lockers installed by the task force to house their gear. The old green wooden storage cabinet had been pushed to the back wall and blocked by stacks of cartons bearing the New York State Police logo. He worked quickly to clear the cabinet. Finally, the doors creaked open on their old hinges to display all the gloves and bats once used by the Makers Village Athletic League. Now that the baseball field had been sold off to a furniture store, he wondered if this equipment would ever be used again.

He pulled out a bat, old but well made. This had been his own contribution to the cabinet, a souvenir from his days with the Yankees rookie league. He hefted it in one hand, testing the weight of the Louisville Slugger.

'Hey, kid,' said a familiar voice behind him.

He turned to see Buddy Sorrel. The senior investigator was staring at the bat, which must seem an oddity in winter.

'Would I want to know what you were planning to do with that, Kendall?'

'I'm gonna play ball.' Rouge pulled the baseball out of his pocket and held it up to the older man as proof.

'Yeah, right. You know, I haven't played the game since I was a kid.' Sorrel cracked a smile at some old memory, and then his expression became rueful. 'Okay, Kendall, you know the rules. If you beat up a reporter, you hit him where it doesn't show – and *no* witnesses. You got that?'

Rouge met with no more questions as he left the police station armed with a bat and a pitcher's glove.

David was standing in the same place at the fringe of light from a lamp post, his white face so pale between the dark ski cap and the collar of a midnight-blue jacket. His eyes were perfectly round as he stared at the bat and the glove.

Rouge pulled the baseball out of his pocket and tossed it. David plucked the ball out of the air and threw it back. Their conversation had begun.

This time Gwen neither drank nor ate anything from the tray, though she was starving and the lure of food was strong. She flushed the cocoa and the biscuit down the toilet, not bothering to crumble the bread, for it would be too tempting to eat just one crumb and then another. With great regret, she watched the precious meal spinning down the bowl and out of sight.

Slowly revolving in a groggy haze, her eyes took in each detail of the large bathroom and finally settled upon the wall hamper. She walked toward it, stumbling once, then falling to the floor and crawling the rest of the way.

Why put a lock and chain on a hamper? Gwen knew this could be worked out if only she could hold on to a thought for two consecutive minutes. She pressed one ear to the metal hamper and held her breath. Not a sound, nothing living inside of it – something dying? Sadie? It was the right size to hold a ten-year-old girl.

150

The child banged on the metal. 'Sadie!' she yelled, and then put her hands over her mouth, suddenly frightened by the sound of her own voice. Well, what did *not* frighten her? Gwen banged her fist on the metal again, this time in frustration. Now she was grateful for the effect of the drug; she was at least not running about the room, screaming and flapping her arms like a goose.

Gwen gripped the hamper's chain and slowly stood up, more steady on her feet now. She began to pace the bathroom in slow circles, willing her mind to clear away the cobwebs of drugs. Turning to the hamper again, she focussed on the padlock of bright-blue paint and chrome. It was like the one St Ursula's had issued to every student with a bicycle.

There had been a rash of bike thefts in September. Boarding students and townies alike had been victims. This padlock was an expensive brand with the option of individual settings. On the day the locks were handed out, the teachers had instructed every student to set the combination to their own birth date, so they wouldn't forget the numbers. Gwen had dutifully done as she was told. But this padlock couldn't be hers. Her own lock was at home, on the bike chain in her knapsack.

Sadie's?

She turned the dial to the day, month and year of Sadie's birth, but it failed to open.

Her head snapped up, and she stood at attention, forgetting to breathe. She could hear the movement of heavy furniture sliding across the floor in the next room.

She returned to her cot and slipped under the sheet. Every muscle was tensing, joints locking up, her whole body freezing into a solid, inert block of fright. Her fear subsided for a moment as she stared at the massive armoire, trying to remember something of importance. It didn't belong in this room – and something that *did* belong here was missing.

On the other side of the bathroom door, she could hear

scraping of wood on wood. Some heavy object was sliding out of the way.

There was no access to the baseball diamond. The field was surrounded with chain-link fencing, and the gate was locked. Rouge motioned David to join him in the wider area of the front lot used by library patrons. The asphalt, marked with yellow lines for parking spaces, was unpopulated in the dinner hour.

He handed David the bat, and in the next moment, the first pitch was in the air. David swung; the bat sounded a loud crack. A long fly ball sailed to the back of the lot, where it bounced once on a dark sedan, then rolled across the wooden ski rack on the roof of a station wagon.

Officer Billy Poor's hand was frozen in the act of reaching for the car door. He stared at the ball, not immediately comprehending what it was doing there, for every fool knew that baseballs only flew in summer. Then he looked toward the front lot. When he saw Rouge and the boy with the bat, Officer Poor grinned.

'Hey, you guys are dangerous. You need a damn outfielder.' And then the village cop was with them in a game of three. In only a few minutes, they were joined by a state trooper in uniform. Then a BCI investigator, with his tie undone, came running out to play, arms laden with baseman's gloves for all. Another village cop, Phil Chapel, came up behind David, who gracefully conceded his place at bat.

The investigators, the troopers and the hometown boys in blue were out in force, and more were on the way down the steps of the station house. Rouge watched their faces glow by lamplight. They had been used up and haggard at the end of a shift and facing another tour of overtime. But now they were reborn, and it was no longer December, but high summer; not night, but day, a warm, dry one; all boys again, gloves reaching out to the long, high curve of a ball in flight, poetry in ballistics, gravity undone.

Buddy Sorrel appeared at the fence gate with a pair of bolt cutters in hand, and soon the chain hung loose and broken. The gate swung open, and the players filed through to the old baseball diamond.

On the sidewalk, Christmas shoppers stopped to stare at them through the links in the fence. The field was well lit by the security lights intended to safeguard a stack of construction materials.

Cops were in the outfield, and one was up at bat. Buddy Sorrel wore a catcher's face mask and crouched behind home plate. David was pitching fastballs and killing the batters off one by one. Now a trooper, still wearing his uniform, hit a long ball into left field, and he began to run the bases in his regulation leather shoes and a glorious grin.

Rouge was up at bat when the children of the Christmas shoppers abandoned their parents on the sidewalk and poured through the opening. Those who hadn't seen the unlocked gate in the parking lot were scrambling up the chain-link fence spanning the sidewalk. Boys and girls dropped into the field, hitting the ground at a dead run. Some ran toward home plate to take a turn at bat, and others scrambled into the outfield.

The cops behind the bases were laughing as each one gave up his baseman's glove to a child. The men backed off to the cheering section by the sidewalk, where the taxpayers were gathering in greater numbers.

A new catcher, much shorter than Sorrel and heavily freckled, tossed the ball back to David on the pitcher's mound; it was a bad throw and wide of the mark. David only stepped to the side, extended his arm in a long, slow reach and caught it with no apparent effort, as though he had taught the ball to fly home to his glove – almost magic. He looked up to the sky of this make-believe summer, and snowflakes fell into his eyes.

Cheers and whistles came from the sidewalk gallery as another boy ran all the bases and skidded into home plate on his little backside. Cars were being moved into position along the parking lot section of the fence, and now the baseball diamond was bright as day, and large, fluffy flakes of snow drifted down in a shower of white confetti.

Every base was loaded with a child set to run, only awaiting the next batter. Rouge handed the bat to a little girl with killer-blue eyes, a brunette heartbreaker with a red beret. He watched as she crouched over the bat like an old pro, and he half expected her to spit chewing tobacco from the side of her mouth. David was on second base when she popped the ball into right field. Off David flew to third base as the girl slid into first, and her red beret went flying. David skidded into third, and the little girl stole second. While the ball was flying back to the pitcher's mound, David touched down on home plate, and a roar went up from the crowd of spectators on the sidewalk.

Now David was startled as the little girl, sans red beret, slammed her small body into the dirt behind him, having stolen one more base against all odds of making it. She jumped to her feet, wrapped her arms around his neck and hugged him in a pure, spontaneous act of joy.

David's eyes were shining, his grin was foolish, his face was red – all the symptoms of a perfectly normal boy in the clutches of a girl.

For the first time in recent memory, Gwen was frighteningly awake. The door opened with a metallic click of the lock, loud as gunfire in the dark. Her eyes were open by the barest slits as the large black shape was silhouetted against a harsh white light from the outer room. Gwen closed her eyes, and the light diffused into a pink blot on the delicate membranes of her eyelids.

Her mind was working through the fear; it was the only part of her that still functioned, trying to disassociate itself from her trapped body with the distraction of new questions. She knew the bathroom door had been locked, for she had just heard the key working the tumblers. But something heavy had also blocked the only exit; she had heard it sliding away from the door. *Why?* Surely the lock was—

The door closed. The glow beyond her eyelids was extinguished, and she was blind to everything now. But there was a terrifying acuity to her sense of hearing. The thing was walking toward her cot. It came on two feet like a human, yet the idea of a large insect prevailed.

Gwen stiffened as the thing settled into the chair by her cot; she heard the wicker sounds of stress and protest as the strands of woven wood gave way beneath a heavy weight.

Utter silence now.

Was the thing also listening to *her?* Did it know that sleep breathing was different? Sadie Green did; she had gone on at great length about the art of shamming sleep in horror movies.

Gwen let her breath come out loud and labored. Was she overdoing it? No. The creature in the chair seemed satisfied with this, for now she could hear the thing breathing too. And there was motion; she had the sense of the giant insect wildly twitching, reaching out with its antennae, growing larger in the dark. The thing was breathing faster, more excited now. When it lightly touched her hair, she could not scream; she was paralysed. It was a fight merely to breathe again.

The chair pulled nearer to the cot. Gwen could smell waves of stale sweat and breath of wine. She could sense it closing in on her. Something was massing just in front of her face. What was it doing with its hands? They might be reaching for her eyes. If it touched her again, would she scream this time? It was coming closer; she could anticipate it, almost see it through her skin, which prickled and grew small bumps.

Was this what David Shore felt like when Mr Beckerman stroked his face or ruffled his hair in class? She thought of the teacher's fat spider fingers touching her classmate. Did David feel this queasiness, this unclean feeling, this desire to take a bath and then another and another? Mr Beckerman had creepy eyes only for the boys, mostly for David, and he hardly knew the girls were alive. And so she knew this thing in the room with her was not Beckerman, yet something akin to the teacher was sitting in the chair by her bed. Perhaps in the absence of light, in the blackness, the blindness, insects were all alike.

Her body was too tense, too rigid. She willed herself to relax each muscle, so if it touched her, it would not know she was awake and terrified.

A hand grazed her face, fingers light in the slow crawl of the spider. It prowled in her hair, and she was filled with loathing. The fingers grazed the more sensitive area of her lips, and now she knew it was not flesh but gloves of rubber. The body of the thing was drawing closer, bending over her now, for she could feel a puffing draft of reeking breath across her face.

A beeping sound began; the repeating tone was low but insistent. The rubbery fingers flew away from her lips, and she heard the rustle of material as the thing fumbled in its clothing and stopped the beeping noise.

The wicker creaked again, this time with relief, as the thing was rising. And now the room had a different feel, a clamminess, and there was the stink of something odious, unclean.

The giant insect was leaving her, stepping quickly on its hind legs and moving toward the door. Gwen kept her eyes shut tight, lest it should turn around and catch her watching.

The door closed. Her eyes opened to the dim glow of the night-light. A gleam sparked off the metal padlock on the hamper, taunting her.

Rouge stood near the window and looked up to the sky. The moon was hidden, but here and there, a star emerged from the lacework of dispersing clouds. The light snowfall had ended, and all the evidence of winter had already melted in a soft rain, dashing every child's hope of a vicious snowball fight to cap off the baseball game.

Cops and kids filled the fast-food restaurant with hollered orders for burgers and fries, chocolate shakes and Cokes. It was a night of hilarity and bragging, and a sight usually reserved for warm evenings after a ball game in the proper season. This might be the last such gathering. By the first day of spring, the baseball diamond would be covered with cement.

David was standing near the cash register, laughing at some aside from a town boy whispering in his ear. Tonight, this quiet child seemed like any other, just another member of the team, and Rouge didn't want that ruined. He plucked the boy from the crowded lineup at the counter and led him to a table at the other end of the room. David seemed relieved to be parting company with the town children. None of them had yet realized that he was too shy to speak, that he was not quite normal, not *really* one of them.

The meal of burgers was eaten over a conversation of words from himself and nods from the boy. Rouge was heeding Mary Hofstra's counsel not to pressure David into speech, framing every question for a nod or a shake of the head. He had just asked if the fries from St Ursula's cafeteria were as good as the fast-food fries.

'They were kidnapped from the boathouse,' said David, ducking his head shyly as he sipped from his milk shake. 'Gwen and Sadie.'

'How do you know?' *Oh, fool.* He amended his question to ease the pressure. 'Are you sure?'

David nodded, and his face was going to a high red color. So they must be close to the hidden thing that David could not confess, not even to Mary Hofstra.

'You saw them go into the boathouse?'

'Yes.'

Another word. More progress.

'Did you see the man who took them?'

David shook his head. 'But he must have been in there the whole time I was—' Words failed David. His face was so miserable, he might be looking at the end of the world as he knew it.

Then David began to speak again, talking faster in an

unbroken stream, a torrent of words. Before the tears could amount to anything, Rouge was bundling the boy into his parka and leading him out the door.

The ten-year-old was silent as they pulled out of the parking lot. During the drive back to St Ursula's, David was more talkative, in rushes and spurts, with no prompting from Rouge. The boy looked ill, possibly because he had eaten more cheese-burgers than any other child at the restaurant. Or it might have been the confession that made him sick. He had admitted to following the girls that day and spying on them. But just now, Rouge was worrying about David's account of the barking dog in the boathouse. He was tying it to Sadie Green's ripped jacket.

'I thought you might think I was weird.' David looked down at his tightly clasped hands. 'I *am* weird.'

'The other kids didn't think so. They know natural talent when they see it. And following girls? You're supposed to do that, David. You're a guy – that's your job in life.'

The boy was smiling at this tossed-off revelation that he might not be a freak of nature, that an interest in girls was more common than he had supposed.

'So, David – got any ideas about that barking dog?'

'I know it wasn't Gwen's poodle. Harpo didn't come with her. He never does, not to the boathouse. And it wasn't Sadie's dog. Mrs Green won't let her have one.'

'Sadie told you that?'

The boy turned his face away to stare out the windshield at the sudden lights of an onrushing vehicle. The other car passed by them, its taillights disappearing around the curve in the road. Safe in the dark again, he said, 'I heard her tell it to Gwen – when I was listening at the boathouse window. But that was another time.'

Rouge pulled into the school's driveway and traveled on to the parking lot at the back of the building. 'So it was a regular meeting place for the girls?'

'Yeah. When Gwen's father wouldn't let them play

together, she'd sneak out and meet Sadie at the boathouse.' David left the car and joined Rouge at the edge of the great lawn and its sprawling view of the lake. 'It was like probation – just Saturdays. So I figured Mr Hubble was mad at Sadie again.'

They descended the slope, casting two shadows by moonlight, heading for the darkened boathouse. A stand of young pine trees hid all but the roof and part of the wharf. When they had passed through the trees and the entire building was visible, David hung back, suddenly regressing to baby steps. Rouge waited for him to catch up and wondered at the look of dread on the boy's face.

The century-old building was forbidding at this hour. Its only window was shuttered like a closed eye. In silhouette, the lines were not quite true and straight. There was almost an attitude in the lean of the walls and the decrepit slope in the spine of the roof. But he thought there might be more to David's new anxiety, which increased with every step.

Rouge looked out over the lake. If David was right, then the kidnapper might be in one of those houses near the water. Anyone with field glasses might note the coming and going of two little girls. But all the lakefront houses had been searched by troopers and town cops.

He turned back to what he could see of St Ursula's main building above the stand of young pines. Beckerman might not be the only pedophile on the faculty. Schools were magnets for freaks.

David touched his sleeve as they stepped onto the wooden planks of the wharf. 'I think they left in one of the canoes. There was no other way to get past me.' He pointed to a cluster of boulders down along the shoreline. 'The rocks would've hidden the canoe if it came from the boat-slip door on the lakeside.'

'We'll check it out.' Rouge opened the narrower wharf-side door. 'They always keep this place unlocked?'

'No, sir, never. There was a padlock on the door. Somebody

broke it. I found the lock and the hasp right there – next to a rock.' He pointed to the smooth boards near the threshold. 'Sadie knew how to open it. She sucked up to the grounds-keeper – followed the old man around for days until she got the combination. That's how I know someone else broke the lock.'

Rouge turned his flashlight on the doorframe. It had been recently painted over with splashes of a brighter white. He could make out the ridges of wood putty filling in long, deep splinters of breakage. Someone had cleaned up the debris, but no one from the school had reported a break-in.

He walked into the building and found the light switch high on the wall, wisely placed beyond the reach of a child. He noted the sailboat and canoes on wooden cradles, all accounted for. David hung back, feet firmly planted on the wharf. The place frightened him, even with the light on.

'When I saw the bike at the bus stop, I thought they were just trying to lose me.' The boy's hands dove into the pockets of his parka as he studied his shoes. 'Nothing made sense that day. It wasn't real till I saw it on television. You know what I mean? That's when I told Mrs Hofstra about Sadie's bike.'

Rouge understood. Most people put more faith in tele-vision than their own eyes. And David had also needed to see events played out like a story before he could make sense of the witnessed bits and pieces.

The boy hovered on the doorsill now, still unwilling to enter the boathouse. 'At first, I thought they must've run away – because of the bike at the bus stop. But why would Sadie double back to move her bike from a good hiding place? Why would she leave it out in the open? You see? It doesn't work. And the dog always bothered me. Then the police came out and searched the school – the boathouse too. So I didn't think they needed me to tell them about it. But I guess they did. I'm really sorry.'

Rouge moved along the wharf to the far edge of the building. Now he was looking at the boatslip doors that would open on to the lake. 'So you figure he took them away in a canoe when it was getting dark? No noise, no one to see. Later, he must've gone back and moved the bike to the bus stop.'

David was beside him, nodding. 'When I finally figured it out—' His hands plunged deeper into the pockets of his coat, and his face turned away from Rouge. 'I was here the whole time it was happening to them.' The boy sank down to the wooden boards, shaking his head from side to side. 'I'm so sorry.'

And now Rouge understood the real shame of David Shore – as if the boy could have known what the man was doing to Sadie and Gwen, as if he could have stopped it. David was sick with guilt.

So they had more in common than baseball.

Susan, lying face down in the snow, so cold. His sister had died alone; that had been the worst of it for Rouge. If only he had been with his twin on that day, to die *for* her or *with* her. Back then, he had wanted nothing more than to lie down to sleep, to death, an end of pain, never awakening to another day of remorse for the sin of being alive. *Susan, my Susan.*

He had been David's age then.

Now he knelt down beside the boy whom Mrs Green had once described as Sadie's shadow. David's arms wrapped tightly around Rouge's neck, and they consoled one another in the dark, both rocking gently in the ancient way of small children seeking solace.

Gwen tried Sadie's birth date again, thinking she might have misdialed the numbers, but the combination still didn't work.

Oddly, she was relieved, not certain anymore that she wanted to see inside the hamper. She abandoned the problem to explore the crack of space between the armoire and the wall. Slowly, she reached one hand into the blackness. Suddenly, she pulled it back with strands of spiderweb on her fingers. A bit of the spider's supper was still kicking its legs. She wiped her hand on one leg of her blue jeans.

The last time she had done this, she must have been too groggy to be put off by the debris of bugs. Gwen plunged her hand back into the opening and touched the wood frame. Then her blind fingers worked downward and found the lower lip of the windowsill.

The child put her shoulder to the armoire, but it would not budge. She returned to the cot and pulled away the sheets to expose the canvas sling stretched across a wooden frame. She flipped it over, viewing the underside with a critical eye to the narrow slats threaded into the canvas hem. With one foot braced on a long board, she tugged at a short slat at the end of the frame. The wood was old and the nails gave with ease. She slipped it out of the canvas and carried it to the armoire, sliding it into the crack between the wall and the wardrobe. When she pulled on her lever, it broke in two. She sat down on the floor and stared at the jagged shard of wood in her hand, genuinely perplexed that such a good idea would not work out in real life with solid materials.

Next, she pulled the cot's remaining frame bars apart and freed them from the loops of canvas. She put the two longest slats together as a single prybar and fitted them into the crevice. This time, the heavy piece of furniture moved a bit when she pulled on the slats.

'Oh, stupid, Gwen,' she whispered. Pushing was easier than pulling. She braced her back against the wall and pushed on the wooden lever. The armoire moved a few inches. Now she put her whole weight into the effort, but this time it would not move at all.

Well, that was not logical, not right. Someone had changed the rules that governed physical objects. Exhausted, she stopped for a moment, and her gaze was pulled back to the hamper again. She averted her eyes and put all her energy into the slats. Nothing happened. Gwen sat down on the floor to rest before the next attempt. Though she never looked at the hamper, it was all but calling her name, daring her to work out another problem of logic: Why lock a hamper? Instead, she turned back to the problem of the immovable object, and then she solved it.

The child was staring down at cracked tiles and the lakes and rivers in the corroded grout between them. The wooden legs had settled into wide gaps where pieces of tiles were missing. She put the prybar slats underneath the armoire and used all of her weight to leverage it back just far enough to kick the small rug under the front legs. One shoulder ached, and she wondered if she had pulled a muscle. Only the suggestion of a possible pulled muscle had caused her father to keep her from gymnastics for a month. But she had been content to sit on the floor of the gymnasium, watching Sadie going through routines on the parallel bars.

Sadie, where are you?

Resting again and taking deep breaths, she avoided looking at the hamper. She knew the answer to the puzzle was in her head. Of course it was Sadie's lock. If the window gave her a way out, could she leave without knowing what was inside that thing? What if she was leaving her best friend behind?

Gwen let these grim questions alone and went back to work. The armoire now sat at a wide angle to the wall, and there was room to stand between its wooden backing and the window. She pressed her face to the cool glass pane. There were trees everywhere, the lines of bare-limbed oaks and birches were silvered by moonlight, and the pines had roundness of form. But there were no electric lights and not a rooftop or a chimney in sight – no one to hear her if she screamed – as if she dared to make any noise.

The ground was a long way down, judging by the scale of the driveway. Her next project was automatic, the stuff of bad movie plots. And her father always said that movies would rot her mind. If only he could see her now.

He'd have a heart attack.

But Sadie would be proud.

What's in the hamper?

Gwen shook her head, saying no to this dark idea. She picked up one of the sheets and tried to tear it down the center to fashion a longer rope. But she was still weak, and now she was frustrated because it would not rip. She dragged it over a nail sticking out of the remaining cot slat until she made a hole in the material. Then she easily tore it down the middle. When all the lengths of two torn sheets were tied together, she anchored them to a back leg of the armoire with a double knot.

Gwen opened the window, and she was foiled again by real life intruding on her scheme to escape by a bedsheet rope. The air was cold – shocking. Shivering, she pushed the mass of sheets over the sill and put her head out the window to watch them unravel along the sideboards of the house. The white material dropped past two dark windows. From the end of the rope to the yard below was how far? One window?

She leaned her upper body over the sill and looked straight down at the ground, focussing on the moonlit shapes of a trash can and a birdbath. The objects telescoped downward, growing smaller and farther away. The yard was spinning; the floor beneath her feet tilted; and her stomach lurched upward in a wave of nausea. She was not breathing – sudden fear had stopped her lungs. Shutting her eyes, she pulled back inside and slammed the window.

Gwen took great gulps of air and flattened her body against the solid, unmoving plaster wall. Her eyeballs rolled back in their sockets, and her breathing quickened while she weighed the fear of going against the fear of staying. Even if she could make herself climb over that windowsill, suppose she lost her grip on the bedsheet? What if the material ripped? She would fall and break her bones in a hundred pieces on the hard ground. Even if she could hold on until she reached the end of the sheets, she might still break her legs in the long drop to the yard. She could not bear pain in any measure. And then there was the cold to deal with. Barefooted she would not get far. How she hated the cold.

Every muscle of her body was pressing up against the wall, limbs and fingers spread across its surface as a second skin to the painted plaster. With effort, she slowly turned her face to the window, the only way out. The night wouldn't last forever. The sky would lighten to gray. Soon the giant insect would come back to her with a tray of orange juice and an egg. His rubber fingers would crawl in her hair, on her face, and this time she would be hideously awake. In her mind, she was already screaming in anticipation of the thing.

There was only one exit.

Sadie could do this; she could climb over that windowsill with no fear of the hard landing. In gym class, Sadie could fly.

Gwen could not.

Not in a million, zillion years could she lower her body out that window. The ground was farther away each time she looked at it with her mind's eye. She was too much a coward even to peer at it through the glass pane one more time.

The child edged along the wall and away from the window, listening to her own heart beating louder, faster, marking time at the speed of frenzy. Soon it would be light. She had to leave, but how? Gwen closed her eyes, and suddenly she was in freefall, dropping past all the dark windows, and the unforgiving ground was spinning, spiraling, rushing up to meet her.

The child's eyes snapped open, and she was staring at the chained hamper. It held less terror for her now. As she returned to this unsolved riddle, a calm settled over her, and she could think clearly again. She had used her birth date as the combination for her own lock, just as she had been instructed.

But since when did her best friend ever follow instructions?

What number did Sadie love the most? Thirteen? Not enough digits. Suppose she added the number 6 for Friday? *Friday the 13th* was a favorite movie title. But now this idea linked to another as she recalled the plot of a better-loved film about a changeling demon.

'And you shall know him by this mark,' she whispered, as she bent over the lock, moving the dial to the right, then left, and for the last digit, right again. The padlock came open in her hand with the mark of the beast, 666.

How appropriate.

At midnight, the boathouse was a swarm of activity. Village policemen and state troopers walked the grounds in close ranks, almost touching shoulders, their eyes trained on the earth. Beyond the glare of large floodlights on metal stalks, flashlight beams combed the grass at the water's edge. Farther up the shore of the lake, another team was working over the rocky beach.

Rouge stood on the wharf just outside the door. The old building had been searched days ago. But the troopers had been looking for two missing girls, not forensic evidence in the disturbance of dust. He made a note on the second broken lock, the one that belonged on the telephone box. He hadn't noticed this in his first perusal of the building. Apparently it had also gone unnoticed by the person who had repaired the splintered doorframe and cleaned up the damage of the broken exterior lock.

Black lights and black dust were the tools used by the FBI technicians inside the boathouse. They were scrutinizing every pore of wood surface, and even opening old paint cans which had been undisturbed for years. One tech stood in the open doorway holding a shred of purple rayon by metal tweezers as he lowered it into an evidence bag.

Buddy Sorrel and Arnie Pyle joined Rouge on the wharf.

'Nice work – for a cop in training pants,' said Agent Pyle, surveying the crime scene.

Sorrel clapped Rouge on the back. 'Kendall, I think you found your niche. So what else did the kid tell you?'

'He said there was a dog in there, and it didn't belong to Gwen or Sadie. He never saw it – just heard it barking.'

'Well, at least we know the bastard has a dog.' Captain

Costello strolled toward them along the smooth wooden boards of the wharf. His eyes were on the plastic evidence bag Agent Pyle was holding. It contained a small electronic device. The plastic casing was smashed. 'A pager. Expensive one, too. Is that a bloodstain?'

'Probably,' said Pyle. 'There's no prints on it, but we think it might belong to our perp.'

'It didn't belong to either one of the kids,' said Sorrel. 'The parents told me the girls never had pagers. Peter Hubble *did* have a transmitter sewn into his kid's knapsack. Too bad Gwen didn't have it with her when she was snatched.'

Captain Costello held up a small address book with a wet and faded cloth cover. 'A trooper found this on the rocks downshore. Looks like it's been in the water for a while.' He handed it to Rouge. 'It's your crime scene, kid. What do you make of it?'

Rouge stared at the tiny book's purple cover. There was no doubt that it belonged to Sadie Green. He thumbed through the pages indexed by tabbed letters of the alphabet, and this was all the legible print to survive the water damage. Everything written on the pages was lost in smears of purple ink. 'This backs up Ali Cray's theory. Sadie wasn't a mistake – the freak needed her to get to Gwen. He tried to force Sadie to call Gwen out, but the kid wouldn't do it.'

'How do you figure that?' Arnie Pyle was looking down at the address book, incredulous.

'The H page is missing,' said Rouge. 'You know Sadie wouldn't tear it out. This was the one with her best friend's phone number. Even if she knew the number better than her own, this was probably the most important page in her book. *He* ripped it out – the pervert. It fits with the broken lock on the phone box. He *had* to use this address book to get Gwen's number. Sadie wouldn't give it to him. I wonder if he killed her for that?'

Of course he did.

The other men stared at the little purple book, then turned

their eyes away, not wanting to see it anymore, nor all the images that fastened themselves to it. The idea of the child standing up to this man was inconceivable, and the violence that must have followed was unthinkable. Yet no one ventured a contrary theory; they had all been struck dumb and sorry, a small troop of four armed men, mourners every one, standing in silent tribute to a ten-year-old girl who was most certainly dead.

Ali Cray had been right about everything.

Costello took the bag with the broken pager from Pyle. 'I think we might've overlooked something.' He seemed to be weighing this bit of high technology in his right hand. 'It's just possible a security freak like Peter Hubble has a trap on his phone line.'

'A wiretap?' Rouge thought he had misunderstood the word. 'But didn't you—'

'No, a *trap*,' said Sorrel. 'I asked about wiretaps first thing. Hubble said no, but I'm not sure I believe him.'

Ah, but Sorrel believed no one.

'Anyway,' said Costello, 'a phone trap would be better than nothing. No conversation, but it would fix local calls, times and numbers.' He turned to Sorrel. 'Buddy, check it out.'

The men turned back to the shore at the sound of a woman's angry voice. Marsha Hubble was trying to force her way past the state troopers on the periphery of the crime scene marked by yellow tape.

Costello put one hand on Rouge's shoulder. 'You're the family liaison. You wanna handle the lieutenant governor? I think she likes you.'

Rouge was silent, only staring at the woman. She wore a flimsy blazer over her pajamas. Her feet were clad in wooden mules with no socks, no protection against the cold night air. People made such odd choices when they were terribly frightened.

'No?' Costello was taking Rouge's silence for reticence. He

turned to his senior investigator. 'Okay, Sorrel, you're with me.'

They walked up the wharf toward the shore. Rouge and Arnie Pyle trailed behind them. Gwen's mother had broken the yellow tape, passing through it like a marathon runner, and now she bore down on Costello with ferocity, pointing one finger at him as though it were a gun. 'I heard about the baseball game!' she yelled. 'Did your boys have a good time tonight?'

Costello put one hand on her arm. 'If you'll just come with—'

'I'm not going *anywhere*!' Marsha Hubble shook off his hand. 'I saw that damn ball game on the news. Everyone saw it. Where in hell do you bastards get off playing silly kid games while Gwen is still missing, and God only—'

'And *Sadie*,' said the captain, ungently reminding her that there were *two* children missing. 'It was the damn baseball game that led us to the crime scene, lady.'

That closed her mouth for the moment. The captain spoke quickly, before she could make a recovery. 'Ma'am, you wanted to take over all the public relations crap – fine. I don't give a shit what the press thinks. And now that I qualify for a pension, I don't care what you *think* you can do to my career. That was your next line, wasn't it? The threat?'

Costello was smiling, but not in any kindly way. In the broad sweep of one hand, he included all the law enforcement officers on the grounds. 'Every single one of these cops is working overtime. You think they might work better if you threaten their jobs too?'

The lieutenant governor backed off a few steps, but Rouge didn't read this as retreat. The lady's eyes narrowed as she shifted the balance of her body; it was almost the dancing stall of a boxer. And now she rallied new anger in a sudden burst of energy for another round with Costello, the only enemy she could identify. 'Somebody has to handle the press. You certainly don't—'

She fell silent as Costello held up the plastic bag containing the broken pager.

'Mrs Hubble, do you recognize this? It's an odd brand, isn't it? And very expensive.'

'It's not my daughter's pager. Gwen's has a brown leather case.'

Costello turned to Sorrel. 'Buddy?'

Sorrel was shaking his head and flipping back through his notebook. 'I talked to Peter Hubble the day the kid disappeared. I asked him – did the kid have a pager or a beeper? He said no.' Now Sorrel held out the notebook's scrawled lines to Costello so he could see it in black and white.

The captain waved the notebook away. 'What about the other kid?'

'Harry Green told me the same thing,' said Sorrel. 'Sadie never had a pager or a beeper. And the kid's mother was there when I talked to him. *No* pager.'

'Sadie has one, too,' said Marsha Hubble, 'with a black case like that one. I gave pagers to the kids so they could keep in touch when Peter wouldn't let them play together. Peter was always putting Sadie on probation. It was—'

Costello raised a hand to cut her off. 'Any reason why you didn't let us in on this?'

'No one asked me. I wasn't thinking – I'm sorry. I gave them the pagers last year. I paid the service a large deposit, so I haven't even seen the first bill yet. I swear I just forgot – there was so much to do—'

'Buddy, forget the phone trap and check out the pager service.' Costello's voice had lost its edge when he turned back to the lieutenant governor. 'Did anyone else have access – the pager codes, the service number? Maybe you wrote it down somewhere, in a Rolodex or an address book? Could one of your staff—'

'No,' said Marsha Hubble. 'It was just for the two of them. No one else had access.'

Sorrel jotted a quick note and shrugged out of his topcoat.

170

'So if Gwen got a printed message on the pager, she'd assume it was from Sadie. Mrs Hubble, I think we should go over everything one more time. There might be a few other things you've forgotten.' And now he draped his coat around her shoulders. 'Sometimes weeks go by before people remember things.' Sorrel removed his scarf and tied it about her neck with surprising gentleness. And it was this last small gesture, a little gallantry on a long cold night, that finally broke the woman.

Marsha Hubble only mouthed the words of thanks. Wrapped in Sorrel's coat, she seemed so much smaller now, making no protest when he put one massive arm around her shoulders and guided her back up the slope toward the parking lot. They had not gone far when she stopped. Sorrel's hand dropped away as she turned quickly to stare at the boathouse strung with lights and yellow crime scene tape. Her mouth went slack, and Rouge knew she had finally put it all together: Gwen could not have been lured from home by a stranger with an adult voice. The little girl had been tricked by a line of electronic type on her pager – a secret gift from her mother. One white hand drifted up to the woman's mouth.

To stifle a scream?

Sorrel put his arm around her again, tighter now, clearly supporting her weight as he all but carried her the rest of the way up the hill.

Costello turned to Rouge. 'I want you to hang around for a while. Check out the kid's story about the lock on the boathouse door, and find out who cleaned up the mess.' The captain inclined his head toward the director, Eliot Caruthers, standing on the periphery of the crime scene. 'Have another chat with that old bastard. He's holding out on us.'

The technician's van was pulling away, and the troopers' cars were heading back to the station house. All the evidence that could be collected had been bagged and tagged. And then the lights went out, one by one, all around the crime scene, as they were disconnected from their battery packs and loaded into a truck. Within twenty minutes, there was not even one uniformed officer to guard what they had left behind. All that marked the activity of the night's work was the yellow tape rippling in the wind as it stretched from tree to tree, from boathouse to wharf post.

And Mr Caruthers had disappeared.

'Rouge?'

The voice came from the spot where he had parked the old tan Volvo, and now he made out the shadowy form of a small boy hiding behind it. 'You should be in bed. It's late.'

'There was something I forgot to tell you.' David stood up straight to look around in all directions. Satisfied that they were alone, he came out from behind the car. 'Mrs Hofstra reminded me. She heard it too.'

'Heard what?'

'There was a gunshot. It was out on the lake, or maybe on the other side. I'm not sure. But it was days afterward, so I didn't think it meant anything.'

'That's fine, David. I'm glad you told me. Are you sure it was a gunshot?'

'Mrs Hofstra was sure. She thought it might be poachers in the woods again. I know she called Mr Caruthers. He'll know what it was. He told her he'd take care of it.'

'Thanks. Now you go back to bed and get some sleep, all right?' He watched David's retreat until the boy was safe home behind the door of Mary Hofstra's cottage.

He turned back to the main building and the single lighted window. The dark rotund shape of Eliot Caruthers was backlit by a bright lamp. The man lifted one hand in salute as Rouge walked across the lawn, keeping his eyes to the window until the director moved away from the light.

Rouge was about to ring the bell beside the rear entrance, but then he tried the knob instead. The door was unlocked and this irritated him, for he knew it was no oversight; his visit was clearly anticipated. Mr Caruthers was expecting a report, as though school days had never ended.

172

Well, this time, everything would be quite different.

He crossed the lush red carpet of the lobby and walked up the familiar grand staircase and down the hall. The door to the director's office was also open; he knew it would be. Mr Caruthers was comfortably ensconced behind a desk in his own element of wood paneling, first-edition books and works of art, all the trappings of wealth and power. He was smiling warmly at his young visitor – his collaborator. In the shadows of a far corner, a bust of Voltaire bore a similar smile – arrogant, superior. Caruthers nodded toward the wooden chair before his desk, granting the young man permission to be seated.

Rouge declined. He stood close to the desk, looking down at the director, wanting this advantage of height. 'There was a break-in at the boathouse. You must have ordered the repair work on the doorframe. Were you ever going to mention that?'

'Actually, I only learned about the broken lock two days ago. It was hardly a secret. The groundskeeper—'

'Tell me about the gunshot on the lake. David heard it, and so did Mrs Hofstra. I have to wonder when you were going to tell me about *that* little detail.'

'Not a related matter, Rouge. We've had trouble with poachers before. You know there are deer in these woods.'

Rouge looked down at the empty chair beside him. He dragged it around to Eliot Caruthers' side of the desk and sat down only inches from the old man's chair. 'I've got all night.'

And now they engaged in an uncomfortable staring contest which threatened to escalate into a pissing contest, the time-honored method of men, boys and dogs to establish who was boss of the world. After ten seconds had elapsed, Mr Caruthers only shrugged, but it was a surrender of sorts. He opened the top drawer of his desk and pulled out a black plastic gun.

'A bit clumsy, isn't it, Rouge? Hardly a lethal weapon. I'm surprised the boys managed to break a window with it. Chief Croft didn't even see fit to report the incident.'

'Or maybe you asked him not to.'

173

'It was only a prank of twelve-year-olds. So, I'm afraid this is a deadend for you.' Mr Caruthers looked down at the gun in his hand. 'I doubt that it makes a very loud noise, probably not the shot Mrs Hofstra heard, but I assure you, this is the only gun I'm aware of. Talk to the village police chief and the medical examiner – they'll tell you the same thing. Two little boys with a toy gun. Hardly a sinister event. However, when rumors get started in a small town—' He waved one hand in an expansive gesture that drew ugly pictures of the villagers storming the castle with flaming torches in hand.

'Where did this *event* happen, and what was a medical examiner doing there?'

'Just across the lake. An old house. The occupant had died some days before – in her sleep. Nothing sinister there either. So when the boys broke the window, they actually assisted the village police in finding the body. In fact, Dr Chainy even thanked them for their help.'

'How did the boys get across the lake? By canoe?'

'Yes.'

'The lock on the boathouse door was broken with a rock. But you already knew that. You saw the rock by the door, didn't you, Mr Caruthers?'

'I can't imagine what that has to do with your investigation. You know how boys are, just—'

'Just boys playing games – with guns.' Rouge looked down at the piece of black plastic lying on the desk blotter.

'Hardly a gun.' Mr Caruthers was smiling again, as though he found this laughable. 'A plaything made by two little boys in their free time.'

'Right.' Rouge picked up the gun. It did look rather like a badly made toy, except for the barrel – too large for ordinary bullets, much less pellets. Only one shot had been heard on the lake and the crude revolving chamber was made to hold two rounds. He looked at the heavy marble bust of Voltaire perched on its pedestal in the corner. 'So the pellet should just bounce off most any surface, right?'

'Well, I know it'll break glass at close range. The boys have already demonstrated that.'

Rouge took careful aim, squeezed the trigger, and Voltaire's head exploded into a hundred fragments of hard stone. The noise had deafened him, and so he never heard the scrape of Caruthers' chair as it was pushed back from the desk, nor the thud of the chair tumbling to the carpet when the director stood up abruptly, his face full of alarm.

The ringing noise in Rouge's ears had abated, and now it was replaced by the ringing of the telephone on the desk. All the call buttons were lit up, one for each housemother. They probably wanted to ask if a bomb had gone off, for real guns were not so loud as this toy.

Mr Caruthers touched a button and silenced the telephone. He found his composure and restored the chair to an upright position. 'I believe I did mention that we had no ordinary students here.' He stared at the gun in Rouge's hand. 'You know what would happen if word got out about that thing.'

'Yeah, I do.' Rouge set the gun down on the blotter, and it quickly disappeared into the director's top drawer. Another deal had been struck.

'I have to wonder what else you might be holding back.' Rouge put his feet up on the desk. It was just possible that Mr Caruthers was more shocked by this act of unparalleled rudeness than by the destruction of Voltaire. He opened his mouth to speak, but nothing came out.

Rouge's slow eyes roved over the debris of the marble bust. 'Maybe you're shielding somebody? Someone who knew the girls – or maybe only Gwen. Beautiful little girl – *you* said that just the other day.'

'Am I a suspect?'

Rouge nodded. 'Let's talk about the shooting party at the house across the lake. I want every damn detail. I could question the boys, but I know you already did that.'

'I note that you're concentrating on Gwen Hubble. Reasonable – but only if you're thinking in terms of ransom.

But now you seem very sure that it's a pedophile. Rouge, if I were the type to fall in love with a child, it would've been Sadie Green. She's a rare little person. You don't—' Caruthers had finally learned to read Rouge's face, and now the man winced. 'She's dead, isn't she?'

Rouge said nothing, and Mr Caruthers dropped his eyes, nodding his understanding of that silence.

'You know everything that goes on here – everything.' Rouge swung his feet off the desk, for his point had been made. 'The break-in at the boathouse happened on the same day the girls were kidnapped. *Before* the boys shot out the window.'

'I swear I didn't know that. I assumed the boys had done it when they took the canoe.'

'Assumed? They gave you another story?'

'They said they found the canoe beached on the rocks downshore by an access road. You know the one. It leads to the foundations of a house that burned down years ago. I swear I thought the boys were lying about the broken lock and the canoe. I thought they were trying to avoid more punishment. You must understand why I had to keep that entire shooting incident quiet.'

The man stumbled about in the silence, losing his composure again, for he must have realized that Rouge did not understand, nor did he forgive. Caruthers stared into the young man's eyes and found something there to be afraid of. He had said it himself: St Ursula's Academy had no ordinary children – and Rouge had come from that lot.

The hamper's chain slithered and clanked to the floor tiles. Gwen sucked in her breath, afraid to move as she listened to the house. But there were no sounds of rushing footsteps or sliding furniture beyond the bathroom door. And now she dared to breathe again.

Stupid Gwen, she chided herself. Hours ago, she had heard the sound of a car pulling away from the house and the noise of its engine fading off. He was probably far away by now, but still she dared not scream, and she took more care to work in silence.

She opened the hamper and reached into the dark space as far as her arm would go. There were only a few towels tightly wadded up at the bottom – nothing more.

So why lock the hamper?

Her brain was working better now, and this question linked up to another and another: Why keep her hungry all the time? Why lock her away in a small room? Could this be the insect's idea of fun? Or maybe the chain on the hamper was closer to the magician's art of misdirection. If the locked hamper was the focus of her curiosity, she might never explore the rest of the bathroom and discover the window – the way out.

But now she pushed this concept farther and smiled for the first time in days as she regarded the hamper in the light of its new possibilities.

This was the way out.

Gwen turned back to the window. She would have to open it again, or the plan wouldn't work. Cold air sliced across her face when she pulled up the sash, and whorls of icy wind followed the shivering child as she turned and walked barefoot to the wall hamper.

The lock was the risky part. But she didn't believe the giant insect would know Sadie's combination. He probably didn't care if he could open it again; he had only cared that the hamper couldn't *be* opened.

She looped the chain from the towel rack to the metal handle in a looser arrangement. Once inside the hamper, she would need more room to reach out and close the padlock. If he thought she had left by the window, he would go outside to look for her. And he might not bother to barricade the bathroom door again. Then she could open the lock and leave the hamper and the house.

A good plan.

Gwen climbed into the small, dark space. She reached back

through the narrow opening and closed the padlock. Then she shifted her weight to rock the hamper back into the wall.

And now the last shred of reason left the world. The hamper's floor of tightly wadded material came loose underneath her feet, and she was falling. Her scrabbling fingers found no traction on the elongating slick metal walls. The mass of towels was being pushed along under her feet, and she was falling down and down, through all the floors of the house in solid blackness.

The towels jammed up around her legs to break her fall as the narrow metal walls bent to a steep incline. At last, her feet were free, waving in the open air. Then she was completely out of the chute and lying in a large wicker basket. Her body was cushioned by the tightly packed laundry she had mistaken for the hamper's floor.

A dim light came from above, and she noticed the smell of detergent and bleach. When she stood up, she could see the faint light from the dials of a large furnace which radiated heat. It was dimmer than the night-light, but she could see a bit of her environs. High above the washing machine was a small window set into a cement wall. Overhead were pipes and ducts. So she had fallen to the basement laundry room.

What should she do now?

She could almost hear Sadie shouting the best line from the worst haunted-house movie – *Get out*!

Gwen crawled up on the washing machine, but the window was too high to reach. She climbed down to the cement floor again. Where was the door? The room was too dark to see any detail, and so she went exploring by touch, trailing one hand along the wall as she walked. She found the doorknob and tried it.

Unlocked.

Beyond the door was blackness. One barefoot inched into the dark and found solid wood, but then, with her next step, she was pitching forward, falling again, and in her descent, there was time for a small outrage – all staircases in a basement

178

should lead *up*. She had learned absolutely nothing from her novel experience of falling through all the floors of the house. Falling downstairs in a basement was somehow unfair.

Her fingers scraped on the wood, and she stopped the roll of her body with only minor pain to her head and one arm, which had made the hard connection of bone to wooden step. She caught her breath and looked up into darkness and a narrowing sliver of bad light. She was sickened by the faint noise of the metal clicks from the top of the stairs. She knew the door would be locked even before she had crawled to the top step and tried the knob.

One small fist pounded on the wooden panel. It must be a self-closing door on a hydraulic pump. Her father had collected every kind of lock known to God and the nervous homeowner. In his opinion, the basement was the weakest point of security with the greatest possibility for human error, and so he had installed a similar door that would lock itself and defeat the carelessness of servants.

So now what?

The only way left was down again. The stairs must lead somewhere. Her father had once talked about digging a sub-cellar to lower his wine racks farther into the earth where it was cooler. Fingertips led her along the wall as Gwen stepped down and down, stone-blind now, guided only by the skin of her hands and feet. At the base of the stairs, her fingers found another knob. It was hard work to push open this door; it was made of thick metal.

And then there was light, though faint and far away. The source was more like a glow in the distance.

This time she took no chances and held on to the knob to keep the door open as one foot reached tentatively into the space beyond. She could feel dirt beneath her toes, but she knew she was still indoors, for the air was a warm, pungent stew of smells – dank earth and manure like the gardener's greenhouse. The humidity was so dense she could almost reach

179

out and touch the drops of moisture hanging in front of her face.

Now she could make out the silhouettes of near shapes, but she could not believe her eyes.

Again, the laws of the universe were failing her. She had expected to enter a shallow cool room with a low ceiling, like her father's plans for the wine cellar. Instead, space expanded outward and upward. What light there was came from the far side of a vast room and beyond a forest of full-grown trees.

She counted only four thick trunks, but *trees?* Growing in a house?

Her eyes traveled up a length of rough bark and into the thick leaves of an oak. Beyond this foliage, she could see vestiges of the old ceiling where it had been cut away, giving the trees more room to grow. One of the four oaks was clearly dead, its arms cruelly amputated, barren stumps reaching up toward the dark high ceiling. Gwen could see more now – a network of criss-crossing pipes and—

Suddenly, there was a burst of strong light, sharp, brilliant and painful. The high ceiling exploded into the brightness of a thousand electric suns. Gwen's hands flew up to protect her eyes. A small scream escaped her mouth and took her by surprise. Slowly, gradually, she learned to see again through the slits of her spread fingers.

All four trees were wide in girth. Her eye for proportion told her that they should be taller than the ceiling would allow, though it was two flights high. They were all twisted, misshapen by their unnatural environment – this sunny and warm summer day in December.

What was that noise?

She was not alone. Gwen's hands dropped away from her face. Her muscles were seizing up again. One hand held fast to the doorknob, fingers pressing hard on the metal. Her knees locked and her body went rigid. She was still sensitive to the bright light, but willing her eyes to see clearly what was coming her way – the misshapen form of a dog.

This animal was another mistake of nature. He had the overlarge head of a mastiff, and he carried it low to the ground, as if he were too weak to hold its weight any higher. The pointed devil ears of a Doberman were flattened back against his skull, and he showed her all his teeth in the stubbed snout of a pit bull. Gray clumps of dirt clung to his dark fur. In a final insult to aesthetics, his tail was crooked. She guessed it had been broken and never properly set.

The animal made no sound as he padded toward her in a slow, stalking gait. This was not the typical family pet which barked at every stranger, but more like one of Mr Stuben's attack dogs, trained for stealth as it closed on the prey. He favored the right forepaw; it hit the ground lightly and picked up quickly.

Her eyes were locked with his, though she knew better than to stare at him. Mr Stuben had taught her never to challenge a hostile animal with direct eye contact. She knew she should drop her eyes and turn sideways to the correct position, but she could not – her feet would not obey. She could only stand and watch.

Now that the dog had lost the advantage of a surprise attack, he barked as he loped toward her. There was something very wrong with the animal. He was in the attack mode, and even with an injured paw, excitement should be moving him faster; he should be running, bounding.

The dog had closed the distance, and now he lunged, rising up on hind legs and hitting her body with his outstretched paws, knocking her to the ground. He hung there in the air above her. His chain would not allow him any farther, not all the way to the wall. Her head had knocked into the metal door. She lost her grip on the knob as her legs went sprawling in the dirt.

The thick panel swung shut.

The dog had her right foot in his mouth. He was dragging her back into the sphere of his chain. He released her foot for a moment, long enough to sink his teeth into the calf muscle of her right leg. With this better grip, he dragged her back a little farther.

The screaming was loud, and at first she did not realize that it came from her own mouth.

The dog released her again, but her face was half covered with leaves and dirt. All she could see was a thin wooden pole jabbing into the dog's pelt. The animal turned on his attacker and snapped at the wood. And now Gwen could hear the sound of running feet in company with the dog's paws and the metal clink of his chain as he moved off in another direction.

Her face flooded with tears of pain, and her vision blurred. But she could move again. She lifted her head from the ground and swiped one hand across her eyes. Now she could make out the fuzzy shape of the dog in pursuit of some bright white quarry kicking up dirt and leaves just beyond the reach of his teeth. The animal ran out of chain and stopped short with a howl of outrage.

Gwen slowly regained her feet and stood up. Her whole body was shaking, and both knees threatened to give out on her. And then the shakes ended; her body began to stiffen again – the dog was turning.

He was walking back, head lowered almost to the dirt, stepping lightly on the injured paw, moving even slower this time.

This was a very damaged animal. She *could* outrun him – if she could move. She didn't even have to run. The dog's chain wouldn't reach the wall; she need only move backward – just a few steps. But first her knees locked, and then paralysis spread through every muscle in her body until she could not even close her eyes against what was going to happen to her. And last – her breathing stopped. Only her heart was alive, beating faster every second, banging out a rush of blood and panic.

The dog was so close.

Gwen's eyes were awash in fresh tears, barely able to make

out the final shock: A blurred, barefoot figure in a white T-shirt and underpants was running toward her – right behind the charging animal.

Impossible!

Sadie Green made the jump of her life, leapfrogging over the back of the dog, flying through space to slam Gwen back against the wall.

Sadie!

The dog's chain would not reach far enough for his teeth to get at her again, but Gwen could feel the hot breath, the spray of froth and the stink from his mouth. Sadie's arms were wrapped tightly around her as they slumped to the floor together and huddled there, pressed up against the rough stone wall. Now Gwen sucked in a ragged breath; her chest burned; the dog barked. He snapped and bit the air only inches away from their faces. Yet Sadie was laughing – triumphant.

CHAPTER 7

Her brain was shutting down, fogging over again. Perhaps the drugs had not yet worn off. 'What?'

'I said it's no use.' Sadie gently pried Gwen's fingers away from the doorknob. 'You can't open it from this side. The knob is frozen.'

Gwen nodded, and then, as if this were something directly related to doorknobs, she said, 'I lost my eye.'

'No you *didn't*.' Alarmed, Sadie gripped her friend by both shoulders and peered into her face. 'You're okay – you look *fine*, just—'

'The amulet you gave me – the one with the all-seeing eye. I lost it.'

Sadie grinned with relief. 'That's okay. I'll buy you a new one. I know where you can get those things by the barrel.'

'You're not mad?'

'At you? Never.'

Gwen weighed nothing anymore; she was unattracted to the earth by gravity, only drifting across the dirt and the dead leaves, a tethered balloon guided by Sadie. As they moved away from the door, keeping close to the walls, Gwen calmly surveyed the damage, as if it were someone else's torn pant leg streaked with thin lines of blood from a dog bite. When she stumbled, Sadie's arm encircled her waist to support her, and they continued along the edge of the small forest of four oak trees. The animal made one last feeble howl as his only chance for a meal was walking away from him.

'I can't believe you made that jump,' said Gwen. 'He could

have killed you. I saw one of Mr Stuben's dogs tear a training dummy to shreds.'

'No way. He's starving – getting weaker every day.' And Sadie obviously took satisfaction in that. 'By this time tomorrow, you could beat up that dog with one hand.'

Sadie's face was so pale her freckles were fading. So despite the brilliant light, this indoor sky was no substitute for the real thing. Gwen stared at the four oaks. Only one had died, but even the survivors had not reached the proper dimensions of grown trees. By their girth, she knew they were old, but the thick trunks were twisted and too short by half. These were dwarfs – twenty feet tall.

They passed by a stand of five upright logs tied together with leather straps and shaded from the ceiling lights by the leaves of the trees. The bark of each log bloomed with mushrooms. Gwen recognized the shiitakes, her mother's favorites, but the shapes and colors on a neighboring stand were strange to her. They passed by three more bundles of logs closer to the wall. All were straight and uniform in girth and length. The last bore plants of lilac with a gelatinous, fleshy texture, and though they more closely resembled misplaced animal organs, she supposed this was also a variety of mushroom.

She looked up through the branches to see patches of the brilliant ceiling. Above the criss-crossing pipes were clusters of common lightbulbs, but so many, perhaps a thousand of them, and they seemed to be growing out of the plaster. There were other shapes she'd never seen before, squared and hexagonal bulbs screwed into upended lamps protruding from holes. Heavier fixtures housed long fluorescent tubes and round ones. Lines of Christmas tree lights dangled from the edge of the electric sky where the ceiling dropped by half its height. It was a dazzling collection of every kind of lightbulb and fixture on the planet.

Gwen winced. Shock was wearing off, and she was feeling the pain of the dog bite. It came on as a stabbing sensation.

She lowered her face to hide the tears from Sadie. 'So you've been down here all this time? With that animal?'

'Yeah, I finally got the dog I always wanted,' said Sadie. 'There's only one snag – he wants to eat me.'

'What've *you* been eating?'

'Mushrooms, and I'm damn sick of them.'

They came abreast of the last log bundle, so different from the others, for this was a mass of twisted, gnarly branches. Gwen recognized these misshapen limbs as the cut off arms of the one oak tree that had died. The mushrooms growing on this bundle were strange and beautiful, resembling fat flower petals of bright pink all melted together.

A low buzzing sound grew in volume as they walked toward a long cave-like area with a low ceiling. This space had irregular stone sides and the more normal proportions of a cellar. An overhang of wood shielded it from the sun-bright ceiling of the forest. One lightbulb shone over a door in the only smooth section of wall. The glow of dimmer lights emanated from row upon row of narrow steel tables, each topped by a rack of metal shelves. Two of the shelving units supported beds of straw and bright fungus, and the rest were stacked with rough blocks of wood chips with mushrooms sprouting from their sides. Some were gray button shapes, others were chunky rounded umbrellas of bright orange and mute green.

This dank cave was not quite as warm as the forest behind them. It was a patch of August shade in winter, and the world became a stranger place with every step. Gwen was distracted from the pain as they passed a shelf of blocks with delicate parasols of purple, and one species that resembled sculptured worms clustered in the loose shape of a mushroom dome. A bright-yellow group had the texture of rounded honeycombs, and at the other extreme were large flat pancakes of reddish brown. The last fruit of the wood blocks in this row were cream-colored goblets lined with pink flesh, resembling wide-mouthed baby birds waiting to be fed. Though botany was a favorite subject, she had no idea there were so many different mushrooms in the world, and in so many colors.

Now she regarded Sadie's plain white underwear. 'Where are your clothes?'

'Too hot for clothes. I stashed them.'

It *was* warm – and muggy. The air was sweating. She looked up to the top of the nearest shelf of wood blocks and saw a tangle of plastic tubing and a nozzle. A fine spray of water washed her face in a miniature rain shower. Her eyes traveled down the shelf boards to the supporting table and a small buzzing pony motor like the one that ran the fish tanks in the biology lab at school. These motors must be powering the plant misters.

Sadie guided her along this wide center aisle. 'Hungry?'

'God yes.'

Sadie stopped by the last table in the row and reached up to a middle shelf to harvest a few mushrooms of a common supermarket species. 'You can only pick them from the back of the block. Remember that, okay?'

Gwen nodded as she took the mushrooms from Sadie's hands and put them into her mouth, trying to eat them all at once.

'*That* hungry.' Sadie made a pouch by lifting up the hem of Gwen's red jersey and filled it with more mushrooms. 'How did you find me?' She waited patiently while Gwen chewed and swallowed.

'I came through the hamper – a laundry chute in an upstairs bathroom. I've been up there for days.'

'In a bathroom?' Sadie walked to a crude flimsy door in a wall of whitewashed board. She opened it to display a small toilet strung with spiderwebs. Rusty pipes lined the back wall of the tiny room, and the floor was dirt. It had the foul wet smell of bad plumbing. 'Was your bathroom as nice as this one?'

'Nicer and larger – big enough for a cot and a chair, and this great—'

'A cot and a chair? Well, that settles it. He definitely likes you best.'

The pain stabbed her again, and Gwen leaned over the table at the end of the row to hide her face, pretending to look at the underside of a shelf. Tiny lightbulbs were hidden by an overhanging slat. She guessed the mushroom blocks needed less light than the oak trees.

The pain subsided, and now she stood back and looked at all the tables along the aisle on both sides. Below each of the shelf tables were narrow wooden carts on wheels. Some of them contained large clear plastic bags with tubes running from white patches. Inside one of the bags was a dark, porous material which must be alive, for some of it was green in striations of mold. Two of the carts contained nothing but the common dirt the floor was made of. And one was filled with sawdust and topped off with purple material – Sadie's sweatshirt and jeans.

'He ripped me off my bike on the way to your house. So how did he get you?'

'Sadie, don't you remember? You told me to meet you at the boathouse.'

Sadie shook her head. 'I never saw you that day. I didn't even get close to your house before he—'

'You left a message on my pager. It said, "Urgent – boathouse – tell no one." '

'No way. I didn't send you any messages. But I think *he* said something like that. I'm not sure. God, he has this really creepy whisper – when he's not yelling at the dog. Damn dog dragged me all over the boathouse. Chewed my parka to shreds. My mom's gonna kill me when she sees it. Then I knocked my head on something, and I woke up here.'

At the end of the aisle, Gwen could see the interior of another room. Sadie pulled her through the open doorway and turned on a light switch. This space was white and perfectly clean. The painted cement floor was cool beneath her bare feet. A chilly, humming breeze came through a small vent near the ceiling of the back wall. Though the door was open, she could barely hear the buzzing of the pony motors outside the room. The air was dry, and the temperature had to be at least ten degrees lower.

A stainless-steel sink gleamed, as did the bottles in the glass-fronted cupboards along one wall. The Formica countertop was lined with racks of test tubes and stacks of petri dishes alongside a tidy row of bound notebooks. Each leather binding bore an old-fashioned script of numerals for successive dates. The first in the row dated back thirty years. One of the journals lay open, and so near the lip of the countertop, it threatened to fall off at any moment. Without thinking, she reached out to push it back from the edge.

'Don't touch that!' Sadie's voice had a rare note of panic, but she was calm again as she explained, 'We have to leave everything just the way we found it, okay?'

Gwen nodded, absorbing this new rule of the game without question. She was distracted by the throbbing pain in her leg, and then hunger won out as a priority. She took more mushrooms from the pouch of her jersey and popped them into her mouth.

A loose collection of petri dishes lay on the counter near the open journal. One was missing a cover and its contents were spoiled, overgrown with black mold. She ate another mushroom. The hunger was subsiding, and the pain was growing again.

'Thirsty?'

Gwen nodded as she sat down on a metal chair with rolling wheels. Sadie filled a glass jar with water from the faucet and placed it on the counter. Gwen drank in big gulps.

'This is where he keeps all the cleaning stuff.' Sadie was rooting around in the closets under the sink, and now she pulled out a roll of thick white gauze, a handful of paper towels and a bottle of liquid soap. She knelt on the floor in front of Gwen and ripped a larger hole in the shredded denim pant leg. After wetting a paper towel, Sadie cleaned the blood away from the wound.

The soap stung. Gwen bit down on her lower lip. Her teeth were grinding; her hands clenched into tight fists. She wiped away the new rush of tears, and now she could see the tip of a bottle on the floor, almost hidden by the edge of the low closets. Small white pills had spilled from the open plastic mouth. 'Are those aspirins?'

Sadie bent low to read the white label on the bottle. 'Tylenol with codeine.'

'Our gardener takes those for his arthritis. Give me some. My leg hurts.'

'We can't touch them. We can't move *anything*.' Sadie stood up and opened a drawer next to Gwen's chair. 'There's more in here. I don't think he'd notice a few pills missing from one of these – as long as we put the bottles back *exactly* the way we found them.' She read off the labels of a large assortment of pharmacy containers. 'Motrin, Advil, Orudis, Soma Flexeril—'

'Give me one of each.'

'Can't.' Sadie was holding up one bottle, reading from the label. 'They all have instructions. Most of them say one pill every four hours.'

'Since when do you care about instructions? I want the pain to stop *now*.'

They compromised with one pill from each of three different containers. Sadie replaced the bottles, carefully rolling each one to show the same portion of the pharmacy label that was visible before she picked them up. Then she knelt down again and stared at Gwen's wound, fascinated by the puncture marks and the reddening welts. 'It's swelling up already. That's fast. Do you remember the giant mosquito at the Museum of Natural History?'

Gwen nodded. The model was monstrous in size, and each time she remembered it, the insect had grown larger and larger, almost reaching the dimensions of the thing that had visited her in the upstairs bathroom. She hated the museum mosquito.

'Totally cool,' said Sadie. 'Biggest bug I ever saw. It was *huge*.' She bent over the wound again, studying a pink fluid oozing up from the deep holes. 'If I didn't know better, I'd say this was the bug's work.'

Sadie was very gentle as she rinsed the soap from the wound and dried it, only dabbing around the holes, constantly looking up to Gwen's face for signs that she might be causing more pain. Finally, the puncture marks disappeared under a winding of white gauze, and the bandage was tied off with a knot, while Gwen read a queer shopping list pinned to a bulletin board over the sink. In faded ink on yellowed paper were mentions of cement bags to finish the floors of the growing room and greenhouse sheeting to line its walls. Another line said, 'Damn bugs,' but named no material to solve the problem.

As Gwen finished eating the last of the mushrooms, the pills were already taking effect. Her leg continued to throb, but the pain was ebbing away. She leaned down and pulled open another low closet to see a wad of purple canvas. 'Isn't that your knapsack?'

'Yeah, but my pager's gone.' Sadie closed this door, then she began to clean the floor with a paper towel and uncharacteristic tidiness. 'He took my phone book too.'

'So that's how he got the number and the code.' And now the hurt was forgotten, and Gwen was feeling light-headed as she pulled the pill drawer open a bit wider. This must be the source of the drugs that had put her to sleep. At the back of the drawer was an open box of disposable rubber gloves – another mystery solved. So these were the monster's rubber fingers. She looked up to an overhead cabinet. Through the glass door, she could see an old microscope. It resembled an outdated model from school which had been recently replaced with a new one. On the higher shelf were rows of jars labeled as bleach and alcohol, yeast and sphagnum. Malt agar? One wall was lined with a standing army of stoppered bottles of dark material. Others were full of sawdust.

'Sort of like the biology lab at school, isn't it?' Sadie walked across the room and opened the door of a large closet to show her a cylindrical metal container with a thermostat on one side. Gwen knew what this was, an oversized pressure cooker. That would fit with the petri dishes on the countertop. These cultures resembled the ones she had grown in lab class.

'Maybe the stories about St Ursula's are true,' said Sadie, grinning. 'We've been sold off for weird science experiments.' She stood in the open doorway and looked out over the fruiting blocks on the rows of tabletop shelves. 'Kidnapped by the mushroom people.'

And now it occurred to Gwen that she was being sucked into another one of Sadie's horror stories. It was such a familiar routine, she forgot for a moment that the horror was real. She smiled at Sadie, consummate spinner of tales. Drowsiness completed the atmosphere of a typical sleepover with her best friend.

'Yup.' Sadie returned to peer into the open petri dish on the counter. 'Definitely weird science.' And now she showed Gwen the label of a package. Her smile was almost evil as she read the line, 'Spawning material.'

'Hmmm.' Gwen looked up at the bottles in the glass-fronted cabinet and read the names of complex chemicals. One jar of green powder was the same potent fertilizer the Hubbles' gardener had used to revive a dying tree. Apparently it had failed to save the barren stumped oak in the cellar forest. The old gardener had called this green mixture a strong potion of last resort. A small amount of undiluted granules had killed one of Mr Stuben's guard dogs. The gardener had almost lost his job for that. Mr Stuben still maintained that the poisoning had been deliberate. But Gwen could not believe the gardener had been that cruel, for the dog had certainly died in pain. Its mouth and tongue had been burned by the corrosive chemicals.

She looked down at the countertop and scanned the scrawled lines on a page of the open journal. She was getting sleepy, and the text began to blur as she came to the last words, which ended mid-sentence in a long, shaky line trailing off the paper.

'So he was inoculating the mushroom cultures, and something must have interrupted him.' Gwen's eyes drifted to a plastic box pushed to the rear of the countertop. She opened the lid and looked down at a cluster of large fungi, dark, marbled and coated with dirt. She sniffed. This was familiar. 'Sadie, do you know what these are? Truffles.'

'Ugly looking, aren't they?'

'A truffle is a—'

'A subterranean fungus,' said Sadie. 'You think I sleep through *all* my classes.'

'Truffles come from Europe, and it costs the world to buy them. Even my dad complains about the price.'

'Really?' Sadie reached into the box, pulled one out and washed it under the sink. 'Maybe they're not so ugly. Take this one for instance.' She held it out for Gwen's inspection. 'It looks like a cute little bird, doesn't it?'

Gwen nodded, drowsing, almost losing her balance on the rolling chair. She stared at the truffle nestled in the palm of Sadie's hand. The small outgrowth at the top might be a beaked head, and the strange shaping in the bulk of it could pass for sweetly folded feathers. Her mouth dropped open when Sadie bit the head off and laughed.

'Not bad.' Sadie held out the box. 'Wanna try one?'

'I don't think so.' Gwen smiled. 'Did you know that truffle spores are usually spread by deposits from the assholes of burrowing rodents?'

'Rodents? Rat shit?' Sadie pulled the truffle out of her mouth and spat into the sink. Gwen was extremely pleased with herself; she had finally grossed out the master.

When Sadie had washed her mouth out with water, she looked up at the clock on the wall. 'We have to be very careful.'

She pulled a rag from the cupboard under the sink and began to clean up each dot of blood on the painted white cement floor. 'He comes back here twice a day. If he finds anything out of place, he'll know I'm still breathing.'

'He thinks you're dead?'

'He's pretty sure I am.' Sadie made a wet ball of the dirty rag and stashed it behind the store of boxes and cans under the sink. 'He buried me alive.'

'Oh, *right*.' By the grace of the pills, Gwen was feeling giddy now, and only deeply ingrained politeness prevented her from laughing out loud.

'He *did*,' said Sadie, insistent and somewhat wounded by this disbelief. 'And I got a real good look at him while he was filling in my grave.' She opened another low closet and hauled out a bulky green trash bag. 'You want to see what he looks like?' The child opened the bag wide to display rolls of black material: the knit of a sweater, the wool cuff of a pant leg and the toe of a large shoe. Sadie dug deep into the bag and plucked out a piece of black felt, a ski mask. She pulled it over her head – instantly morphing into an entirely different creature.

Gwen was jolted awake, eyes wide and all her attention riveted to the black felt mask. So this was the thing that had come to sit by her cot in the bathroom. The eyes were cruel slits crowned by slashes of white stitching that resembled angry eyebrows. The mouth was sewn shut with thick white embroidery thread to create the outline of intermeshed triangular fangs. Sadie was showing her the face of the monster.

'What do you think?' Sadie's words were muffled by the material, her voice unrecognizable and barely understood.

'Take it off! *Please*, take it off!'

'Okay, okay.' Sadie hurriedly removed the mask and plunged it back into the bag. 'We have to hide soon. When he knows you're gone, he's gonna tear this place apart looking for you.'

'He'll think I'm outside. I tied the bedsheets together and left them dangling out the bathroom window.'

Sadie nodded with approval. 'Good job. But he'll be back soon, and he's still gonna search the house. *I* would. We'll know when he's here – you can hear the car engine. We have to find a place to hide.'

They walked out of the sterile room and back into the vast space of the mushroom farm and the hum of tiny motors. Any one of the carts beneath the rows of tabletop shelves would make a good hiding place with room to spare.

The dog barked again. Gwen turned toward the trees, the realm of the chained animal. 'If he lets that dog loose, there won't be *any* place to hide.'

'There's one safe place.' Sadie led the way to the center of the aisle of tables and pulled out a wheeled cart full of dirt. She pointed under the table to a dark rectangular hole between the cart tracks. Small mounds of soil were piled on the sides of it, and all the dirt in the cart would account for the rest. 'That's it. He didn't finish filling it in. His beeper went off and he left. But that's where he buried me.'

'You're not serious.'

Sadie smiled. 'That's my grave. I *told* you he buried me alive.'

Gwen covered her ears. 'He didn't.'

'Hell yes, he did.'

'Stop, it's not funny.'

'He thought I was dead.' Sadie pulled Gwen's hands away from her ears. 'No, listen. It was some of my best work. The trick is the open eyes.'

Gwen hugged herself and shook her head. 'No.' But now she looked at the hole in the ground, and it *was* very like a small grave.

Sadie reached into a cart under the next table and pulled out her clothes all caked with dirt – more proof. 'I have to put these on first. He buried me in my clothes.' She pulled the purple sweatshirt over her head. 'I've given this a lot of thought. The best death is with open eyes. Of course it's harder. You can't blink. But if I'd closed my eyes, he might've listened to my heart.'

Sadie stepped into her purple jeans and zipped them. 'Oh, and another nice touch? I went stiff all over. He came down to check on me later, just enough time for rigor mortis to set in. It was perfect. I didn't have my parka on, and I was lying three feet down in cold dirt. You see, Gwen? Cold? Stiff?' She sprawled out in the hole and folded her arms across her chest in the best tradition of a movie corpse. She stared open-eyed at the ceiling. 'See? *Dead.*' She grinned. 'Neat?'

Gwen nodded, dumbfounded, not really letting it sink in that Sadie was lying in her own grave.

'If the dog leads him here, he'll think the dog just wants to finish what he started in the boathouse.' Sadie sat up and scooped more dirt from the ground, deepening the hole. 'This is the best hiding place – the *only* hiding place.'

'I'm not going in there.'

'Well, yes you are, Gwen. It's the only way.'

And now they heard the car engine, only faint at first, but it was coming closer. Sadie ran back to the sterile room, calling out to Gwen, 'Get into the hole. I forgot to put the bag back in the closet. I have to put it back or he'll know.'

Gwen crawled under the table and reluctantly settled into the hole, lying back on the dirt as Sadie had done. It was not so bad really, and it was cooler here. Her eyelids felt so heavy now, closing slowly. She crossed her arms over her chest and wondered if it would be appropriate or helpful to say her prayers while lying in a grave.

'Now I lay me down to sleep,' she whispered.

The car engine was directly overhead. Where was Sadie? There was no panic, no urgency in this thought, merely sleepy speculation. Perhaps the next time, she would only take *two* of the pills.

'I pray the Lord my soul to keep.' And then she remembered a better prayer, an ancient relic of folklore and more powerful. This had been yet another gift from her best friend, a magic charm to stave off the nightmares of a perpetually frightened child – so they might get on with the hard-core therapy of watching horror films. 'From ghoulies and ghosties, and long-leggety beasties, and things that go bump in the night, Good Lord, deliver us.'

She could hear bare feet pounding back to her. And now Sadie was piling into the grave and scooping the dirt in around them. 'He didn't have time to shovel in much, so it won't be so bad. Just enough to make it look like I never left, okay?' She pulled Gwen's shirt up over her face. 'This'll keep the dirt out of your eyes and your mouth.'

Gwen had heard no footsteps overhead, but she knew the man was in the house. She could feel his presence. In her mind, she followed him upstairs to the bathroom. She imagined his outrage when he saw the open window, the sheets, all the evidence of her escape.

Bad girl. Oh, he's so angry.

Now he would be running down the stairs to search outside the house, perhaps believing that she had made that jump from the end of the sheets to the hard ground, not knowing what a miserable coward she was.

Bad girl.

She closed her eyes and held on to Sadie, who was reaching up to pull the cart back into place over the open hole, their coffin lid on wheels. Gwen was feeling light-headed again and breathing deeply. The ruthless need for sleep was overtaking her entire body, relaxing every muscle. But now her eyes shot open in the dark. Things were moving in the earth beneath her. The ground was alive with insects, and they were inside her clothes and crawling on her flesh. She wanted to scream, but at the height of terror, her foot kicked out with an involuntary stumble, falling into sleep. And then her fast-beating heart settled into the gentle rhythm of an exhausted child.

Ellen Kendall removed her reading glasses and rubbed her

eyes. At the center of the kitchen table lay the bound trial transcript awash in the first light of morning. She turned to look out the window. Noisy blackbirds were gathering around the garbage can in the yard, flapping their wings and screeching. A lean starling alighted on the windowsill. Grease glistened on his feet, and now it smeared the sill.

Filthy little beast.

She waved her hand at the glass to shoo him away. But the scavenger only cocked his head and glared at her, fearless and oblivious to warnings.

Well, what could one expect of a bird too stupid to fly south for the winter?

She looked down at the transcript. Hours ago, when it was still night, she had closed the heavy volume, retiring to her bed and the warm comfort of a down quilt. But compulsion had killed her only chance for sleep and called her back to the kitchen, cold and barefooted, to finish her reading. Now her eyes were sore, and her mind was flooded with odd thoughts.

What if the priest was innocent?

She had not seen Paul Marie since the day a jury had found him guilty of murdering her daughter. He had been dressed all in black, but for the white of the priest's collar.

The starling flew off.

Ellen turned to her son. Rouge sipped his coffee as he leaned against the doorframe. He was dressed in jeans and one of his father's old pinstriped shirts. A red tie hung around his neck, undone, and his smile was wry. She admired her handsome child and envied his youth; young faces were indestructible and never showed wear or sag. Ah, but then Rouge had slept soundly, hadn't he? And perhaps that was what his smile was about – an apology for ruining her entire night.

Ellen tapped her reading glasses against her teeth. 'You were right. The defense attorney was definitely dirty.' She opened the transcript and riffled the pages. 'It's all here, babe. A first-year law student would've put on a better show in court. Too bad the priest's lawyer is dead. You could've fried him with the receipt for the police reports on the bogus witness.'

'So somebody bought him off.'

She nodded. Not *somebody*, though, not just anybody. 'The most likely suspect in that maneuver is your dad. He was obsessed with nailing the priest. But Paul Marie was really convicted in the family newspapers – all three of them. The courtroom débâcle was only a formality.'

Doctors had kept her heavily sedated for most of that year, and she had also self-medicated with alcohol, but something of the carnival atmosphere had sifted through the curtain of Valium and whiskey fumes. As she recalled, it had been a good year for priest bashing all over the country.

'You want me to track down the payoff?' Years ago she would not have asked; she would have run with this story. But she was no longer in the game, not a reporter anymore. Oh, and this time, she was the widow of her prime suspect.

Rouge stood at the counter and filled his coffee mug again. He brought the carafe back to the table. 'I'm more interested in Dad's financial arrangement with Oz Almo.'

'Sorry, babe. I was kept out of that. I only know your father paid an enormous amount for the ransom.' But her son would know more about the dollar-and-cents details of Bradly Kendall's affairs. Rouge, at nineteen, had settled the estate and done the financial planning to save the house and keep them both afloat. She had been sober by then, but of little use to her son.

Rouge tipped the carafe to fill her cup with an aromatic stream of black coffee. Ellen smiled at this small service her son had once performed by habit. It reminded her of the old days when she had been too drunk to be trusted with the pouring of hot liquids. She sometimes wondered what passed for nostalgia in less dysfunctional families.

'I know the amount of the ransom money,' said Rouge. 'But a lot more disappeared from the stock portfolios, and all the real estate holdings were mortgaged to the hilt. I couldn't account for half of what was missing when Dad died.'

'So you figure he was giving money to Oz Almo? Bribes for the lawyer? That might work.'

'Whatever Dad was up to, he was using cash – no paper trail. Almo is the logical go-between for payoffs.'

'God, I despised that nasty little bastard, but your father had a lot of confidence in him. Oz was still on the force then, and he did make a great prosecution witness. Of course, with the defense attorney working for the prosecution—'

'Why didn't the church get Paul Marie a decent lawyer?'

She let this oxymoron slide. 'They got him the best shark that money could buy. But the priest fired that one.' She lifted up the transcript, and beneath it lay her late husband's grisly scrapbook containing every public detail of their daughter's murder in yellowed strips of newsprint. 'It's all in there. The first attorney wanted to plea-bargain, but Father Marie kept insisting he was innocent.' She made rough notes on a yellow pad. 'I can trace some of Oz's financial history with a credit report. It's a start. I can probably get the rest through a bank officer in Manhattan. She owes me one. The banks are all hooked up to one big goldfish bowl.'

'And could you look into Almo's business clients over the past fifteen years? He seems to have a lot of money – nice clothes, big house. I wonder if it comes from case work—'

'Or ransom money?' And now she could see that Rouge had also thought of this ugly little possibility. 'Consider it done.' She understood her son's need for the help of an outsider. The State Police would not take kindly to their brand-new rookie investigator going after an ex-BCI man. 'I'll start calling in my markers today. Anything else?'

Rouge nodded. 'Ali Cray thinks someone screwed up Paul Marie's paperwork to put him in the general population. Considering the crime, that would border on attempted murder. That might account for some of the missing money. If Oz Almo had to bribe the prison—'

'No, babe.' Ellen shook her head. 'As conspiracy theories go, that angle is a real yawn. And it shows a certain naiveté about our screwed-up penal system.'

'That prison has a segregation policy for sex offenders. I checked.'

'And this is the logic supporting Ali Cray? Pay attention, Rouge. Mommy's going to educate you. People get lost in the shuffle all the time – it's a common event. So beware of logical deduction. No, let me put it another way – screw logic. Stick to the facts. Operate in real time, in real life. Don't get caught up in anybody's conspiracy theories.'

'If she's right, the priest might—'

'Forget the just and noble cause, okay? There isn't any justice. You want the truth? Then you can't afford to become a believer – not in anybody's cause. Not the priest's – not your own.'

Rouge lightly slapped the transcript binder. 'You've got the proof that Oz was a dirty cop. That bracelet—'

'No, babe. I've got a lead on a *possible* payoff. And suppose it pans out? This is proof he planted evidence? No. But what if he did? So what? Cops do this kind of thing all the time – another yawn. When I was a reporter in Chicago, cops used to carry *spare* evidence in their damn cars – usually drugs.'

'The silver bracelet—'

'That *was* Susan's bracelet. Your father gave it to her on her last birthday. And she *was* wearing it that day. Oz did *not* get it from your father so he could plant it. These are facts.' She flipped through the pages of the transcript. 'The priest didn't get a fair trial, but there's nothing here to say he's innocent – so that's not a fact. Don't touch Oz till you get something solid.'

'Suppose I question Oz – alone.'

'No. Bad idea. Don't listen to your heart or your gut, babe. They're both pickled in testosterone. Listen to your mother.'

'I'm not going to hit him. I just want to—'

'Rouge? Take notes.' She held up the transcript as an exhibit. 'You can't put your faith in the cops or the courts.' Now she held up the scrapbook of clippings, exhibit number two. 'And you can't believe what you read in the newspapers. So, if you won't trust your own mother – who's left?'

At last she had the sense that they were in accord. He leaned back against the slats of his chair, smiling as he finished his coffee.

They were a team.

How many years had passed since she had felt so close to her son? And now she realized this was revisionist history. When her daughter was alive, Ellen had left the twins largely to the care of other women and not worried over them. Her children had always been so self-sufficient, wanting no company but their own. After Susan's death, she had been immersed in guilt for the botched parenting. And she had never gotten any better at the mother's trade, drinking heavily and utterly oblivious to her small son when he was the most needy. Had she frightened Rouge in the days when she slurred her good mornings as well as her good nights? What had it been like for a ten-year-old to see his mother fall asleep in a stupor, hours before the bedtime of a little boy?

But now she had a second chance: her surviving child needed a covert source of facts, the help of a dirty, backdoor invader, a professional destroyer of private lives, who well understood the loathsome workings of the world's worst scum.

So this is motherhood.

Gwen woke to the sounds of crashing glass. The thing was in the basement with them – searching the white room, and very close to the hiding place beneath the cart. She could hear the clipped barks of the dog; she could feel the footsteps walking down the aisle of mushroom tables. Sadie was on top of her, both hands furiously working more dirt around Gwen's body. The dog was more excited now, barking louder, and she could imagine him straining at the leash as they came closer. The barks subsided to small cries from deep in the dog's throat, heavy breathing and snorting.

Gwen listened to the man's footsteps and the panting of the dog. She flinched when the cart was kicked, and her jersey slipped down under her chin, letting dirt into her eyes and her mouth. She was gagging. She could hear the cart wheels rolling back. Her eyes were shut tight against the crumbles of dirt spilling from Sadie's sweatshirt. And then the cart was slammed back into place under the table. The dog barked once, but the sound ended abruptly and was followed by a yelp of pain.

'Stupid animal,' said the whispery voice outside.

So he had seen what he expected to see – the one dead child lying in her grave, all stiff, eyes wide and staring in the dim light under the table.

Now the panting of the dog was trailing back toward the far side of the cellar with the man's footsteps. The cellar door slammed shut, and finally there was silence.

Sadie rolled off to one side. Gwen tried to sit up, bumping her head on the wood of the cart as she spat out the dirt. The pain in her leg was back, and it was worse now. *More pills. I need more pills.* She was climbing out of the hole and pushing against the rolling cart when Sadie stopped her.

'Not yet. He hasn't gone away. The car's still here. Wait for the sound of the engine.'

'Sadie, I have to have those pills. I can't—'

'You stay here. I'll get them.' And then she was working her way out of the ground, the grave, crawling between the wheels of the cart.

Gwen sat alone in the dark. Light streamed under the cart, petering out above the wound and the torn-away denim. Swollen flesh bulged around the edges of the bandage. The damage was spreading beyond the wound. She stretched her leg into stronger light and untied the knot in the gauze.

And now she was frightened.

The skin around the puncture marks had turned from

bright red to a dusky color. She touched the small holes from the dog's teeth, and her body was shot through with a searing-hot skewer. She screamed in one long continuous cry, unaware that Sadie was back with her, climbing into the hole. Sadie forced the pills into her mouth and chased them down Gwen's throat with water from a jar.

They sat in silence for a little while, time enough for the pain to dull. A beetle crawled out from the sleeve of Gwen's jersey, and she slapped it away, suddenly cold and clammy in her skin.

'Lie down,' said Sadie. 'Just till we hear the car pull away.'

'I can't do this. It's the bugs.' Gwen covered her face with dirty hands. 'I don't know what's happening to me. Bugs never bothered me before.' She was crying now. 'Remember the games, the bug races?'

'We were eight.' Sadie smiled as she stroked Gwen's hair. 'Your bugs always won.'

'But now I've got them in my clothes, and I can't stand it. What's happening to me?'

'You're becoming a woman.' All the resignation in Sadie's voice said that this was fated, and there was nothing to be done about it.

'And that *man*, Sadie. It's the same feeling, like the big mosquito model at the museum – a big bug.'

'*The Fly.*'

'The 1958 version? Or the remake in 1986?' Gwen had automatically slipped into the old game of film trivia. This was deep, long-term conditioning. Studying for Sadie's horror quizzes had taken precedence over her homework assignments for years.

'I like it,' said Sadie. 'So that's his name – The Fly.'

And now for the last bit of madness in her strange odyssey, Gwen heard the sound of raindrops on the leaves of the trees. She looked out between the cart wheels and craned her neck to see a bit of the lightbulb ceiling beyond the cave of the mushroom farm. Great dollops of water were falling from the pipes that spanned the electric sky.

It was raining indoors.

'Would you say you've always been a little obsessive about the idea of a kidnapping?' Arnie Pyle turned his sad brown eyes on Peter Hubble, but Rouge saw no sympathy or empathy in the agent's manner.

Peter Hubble only nodded, agreeing that this was a fact and then tilting his head to say, *So?* As if every father in America had sewn a transmitter into the lining of his child's knapsack; and what man did not ink his little girl's hands and roll the tips of each tiny digit onto the proper square of the card labeled for the impressions of fingers and thumbs; surely every parent had a frozen blood sample in the refrigerator, just in case the need should arise for a DNA match.

And then there was the pack of cards lying on the conference table, bearing yearly sets of Gwen's footprints from the day she was born. Delicate loops and whorls described her toes and soles, so tiny, more heartbreaking than any photograph could be. None of the men seated at the long table would look at them again.

Three federal agents lined up on Pyle's side. Peter Hubble was flanked by Rouge and Buddy Sorrel. The senior investigator had been silent for the entire time, only occasionally making notes. Another BCI man was slumped against the door, not making any indication that he was even listening to the conversation.

An hour ago in Captain Costello's office, Agent Pyle had made it clear that, with the advent of a ransom note and its out-of-state postmark, this was now a federal investigation. The captain had responded with an enigmatic smile. Rouge had to wonder what Costello knew about the ransom note that Pyle did not. None of the parents had seen it yet, for the FBI had taken on the chore of sorting through the Hubbles' incoming mail. Rouge wondered when the feds were planning to mention this note to the families – and how.

Agent Pyle had his mouth set in a tight line as he drummed his pencil on the table. 'Sir, could your ex-wife have taken Gwen?'

'Marsha?' Peter Hubble was obviously taking the FBI agent for a lunatic. 'No, of course not.' And now the man's eyes were angry. He was rising from the table. 'Pyle, you can't even get your facts straight. My wife and I are separated, not divorced. Why are you wasting time with this nonsense? Why aren't you out looking for Gwen? At least let me go out and—'

'You're not going anywhere,' said Arnie Pyle. 'But if you need a lawyer, I can arrange that. Whatever it takes, you're gonna talk to me.'

Peter Hubble sank back in his chair, eyes rolling to the ceiling, as if to ask, *What next?* And Rouge did wonder if Kafka had scripted this interview with the devastated father. Any fool could see this man was in pain.

'Your wife fought you for custody of Gwen.' Pyle's words were dry and clipped.

'That was two years ago.' Hubble spoke to the ceiling. 'Marsha and I worked it out.'

'You take a lot of precautions with your daughter's security, sir.' There was courtesy in Pyle's language but not his tone. 'You thought your wife would come after Gwen. Isn't that right?'

'I'm a wealthy man,' said Peter Hubble, calmer now, or perhaps merely tired. 'The reasons for the security should be obvious.' Unspoken were the words *Even to an idiot like you.*

Sorrel smiled but never looked up from his notebook. Rouge wished he had the senior man's eye, for he was confused. No one in the room, not even Pyle, had ever speculated on the possibility that Marsha Hubble had kidnapped the children. She had been in Albany at the time of the disappearance, and in full view of a staff of eight people, all royally pissed off at the loss of their weekend. The alibi of the noncustodial parent was always checked very carefully by the State Police, and the FBI man would know that. So where was the agent going with this line of questioning?

Arnie Pyle made a small production of receiving a file from the agent next to him. He was slow to open it. He shuffled the papers and extracted one with a bold-face heading for Family Court. 'Last summer your wife accused you of child abuse. Were you slapping the kid around?'

'No!' Peter Hubble was on his feet again. 'Why are you twisting this, Pyle? My wife claimed *psychological* abuse, and I think you know the difference. She said I was overly protective.' Hubble leaned over, both hands on the table. He was looking less like a victim now and more like a man about to stomp another man into the ground. Rouge wondered if any of the cops in the room would stop Gwen's father from decking the fed. He thought not. But it would further complicate Hubble's life if Arnie Pyle filed charges for assault.

Rising from the table, Rouge put one hand gently on Hubble's shoulder, and though his touch was light, it was sufficient to settle the man back into his chair. 'Your wife's a politician, sir. So I'm guessing that she fights dirty, but I don't know what the feds have. Will you tell me about the abuse charge?'

Hubble seemed to respond better to Rouge's more reasonable voice. 'Marsha took me to court to force an issue. The charge was dropped when I allowed Gwen to go to summer camp with Sadie Green. I had plans to take my daughter on a tour of the Greek Islands. Apparently, my wife thought a summer with Sadie would be more educational. And she was right about that. Gwen can now quote lines of dialogue from horror films verbatim. And sometimes her language is objectionable.'

Rouge repressed a smile. 'I gather you don't approve of Sadie.'

'No, I don't – never did.' His face softened. 'But I have

always liked her tremendously. So would you – if you knew her.' His words trailed off.

Rouge could see the sniper shot coming from Pyle, for this was a moment of extreme vulnerability. He warned the agent off with a slow shake of the head.

But Pyle's voice was no more civil when he said, 'We found your daughter's prints on the button pad for the security alarm. Gwen turned the system off so she could leave by the back door without anyone knowing. Who besides your wife could have called her out? Any friends of the family, people your wife works with?'

'Only Sadie. She's the only person in the world who has more influence over my daughter than I do.'

Arnie Pyle leaned forward, his face all suspicion now. 'We know it wasn't Sadie. Anyone else? Mrs Hubble has a lot of enemies between the governor's office and Senator Berman's camp.'

Hubble shook his head, more in wonder over the far-fetched political motive than as a negative response.

'I know you have the reputation of being a recluse,' said the agent. 'But your wife does a lot of socializing. Could you give us a list of people who—'

'You're wasting time with this.' Peter Hubble pushed his chair away from the table, giving Rouge a clear view of Sorrel, and this time he did catch the older man's eye. Sorrel nodded. Now they both knew where Pyle was headed with this inter-view. It was a seek-and-destroy mission in the political arena, and nothing to do with apolitical little girls. Sorrel shook his head to reiterate Peter Hubble's sentiment that this was a waste of time.

'I'm looking for names in the family's inner circle, someone who knew your kid.' Arnie Pyle slammed both hands flat on the table. 'We know Gwen was in the habit of slipping past the nanny and sneaking out.'

'Well then, you know more than I do. This is news to me.' And it was clear that he did not believe Agent Pyle.

Rouge nodded. 'It's true, Mr Hubble. We got that from a little boy – the one who spotted Sadie's bike at the bus stop. He says Gwen used to sneak out to meet her friend at the boathouse when you wouldn't let them play together.'

'I didn't know that.' Peter Hubble seemed genuinely startled and perhaps a bit foolish. Even Pyle could have no doubt that this man of a thousand locks and state-of-the-art monitoring equipment was truly ignorant of his daughter's secret life.

Rouge leaned forward, ignoring Pyle's sign language to back off and speaking only to Peter Hubble. 'The last time David Shore talked to me—'

'David actually *spoke* to you?' Peter Hubble was incredulous as he sat back in his chair, digesting this new information. There was a sardonic twist to one side of his mouth, only the suggestion of humor. 'When she was eight years old, Sadie told me David Shore's tongue was cut out at birth. Some strange religious ritual, she said. Sadie thought he might be a Protestant.'

Now Gwen's father and a table full of investigators and agents were smiling against their will.

The insane indoor raining had ceased, and the door opened. The man was back. The dog cried out in pain once more, and the thick metal door closed with a bang. The children stayed in the ground until they heard the sound of the car engine starting up and then fading away in the distance.

Sadie pushed back the cart and climbed out of the hole. She ran to the end of the aisle of shelf tables. 'Look.' She was pointing into the trees where the dog sprawled in the dirt, not moving. Gwen was limping on her wounded leg and slow to catch up. Now she could see the bundle on the ground near the prone body of the chained animal. Inside the clear plastic bag was a wad of bright red material.

'Gwen, that's your parka, isn't it?'

'He must have gone to look for me outside. That's why

he took the dog and the parka – it has my scent. Maybe he thinks all dogs can track. Mr Stuben says it takes a long time to train a dog that way.'

The animal rolled over on its side and moaned.

Gwen was poring through the bags in a near cart. One was labeled for dog biscuits. Another was a familiar brand of dry mix that had to be blended with hot water to make something approximating meat and gravy. She pushed her hand deep into the cart and extracted a can of dog food. This was what she fed to her poodle Harpo. Mr Stuben had said it was the best money could buy.

The dog was on his feet again and in motion, paws hitting the ground in the wobbling gait of a weak and badly injured animal. He stopped short of his chain, having learned his limitations by the painful choke at the end of his tether.

'The chain won't reach this far,' said Sadie. 'Don't be afraid.'

But Gwen wasn't afraid of the dog anymore, and this was not due to the calming effect of the pills. The savage, barking animal before her sounded the only familiar note in a brand-new world of alien mushrooms and tall oaken dwarfs, where it rained indoors while a multitude of electric suns burned bright – and a monster roamed.

The *dog* she understood.

There was no hate between them; the child held no grudge for the bite, for it had been nothing personal. A starving animal had to find his meals where he could. The dog was behaving normally, predictably, and the rest of the world was not. She entertained the odd idea that they might become friends, for she already knew so much about him. The silent attack had proved that he was professionally trained, perhaps as a police dog. He had only barked once before the lunge. And this told her the dog had been frightened too.

Of course he was. He had sensed the fear in her, and instinct told him that every frightened animal was dangerous. Now she was also wounded, and thus she was twice as dangerous, a double threat to the dog. He was terrified this very minute, even as he curled his black lips back over his fangs and snarled. The animal was injured and afraid for his life, but he was no coward. Mr Stuben would have said this creature had great heart.

In the dog trainer's opinion, there was much to be learned from animals – specifically, the great distinction between cowardice and fear. In training sessions, he took advantage of the dog's duality, the love and fear of humans, but he never beat an animal. If the dog's survival was threatened by cruelty, the great heart would overrule fear and the dog would even turn against his master. Gwen stared at the animal, finally connecting with his terrified eyes.

Yes, it was all about survival now. But she had Sadie on her side; the dog was alone.

Gwen was ten years old and lived in fear of the whole world, all except this snarling animal, straining to get at her again. Far from fearing him, he became her only bridge to all that was left that she could understand and control. 'We might be able to do something with the dog.'

'I'm working on it.' Sadie reached into a cart filled with tools and pulled out a long blade with a circular handle. It was a gardener's shear, one half of a broken pair. 'It's not sharp enough yet.' She walked to the stone wall and rubbed the metal against a rough outcrop, honing the blade carefully, lovingly.

'You'd never get a chance to use that,' said Gwen. 'It'll only take him a second to rip out your throat. Wouldn't you rather have the dog for a friend?'

'Gwen, he'd rather have me for dinner.'

'You said you always wanted a dog.'

'I don't want to lose a hand petting him, okay?'

'He does look pretty weak. Wanna give him some food?'

'Haven't you been paying attention?' Sadie looked at the other child, as though her old friend might be addled. 'I hate the dog. And look at what he did to you.'

Gwen looked down at the bandaged leg with a curious detachment. This time, she had only taken two pills. Her head was a bit clearer and the pain was still kept at bay. There was more weight to the leg now, as if she carried some small and heavy object inside her calf muscle. But there was no pain, and now she regarded her own leg as some alien thing attached to her body.

Back to the problem of the dog. 'Well, Sadie, as Mr Caruthers would say – let's approach this with logic. Wouldn't it make more *sense* to be friends with the dog?'

'Oh, sure it would. But I'm gonna kill him.'

'Do you know the dog's name?'

'The Fly never calls him by name. Never feeds him much, either. I bet the dog didn't eat anything today.' The knife blade made a grating noise on the stone as she moved it back and forth with definite relish. 'This is gonna be real easy.'

Gwen spotted the shiny metal bowl at the base of the nearest tree. 'There's no water in the dog's bowl.'

'He gets water when it rains from the pipes in the ceiling.'

But the bowl was so close to the tree trunk, the thick leaves would prevent any water from accumulating. 'I think the man wants the dog to be mean. Mr Stuben says an animal that's crazy with hunger and thirst is a good watchdog because he hates the world. We could give him water. That's a start.' She picked up the broom and got down on her hands and knees.

'I told you I'm gonna—' Sadie broke off her honing. 'What are you doing?'

Gwen stretched out the broom to reach the dog's bowl. 'What do you think?' The animal was watching her, crouching now, set to spring as she maneuvered the broom handle to move the bowl, sliding it in a wide arc away from the tree trunk.

'Gwen, get back! You don't—'

The moment she grabbed the bowl, the dog came running. And now Sadie was dragging her back by the heels. Gwen had underestimated the limits of the dog-chain circle, and his massive jaws were within a foot of her hand when Sadie finally dropped her feet in the dirt on the safe side of the invisible line of demarcation. But Gwen had held onto the bowl and felt enormously proud.

Sadie hunkered down beside her. 'I think you're drunk. It's those pills.'

'Stoned,' Gwen corrected her. '*Drunk* is for alcohol, *stoned* is for drugs.' But now she did wonder how much of her newfound bravery was owed to the pharmacy bottles.

Sadie shook her head as she took the bowl from Gwen. 'You almost lost your hand for this stupid piece of tin. And now you want to give him water?'

'Not giving him water is like torture.'

'What if that creep sees the dog's water bowl filled? You want The Fly to know we're down here?'

'And what about that?' Gwen pointed to the sharpened blade lying on the ground where Sadie had dropped it. 'When he finds the dog with that thing stuck in his heart – you don't think he's going to suspect something? Or were you planning to make it look like a suicide?'

Sadie was very quiet as she stood up with the bowl in her hands. Her face was grim when she turned her back on Gwen and walked down the wide aisle between the mushroom tables.

'Where are you going?'

'To the sink, to get your damn water.'

Gwen caught up to her, limping on the injured leg. 'I'm sorry.' But she was not. She was still pleased with herself, feeling less the coward now. She stood by the sink in the white room while Sadie filled the bowl with water. 'Do you remember any words the man used with the dog? Command words?'

'He does it with Indians,' said Sadie. 'When he set the dog on me, he said, "Geronimo". When he called the dog off, he said, "Sitting Bull." ' She turned toward the door with a full bowl of water in her hands. Her tongue stuck out between her teeth as she concentrated on not spilling any.

They walked slowly back to the edge of the small forest. Gwen stopped to grab a handful of biscuits from the dog-food cart while Sadie put the tin bowl on the edge of the magic circle, the outer limit of the dog chain, and pushed it forward with the broom handle. The dog came creeping forward on tender feet, ears high, nose pointing.

Gwen studied the mongrel's aggressive family tree in the characteristics of three fierce breeds of biters. 'Here, take one of these.' She handed Sadie a biscuit. 'Throw it to him.'

'You want him to get his strength back? Are you nuts?'

'All right, throw him *half* a biscuit.'

The dog had drunk the contents of the bowl, almost inhaling the water. His head went up, and his ears flattened back with renewed suspicion. Sadie broke one biscuit in half and threw it to the dog. He fell on the morsel and devoured it. When he raised his head again, something like a human crying came from his throat, dogspeak for, *More Please.*

'Hold up the other half of the biscuit so he can see it,' said Gwen. 'Yell, "Sitting Bull".'

'Sitting Bull!'

The dog backed off a few feet and sat down, all his muscles tensing, eyes fixed on the bit of biscuit in Sadie's hand.

'Throw it to him.'

Sadie did, and the dog caught the biscuit in the air, jaws clamping down on it. Even above the mechanical hum of all the tiny motors behind them, the girls could hear the rows of sharp teeth gnashing and chewing.

'Nice throw,' said Gwen. 'Now we're going to do it again with another biscuit. We'll keep it simple – just work with the tricks he already knows. But it's important that he takes orders from you.'

'Why me? You're the dog expert. You trained Harpo to—'

'But you make a better Alpha wolf – a pack leader.'

Sadie was neither wounded nor afraid. Gwen was a coward, and the dog knew it, even if her best friend did not. She could never command this animal; she respected him that much.

'Everything he does from now on is all about staying alive. But even wolves take orders.'

'From the Alpha wolf.'

'Right.' And once he became Sadie's dog, she would be less inclined to kill him. It would have been just a matter of time before Sadie began to experiment with the dog's food and the chemicals in the white room. One would only have to inhale the green powder to know that it was lethal.

'Whoever feeds him gives the orders,' said Gwen. 'So Geronimo is the attack command. He needs something to attack.'

'I got just the thing.' Sadie ran down the aisle of mushroom tables and disappeared into the white room. In another minute, she came strolling back with the black felt mask held up high. 'Like it?' She stopped by a cart, picked up a handful of plastic bags and stuffed them into the mask as she walked. When she handed it to Gwen, it was rounded out in the shape of a human head.

Gwen threw it to the center of the dog circle. 'Now yell—'

'I know. Geronimo!'

The dog fell on the mask. He sank his teeth in and shook it until Gwen whispered the counter command, and Sadie yelled, 'Sitting Bull!'

The dog broke off the attack, and she was about to break a biscuit.

'No,' said Gwen. 'Throw him a *whole* biscuit. And then you have to praise him. Mr Stuben says that's very important.'

Sadie begrudgingly threw him the biscuit, but seemed reluctant to say anything nice to the dog.

'Sadie, do it,' whispered Gwen.

'Good dog.'

'Louder. And say it like you *mean* it, Sadie.'

'*Really* good dog.'

Over the next hour, they made more trips to the biscuit bag.

'I think the dog likes you, Sadie. He doesn't growl anymore. Look at his eyes. Friendly, right? Isn't that nice?'

The other child seemed unconvinced. 'Geronimo! Yeah, look at him rip into that head. What a nice dog.'

Gwen watched, smiling as the animal's teeth closed on the dark cloth head. He whipped it back and forth, tearing the felt skin. 'Our parents are probably going crazy right now.'

'Not mine,' said Sadie. 'Sitting Bull! My mother's pregnant.' She tossed the dog a biscuit in a languid fashion, already bored with this new game of shuttling the animal between frenzy and repose. 'Right now, the school shrink is probably telling my parents I ran away from home – acting out my anxiety with a bid for attention.' Sadie knew all the jargon words. She had been sent to the school counselor that many times.

'Dr Moffit is such an ass. But parents are really into that crap, aren't they?'

'Geronimo! Gwen, I've been meaning to talk to you about your language.'

'*My* language?'

'Sitting Bull!' Sadie tossed another biscuit. It was not a long throw, for they were sitting closer to the animal, only a few feet from the invisible border of the circle. 'If you say *crap* to your dad one more time, he'll never let me sleep over again. I never say crap in front of *my* parents.'

'Crap, crap, crap.'

'*Shit, shit, shit,*' sang Sadie in the higher register for the second bar of 'Jingle Bells'.

'*Crap, crap crap,*' chimed Gwen.

And they harmonized on '*Shit, fart*' for the finale.

Gwen applauded, and though it was difficult to lose her balance from a sitting position, she managed it, falling backward like a toppled bowling pin. Perhaps Sadie was right about the pills; maybe she was a little stoned. But at least there was no pain – she could not bear pain. The child was grinning entirely too wide as she righted herself to a cross-legged sit. 'Now let's do "Silent Night". *Shi-i-i-it*—'

Sadie put up one hand to stop her. 'That's a movie title. You remember it? I taped it for you last year.'

'*Silent Night, Deadly Night*, 1984? Killer Santa Claus versus the evil nun?'

'Yeah.' In a rather good imitation of Mr Caruthers, the closest thing to Santa in the flesh, Sadie puffed out her stomach and lowered her voice. 'And what did we learn from this movie, Gwen?'

'Never trust a nun?'

'Close.' Sadie whispered, as though the dog might be listening, 'This movie has *two* monsters, right?'

The chained animal barked.

'David told you that? David the Alien?' Sadie's father smiled for the first time since the interview had begun.

'He's a strange little boy, isn't he, Mr Green?' said Arnie Pyle.

'Yeah, but some of the weirdest people I know are children.' He smiled at the FBI agent. 'Call me Harry.'

'Do you know a lot of small children, Mr Green?'

'Oh, sure,' he said affably. Innuendo and rudeness had sailed past him. 'I started coaching Pee Wee League baseball when Sadie was big enough to swing a baseball bat. But my kid *really* shines in gymnastics.'

Rouge cut off Arnie Pyle's response and said in a softer tone, 'So you didn't know anything about these meetings at the boathouse?'

'No, I had no idea that probation nonsense was going on. Peter Hubble's an odd bird. I don't know why he'd want to keep them apart. He didn't much care for the films they were watching, but I figured he was over—'

'What films?' asked Pyle. He had not been privy to Rouge's detailed report on Sadie's genre of choice.

'On Saturdays,' said Harry Green, 'I used to drive the kids

217

down to Milltown. There's this little theater on George Street.' He turned to Rouge, a local man. 'You know the place with eight million kids lined up to see vintage horror movies? Ever been there?'

Arnie Pyle leaned forward to get the man's attention back. 'You exposed the girls to horror movies?' He might as well have suggested that this big man with the sad smile had exposed his naked body. But again, Pyle failed to place his shot.

'Pretty tame stuff really.' Harry Green seemed to take no offense. 'You'd laugh at them. The kids do. Sometimes you can see the seams in the monster suits, the wires and the wheels. But then Peter Hubble made the theater off limits for Gwen. So now the kids tape the same old movies from cable TV and watch them on the VCR.' He shrugged. 'But Peter doesn't seem to mind that. Go figure.'

Arnie Pyle stood up as a signal that the interview was ended. There was nothing to be had from this large and friendly man who refused to acknowledge an insult. Another agent escorted Harry Green out the door.

Buddy Sorrel also rose from his chair and motioned Rouge to join him in the next room. 'Nice job. Now you're on your own.' Sorrel gave him a stiff smile. 'Go back in there and hang out with the feds. The captain doesn't want any part of the interview with Mrs Hubble. This time, you play it Pyle's way. I don't care what he does to the lady, you let it blow back in *his* face – not ours. Got it?'

Yes, he got it. He was to be Captain Costello's fly on the wall and nothing more. Rouge looked through the open door. A technician stood at the end of the long table, face averted as he leaned over to set down the polygraph equipment. When Rouge walked back into the room, Arnie Pyle did not seem happy to see him. The agent turned his back and looked down at the machine.

'Why a lie detector?' Rouge watched the tech adjust his

dials. 'The parents have already been through this – all of them.'

Without turning, Pyle said, 'Well, Mrs Hubble is going through it again.'

'Why her and not the others?'

'Because I have a few questions you guys never asked.' Paper was scrolling across the machine bed, and the FBI agent was intent on the test of waving black lines beneath three moving needles. 'And she's a politician, isn't she? A professional liar.' His back was still turned when he said, 'It works better when there are fewer people in the room.' He waved vaguely toward the door. 'You mind, kid?'

Rouge sat down at the table. The fed smiled. 'Fine.' He turned to a trooper standing near the door. 'Bring her in.'

'*Ask* her to come in,' said Rouge to the same officer.

The man in uniform grinned, touching his cap in a non-regulation salute as he walked out the door.

Arnie Pyle nodded in recognition of the point scored. 'This time, I'll handle the questions, okay?'

'Sure. But if she breaks you in half, I'm not gonna shoot her for that.'

'Oh, I think you might even drive the lady's getaway car. I believe you found your calling, kid – white knight.'

'Why don't we do a deal, you and me. You don't call me *kid* anymore, and I don't call you *shithead*.'

'But that's his name,' said the silver-haired man standing just inside the door. Taken by surprise, Rouge was slow to extend his hand to this old friend of the family. It had been years since they last met. Julian Garret had once been a regular at the Kendall dinner table. But the famous political journalist showed no recognition as his eyes passed over the younger man. Nor did Garret notice the hand suspended in the air as he turned his back on Rouge.

Julie, don't you know me?

'Buzz off,' said Arnie Pyle to the journalist, 'and right now.'

Pyle was too anxious to get rid of this man, and Rouge had to wonder why. He was certainly not protecting the lieutenant governor from the press. All the reporters had round-the-clock access to Marsha Hubble.

Julian Garret turned his head to smile at Rouge as he shrugged off this blatant rudeness. 'I blame Arnie's bad manners on his mother. It was a tragic incident in his formative years.' The old man sat down on the edge of the desk.

'Go away,' said Pyle.

Did Julie's presence make him nervous? Yes.

Garret ignored the FBI man, speaking only to Rouge, still regarding him as a stranger. 'It happened after school one day. Little Arnie – poor child – never heard so much as a warning bark before his mother ran out from under the front porch and bit him.' Julie feigned interest in his manicured fingernails. 'I'm told Mrs Pyle also chased buses and cars.' He turned back to the FBI agent. 'Planning to wire the lady politician, I see. You're probably wondering how I—'

'Get out, Julie,' said Pyle. 'I mean it.'

That had the tone of an implied threat, and perhaps the unraveling of a deal. With a political columnist? Suppose the famed reporter was not merely covering the press conference of a high-profile senator with a governor in his pocket and alleged mob connections – though Rouge's mother had not used the word *alleged*.

The journalist smiled, inclining his head a bare inch in farewell. Garret swung his walking stick across the outer room with well-remembered panache.

Rouge closed the door, saying, very casually, 'So why do I think your interest in Marsha Hubble has nothing to do with her missing daughter? Who's the target? Senator Berman?'

The look of surprise on Arnie Pyle's face told Rouge that he had been sorely underestimated, but that was all changing behind the agent's eyes. So dirty politics held sway over missing children. The fed was that cold. *You bet your ass, babe*, as his mother would say.

They sat in uneasy silence for the next few minutes, and then Gwen's mother was escorted into the room. There was no polite conversation, not even a hello from Arnie Pyle. But the lady seemed not to care about this slight. Her eyes were riveted to the machine; what it implied was not lost on her. Pyle ignored her while the young civilian technician was taping the wires to her skin. Her look of disbelief was blending into resignation.

Pyle stood to one side, giving Rouge his first clear view of the polygraph tech, a very young man with boyish cowlicks and freckles across the bridge of his nose. The FBI had more seasoned pros at their disposal, and Rouge had to wonder if this examination was all for show.

When the technician was done with the mundane test questions, Pyle stood over Marsha Hubble, almost threatening in his posture and proximity. He had bound the woman with wires, and now she must know he was about to hurt her. Her hands balled into fists, and she sat a little straighter, bracing for the first salvo.

'You have no idea what happened to the kids?'

'No,' she said.

'But you still resist the idea that Gwen ran away?'

'It's not in my daughter's character.'

The young technician leaned forward and said, 'Ma'am, could you please restrict your answers to yes and no?'

'Shut up,' she said, never taking her eyes off Pyle.

And the technician did shut up. His broad farmboy face was reddening as he ducked his head to look down at his waving needles and rolling graph paper.

Agent Pyle stood behind her and rested his hands on the back of her chair. 'Your husband says Sadie's a bad influence on Gwen.'

The technician's voice was more timid now. 'Sir, if you could structure your questions—'

'Butt out!' The FBI agent raised one hand in a futile gesture, perhaps wishing he could call the words back. All pretense of a polygraph exam was blown – that much was in the lady's face. Rouge wished that Arnie Pyle could see the disturbing new light in Marsha Hubble's eyes.

The agent ran his hands down the sides of her chair. She must have felt his fingers brushing against her clothes, but she gave no indication of it. Rouge was becoming more fascinated with every passing second, for Pyle did not seem to realize that the game was up. His voice was even and low. 'Your husband is a very worried man.'

'And a humorless man. Sadie believes *he's* the bad influence. I tend to side with the kid.' She was more testy now.

'I think your husband worries about other people too, enemies who—'

'Worrying is a way of life with Peter. He'd keep Gwen wrapped up in velvet padding if my lawyer wasn't smarter than his.' Her voice was getting louder, stronger.

'You have some formidable enemies, lady. I don't blame him for being worried.'

'What the hell are you getting at, Pyle?' She was done playing with him.

He came out from behind the chair and leaned one hand on the table. He regarded Marsha Hubble with mild contempt, not even acknowledging the anger in her face.

Bad mistake, Pyle.

In Rouge's experience, it was always a good idea to keep one eye on the end of a fuse – so a man could pull back before his balls were ripped off by the blast. All women carried dynamite; it was issued to them at birth, along with many packs of matches for lighting fuses.

'I think you *know* who took the kids.'

'So now *I* planned it? You moron. What do you think I did with the extra kid?'

Pyle obviously didn't hear the tension in her voice, a woman's only warning that she was striking the matches. The agent settled into a chair next to hers and leaned back, folding his hands behind his head. He was entirely too comfortable with what he was doing to her. 'Lady, you made—'

'You're so smart, you little bastard? You try making a baby from scratch materials.'

Rouge could smell sulfur and smoke in the air.

'Okay,' said Pyle, so glib he annoyed her even more – another error. 'Let's talk about your enemies. Senator Berman really wanted to knock you off the governor's ticket. But you managed to stay on for another election. So I gotta wonder what kind of leverage you used. You must've considered the mob as a possible—'

'I know your background, Pyle. I mean *after* you left the Center for Missing and Exploited Children.' She ripped off the lie detector wires, one by one, with great deliberation and no hurried motions. 'I understand you received a commendation for your work on New York crime families.' The last wire was gone; the lady was unbound and rising. 'You would use my little girl to build a damn mob case against Berman?'

Rouge thought her voice was entirely too calm as she hovered over Arnie Pyle. The FBI man never blinked. Rouge wondered if Pyle simply lacked the good sense to move away from her before—

'You son of a bitch!' Her closed fist connected with the agent's right eye, hard enough to rock Arnie Pyle on the rear legs of his chair, to tip him backward and send his head slamming into the wall as the chair slid out from under him.

The civilian polygraph technician was stunned, and then his mouth widened in a boy's grin. 'Nice one, ma'am.'

She had quit the room by the time Arnie Pyle had risen from the floor. His hand went to the back of his head. 'She acts like a bitch, but she's got those humongous balls. I'm so confused.'

'And so full of yourself.' Becca Green was standing on the threshold. She entered the room, followed by Captain Costello. 'I don't know what you did to Gwen's mother, but if you do it again, I hope she beats the crap out of you.' She advanced on him and put one pointing finger into the middle of his chest.

Pyle backed up a step. He had suddenly learned some measure of respect for mothers. 'I'm not her enemy, Mrs Green.'

'Damn right you're not. You're just something she bumped into in the dark. So, you wanna tell me about the ransom note *now*, or do I call that woman back in here to finish you off?'

Arnie Pyle was reaching inside his jacket. 'I was going to share this with all of you when—'

'Sure you were. Cut the bull, okay? Give it to me.'

He pulled out a folded sheet of paper, and she ripped it from his hand. She read the scrawl of lines on the page and looked up at Captain Costello. 'You're right, it's a fake. Sadie doesn't wear purple underwear.' She crumpled the paper into a tight ball and delicately held it between her thumb and forefinger as she placed it in the breast pocket of Pyle's suit. She patted down the bulge in the material. 'I do have *some* control over my daughter. Not everything in her life is purple.' She smiled at the agent with overdone sympathy. 'I guess you just got demoted back to the *B* team.' She turned to Captain Costello. 'Right?'

Captain Costello was smiling. Marsha Hubble put a stop to that when she walked back into the room.

'Get a car to take me home. *Now.*'

Rouge knew the lieutenant governor's tone would have been more polite had she been talking to a taxi dispatcher. Captain Costello let the insult slide. 'In a few minutes, Mrs Hubble. There's something I have to discuss with—'

'I haven't got time for this,' she said. 'I have press interviews and citizens groups waiting to—'

'No you don't,' said Costello. 'I'm sorry about the press command post – that's over. I'm shutting it down. From now on the media will be channeled through my office.'

'You can't tell me what to—'

'Well, yes I can – if you're obstructing the case. And you are.'

'This is ridiculous. You have no idea how to use the media. I do.'

Captain Costello turned to Mrs Green. 'Is that how you feel too, ma'am?'

'I wouldn't know about any of that,' said Becca Green. 'I wasn't invited to the command post. That's at Marsha's house, isn't it?'

Rouge thought Marsha Hubble smiled with a bit too much condescension as she put one hand on the other woman's shoulder. 'Becca, I know what an ordeal this has been for you. That's why I made a deal with the press. They get access to me anytime they want it, and all the FBI bulletins – as long as they leave you in peace. I didn't want you and Harry to put up with those jackals calling day and night.'

And perhaps she didn't think Sadie's mother would know how to use the media, either. Rouge watched the anger in Costello's eyes as the politician went on with her performance, flashing her best public relations smile, her eyes radiating warmth all over Mrs Green. Marsha Hubble's tone could not have been more solicitous. 'I can handle everything myself. You can trust me to—'

Her mouth closed softly, and her eyes were quizzical as she stared at her husband. Peter Hubble was seated close to Sadie's father on a bench facing the door. The two of them were poring over a road map heavily scored with pencil lines and ink. 'What are they doing?'

'They're planning their day,' said Becca Green, matter-of-factly. 'You didn't know? They drive around all day long, looking for the kids. They used to do that at night, but I convinced them they could see more when the sun was out. In my experience, men often miss little details like that. They need direction.'

'And what about you?' The concern in Marsha Hubble's

voice had the ring of the genuine article. Her arm circled Mrs Green's shoulders. 'How do *you* spend the days?'

'Me? Oh, early in the morning I make up sandwiches for the guys to take on the road. I'm afraid they'd forget to eat if I didn't. Men – they're children. After that, I make breakfast. I like to send them off with a good meal. And then I spend hours waiting for the phone to ring. It never does, but you never know.' She nodded toward the men and their maps. 'When it gets dark, I start cooking a hot dinner for those two. I spend the rest of my time crying for the kids. And sometimes I cry for their fathers. It's a lot of work, but it fills up my day.'

The politician's arm fell away to hang limp at her side. 'I didn't know—' Softer now, in the smaller voice of a mechanical doll, 'Oh, God, no.'

'So you don't think God is moved by tears?' Becca Green seemed to be weighing this misunderstood opinion. 'Well, maybe you're right. But you gotta try everything – crying – everything.'

The lieutenant governor was not standing very straight anymore, and Rouge worried that she might fall to her knees, for every bit of her energy was gone; the fight was finally over. A wet streak of mascara marred the careful mask of her makeup.

'That's the spirit.' Mrs Green enfolded the taller woman in her big arms and held her close. The golden head slowly bent to Becca's shoulder. 'Then, later on,' Sadie's mother whispered, 'if crying doesn't work, we'll try something else.'

Gwen sat in the dirt a safe distance from the dog circle. She was surrounded by small stacks of journals and shaded from the bright light by the boughs of an oak. The journals were arranged by the order of their dates. She picked up one after the other, leafing through the pages, scanning the maintenance entries penned on the first day of every month. And now she understood why the cellar thermostat was registering seventy-nine degrees, though no heat was coming from the steam radiators along the rear walls.

'Sadie, the pipes aren't for watering the trees – there's an underground irrigation system for that. The rain lowers the temperature of the room. All those bulbs make it too hot, but oak trees need fabulous amounts of light. So she installed the—'

'*She*? The Fly isn't a woman. You saw him, you heard him.' Sadie broke another biscuit in half and yelled, 'Sitting Bull!' When the dog backed away from the stuffed felt head, she threw him the piece of biscuit. Then she reached down to touch Gwen's forehead. 'You've got a little fever. So what is this *she* business?'

'Okay, I'm not sure it's a woman. That's just a feeling, but whoever writes these journals is a *different* person.'

Sadie seemed skeptical.

'It's the way she treats the dog.' Gwen picked up another journal and opened it to a page marked by a turned-down corner. 'Here,' she said, one hand moving down the lines of writing. 'She bought him from a kennel that was going out of business. Oh, and it turns out he *is* good at tracking scents. He digs up her truffles.'

Gwen riffled through another journal, passing by all the entries for experiments on new cultures, until she found another turned-back corner. 'Listen to this. "The dog was mean as they come, but in time, I taught him to be gentle. Now he licks my hand a hundred times a day and never leaves my side." ' She closed the notebook and pointed to the cart containing the dog's food. 'All those cans and bags are very expensive. This person doesn't mistreat animals. This is someone *else*.'

'Maybe he's a split personality – *Dr Jekyll and Mr Hyde*.'

'Conrad Veidt, 1920.' There were many films by the same title, but this German version was a favorite because the butler was played by Bela Lugosi. 'No, that doesn't work for me. I think it's two different people.'

Sadie shrugged. 'Find anything on the lock?' Turning back to the dog she yelled, 'Geronimo!'

'Not yet.' Gwen raised her voice to be heard over the snarling. 'But I know why there's no ladder for changing the lightbulbs. There's a crawl space between the ceiling and the top floor. She replaces the bulbs from up there, about three feet under the first floor.'

'Sitting Bull!' Sadie tossed another biscuit. 'So that's why you can't hear his footsteps when he comes into the house.' She turned away from the dog and hunkered down on the ground near a pile of dark clothing.

'Right. So then she crawls around up there replacing the bulbs. And it really hurts her to do that. She has arthritis – that's what all those pain pills are for – but she keeps going into that crawl space on her hands and knees.' Gwen bowed her head to read from the page, ' "All doubled up in agony, not caring about the pain, always for the love of the trees." '

Sadie looked up from her project of stuffing shredded magazines and plastic bags into a large black sweater, filling it out in the shape of an adult-size torso. She held up half a biscuit and yelled, 'Geronimo!' And once again the dog attacked the stuffed mask, so like a human head.

'Don't let him chew on it anymore. He's going to demolish it.' The dog had ripped away some of the stitches shaped like fangs. Part of the felt mouth hung open. With each biscuit, the dog grew a little more violent, more powerful.

'Cool.' Sadie smiled her approval as he whipped the mask in a particularly vicious frenzy. 'Sitting Bull!'

The dog backed away and sat down, his eyes fixed on Sadie's hand, from whence came all food.

Gwen bit into a shiitake mushroom from the stand of logs by the wall. She had been tempted to eat the beautiful mushrooms that grew on the log bundle next to it, but she hesitated out of respect. According to the journals, she had guessed right about those gnarly logs; they had come from the dead tree with stumps for arms. The tree had a name like a person.

Sadie knotted loosened threads from the sweater's hem into the belt loops of the stuffed pants. Now she laid the headless body out on the floor. 'Well, what do you think?'

'Looks good, but you need his shoes.' Gwen put her thumb in the book to mark her place as she closed it. 'The shoes have the strongest scent. Maybe you can tie them to the pant legs with the laces.'

'Too bad Mark isn't here. I bet he could make blasting powder with the chemicals in the white room. Then we could just blow the door open.' Sadie bent over the torso again. 'You think Mark and Jesse ever got the gun to work?'

'No way.' Gwen resumed her reading. She had found a pattern in the written lines, and now she reached into the stack of journals and went to the same dates in each one. 'It was pretty dumb of Jesse to encode all the gun designs from the Internet. It was like flagging the file for Mr Caruthers. He was the one who *bought* them the encryption program.'

'Stupid boys.' Sadie had succeeded in fastening the shoes to the pant legs. All that remained was to attach the head. She turned to the dog, who seemed to like the head more than she did. He was holding his Sitting Bull pose, but drooled as he stared at the round dark object. 'But suppose they do get the gun to work?'

'Never happen,' said Gwen. 'They always talk big. Make the dog hold that pose for a while. I want to see how long he'll keep it.' In journal after journal, the same dates were panning out.

Sadie's eyes wandered from the dog to the head and back again. He really coveted that head.

Gwen opened another book, scanning for a reference to the lock. 'I think the boys are full of it – all talk.'

'I don't,' said Sadie. 'I think they make Mr Caruthers really nervous.'

'Jealous?'

'Yeah.'

'I found the door problem.' Gwen looked up from the journal. 'I know what's wrong with it. The metal was too thick for a regular lock, so she had a special one made. But it broke down after twenty years. The knob on the other side will open the bolt. But the inside knob won't turn at all – it's fused. Whenever she's down here working, she props the door open with that block of concrete by the wall. The door is set on an angle. That's why it closes by itself.'

'Why didn't she just get the lock fixed?' Sadie was examining a handful of dog biscuits, perhaps with a view to a trade – biscuits for the head.

After a few minutes' reading, Gwen said, 'She didn't want to call a locksmith. Listen. She says, "All I need is for some fool to go to town and talk about the oak trees. They'll put me away." '

'It *is* crazy – growing trees in the house.'

'She needed the tree roots to grow truffles. She wanted a sample of every fungus in the— Wait.' Gwen picked up another journal and flipped through the pages until she found the date she was looking for. 'Here. She wrote this when one of the trees died. "In the beginning, my work was all about the fungus collection. But now it is all about the trees. I must not lose any more of them. It is so hard to make new friends when you are old." She blames herself for the tree that died. Grieves over it like it was a person.'

'Well, what does she want with us? And who's The Fly?'

'Maybe he's a relative or something, but this woman probably doesn't know we're here.'

'How do you figure that?' Sadie had turned away from the dog, and he crept a few inches closer to the head.

'She's not even in the house.' Gwen rested one hand on the stack of journals on the ground beside her. 'Each notebook covers one year. Every year, she breaks off on the same day. I checked the dates for every journal. And she always makes an entry *exactly* nine days later. So she'll be back the day after

Christmas. If we just hold on till then, we won't have to use the dog.'

Sadie looked back at the animal, and he immediately stopped edging toward the mask. Gwen thought he looked shamefaced to be caught. Sadie turned away from him, and the dog crept closer to the mask again. Though Gwen was still watching, apparently he didn't care what she thought of him, for she was no Alpha wolf, not even close.

'You don't think the dog can really do this, do you?'

'He can. He wants to,' said Gwen. 'When we were in the ground, I know the man hurt him, and—'

'The Fly. Call him *The Fly*.' Sadie's correction was gentle but firm, for this distinction between man and insect was very important to her – more than a movie title. In her own way, Sadie had already defeated the man – the bug, The Fly.

'Right,' said Gwen. 'The dog was already limping when I got here. The Fly probably mistreats him a lot. If you keep hurting an animal that way, he'll turn on you.'

'So we're training the dog to do what he really wants to do.'

'Yes. I don't think that man— Sorry. The *Fly* doesn't know anything about animals. The dog is the journal lady's pet, not his.'

'Why do you think she isn't part of this? For all you know—'

'She's not mean enough, not mean at all. That dead tree over there?' Gwen pointed to the barren oak. Its arms ended in cruel, flat cuts. 'She feels guilty because she couldn't keep it alive. This is the book she started when the tree died.' Gwen held up a journal and opened it to a turned-back page. 'She says she's in mourning. She named all the trees for people she loved. The dead tree was called Samuel. He was a soldier, I think. It says he died in a war.'

Sadie turned to the dog. He had moved a bit closer to the black felt head, breaking the Sitting Bull pose again – cheating. A cross look from the Alpha wolf made him back up a few steps. 'So she named a *tree* after a dead soldier? My family names *kids* for dead people. But a tree?'

'Hmm. She kept it alive for more than twenty years.' Gwen ran one finger down the page until she found the line she wanted. 'And when the tree died, she wrote, "I must have a penchant for grief. He went to war, he said, for my sake. And now Samuel is killed again. Forgive me twice, my love." '

Gwen was first to notice the silence. The plant misters no longer shushed fine sprays of water into the air over the mushroom tables, and the pumps had ceased to buzz and chug. The brilliant ceiling went dark, and all the table bulbs blinked off beneath each shelf of mushroom blocks.

'This happens every night,' said Sadie.

'But the lights – the heat.' The pills were wearing off. Pain was stealing over her, and Gwen could hear the fear creep back into her voice.

'Don't worry. The furnace will kick in when the temperature drops. You'll hear the hiss of the radiators in a little while.'

But for now it was dead quiet, and the only remaining illumination was from a single bulb over the door of the white room. It wore a halo of refracted light from the drops of moisture in the air, and it appeared to hang there as an independent thing, a floating disk, an electric moon.

The girls sat very close together in the darkness and listened to the sound of the dog chewing on the head.

CHAPTER 8

Dr Mortimer Cray signed the paper acknowledging that his life was worthless should the inmates take him hostage; understanding that there would be no negotiation to save him; and agreeing that neither he nor his heirs would hold a harsh or legal grudge against the State of New York for his mutilation or demise. Then he deposited his keys in a plastic tray, for they might be used as weapons – or so the prison authorities maintained.

The psychiatrist opened his arms and spread his legs for the man in the dark uniform. After probing all the forbidden zones, the corrections officer was satisfied that the doctor possessed no contraband. Finally, Mortimer Cray passed into a long room where the prisoner awaited him, shackled hand and foot, seated behind a table near the opposite wall.

A guard was posted by the door, far enough from the table to prevent eavesdropping on a normal level of conversation. This was not the privacy the psychiatrist had hoped for, but it would do. He did not trust the telephones in the common visiting area, nor did he want a wall of glass to hamper intimacy.

Mortimer adjusted his glasses as he approached the prisoner. He was about to turn to the guard and tell him this was the wrong convict; this hulk was not Paul Marie. The man he wanted was of slight, almost delicate build. Then the prisoner raised his head and Mortimer beheld the man's eyes, large, dark-brown and liquid – so beautiful. Once they had been the priest's only truly outstanding feature.

From the moment the psychiatrist sat down at the table,

the prisoner began to grow in size. The doctor blinked, but the illusion persisted. The man's shoulders grew wider, his thick arms more muscular. The chains seemed less substantial now. Mortimer glanced quickly over one shoulder to see the guard engrossed in his newspaper, taking no notice of this frightening metamorphosis.

The doctor diagnosed his own delusion as a by-product of increasing tension over recent days – and all the long years of fear.

'*Mr* Marie,' the psychiatrist began, deliberately using the wrong form of address. But the prisoner did not correct him, nor was there any outward sign that he minded being stripped of his proper title. Perhaps Paul Marie no longer thought of himself as a priest.

'I don't believe you'll remember me, sir.' Mortimer could not look away from the man's eyes. They were invasive, probing. The prisoner was clearly sizing up his visitor. And now, as Paul Marie settled back in his chair and his chains, the doctor wondered how he had fared in the analysis. 'I'm a psychiatrist. I was—'

'You're Ali's uncle.' The tone was so civilized, that of a gentleman, but with each slight movement, his chains clanked. A warning? A reminder that this was a most uncivil place? 'When I was a parish priest, you never came to the services. But the checks you've sent to Father Domina – since then – they were all very generous.'

The last phrase was close to sarcasm, but so subtle that Mortimer was unsure. How much could a priest extrapolate from tithings?

'I read the report of your last hearing, Mr Marie. You showed no remorse for the crime. I expect that's why they denied your parole. You never admitted to—'

'It's against my religion to make a false confession.'

The doctor's skin prickled. He turned his head quickly, but there was no one beside him or behind him. The guard was still seated near the door and half hidden by the opened pages of his newspaper.

At odd moments over the past few days, Mortimer had sensed someone standing close to him. And several times he had seen shadows behind the reflection in his shaving mirror and wondered if he was alone in his own bathroom. Again, he diagnosed himself: he was never alone; death was always close by – and closer now that he had ceased to take his medication. One must expect unusual symptoms and reactions – the racing heart, its missing beats. And breath itself was no longer taken for granted. He tried to remember what his respiration had been like only minutes ago – not too shallow, not too deep. Mortimer lowered his voice, though he was confident that the guard was oblivious to all conversation. 'It might be possible to get you a new trial. I have a certain amount of—'

Had he given something away? Paul Marie was shaking his head from side to side, as if the psychiatrist had already named his price for this miracle.

No deal, said the eyes of the priest.

The doctor was more and more deliberate in his breathing, deeper now and slower. Yet his heart quickened, heedless of the fact that it contained a finite number of beats, and they were being used up by irrational fear. He pressed on in a virtual race with his reckless heart, wanting to finish this business before the final beat and endgame. 'But first, I wonder if we might discuss another matter – Father Marie – in strictest confidence, you understand.'

More had been given away with the restoration of the priest's title. Paul Marie was clearly offended, that much was in his face. Could the man already suspect a prelude to a religious ritual?

'Dr Cray – this is about the missing children?' Paul Marie folded his massive arms across his chest. 'I'm tired of eating sins. That's no longer my line of work.' He glanced at the guard and in a louder voice, he said, 'I'll tell that man whatever you tell me.'

The guard looked up from his newspaper, and in that instant, Mortimer knew that the priest was lying, that he held to the holy sacraments and always would. Father Marie had merely condemned his visitor to a more public truthtelling, not allowing an unethical side street of protected confession.

'I want to tell you something, Father. I'm a very sick man. I don't have much time—'

'But you want more than absolution, don't you?'

Mortimer felt the drain of blood between the slow beats, the loss of air, breath coming in shallow sips – the fear. Mind and body were surrendering to the priest, who seemed the better man in this art of reading psyche.

Paul Marie's voice was lower now, less public. 'Pious men believe in a burning hell. You're perspiring, Dr Cray, and that tells me you're close to the fire – a true believer.' He leaned across the table, bringing his body as near to the old man as restraints would allow. 'Where are the children, you bastard?'

The psychiatrist's skeletal body sat at attention, suddenly stiffening in every frail joint of brittle bone. His mouth formed the word *no* – more in wonder than denial. This priest was a throwback to diviners of entrails, reading the sweat of hellfire, guilt from a sinner's pores. Though Father Marie had never touched him, Mortimer was pressed back in his chair. He had the sense that the priest was growing larger again as the man rose from the table, chains clattering.

They had the guard's attention now, and he was also rising, stepping forward, but Mortimer waved the man back. After a moment of uncertainty, the guard settled down to his chair, but his cautious gaze remained on the prisoner.

The priest was standing very still, but he continued to grow in Mortimer's eyes, massing with energy and form. Soon Father Marie would be a giant.

And himself? Altogether gone.

'I don't remember you as a religious man, Dr Cray. Come lately to God? Seeking forgiveness? Or did you only plan to shift the burden?'

'Would you tell?'

'In a heartbeat. I wouldn't send those little girls to God under any circumstances. It's pretty obvious He doesn't know how to take care of them.'

Liar. 'Forgive me, Father, for I have sinned. My last confession was forty—'

'Enough!' The chained hands were rising. Then the priest's anger subsided, and his hands lowered. 'The children are dying, Dr Cray. You have to tell someone, don't you?' There was a cunning aspect in the face of the priest. 'I can see the pressure building. Your fists are clenched, your knuckles are white, the vein in your temple is throbbing – and you're sweating even more now. Proximity to the fire?'

Mortimer began again – the magic words, 'Bless me, Father, for I—'

'Never.'

'For I have sinned.'

'May you burn in hell.'

The priest stretched out one hand toward Mortimer. The guard left his chair again and started across the room, the newspaper crackling in his tight grip.

'I'd rather kill you than hear your confession.' The priest's hand dropped to the table, and the chains clanked on the wood. And now, in the manner of a perfectly rational man, he said, 'But I won't do that.'

The guard stopped and only gaped at the prisoner, not moving any closer. Was this man also frightened of the priest? Perhaps it was no illusion, but—

'You wouldn't mind dying, would you, Dr Cray? The long, sweet sleep? What if the last second of life is the real eternity, expanding out for all time – forever fear, forever guilt. And all that physical pain you're feeling right now? Is your heart bothering you, sir?'

The priest's eyes were following the slow crawl of Mortimer's hand to that place where his organ was hammering wildly out of rhythm.

'The soft gloved hand of Death? Is that how you see it? I don't think so. I see a fist with all the implements of torture – all for you.' Paul Marie leaned forward, hands flat on the table, looming closer.

The guard was edging toward them. His newspaper fell to the floor with a soft rustle.

'Not appealing? So that leaves you with what, *Mortimer*?' The priest spat out the more familiar Christian name. 'To go on living, knowing that children are dying in pain? Can you do that?' Paul Marie rose to his full height. 'Of course you can. What was I thinking? How many times?' The priest pointed one damning finger, but not at the old man's face – at his heart. 'How many children?'

Father Marie, nine feet tall in Mortimer's eyes, sent his hands and chains crashing to the table, and he roared, 'Tell me where those children are!'

Mortimer could feel the hot flush rising in his face, and the tight clenching of the heart muscle, a fist inside his breast. And now his eyes were playing tricks on him again. Flashing white stars shot across his field of vision. Then he saw balls of bright red fire and black lakes. Hysteria heightened to a crescendo as he detected a slow-crawling shadow along a brightly lit wall behind the table. Not the guard's shadow – not the priest's.

Suddenly, a great buzzing filled his ears and grew in volume. He stared up at Paul Marie. The buzzing drowned out his very thoughts; it was deafening, unremitting, insectile. His mind was cracking open, reason and logic escaping him, swept away by mounting terror and panic. The buzzing came from within, and the volume grew as the priest raised his fists high in the air, as though commanding, orchestrating the madness.

Mortimer stumbled to his feet, knocking into the table. He slapped away the guard's outstretched hands. The shadow was all around him now, engulfing him as he fled across the room to the door.

It was locked. *No! No! No!*

He banged his clenched hands against the metal, and the buzzing of a million winged insects drowned out the voice of the worried-looking guard, who was fumbling at the intercom buttons. Mortimer's legs failed him. He ceased to struggle and sank to the ground; his eyes were closing as his gray, sunken cheek met the hard floor. His last clear image was of the priest slowly lowering his hands. Then the buzzing stopped, and the ensuing darkness obscured the Lord of the Flies.

Sadie took the journal from Gwen's limp hand and set it on the stack by the wall of the white room. 'You shouldn't have stayed awake so late.' She looked up at the burnt-out bulb over the door. 'When we hear his car, we'll have to move fast.'

'I'm sorry.' Gwen had fallen asleep propped up against the wall under the only source of light. Every muscle ached, but the leg was a separate pain; it came on quickly with no warning, stabbing, stabbing. She accepted a single pill from Sadie's hand and then the glass jar. She wolfed down the painkiller and looked up to see her friend balancing on the rolling chair from the white room, changing the burnt-out bulb for a new one.

'That was only one pill, Sadie.'

'Why don't we see if that's enough, okay?' She climbed down from the chair and pointed to the trunk of the nearest oak tree. 'So what did your journal lady name that one?'

'She calls it Elvira, after a baby who was killed before she was born. Elvira never even had a gravestone, but now she has an oak tree. I think that's sweet.'

'Oh, yeah? What about the poor Samuel tree?' Sadie was looking at the nearby stand of gnarly logs, limbs from the dead oak, namesake of a soldier. 'Samuel dies, and then she hacks off his arms to make more mushrooms. How sweet is that?'

'I need another pill, Sadie.'

'Give it a little time, okay?'

It was time that frightened her. She could not even bear the expectation of pain. Her leg was throbbing, and when she stood up, she felt the dead weight at the center of her shin where the punctures were. Something had gone horribly wrong with her body, and this thought kept coming back, no matter how fervently she denied that this destruction was part of her. 'What do you think happens after you die?'

'After they bury you? Who cares? The funeral is the main event.' Sadie wheeled the chair back into the white room, and Gwen trailed behind her. 'If you're a cop, they play bagpipes and drape your coffin with a flag. Before they put you in the ground, they fold up the flag and give it to your mom. Pretty cool.' Sadie looked at the burnt-out lightbulb in her hand. 'But now that I've been buried alive, I can't come up with anything to top it.' She hurled the bulb at the wall. It exploded into tiny fragments of a glass shower, and the silver metal base went careening off to a corner.

Sadie no longer cared about putting each thing back in its place. Gwen tried not to think about what this implied, hiding it from her own mind with thoughts of death. 'But, *after* you're buried. What then, Sadie?'

'You're bug food.'

The dog barked, calling for their attention, and they ran out of the room to find him sitting under a tree near the chewed body of clothes and stuffing.

'How long has he been holding that pose?'

Sadie craned her neck to look back through the open door to the clock on the wall. 'Fifteen minutes – a new record.'

'Give him the attack command and another biscuit.'

'Geronimo!' yelled Sadie. The dog hit the body of the dummy and began to gnaw on it. Then he ripped a shoe loose as he whipped the dummy from side to side.

'Call him off before he wrecks it.'

'I thought that was the general idea. Sitting Bull!'

The dog backed off to the trunk of a tree and sat there, waiting on his biscuit. Sadie tossed it to him. He leapt into the air and his jaws clamped on the food. 'Good boy! So, all that reading last night – did you find the dog's name?'

'He doesn't have one.' She had finished scanning all the pages, hunting key words for every reference to the dog. 'When the kennel closed down, the animals were auctioned off by strangers. No registration papers – there wouldn't be any on a mongrel.'

'The journal lady never gave him a name? She had to call him something.'

'She only writes about him as "my friend, the dog". I guess you can call him whatever you want. *The Blood Beast?*'

'*Night of the Blood Beast*, Ross Sturlin, 1958. No good,' said Sadie. 'The dog had a name once. I can't change it.'

Gwen struggled with this, for Sadie had no trouble with naming the man for a famous insect. This might be a measure of her greater respect for the dog, an echo of the journal lady, who had not named him either – she didn't feel she had the right.

Sadie threw him another, unearned biscuit. 'He's as ready as he'll ever be.'

'No, not yet.' *Not ever.* 'We have to be sure he takes orders only from you.' And now that Sadie was less inclined to kill the dog, they might all get out of this together – if they could only hold on until the journal lady came home. 'Maybe tomorrow or the next day.'

Sadie turned on her, and the small pale face was all but screaming, *What? Are you nuts?*

Gwen looked around at the debris of the torn dummy. Plastic bags had come out of the pants and the sweater. All this mess had to be cleaned up. How were they going to retrieve what was lying within the circle of the dog's chain? It would be a mistake to trust the animal within harming distance. And where *was* the man – The Fly? Why hadn't he come back again? 'The Fly must be going crazy wondering where I am. Maybe he figured I went to the police. Maybe he ran away.'

Sadie shook her head very slowly, to say, *No, don't hope for things like that.* Aloud, she said, 'We should change your bandage. It's really dirty.' She pressed one cool hand to Gwen's forehead. 'And you're burning up.'

'I need another pill. My leg *really* hurts.' No – *really*, it only throbbed, but the pain was surely on the way back to get her again.

They walked down the aisle of tables and shelves to the white room and its precious store of pharmacy bottles. Sadie lagged behind for a moment and then caught up. 'Your limp is getting worse.'

'I probably pulled a muscle. Remember when you did that in gym class? You limped for days.'

Sadie preceded her into the room and pulled open the medicine drawer. 'There must be a zillion drugs in here.' She picked up a bottle and perused the label. 'We won't do this one again. I think it's what kept you awake.'

Gwen picked up another bottle and read the label. 'Why don't we try one of these? Flurazepam hydrochloride?'

Sadie gently took it from her hand and put it back. 'No, that's old stuff. The label is all yellow.'

'Here's a newer one, same thing.'

'No.' Sadie's hand covered hers before she could pick it up. 'Read the *whole* label. "One pill at bedtime." That probably means it'll make you fall asleep. Bad timing for that.' Finally she selected one that she approved of and handed over the pill with a fresh jar of water.

The moment Sadie's back was turned, Gwen slipped one more pill from the bottle, and then she caught her friend's eyes on her in the reflection of a glass cupboard. But there was no scolding; Sadie said nothing at all; she only rolled the bottles absently with one finger.

'Is there a name on one of the labels?' Gwen drained the jar of water. She was thirsty all the time now. 'My mother's name is on the pills she takes for migraines.'

Sadie picked up one bottle after the other. 'Most of them

say, "Sample, not for sale". This one has two names. E. Vickers – that's probably your journal lady.'

'And the other name?'

'Dr W. Penny.'

'I know that name,' said Gwen. '*William* Penny. He's in the journals.'

Sadie put the pills back in the drawer, but took no care to leave the labels as she had found them. The child was no longer afraid of discovery. So she meant to use the dog *today*.

But Gwen knew it wasn't going to work. The man was bigger and more frightening to the dog – a superior Alpha wolf. When the man found out what they had done, when he saw this mess, he was going to be so mad.

Sadie knelt on the floor in front of Gwen and unwound the gauze bandage, exposing the puncture wounds to the light. The small holes had not healed; they oozed with yellow-green pus. The surrounding skin was bronze in color, darker today, and the leg was bloated. 'It smells.' Sadie leaned closer to the wound.

Gwen looked away, not wanting to see it. 'E. Vickers. I wonder what the *E* stands for?'

'We have to get out of here. You're getting worse, not better. You need a doctor.'

Gwen picked up the pill bottle from the drawer and stared at the name on the label. 'Dr Penny. Miss Vickers writes about him a lot.'

'Listen to me, Gwen. Your leg—'

'Dr Penny is her heart specialist. He makes lots of house-calls. But Miss Vickers thinks he only comes by to see the hired woman, Rita. She hears them whispering together all the time. Rita is on vacation too. They'll all be back in a few days.'

'Don't count on it. We have to get out of here – soon. The dog is ready.' Sadie was soaping the wound very gently.

A stab of pain made it through the barrier of drugs, and Gwen bit down on her lip until it went away. 'They all go on vacation at the same time every year, Miss Vickers, Rita and Proper William – that's what everyone calls the doctor behind his back.' Another stab. Gwen stared down at the bottle in her clenched hand, willing the pain to end before she cried and broke down, confessing the depth of her cowardice and the terrible cost of it.

But surely Sadie must already know what a fraud her best friend was, for she could add sums, couldn't she? She could figure the length of two sheets torn into halves, how far the bedsheet rope would dangle, how close to the ground. But she never asked why Gwen had not gone out the bathroom window. Gallant Sadie was such a good friend, she was capable of keeping this nasty secret even from herself.

The man was going to be so mad when he found them.

Gwen stared at the container of pills. How many would it take to kill the panic? The bottle was slapped out of her hand as she was opening it. 'What did you do that for?'

Did Sadie look a little frightened? Yes. And now Gwen remembered that she had already taken three pills. Ah, well. She was calmer now, and the pain was gone again. Nothing else mattered.

In Rouge's estimation, Dr Lorimer looked more like a well-to-do undertaker. The heart specialist was dressed in dark and expensive materials, and when he stepped back from Mortimer Cray's bedside, his somber eyes took in the entire patient, as though wondering if body and coffin would be a good fit.

Lorimer's funereal attire was quite a contrast to Myles Penny's wrinkled white coat, mismatched socks and baggy pants. Dr Penny stood at the foot of the bed, staring at sheets of ragged lines scrolling from the mouth of a machine. The general practitioner spoke to his patient with a dismissive tone, suggesting that Mortimer Cray was wasting his time. 'Your old pump isn't any worse off than the last time William examined you. I guess we don't have to crack your chest open today.' He pointed to the heart specialist. 'See? Dr Lorimer's packing up his bag and going home.'

And now Dr Penny turned to Captain Costello and Rouge Kendall. 'I'm forgetting my manners, boys. This here is Ed Lorimer. He's covering my brother's end of the practice this week.'

Lorimer only nodded to the two police officers as he closed his gladstone bag and reached for the door. When the best-dressed doctor had left the room, Captain Costello turned to Myles Penny. 'I'd like to do the interview in private, if you—'

'Not a shot in hell,' said the doctor, frowning. 'I'm staying. Mortimer doesn't need surgery, but he's not quite out of the woods. Find his niece yet?'

'Yeah,' said Costello. 'One of the FBI men tracked her down. He's bringing her over now.'

The patient never stirred in his bed, but he followed the conversation with his eyes. His thin face was nearly as white as the bedding, and Rouge thought the old man looked badly frightened. A heart attack could do that. Or maybe the psychiatrist had another reason to be fearful. Captain Costello's presence here would not be a comfort. The last time they met, the captain had all but accused him of conspiracy to murder a child.

'I promise you', said Costello, 'we'll be brief, but I think he'd be more inclined to—'

'Nope.' Myles Penny settled himself into a chair near the door. He waved his hand at Costello. 'Now you just get on with your business. Don't mind me.' The doctor opened his magazine; the discussion was over.

Rouge leaned back against the wall as Captain Costello pulled the remaining chair close to the patient's bed. Mortimer Cray was staring at the ceiling, not showing any sign of awareness anymore.

'Dr Cray, we believe you can give us helpful information.'

No response. The room was silent, except for the mechanical noises of the equipment by the bed and the rustle of Dr Penny's magazine pages.

Costello waited a moment more, and then he edged his chair closer, scratching and screeching the legs across the floor. He could not be ignored unless the patient was stone deaf, and judging by the old man's pained expression, he was not.

'Dr Cray, was the priest ever one of your patients?'

Mortimer Cray turned his head to look at the man for the first time. 'I can't answer that. Surely you can understand why.'

'No, I can't understand a damn thing anymore, Dr Cray.' Costello was too loud this time, showing too much emotion, and too quickly. Rouge had to wonder if the case was getting to the captain, or was this acting? Costello lowered his voice, more reasonable this time. 'Help me understand. Why won't you give me this lousy little shred of information?'

Rouge understood the psychiatrist's code of ethics. Dr Cray wouldn't allow the police to close in on a patient by process of elimination, not even to the extent of eliminating a man with a prisoner's alibi. He would do nothing to help them.

'If this is a matter of patient confidentiality,' said Costello, 'we can compel you to assist us.'

A small burst of air escaped Dr Cray's cracked lips. A weak attempt at a laugh? Perhaps the old man felt he was beyond the law, closer to death, not believing in the good news of medical science and heart monitors.

The captain reached into his pocket and pulled out his wallet. He opened it to display pictures of two little boys.

Mortimer Cray glanced at the photos and looked away.

'My grandchildren,' said Costello. 'I used to show their baby pictures to everyone.' He put the wallet back in his pocket. 'But I don't do that anymore. None of my investigators do. You see, we're all beginning to think like perverts. Your niece says a lot of little kids died because some freak fell in love with their photographs in a magazine or a newspaper.'

Dr Cray was staring at some dot on the ceiling. He had the look of a trapped animal – too much white in his eyes.

'Gwen Hubble's pictures never appeared in public,' said Costello. 'And I can't see the parents flashing wallet snapshots to strangers. The mother doesn't even have the kid's picture on her desk. Of course, Mrs Hubble lives in the public eye. And I think she realizes that some of the eyes are insane – and the mouths drool. But the pervert didn't need to see a photograph. He lives right here in town, doesn't he, Dr Cray?'

Mortimer Cray was looking at Myles Penny, but the general practitioner was involved in the pages of the *New England Journal of Medicine*. There was no help coming from that quarter.

The door opened, and Ali Cray entered the room. When she looked down at the old man in the bed, she seemed relieved. Agent Arnie Pyle walked in behind her, sporting a black eye, his souvenir from Marsha Hubble's interrogation.

Costello gave no sign that he was even aware of the new visitors. He was totally focussed on Mortimer Cray. 'We've taken statements from Paul Marie and the prison guard. The priest was really angry, wasn't he, sir? I know what set him off. It would be better if you made a statement in your own words.'

Mortimer Cray stared at the ceiling. Costello was at his ear, only inches away. 'It's Christmas Eve. If your niece is right – and she's been right about a lot of things – one of those kids is alive. She'll die on Christmas morning. Isn't that the way it works?'

Ali Cray's reaction was not what Rouge had expected. After the silence had dragged out for a few more seconds, she walked over to the bed. 'Tell him.' When she looked down at the old man, her face displayed no emotion whatever. 'I know this pervert is one of your patients.'

The psychiatrist turned his eyes toward his doctor again. And now Myles Penny closed his medical journal and set it down on a low table. 'Ali, if that's the case, you're wasting your time. He'll never tell you anything about a patient. You know that.'

The general practitioner stood up and moved Ali to one side, as though she were a piece of furniture. He leaned down and held a pen light to each of Mortimer Cray's eyes. 'Ethical conduct is Mortimer's religion. Isn't that right, you old bastard?' The insult was almost endearing. 'He'll never give up the name of that patient. Am I right, Mortimer?'

The old man nodded his head. And then his eyes widened, for he had just confirmed Ali's charge; he had been duped by his own physician. The patient's head pressed deep into the pillows, and judging from his expression, Rouge guessed the unspoken sentiment was some genteel variation on *Oh, shit.*

Myles Penny seemed rather pleased by the success of this gambit. Costello certainly was. Rouge had more difficulty assessing Ali's state of mind. She was so utterly without emotion. And then he understood this as extreme control, and she was about to lose it. The stress was showing in her eyes.

She leaned over the bed. 'Give it up, Uncle Mortimer. A name, a place – something.' Ali's face was close to her uncle's. She was the only woman in Rouge's experience who could scream with a whisper. 'I know Gwen Hubble is alive. That's the pattern. There's still hope for one child.'

Myles Penny shook his head to say, *No use,* as he moved down to the foot of the bed and picked up a chart chained to the iron frame. 'Damn waste of time, Ali. A hundred little girls could die before he ever told you a thing.'

Ali Cray was nodding as she glared at her uncle. Rouge sensed a line of tension strung out between these two people; it was taut and tightening. Mortimer Cray appeared to be anticipating something, drawing in his frail shoulders, bracing. The room was so quiet. One gnarly finger tapped the blanket, perhaps keeping to the beat of some inner clock, ticking off the passing seconds. And now the old man closed his eyes against whatever might happen to him; some act was impending.

Agent Pyle had been quiet through all of this. He was looking at Ali with something approaching tenderness, even as she raised her hand to strike the utterly helpless old man on the bed.

'Ali!' Myles Penny dropped the chart, and it swung by its chain.

Rouge read a mix of sorrow and frustration in the simple motion of Ali Cray's arm slowly dropping to her side.

Costello abruptly stood up and moved his chair to the wall, making a great show of preparing to leave. He turned back to the man on the bed. 'Just one more thing, sir. Why did you visit the priest today? Just tell me if Paul Marie was ever a patient.'

Mortimer Cray opened his eyes, but said nothing.

'No, he wasn't my uncle's patient,' said Ali. 'Father Marie was never in therapy of any kind.'

'Not even as a prisoner?' Costello seemed dubious. 'I thought the therapy program was mandatory for the perverts.'

'No, it's voluntary,' she said. 'According to the warden, Father Marie never participated.'

The captain was unconvinced. 'That's odd, isn't it, Ali? I know a therapy program carries weight with the parole board.'

'I know. That's the reason most prisoners go along with it. But not Father Marie.' Ali looked down at Mortimer again. 'I interviewed the priest. He has a dim view of psychiatrists – takes them for prancing con artists, all smoke and mirrors.' She turned back to Costello. 'So he would never have sought out my uncle. Don't you see? It had to be the other way around.'

And now they had a brand-new game. Costello moved back to the bedside. 'The priest said you knew who the perp was. So we can—'

'He never told you anything.' Mortimer Cray looked up at the captain, with a brief, bitter flicker of a smile.

249

'You don't think so?' Costello was incredulous. 'Why? Because he used to be a priest?'

'He *is* a priest.' Mortimer Cray said this quietly, but with unmistakable conviction. 'You called him that yourself, Captain. The *priest* never said anything.'

'You're right,' said Costello. 'It was the guard. *He* said you could tell us where the kids were.'

Ali Cray stepped back to the bedside and bent low over her uncle. 'Was Father Marie your confessor?'

The old man looked away, refusing to meet her eyes.

With one hand, she turned his face to hers, and she was not gentle. 'Am I right, Uncle Mortimer? You wanted the priest to break his oath because you wouldn't break yours?' Rouge could see the deep indents Ali's fingers were making in the crepe flesh of her uncle's face. 'You weren't there for religious reasons – not you, the professional atheist. *Talk* to me!'

'That's enough!' Myles Penny was standing close behind her. 'Ali, don't press your luck with me, or I'll push you right out the door.'

Ali didn't seem to hear him, though she moved her hand to rest on the pillow beside Mortimer Cray's head. 'Did you confess to the priest? Did you tell Father Marie who it was?' Her hand drifted to her uncle's chest, a none too subtle threat to an old man with a heart condition.

'Uncle Mortimer, what kind of trophy did the killer take from Gwen Hubble? Has he told you yet? Or does he always wait until the child is dead?' She gripped him by the shoulders, as if she intended to shake the answer out of him. 'Gwen is only ten years old!'

Mortimer Cray's eyes were wide and staring in disbelief, full of horror. His head shook from side to side, and he began to thrash under her hands.

Myles Penny was true to his promise, grabbing Ali by the shoulders and roughly pulling her back from the bed. She didn't resist him while he ungently propelled her to the door and pushed her into the corridor. Now he silently motioned the others to follow suit.

Rouge was the last visitor to quit the room, closing the door behind him as Dr Penny was filling a syringe from a bottle. The last thing he heard was the doctor saying, 'This anxiety is going to kill you, Mortimer.' And then he heard a soft moan from the patient, which he took for affirmation.

'Don't even try to bullshit me. I know all about the boys with the gun.' Investigator Sorrel was holding the local police report over the head of the medical examiner. 'Doc, I gotta wonder who leaned on you.'

'What? Buddy, will you talk sense?' Dr Howard Chainy pushed his chair away from the desk and adjusted his glasses, as if this would help him to see the BCI man's logic more clearly.

'The local police chief says you told him to leave the kids and the gun out of his incident report.'

'The *gun*? Oh, Jesus Christ, Buddy, it was only a damn pellet gun. A kid's toy. The boys broke a window and found a dead body – three *days* dead. Now that's all there was to it.' He turned back to the mass of paperwork on his desk.

'Then why go out of your way to withhold—'

'The people in this town just love their rumors about St Ursula's,' said Dr Chainy. 'If you stir this thing up that silly toy will turn into a full-blown tank gun before the week is out.'

'You could save me a trip out to the house, if I could just nail down the loose ends.'

Chainy shook his head in disbelief. 'You're not really going to waste any more of my time with this nonsense, are you?'

Investigator Sorrel was planning to do just that, for he was one neat ex-marine. His wife always deferred to him in the chore of making the bed in the morning, for he could bounce a marble off the blankets when he was done. How he hated the sight of wrinkles in the fabric, loose threads on a bedspread, and loose ends in a police report. Unanswered questions made him totally crazy and a very good policeman. He would go to the freaking moon to nail down one inconsistency.

Yes, he was a damn tidy man and royally pissed off. The incident on the lake might have nothing to do with the case at hand. According to the report, every room of the house had been thoroughly searched by the chief and two local cops. But there were *loose* ends. 'Whose idea was it to amend the report? Yours or that school dir—'

'Mine. Satisfied?'

No, he wasn't.

Howard Chainy smiled, almost evil for a moment, then raised his voice. 'So, how goes the great *truffle* hunt, Buddy?'

The doctor's assistant looked up from his work at the next table. Chainy had promised to keep the truffle angle quiet, but he was bordering on blackmail. The pathologist spun around on his stool to face the young man in the lab coat. 'Hastings? You ever hear of doing an autopsy on a damn fungus?' And this was a blatant threat.

Sorrel pushed through the swinging doors of the autopsy room and stormed down the hall leading to the parking lot. He passed through another set of doors that closed behind him with maddening slowness. Finally, outside in the parking lot, his car door made the satisfying slam that his angry exit from the building had denied him.

It had been a long morning of irritations. Another BCI investigator had been assigned to oversee the daily logs of the local police department, and the man had not cared that the bones of this particular incident report were suspiciously bare. The local chief of police had been entirely too blasé about filling in the missing pieces, as he had not yet finished collecting them. More irritation. And now the damned medical examiner, supposedly on the same side of the law – that old bastard was holding out on him, *threatening* him.

Driving back to the station house, Sorrel was not any calmer as he moved on to the next loose end. The deceased householder had a cleaning lady, but no one had questioned this woman. A village cop, Phil Chapel, had been on that search party, and according to Chief Croft, this officer had been in charge of tracking down the hired woman to find out why she never reported the death of her employer. 'Closest neighbor says she's on vacation' read the badly typed line of the report – not even a name for the woman. And the cop had made three typos in a single sentence; this alone was cause to despise the little weasel, sight unseen.

Sorrel used his car phone to call the state trooper manning the front desk at the station house. The trooper assured him the local police patrol was due to check in, and Officer Chapel would not be allowed to escape until the senior BCI investigator arrived to take a shot at him.

Fifteen minutes later, Sorrel was seated at his desk in the second-floor makeshift squad room. The place was deserted. Everyone else was out on assignment, and the civilian secretary was not at her post.

Officer Phil Chapel was standing at attention. He was very young and had the look of a guilty child; he knew he had done something wrong, but hadn't a clue as to what that might be.

'What about the cleaning lady?' Sorrel barked; Chapel flinched.

'She's more like general help, sir. She cooked and—'

'Where's her statement?'

'She won't be back in town till the day after Christmas, sir.'

'You didn't want to disturb her while she was on vacation. How sweet. You don't even have a name for this woman, do you, Chapel?'

'Ah, no, sir. The neighbor on the west side never mentioned it. The hired woman didn't take anything from the house, so I didn't—'

'And the old lady who died? What about her family?' Sorrel

held up the single, uncompleted page of the incident report. 'There's nothing here to say they were ever notified.'

'I thought the chief was going to take care of that, sir.'

'Charlie Croft says he told *you* to do it.'

'I guess he did, sir. But you see, her regular doctor was on vacation. So without—'

'Never mind, Chapel. Let's get back to the hired woman. You think the neighbor knows where we can reach her?'

'No, sir. She takes her vacation the same time as the old mushroom lady. But she never says where—'

'The old *what*?'

'The *dead woman*, sir,' said Chapel, perhaps thinking he had messed up with the informality of a nickname.

'You said *mushroom* lady.'

'Well, the whole house was full of mushrooms, sir. Little statues, drawings. All those books with mushrooms on the covers.'

'Son, did you see an actual, edible mushroom?'

'No, sir, not a damn one.'

'How could you let my uncle go home?'

'Oh, *now* you're concerned.' Myles Penny talked out of the side of his mouth, never looking up from the desk as his pencil moved across the open pages of his appointment calendar. 'It wasn't my decision to send him home. That was Mortimer's call.' He pushed the papers to one side and tapped his pencil on the blotter, indicating that he had more pressing business to get on with, and that Ali Cray should get out of his office – this minute.

'Myles, the man just had a heart attack.'

'Well, no he didn't. Your uncle had a massive *anxiety* attack. It all fits – the vision problems, the buzzing, the chest pain. Probably couldn't catch his breath, and that brought on the blackout.' He shrugged his shoulders to say, *Enough?*

'When I saw him, he looked about two inches away from death.'

'Well, he's *not.*' Myles was more irritable now, and she could guess why. Her worries would not ring true, not after her performance in the sickroom. The doctor was an excellent judge of character.

'After I talked to Dr Lorimer, I got a second opinion – your uncle's. Old Mortimer diagnosed his own symptoms. Nobody in town's better qualified. He'll live a good long while if he stays on the medication William prescribed.' And something in his eyes said, *Not that you care.*

'Can't you reach William?'

'Wouldn't know where to try, Ali. Now Dr Lorimer's a good man. He always covers William's heart patients, and he hasn't lost one yet. Trust me, the diagnosis is sound. He'll be miles more comfortable at home – if you wanna be a good sport and not tell the cops where to find him. You don't really think he's involved in this, do you?'

'I don't know what to think,' she lied. 'I'm sorry about the way I acted.' Another lie.

'Ali, if there's nothing else I can do for—'

'Doesn't William's service have a number where he can be reached?'

'I wish they did. Every time William leaves town, it's hell around here. Every damn one of his patients knows the day he's gonna leave town. And then the perverse little bastards start calling in every ache and pain you could imagine. Now I told you, Lorimer is a good—'

'I believe you, but I was thinking of something else. Maybe you can help me. There's a question I forgot to ask William the last time I—'

'Is this about Susan Kendall?'

'Yes. I know it was a long time ago, but when he filled in for Howard Chainy—'

'You're wondering why a top-ranked surgeon took on the job as acting medical examiner? He owed Howard a favor, Ali. They go back a long way.'

'No. I was thinking about the test for the monozygotic

twins. He needed a blood sample from each child to prove that, didn't he? Did the parents consent to—'

'No, my brother did *not* ask the parents if he could blood-suck their only remaining child.'

'So how did he manage the test?'

'No idea. Unless he kept a blood sample from the previous winter. William stitched Rouge's finger back on after an accident. Now when was that? I guess the boy was nine years old.'

'I was there,' said Ali. 'He took a fall on the ice, and another skater ran over his hand.'

'Well, the priest brought him straight here in a car. Smart man, even if he is a damn pervert. Didn't wait for our crack ambulance crew that can't find its way from one end of town to another. The boy's finger was almost severed. Now William is one fine surgeon, no matter what part of the body he's stitching. In fact, he was probably the only doctor for fifty miles who could've done an operation that delicate. The human hand is a major surgical challenge, tricky as hell. But afterwards, the boy's finger had full mobility. A real nice job.'

'Did Susan come in with her brother?'

'Are you kidding? We couldn't pry the twins apart. It was William's idea to let Susan stay for the operation. Oh, I know, he comes off as a self-important twit. But he's very sensitive to every kind of pain. He was planning emergency surgery with a local anesthetic, and I guess he figured one twin would calm the other.'

'You think that's when William suspected they were mono-zygotic?'

'I'm sure they piqued his curiosity. Except for the haircuts, the Kendall kids were identical. I've seen a fair share of twins, but nothing like that pair. Let me tell you the eerie part. Susan was in pain too, and showing symptoms of shock. None of that psychosomatic bullshit. She was *feeling* pain. I gave Rouge the local anesthetic while we were prepping him for surgery. The nurse was gowning and masking Susan – so the little girl never saw that needle. But the anesthetic also worked on her. It was like treating one child with two bodies.'

Ali wondered if Rouge had felt pain while his sister was dying. Could he have known the moment when her neck was broken? Had the little boy experienced a sympathetic death?

Myles stood up, and this time there should be no misunderstanding that he meant to throw her out. Charm had never been his forte. She lifted one hand in a listless goodbye and left the room, pulling the door closed behind her.

She had told Arnie Pyle not to wait for her, but there he was, seated in the clinic reception area, half concealed by the fronds of a potted palm. His black eye was hidden by the spread pages of a newspaper, perhaps to dodge the queries of patients and visitors. Arnie had not volunteered any explanation for the dark bruise. She had decided it must be a sore point, something he took no macho pride in, and tactfully, she left it alone. But when he stood up and emerged from the palm fronds, she was startled anew.

There was something very wrong here.

The other day, she had thought nothing of the smirk; it fit so well with his sarcasm. But now he still smiled with only half his mouth. There had been several years of angry distance between them, and Ali truly could not remember if he had always smiled in this odd way. In a disturbing flight of fancy, she wondered if he could have picked up this mannerism during that year of living with her, as though this mirror image of her own twisted mouth might be the result of close association – a contagion of damage.

The smile evaporated quickly. Perhaps he was embarrassed – caught with a genuine emotion. The agent jammed his hands into his pants pockets and made his stand in the center of the room. 'Gonna tell me what you and Dr Penny talked about? I always share with you.'

'Sure you do.' She intended to walk past him, but he

moved to block her way. 'All right, Arnie. It was a consultation.'

'For the scar? Cool. So, it isn't hereditary, is it? Like maybe you had a gigantic mole removed? I'm just thinking about our kids, Ali. But I guess we could always adopt.'

'Yeah, I'm trying to picture baby drunks staggering around the house and throwing up on the carpet.' Did that sound bitter? She hoped so.

His half smile was back. 'I cleaned your carpet, Ali – on my hands and knees. You forget these little things.'

He moved toward her, and she took two steps back. It was the same old dance. 'You're right, Arnie. And the time you vomited on my shoes, you bought me new shoes.' To hell with tact. She pointed to his black eye. 'How did you get that?'

He waved it off. 'Oh, the usual thing.'

'A *woman* did that to you?'

'But she didn't have your touch, Ali. And I never loved her. It was just a fling, a little meaningless brutality on the side.' He pulled out a pack of cigarettes and lit one. 'Okay, fight's over. You got anything solid on this sick bastard?'

'You're breaking the law, Arnie. This is a public building.'

'What've you got? Speak up, or I'll blow a smoke ring – right here, right now. And then I might get a little crazy and drop an ash on the rug.'

'But you don't like my theories. You said as much in a room full of cops and feds. Why don't you ask the team from Quantico?'

'You know I don't let the witch doctors mess with my cases. If you've got something on this lunatic, I wanna hear it. Or I could go have a chat with your dear old uncle.' He was smiling again. 'You really think he's treating this pervert?'

'The pervert is a *sadist*. Concentrate on that.' She could not stop staring at his mouth. 'He'd get off on sharing the kill with a psychiatrist. It would be a rush for him – immediate gratification.' *Please stop smiling, Arnie.* 'It would extend the circle of victims beyond the child and her family. He could draw out the sadism as long as he liked – almost heaven.'

'So our perp tortures the shrink, and the shrink can only unload on a priest.'

'Right.' *Or another psychiatrist.* And now she stopped to wonder why Uncle Mortimer had not taken that route. However, this was not an idea to explore with Arnie Pyle. 'But going to a psychiatrist doesn't mean the pervert is insane, just smart and sadistic – much like yourself.'

'Thank you. But if you're right about all those other cases, you gotta know this guy is royally screwed up.'

'Tell me if I've got this wrong, Arnie. You think he's mentally incompetent because his fantasy revolves around a little princess. Are *you* crazy because you have wet dreams about a supermodel knocking on your door to ask you for sex?'

'So you're saying he's just more *realistic?*'

'It's all about control.' She stared at the cigarette in his hand and avoided looking at his face again. 'That's why he favors a small target. He has absolute control over a child. In your fantasy, you're all sweaty and grateful to the goddess. In his scenario, he's a god.'

'Okay, twisted but sane. So how do you like the death penalty *now*, Ali?'

'My feelings haven't changed.'

'Oh, come off it. You want this freak dead as bad as I do.'

'When the Russians increased the penalties for pedophilia, the freaks killed more of the children. Call me a fool, Arnie, but I think the parents would rather get the kids back alive.'

And now they realized there was someone standing close to them and listening to every word, quietly, politely waiting until they were done. It was Rouge Kendall, whose sister had not come back alive. He inclined his head to say hello to her. 'The woman at the desk told me your uncle was released from the clinic.' He was pointedly ignoring Arnie Pyle.

What had Arnie done to antagonize this man?

'Rouge? Could you keep that to yourself for a while? Dr Penny doesn't think my uncle's up to another interrogation.'

'Sure, no problem. But there's one more thing – if you've got a minute.' The young investigator was speaking to her but looking at the FBI man. Arnie only smiled at him, pretending to be too obtuse to allow them any privacy.

Rouge was more graceful, only *thinking* the word *asshole*, only making this opinion clear with his expression, and thus refusing to engage in Arnie's favorite game – Two Dogs Barking. The young cop turned to Ali. 'Back in the hospital room, you said the pervert takes trophies. That wasn't in the case notes you gave us.'

'Costello's idea. He didn't want the details of the trophies floating around in fifty printed copies.'

'So you have a list?'

Ali nodded. Slipping her arm through his, she led him to the far side of the room and away from the hearing of clinic visitors and the FBI agent. She looked back at Arnie. The command in her eyes said, *Stay.*

'Your man only takes very small items, Rouge. One was a ring. Another child was missing a tiny pin shaped like a flower. Other things – a religious medal, a fine gold chain with a single pearl. Always something delicate.'

'So this wouldn't fit?' He pulled a piece of silver from his pocket and held it out to her. 'This was used as evidence against the priest. It's my sister's bracelet.'

Ali accepted the proffered jewelry and turned it over in her hand. The circular opening was very small, but the silver was in a broad, flat design, and it was heavy in her hand. 'I guess it's possible. But this would be the largest thing he ever took. If this was all she had on her, but you—'

'I know. I read the list of Susan's personal effects. There was a religious medal around her neck. So he should have taken that before he took the bracelet, right?'

Ali nodded. They both knew Susan was still wearing the medal when they found her body.

'There was something else,' said Rouge. 'I gave Susan an ankle chain when I left for military school. She wore it every day, but under her sock, so no one else would know about it. That's what she said in her letters – that's the way she put it. The chain was thin, very fragile, with a small engraved oval of gold.'

'Then that's the trophy. If you find the anklet, you'll find the man who killed her.'

'You wouldn't actually need the ankle chain to find him,' said Arnie Pyle. He had crept into their space.

Ali glared at the agent to say, *Bad boy.* 'He's right, Rouge. You only need to find a man who knew she wore it. Unless she told someone in the family or a—'

'Even my parents didn't know. It was just between us.'

Ali imagined the delicate chain on the small ankle of a ten-year-old girl, a tiny secret beneath a white sock, gleaming warm against her skin, something her twin had given her with the sweet love of a child. She could see Susan's murderer taking it out every night and using it to relive the violation and the murder. Perhaps he masturbated when he held it.

Buddy Sorrel parked his car by the access road. He walked down the long driveway to the lakehouse, looking to his right and left for signs of mushrooms. According to the tax assessor's aerial photographs, there was no atrium on this property. The BCI investigator felt like a fool wasting his time here, but the captain had made him the official mushroom man, and all the details of fungus were now his province.

Maybe he should call out a patrol car to help him search the woods for a grower's shed. The trees could hide such a structure from the tax office aerial photographs.

No, scratch that idea. The captain wouldn't like it if he tipped this lead to one of the uniforms. And even with a hundred state troopers, he wouldn't find the elusive truffle in a search above ground. That particular fungus would be hiding in the earth, possibly keeping company with a small corpse.

However, oaks were plentiful along this private road, and Dr Mortimer Cray, amateur botanist, had claimed the roots of these trees were vital to the growth of truffles. Could a dog sniff them out? The Canine Corps could sniff out explosives – why not truffles?

What was he going to accomplish here? Probably nothing. Three local cops had searched the house, and evidence of two kids could not have escaped them. But the loose ends must be tied.

After clearing a bend of evergreen trees, he could see the entire ramble of the house, a sprawling, bastard thing of wooden walls joining brick ones and linking to a common plane of rough stone four stories high. He hung back by the trees and stared up at the fourth floor. There was a bit of white material sticking out from the sash of a closed window, waving in the breeze like a nagging three-dimensional metaphor for the despicable, intolerable loose end.

He walked up the flagstone path to the back door. The property seal was fixed to the doorframe. On closer inspection, he knew the adhesive material had been peeled back and replaced several times.

Well, that could be kids. In his younger days as a beat cop, he had spent a lot of nights routing teenagers out of the damndest places.

He reached up to the ledge over the door and found the key where the local police chief had left it. However, Chief Croft could not be sure that he had actually bothered to lock the door. According to the chief, some older residents of Makers Village didn't even own keys to their original turn-of-the-century locks.

Sorrel ripped off the tape and tried the knob. The door opened with ease. He walked into the kitchen, which should have been on the other side of the house, for the back doors were usually lakeside. He looked around at the dust settling on stacks of mushroom cookbooks at the center of the kitchen table. And on the wall was a clock in the shape of a common toadstool. Too bad Costello had held this aspect back from the uniforms. He could have sent a trooper on this wild-goose chase.

Sorrel headed for the stairs, mindful of the shifting directions as he climbed a twisting route toward the fourth floor, where he had seen the white material sticking out at him like a tongue. When he entered the bedroom at the top of the stairs, he knew there was something wrong with the floor plan. Well, a lot was wrong with it, given the careless architecture of the house and all its add-ons. But one thing troubled him: there was no window where he expected to see one. He stepped back into the hall to get his bearings by the window at the end of the corridor. Odd. He returned to the corner bedroom. Only one of its walls had windows.

And now he noted a rectangle of brighter wallpaper next to the large armoire, and this large, light patch was shaped with the wardrobe's rounded corners. So the heavy piece of furniture had been recently moved. He reached around the back of it, but his hand would not fit into the narrow crack of space between the wood and the wall. He rocked the armoire on its front legs, intending to slide it to one side, but it toppled to the hardwood floor. Riding over the sound of the crash, he thought he heard a car engine out in the yard. But the door behind the armoire had his full attention.

When he turned the knob, the door would not open. And now the old house suddenly became miles more interesting. This door was locked, while the downstairs door was open to any tramp who happened by. The wood panel was solid construction, and he was not about to break his foot trying to kick it in. He wrestled with the weight of the toppled armoire and moved it out of his way. Once he had space enough to maneuver, he put all his strength behind the twist of the knob to force the metal lock. It was an old mechanism, and it broke easily. The door opened on to a large bathroom with a second armoire pulled out from a window. A loop of knotted sheet dangled from the windowsill. One end was caught in the sash, and the other end was tied to a back leg of the wardrobe. And now he saw the remnants of a cot, its crumpled canvas and broken slats.

Somewhere beyond this room, he thought he heard the creak of wood. He stood very still. Then he heard it again. Something stirred on the floor below, or was it on the stairs? He stopped to listen for a few seconds more, but heard no further noise.

Well, old houses had old bones; their joints gave in to every breeze and creaked with the motion. And these centenarians were not airtight, but breathed in and out. He decided it was only the wind, nothing more.

He was reaching for his cell phone to call for the troopers when his eyes focussed on something else. Sorrel knelt down beside the discarded cot canvas. He plucked up one long blond strand of baby-fine hair and held it up to the light – so delicate, so bright.

The strand of gold was the last thing he ever saw; the blow to the back of his head was that swift, that sure.

Minutes had passed since they heard the car engine pulling up to the house. Gwen carried the stack of journals, moving slowly, awkwardly.

'Help me, Sadie.' She deposited her load on the countertop and limped out of the white room and down the wide aisle of tables toward the trees. 'We've got to put everything back the way it was. If he sees this mess—' And now she stopped, dismayed. Too many bits of the dummy's head and torso lay within the dog-chain circle. An unholy mess was this body of an artificial man.

Where had Sadie gone?

Gwen got down on her knees and stretched out her body. Lying flat on her stomach, she batted the head with the broomstick. The dog held his Sitting Bull pose, but she knew better than to trust him. After she snagged the head, she stared at the rest of the torso beyond her reach, pondering how to

264

recover it. 'And all that stuffing.' Gwen could see the shredded bits of the plastic bags strewn everywhere.

'Not enough time to clean up,' said Sadie, appearing beside her. 'And it doesn't matter anymore. When The Fly comes through the door, we'll put the dog on him.'

'No, the dog's not ready.'

The dog was waiting on his biscuit. Sadie threw it to him. He leapt into the air and snatched it with amazing speed and sureness. Then he pranced to the limit of his chain, eager for another round of Geronimo and Sitting Bull.

'The dog's ready. We have to do it now. You need a doctor.'

Gwen held the felt head in her hand, squeezing the material. 'No, it's too soon. We can't do this.' She slowly sank down to the ground and sat cross-legged, staring at the ceiling until the brilliant light burned her eyes.

Sadie hunkered down beside her. 'Why doesn't he come down?' Now she was also looking at the ceiling. 'What do you think he's doing up there?'

'I don't think he's in the house.' She hugged herself with tight-wrapped arms.

'But the car hasn't pulled out yet.'

How could she explain to Sadie that she could not feel the man anymore. He was somewhere else now, and she was sure of it. So there was more time to clean up the mess. 'The dog needs another—'

'Look at me.' Sadie put her hands on Gwen's shoulders. 'You don't want to do this. You're the one who isn't ready, and you never will be. You're still waiting for someone to come and get us.'

'Okay, you're right! And you know why? Because it isn't going to work. This is not a movie. It's real! He's not The Fly, Sadie. He's a *real* living man. You can't kill him, you can't even hurt him. All you can do is give us away.' She gripped her friend's arm, pleading now. 'He'll be so mad, Sadie. We have to wait till—'

'We can't wait any longer. Your leg is getting worse all the time.'

Gwen folded up, drawing in her knees, pressing both hands over her ears. She disowned her leg and its darkening flesh, its foul smell. She shut her eyes, until she felt Sadie's hand on her hair, stroking her, calming her.

'Okay, we'll put everything back the way it was.' Sadie stood up and walked over the invisible edge of the dog's circle. She was holding the broom and keeping one eye on the dog. She stretched the broomstick out to the torso and began to nudge it back toward her.

The dog came at her, stealthy, head low to the ground. Surprised, Sadie could only stare, taking slow backward steps not wanting to turn away from the animal.

'Don't look directly at him.' Gwen tried to keep the panic from her voice as she crawled to the edge of the circle, making no sudden movements to set off the animal. 'When you look at him, he takes that as a challenge. Stand sideways and look at me.'

Too late – there was a light in the animal's eyes, a hint of something crafty from out of the woods, out of the wild. His muscles were bunching, tensing. And now he was almost in flight, running fast. Sadie thrust out the broom handle. The dog stopped short, taking the wood pole in his teeth and splintering it as he dragged it backward and Sadie with it. She dropped the handle and ran back to the edge of the circle, just ahead of the dog's snapping teeth.

Sadie stood beyond the dog's reach and watched him straining at his chain, wanting to get at her. She was shaking.

Gwen slowly got to her feet, crying and yelling at once. 'You see? You don't know what you're doing!' And now the wounded leg failed her. She fell to the dirt and lay there, pounding the ground with one closed fist. 'It won't work! Can't you *see* that? The dog won't hold a pose.' She was screaming now. 'He'll rush the man before he gets a chance to prop the door open. Then when the man figures out what we did—' Her voice was lower, full of anger and frustration. 'Then he's going to hurt us *really bad*, Sadie. It's stupid, just *stupid* to think this is going to work.'

Sadie looked as though she had just been slapped by her best friend. Her face was white. 'I'm sorry.' The child's voice was smaller now, almost a whisper, and her eyes were full of hurt. 'I'm doing the best I can.'

Christmas Eve services were being held in the prison chapel, but Paul Marie was not in attendance. He stared out the window at the gray walls of an air shaft.

His most constant visitor had been inadvertently amusing tonight. At the end of their hour together, Father Domina had wished him a very merry Christmas and a happy and prosperous New Year. The elderly priest had detected no irony in the prisoner's sudden hilarity. The good old man had even taken great pleasure in Paul Marie's tears as they rolled down the laughing man's face.

Years ago, Jane Norris had also been a steady visitor. Their old love had become corrupted over time, but not entirely dispensed with, not on every level. He still had dreams about her body, but not her soul.

At his trial, she had seen it as her Christian duty to stand up in a public courtroom and tell every detail of their teenage couplings, the exact number of penetrations – not how many times they had made love. In her sworn testimony it had seemed very important to Jane that she had been his first – penetration.

For ten years, she had visited the prison, faithfully, religiously, using her allotted time to pray aloud for his soul, murdering it with each dryly uttered word of forgiveness for every act of love. Jane had never married, never taken another lover. She had become rather like an insane nun in her devotions to his salvation.

Five years ago, she had died by her own hand, and he sometimes wondered if it had been a sane act done in her only lucid moment of the decade. Perhaps toward the end of her life, unlike Father Domina, Jane had finally grasped irony – and then put her head in that oven.

Other people had replaced her in the visitors' room, most of them policemen wanting to close old homicide cases with similar characteristics. And every two years, a different FBI agent would come by to chat for an hour and then go away with nothing for his trouble. The priest was far from lonely.

Even now he had a companion. The shadow under his bed was a constant presence, a reminder that his own mind was far from stable. This evening, he had given up the fight to call the thing by its true name – insanity. He accepted it now, and at the same time, he despised this debased entity, so smitten with him that it lay on the floor of his cell only to be near him.

The shadow had forgiven Mortimer Cray.

And the priest? He never would – never.

The shadow was apparently less sure of this, for hope emanated from the darkness under the bed.

The Christmas bells of three churches were tolling in the distance. Mortimer Cray stood in the greenhouse among his flowers, beholding a young fruit tree he had raised from a seedling. Its shape was almost feminine, thick leaves rounding out its form in an hour-glass essence of the Lady Nature, the deity he loved best.

He looked away from the tree and turned inward to listen to the more insistent Old Testament God, a petulant Being prone to temper tantrums, Who was always shooting craps with the Devil and losing, then taking His losses out on the faithful. Poor Job had the bad luck to be created in the wrong half of the Bible.

Mortimer looked down on his shaking hands. He should have died years ago. Keeping him alive so long was the ultimate sadism. A gun lay in the top drawer of his bedside table. He visualized it in his hand and raised one finger to his temple, but failed with a sudden trembling, too much the coward to pull an imagined trigger.

Now a movement in the greenhouse glass had his full attention. Someone out in the yard was staring at him. It was a smooth young face so like Susan Kendall's. Mortimer stepped backward and knocked a plant off the table. The pot shattered in a hundred pieces, but his attention was riveted on the young policeman beyond the transparent wall.

Rouge Kendall had been his youngest patient, the one he held responsible for the resurrection of his own long-dormant emotions. All through the long process of grief counseling, the child had unwittingly tortured his doctor by crying with Susan's eyes, innocently opening up Mortimer's soft underbelly, forcing him to empathize with a ten-year-old's pain.

It seemed that young Rouge had lost his sister and then lost his sanity on the following day. The little boy had sat with his doctor, expressing fears over the selection of Susan's small custom casket, for it left her no room to grow. Rather than point out the irrationality of this idea, Mortimer had interceded with the parents to give Susan an adult's casket. At the time, he thought they would find the request absurd, but they had ordered it without protest to quell the anxiety of their living child.

At the service, he had been appalled by the effect of that tiny girl lost in the cavernous space of the white satin lining. His meddling had been a tragic mistake. He whispered a few words of apology to her corpse. And then, just for a blurred moment, her image had doubled, and he believed he had seen two children lying together. He had rubbed his eyes and told himself this was only stress. Or was it an insight into the dark mind and desires of the surviving twin? A hidden agenda for the larger casket? Suicidal ideation in a ten-year-old boy?

When faulty vision had corrected itself, and Susan was restored to her singular self, he had looked everywhere for her brother and found the child at the edge of the mourning crowd. Rouge was watching him with grave suspicion, as though, in the previous moment, he been staring at Mortimer from the casket – from Susan's point of view.

Muddled old fool. This was no child in the window glass, but a full-grown man. Rouge was reaching into his coat, exposing the gun in its holster.

Yes, let's get this done and quickly.

But it was not a gun that the young policeman was holding up to the glass. It was a black-and-white portrait of two little girls with their arms entwined around one another. He secured the paper to the window with bits of tape.

Mortimer had seen these posters everywhere in town, yet now it took him forever to read the single word below the photograph: Please.

When he lifted his eyes from the page, Rouge Kendall was gone.

In the smoky light of Dame's Tavern, Rouge put up one hand to hail the bartender, then pointed to his companion, Arnie Pyle, who needed another round of bourbon.

The FBI agent was still apologizing for his ignorance. 'I swear, I had no idea your sister was a kidnap victim. I never saw any material on her case.'

'The State Police found the killer on their own, and pretty quick. There was no reason to call in the FBI.'

'Short shot me again,' said the agent to the waiting bartender. 'Really thin it out this time, okay? Watered-down bourbon is my version of abstinence.'

When Pyle's drink arrived on the coaster in front of him, it was already paid for. The bartender pointed to a silver-haired man at the end of the bar. Julian Garret lifted his own glass in salute, drained it and walked away. The FBI man seemed relieved as he watched Garret's progress toward the door. Then he swiveled his stool around to face Rouge. 'So we have a deal? From now on we share?'

They clinked glasses to seal a bargain that Rouge had not actually agreed to.

'Good.' Pyle took a healthy swig from his glass. 'I already know what you got from Caruthers. The old access road down-shore from the boathouse? I hear the BCI techs pulled a few tire molds from the tracks.'

Rouge nodded. He was not inclined to elaborate.

'So you figure that's where the perp stashed his car,' said Pyle. 'Nice work. Now here's the deal. You get me those molds and the FBI lab will tell you where the perp shops for tires – and real fast. Our guys are the best.'

'No, you don't want those molds.' Rouge smiled, aiming at coyness and succeeding, for the agent was already rearranging himself on the stool and cocking his mouth for an argument. Rouge put up one hand to stop him. 'We only got fragments of tracks. Maybe ten or twelve different tire treads and some partial shoe prints.'

'We can do a lot with that, kid. The lab can tell you—'

'Arnie, I already know where most of them came from. That road leads to the foundations of a burnt-out house. It's a hangout for teenagers. They drink beer, smoke a little weed.'

'Our guys could still make a pass for fibers and tread frag-ments. Might match what we got from the boathouse. Then when we catch the perp, we can place his car near the crime scene. Deal?'

Rouge shrugged, conveying boredom and reluctance with that single gesture – less work. 'Okay, Arnie, I'll get the molds for you.' And that neatly solved Captain Costello's problem of how to get the feds to do tedious forensic work without demanding payback. 'My turn.' Rouge ran one finger around his glass. He had not yet touched his first shot of whiskey, ordered twenty minutes ago. 'You seem to know Julian Garret pretty well. Are you one of his sources?'

'Absolutely not, but we've done a lot of drinking together.' Pyle smiled over the rim of his glass. 'Julie's not gonna hear anything from me, if that's what you're worried about. No leaks.'

'No, that doesn't worry me at all – since he's a political columnist. He's not here for the kidnappings. Are you?'

Arnie Pyle looked deep into his glass, as if his next strategy might be written on the ice cubes. Finally, he faced Rouge with a smile that might be genuine. 'My compliments, kid. All right, Julie Garret thinks my only interest is Mrs Hubble – developing her as a witness against Senator Berman. And I *do* think she could tie that little rat bastard to mob money. So Julie was *almost* right. But I had better leads to work in Washington. If not for Ali Cray, it wouldn't have been worth the trip.'

'How did you know Ali was in Makers Village?'

'I always know where Ali is.' The agent worked on his bourbon and never seemed to notice that Rouge's glass remained full.

'Did Ali ever tell you that you reminded her of someone?'

'No. Why do you ask? You know her from someplace?'

'She lived in Makers Village when she was a little girl. You didn't know that?'

'I didn't even know she had an uncle in this town,' said Pyle. 'Not till Costello asked me to bring her to the hospital. All the early paperwork I could find on Ali Cray came from the Midwest. So you knew her when she was a kid?'

'We were both in the church choir when I was nine. The next year, I was shipped off to military school, and Ali's family left town. That's it. Now let's hear your story.'

'My history with Ali?' Pyle drained his glass. 'I met her when I was working a case in Boston. In those days, I was still hunting for missing kids full-time – and I was the best. But Ali knew more about pedophiles than the freaks knew about themselves. I tried to recruit her for the Bureau. She turned me down flat.'

The agent put up one finger to the bartender to request another round. 'So, Rouge – what you were saying before – about me reminding her of somebody. Who would that be?'

He shook his head. 'You just looked familiar is all. Ever sing in a church choir?'

'Only in my mother's dreams.' Pyle's drink arrived and barely had time to settle on the bar before the glass was in his hand and on the rise.

'I had the impression you didn't like Ali very much.'

'Wrong.' The agent settled his glass in the exact center of the cocktail napkin, with a precision practiced by drunks affecting sobriety. 'I'm gonna be in love with Ali Cray until the day I die.'

'You have a strange way of showing it.'

Pyle was staring at Rouge's virgin glass, untouched, and perhaps he was trying to count his own shots, for he was slow to answer. 'Well, I'm not a sensitive, New Age kind of guy.'

'She dumped you, right?'

'You got it.' Pyle pushed his glass away.

'Because she was frigid, or because she was a lesbian?'

He grinned. 'It was the scar. I just had to know how she got it. It was the one thing she didn't want to tell me – so I had to know. It got to be an obsession with me. I drove that woman nuts – *never* let up on her. And then I drove her away – my own fault. But I could never quite let go of Ali. I used to follow her everywhere. She could've ruined my life with a stalking charge, but she didn't. One time, I banged on her apartment door all through the night – drunk out of my mind and screaming in pain. The next morning I woke up in the hall outside her door. There was a blanket wrapped around me. After I passed out, she'd covered me up with a damn blanket. I think she understands pain like nobody I've ever met before.'

'Still no idea how she got the scar?'

'No, but I think about it a lot.' Pyle was staring at his glass, and perhaps his head had cleared enough to realize that he was doing most of the giving in this new relationship of share and share alike. 'Do you know how she got it, Rouge? Any theories?'

'Nope. Sorry.'

'Are you at least gonna tell me why you stopped by Mortimer Cray's place?' Pyle had just a slight edge of suspicion in his voice. 'You sure didn't stick around very long.'

'I wanted to ask him something about Paul Marie. Then I decided it might be a better idea to drive out to the prison tomorrow and talk to the man myself.'

'You mean the priest? Let me save you a trip, kid. That little scene at the hospital – that was the first I'd heard of Paul Marie. So I asked Costello, and he tells me the guy is a child killer who just blew parole. Now this freak will probably never get out of prison, but as long as he thinks he has a chance of winning over the next parole board, he won't cooperate with you. I've been through this a hun—'

'Here's something you didn't hear from Costello. The guard at the prison said the priest wanted to kill Mortimer Cray this morning. Paul Marie has something solid. If he can trade information for parole—'

'Well, that changes everything,' said Pyle. 'Mind if I come along?'

'I don't care. Sure, come along.' And since this invitation to the prison was the last item on his wish list, Rouge slid off the barstool. 'I have to get home. My mother's waiting dinner on me. I'll pick you up at your hotel. Eight in the morning?'

'Eight it is. But before you go – there's something I want you to think about, kid. You should go back to school and finish your degree. Then I can get you into the Bureau with no trouble. You got the talent to—'

'I don't think so, Arnie. But thanks.'

'Like you're gonna get a better offer? You got a first-class brain, Rouge. You're wasted in a toy town with one cop car and one traffic light.'

'But we have *four* fire engines. We're real big on fires around here. If we ever have one, we'll be ready.'

'Makers Village doesn't even have Chinese take-out, for Christ's sake.'

'No need.' Rouge bent down to the table behind the barstool to pluck a sugar packet from a bowl. He read the text printed on the back and then handed it to Pyle.

Now the man could read his proverb without the trouble of cracking open a Chinese fortune cookie. ' "If the fool would persist in his folly, he would become wise." '

Arnie Pyle put up his hands in surrender, only quibbling that this quotation belonged to William Blake, who was not actually Chinese.

'All right,' said Gwen. 'Suppose we get him to hold the Sitting Bull pose long enough. If it *does* work, that dog's going to rip the man—'

'The Fly.'

'He's going to rip The Fly to shreds. He'll kill the—'

'Good. The Fly dies. That's the idea.'

'No, Sadie. You never think things through.' Gwen covered her mouth. 'I'm sorry. I'm such a—'

'No, no more.' Her arms wound around Gwen, perhaps afraid that she was going to cry again. Stubborn Sadie had not accepted any apologies during the past half hour of tears, and she would not listen to them now. In Sadie's eyes, her best friend could do no wrong.

'Okay.' Gwen put her hands up to say that she was in control of her emotions again. 'Maybe what he did to you was an accident. Suppose he didn't really mean to *kill* you. But when he put you in the ground, he *thought* you were dead, didn't he? You *made* him think that. You don't know what—'

'It's been hours and hours.' Sadie moved off to the edge of the dog circle for a better view of the door. 'He couldn't be outside all this time. He's got to be in the house. Why doesn't he come down here?'

'He's already searched the basement with the dog. He may never come back here.' Gwen didn't believe that any longer, but it seemed important to keep saying it, thinking it, to ward off all the ugly pictures in her head. He would be so angry when he came back, when he saw all the—

'Then what is he doing? Why didn't he take the car?'

'Maybe he walked home.' Gwen winced as one of the journals fell from her hand and grazed the injured leg, rousing the dead weight in her calf muscle. She felt the little monsters stirring inside her flesh, uncurling their small hands of sharp nails to stab her from within. But it was only a feeble gesture this time, a weak theme of aches and little pricks. She was learning the scale of relative pain, songs from hell. The drugs in her system forced the monsters back to sleep. She touched her leg. They stirred again and sang to her upon request this time. Each puncture was a separate mouth screaming through her nerve endings.

And now there was something else in this strange world which she could control.

'Hurts, doesn't it?' Sadie sat down in the dirt beside her. 'Time for a pill?'

Gwen shook her head. 'You were right about the pills. They slow me down.' And if Sadie meant to do this thing, then it would take proper timing. The man had to get inside the door and prop it open with the concrete block before Sadie gave the Geronimo command. Timing was everything.

'Your leg hurts a lot now, doesn't it?'

'I'm all right.' She was not, but the anticipation of the pain had been worse than the real thing. 'It's not so bad.' And wasn't she thinking more clearly now? Yes, she could list every possible error, every opportunity for disaster. Her fear was mounting, the leg was throbbing, and the pain was insistent, constant in its song. 'I'm fine.'

'Sure you are.' Sadie, the unbeliever, ran off down the aisle and disappeared into the white room. She came back with a pharmacy bottle and a jar of water. 'These you can take every three hours. It's been about that long.'

'Just one.' Gwen took the pill and the jar.

'Should I throw him another biscuit?'

'No. He should stay hungry for a while. I can use that to reinforce the pose.' She set the jar down on the dirt beside the pile of journals. 'It's Christmas Eve, isn't it? Maybe he won't come back, maybe we can—'

'Best line from the killer-Santa movie – "Christmas Eve is the scariest night of the year." ' She squeezed Gwen's arm and offered her a smile, a small one. 'I know this isn't a movie – and I know you don't want to do this, but we can't wait any longer.'

'Miss Vickers will be back the day after Christmas.' If she could only convince Sadie to bide time, to hide and wait. She could not yet wrap her mind around what they were planning to do to The Fly – no – the man, the real and solid man. He would hurt her when—

'So she'll be home soon,' said Sadie. 'All the more reason why he has to find us now, before Miss Vickers comes back.' Sadie helped her to stand up and then led her to a cart alongside the one which covered the shallow grave. This one was also filled with loose soil.

'I didn't want you to see this. But now I think it's time you did.' Sadie pulled out the cart to reveal a second hole, a shallow rectangle in the earth.

'That's my grave, isn't it, Sadie?'

'Yes. Nothing happened by accident. He didn't *accidentally* hurt me. He *meant* to murder me. You're alive, but here's your grave – waiting for you.'

'Let's kill him,' said Gwen.

Rouge turned off the road and into the private driveway. His foot slammed on the brake yards short of the house. It was the sight of the Christmas tree lights that shocked him. They blinked in soft diffusion through the drapes of the front windows.

He took his foot off the brake pedal and drove the car under the portico that had once sheltered the carriage horses of another century. And now he could see more of the twinkling

Christmas decorations. All the first-floor windows were ablaze with interior lights strung around their frames.

He turned off the ignition and left the car, ignoring the flagstone path, his shoes pounding across the yard. He was through the door and staring at the Norwegian pine beyond the foyer. It was huge, dominating the center of the wide parlor.

His mother had not put up a Christmas tree in fifteen years. The last time he had seen one in this house was the morning when his twin was found. He knew his sister was dead before the policemen came with the news. He remembered looking at his watch, because he wanted to know the precise time when Susan's life had stopped.

In the early light of dawn, he had walked barefoot down the stairs to find his mother sitting by the Christmas tree. For the first time since Susan's disappearance, Ellen Kendall had been without fear in her eyes. She was beyond that.

She also knew.

Mother and son had only exchanged glances when the policemen had come to the door an hour later, two grown men in tears. Bradly Kendall had ushered them into the house. Five people stood in front of the tree that Christmas morning, and his father was the last one to know that Susan was dead.

And now Rouge was staring at the same decorations, the same blinking lights. He turned to see his mother seated near the fireplace. It roared and crackled with burning Yule logs.

'It's Christmas Eve,' she said in answer to his confusion. 'Half-price sale on trees. What woman could resist?'

Her face was glowing with firelight. She stood up and crossed the room to kiss him warmly on both cheeks. When she hugged him, he wished it could go on forever. He had missed her so much. Too soon, she stepped away from him.

'Rouge, you remember Julie.'

The Washington columnist was sitting on the other side of the fireplace. The old man was drinking from a brandy snifter, but there was only a coffee cup by his mother's chair. Rouge caught her smiling at him, as she caught him checking on her. There was a teasing brightness in her eyes, a haunt of the old days.

Hello, Mom. So you've come back – all the way home.

'Look at this, babe.' She was holding up a press pass. 'Julie got it for me. Useful little thing.' She flashed a smile at the older man.

The columnist stood up to take Rouge's hand in his. 'My apologies for not acknowledging you at the police station. You must have thought I was rude.'

'No, sir. Not at—'

'Yes you did.' Julie turned to Ellen. 'The boy made me feel like I'd just kicked a puppy.' He clapped Rouge on the back. 'But there was no point in tipping off Arnie Pyle. He never learned to share his toys or his friends. You understand. Of course you do. You were such a brilliant child. I'll be watching your career with great interest, Rouge.'

The reporter was pulling on his topcoat as Ellen handed him his scarf. 'Julie's heading back to Washington tonight.'

'I wish I could stay longer, but I'm running late.' He shook Rouge's hand. 'Son, you turned out well. Before I saw you at the police station, I thought your mother was only bragging.' Now he turned to his hostess and made a subtle elegant gesture, the mere suggestion of a bow from the waist. 'Ellen, I hope you found the evening profitable. I wish you both – good night.'

Rouge knew this was an amendment of the automatic phrase for the holiday season. Despite the festive tree in the center of the room, this was also the eve of a dark anniversary, and Julie was a very gentle man. So it surprised Rouge when his mother kissed the reporter's cheek and said, 'Merry Christmas, Julie.'

From different sides of the cellar, the children watched the door in silent anticipation, as they would await the rising of a theater curtain. The dog was holding the Sitting Bull pose longer than he ever had before.

Timing was everything.

Oh, why couldn't they just stay here in the dark, lost in the trees and the mushroom aisles? Gwen looked over at Sadie, lit only by the single bulb over the door to the white room – all else was darkness. The ceiling had shut down for the night, and the mushroom tables were dark shapes standing in rigid formation. The only sound was the hiss from the radiators coming to life after the artificial day had ended.

Sadie turned her head so Gwen could see her face. There was no fear in it – there never was. But Sadie didn't know how many things could go wrong. And then the man would be furious. He would want to get even, to hurt back. This was so crazy. She wanted to end it, to stop it. Perhaps if she warned the man, he wouldn't be so mad.

But what about Sadie? She would never understand that. She would only wonder what had happened to all of Gwen's good intentions to help her kill a man.

Gwen looked back at the door. Maybe he wouldn't come. Maybe he thought she was lost in the woods, frozen to death. He might have run away.

What was that? Was it the door? She tried to sort out this sound from the hiss of the radiator. Yes, the door was opening. He was coming. She could see the dark shape moving into the cellar.

Don't panic, not yet.

She watched him nudge the concrete block into place with his foot. The door was propped.

Not yet.

He was advancing through the trees. All the while, the dog was silent, holding the pose, waiting, just as Sadie was waiting on the signal. Now Gwen clicked on the flashlight, and Sadie screamed, 'Geronimo!'

The dog was bounding forward. The man didn't move until it was too late. Shock had pinned him to the spot. The dog was almost upon him, crouching for the lunge. The man turned and started back to the door. The dog had his paws on the man's back, angling for the neck.

Man and dog were going down.

And now the whole world exploded with a bang. The crack of thunder filled the basement with noise. Sound bounced off the walls; it filled her brain and sent her reeling away from the tree. She scrambled back to her hiding place, putting her hand to the wound to make it hurt, to keep her focussed on what was happening – and not what *might* happen.

The dog was not moving anymore. The man was getting to his feet and walking to the door, bent grotesquely with one hand pressed to his leg. She could barely make out the shape of the gun in his other hand. He fell to the ground. Perhaps he was hurt worse than she thought. But no, he was on his feet again, moving into the light from the staircase beyond the door, and there was no trace of a limp. This was her worst-case scenario: the man was only slightly wounded, hardly harmed at all.

The dog made no noise. He lay so very still he might be dead. What had they done?

The man used his foot to move the concrete prop, and then the door closed behind him. Gwen waited, hardly breathing, listening for the car engine. The lightbulb over the door to the white room went out, and she sat in total darkness.

Then Sadie was by her side, taking the flashlight. She clicked it on and held the beam under her face; it took on a savage cast of shadow in the underlight. She pointed in the direction of the white room. 'That was a brand-new lightbulb over the door. It didn't just burn out. I think he switched off the fuses.'

They waited in silence until they heard the car engine dying away. They crept close to the walls, then hurried down the aisle of mushroom tables. Sadie was first into the white room. She tried the switch on the wall.

Nothing. So it would always be night from now on. He had killed the light.

'It's not so bad,' said Sadie. 'There's loads of batteries under the sink. We can keep the flashlight going forever.' She went down on hands and knees to root through the lower cabinets. 'I'm sorry it didn't work. Really sorry. You were right.'

Gwen sat in the middle of the floor, hugging herself in the dark. 'It's all right, Sadie. We did the best we could.' She felt the first calm that did not come from a pill. The worst thing she could have imagined had come and gone, and she was not broken in every bone and bleeding rivers on the ground. Nothing from her imagination had harmed her yet. 'I wonder if the dog is dead.'

'Doesn't matter. He might as well be dead. You know he's been shot. Probably useless now. A gun. Damn – a gun. Who could've figured on that? You want me to check him?'

'No,' said Gwen. 'You can't go near him now. He's so badly wounded, he's more dangerous than he's ever been.' She had watched this animal go from repose to attack mode in the fraction of a second. *Brave dog*. The man would at least never kick him again. And now he could not even be touched, for a wounded animal could not be trusted. He was going to die all alone.

Sadie opened a bottle of pills, then filled the jar at the sink.

Gwen took a pill – only one. Sadie held out another. 'To help you sleep.'

As if she could. She waved off the second pill. 'Let's get out of here. It's too cold in this room.' Gwen turned the flashlight on the vent. A ribbon was flying straight out to signal the air flow. 'How come the air conditioner works if the light switch doesn't?'

'Separate fuses,' said Sadie. 'On the fuse box at my house, there are labels for everything, and one is just for the air conditioner.'

They walked out of the white room, but they were not

greeted by the same old wall of warm air. The temperature had dropped and the hissing sound was gone.

'That creep.' Sadie shined the flashlight on the far wall of radiators. 'It wasn't just the light fuses. He turned off the furnace too.' The yellow beam lowered to flash on bare feet, and Sadie's disembodied voice said, 'I can't believe the heat could go down so fast.'

'No,' said Gwen. 'Heat rises.' She took the flashlight from Sadie's hand and pointed it up to the high ceiling beyond the cave of the mushroom farm.

And the temperature continued to drop.

Long after Rouge Kendall had left the bar, Agent Pyle sat alone, his hand inches from the bourbon glass. He didn't want it anymore. Arnie was only craving sobriety and clarity as he became more engrossed in the enigma of the rookie investigator with the auburn hair.

Either Rouge Kendall was wasting his brain or using it rather well. Arnie thought about his own cramped Washington apartment with the view of a wall, his long hours and lack of satisfaction. He might come back to Makers Village one day when Rouge was running this place, and maybe he would hit the man up for a job.

Arnie stared out the front window of the bar, past the gold lettering on the glass to the sight of last-minute shoppers, adults and children. Music began to pour from loudspeakers on the other side of the street, and now he listened to the Christmas carols of a boys' choir. The shoppers slowed their steps, turning their faces up to the source of music, craning their necks the better to catch the strains of 'Silent Night'.

Two children stopped awhile on the sidewalk to torture a third child, playing keepaway with the middle youngster's hat as he ran from one to the other, screaming obscenities.

What a place to raise kids. He wondered if Ali wanted children. Well, she might have to wear a bag over her head during the formative years, so she wouldn't traumatize their kids with her face.

He shook his head.

Naw, the brats would take a lot of pride in Ali's scar.

Children loved things like that, the scarier the better. His real fear was that she would tell the kids how she got the scar, but never tell him.

It was impossible to shake the eerie feeling that his erstwhile barstool companion knew what had happened to Ali. Ah, Rouge – strange kid, so subtle with his loss leaders posed as innocent questions, and perhaps they were. But what if Rouge did know – without being told? Given what the young cop would have to go on—

Arnie Pyle jerked up his head to stare at the fool in the mirror. He had worked through the riddle. And now he laid his head down on the bar.

Oh, Ali, no.

CHAPTER 9

'No, Rouge, don't touch it.' Ellen Kendall was heading down the hallway toward the kitchen where the extension phone was just a ring away from picking up the call. 'Let it ring through.'

Her son stood beside the telephone table in the living room, saying to his mother's back, 'Ring *through*?'

'To the answering machine,' Ellen shouted on the run. She had forgotten that this newly installed device would be a surprise to him, as would the fax machine connected to it.

The phone apparatus sounded a beep, and she hovered over it, waiting to see if it would print out a message or produce a human voice. She turned to see her son at the kitchen door, surveying the mess. Every bit of surface was littered with piles of papers, notebooks and electronic equipment.

'If you pick up the phone, you might interrupt a fax.' And now the paper began to scroll out of the machine mouth. 'Coffee's ready, babe. How come you're up so early?' She had not yet been to bed. Mastering the technology was taking longer than she had expected.

'I've got errands to run before I start my shift.' He walked to the coffee machine, which kept company with a laser printer on the kitchen countertop.

Ellen smiled. He was probably wondering what she had done with the toaster, his only source of breakfast for many years. She tossed him a bran muffin in an easy overhand pitch. Rouge plucked it out of the air and stared at it with vague suspicion, for this was more nutritious than the cinnamon toast he had been eating every day since the age of ten. This was mom food.

The world had changed.

He poured his coffee from the carafe, and then sat down at the table. He piled one mound of paper on top of another to make room for his steaming mug, and now he was staring at the laptop computer.

'That's a present from Julie Garret. So is the fax.' And now she held up her press credential, another gift. 'It's all attached to a solid job offer from Julie's paper. Your old lady's back in harness.' Actually, this announcement was a bit belated. Last night, Julie had left town with the copy for her first story, the best work of her career. But her son didn't need to know about that yet. He was a close relative, true, but also a cop.

Ellen put on her glasses to read each line as it appeared above the edge of the fax machine. 'Merry Christmas, Rouge. I know how Ali Cray got that scar. And Oz Almo's definitely into something shady. Which one of those gifts would you like to open first?'

'Oz.'

Without turning away from the scrolling lines of type, she pointed to the center of the table. 'Check out the red folder. It's all there. Credit history, financial sheets. Oz has a steady flow of wire transfers from banks outside the area. None of the payments are retainers. They won't match up with the dates on his client list.'

He pulled the red folder from the pile and scanned the first paragraph of the paperwork inside. 'Who is Rita Anderson?'

'She's a cleaning woman. First clue – Rita comes in once a week to dust, and Oz pays her fifty thousand a year. Next, the sources of the wire transfers are summer people with houses on the lake. They're all wealthy. I only contacted three of them. Asked if they could give a reference for Rita Anderson. Two of them used her as a cleaning woman. One old lady said Rita was a home healthcare provider.'

'So Rita gets the dirt on these people, and Almo does the blackmail.'

'Works for me, babe.' Though it had taken her entire minutes to work out a pattern of blackmail using an overpaid cleaning woman as an operative. 'It gets better. Julie Garret went out drinking with a source the other night. This source wanted to derail him from another story – threw out Almo's name as a mob connection to Senator Berman. Then the guy tells him it didn't pan out. Now Julie always knows when this guy's trying to throw him off. But he figures there might be some truth in it. That's the source's style, misdirection with accurate information. So Julie listens. The source tells him Almo is a dead end, all mouth, just throws the senator's name around to scare the marks into thinking he's a bigger fish than he is.'

'So the feds followed a rumor and put a wiretap on Oz. They were looking for a mob tie and stumbled on the blackmail?'

'Did I say that? Did I say *wiretap* or *feds*? And Julie's source never mentioned blackmail.' Though the word 'mark' implied some kind of scam ten times out of ten.

Rouge went through the sheets more carefully now, reading all the words, never looking up as he said, 'You know who Julie's source is. I know you do. Tell me.'

'You interrogate like a cop. I'm your mother – stop that.'

Rouge sat back in his chair and sipped from the mug. 'Okay, I'll guess, and you tell me if I'm warm or cold.'

He *would* pick that old childhood game, the one she always lost. It had been his favorite from the time he learned to talk. Ellen was still mystified by his methods for winning every round. And now she was debating whether or not to risk it when he began the game without her.

'The source is a fed on the organized crime task force,' said Rouge, 'and his name is Arnie Pyle.'

Her face must have told him that he was dead on target. His smile was very faint; even as a small child, he had always

287

been too gracious a winner to gloat. Or perhaps every win had been entirely too easy for him.

'Rouge, you can't repeat that. Oz Almo was just one small detail in a task force investigation. You can't compromise a—'

'And what Pyle told Julie could only be gotten with federal wiretaps.'

'I owe Julie bigtime. I can't burn one of his sources.'

'So Pyle was going to sit on the blackmail evidence.' Rouge held up the financial sheets. 'Two of these wire transfers are from banks in New Jersey. Extortion across state lines is a federal crime. Holding back evidence only makes sense if the fed's wiretap wasn't legal. So I can assume it wasn't.'

'No, Rouge, you can't assume that. Stick to the facts. Exposing a wiretap might only jeopardize a legal investigation. So if you're thinking of trying your own extortion on the FBI, it'll blow up in your face.' Now this was more like parenthood, warning the baby not to play with fire. 'If you threaten Pyle, you'll burn Julie. Oh, and I get burned too. I'd have to nail you for that, babe – child of mine or no. You never burn your sources, and particularly not your own mother.'

He nodded absently, and ran one finger down the asset column of a banking sheet. 'I don't see any major investments.'

'No, I haven't found any yet. Just a few T-bills, mutual funds, standard accounts – things like that. I don't think Oz is bright enough to play the stock market. No big-ticket items either. He doesn't even own the lakehouse. It belongs to his aunt. He strong-armed the old lady into a nursing home. So the ransom money looks like a dead end, babe. Money leaves tracks, and my financial sources are solid. If they can't find the ransom, it isn't there. It's not like he could pull off a money-laundering scheme. Given what the fed said about him, Oz has zero connections for that kind of a racket.'

'Dad marked the money. Oz might've been afraid to spend it.'

'There's a limit to my talents. I can't tell you what the little bastard has stashed under his bed.' She tore a long rolling sheet off the fax machine. 'And now, best for last – the mystery scar. When she was a little girl, her name was *Sally* Cray, not Ali. But that much I knew yesterday. Got it from the baptismal records at the church.'

She handed him this sheet as another one was rolling through the machine. 'The background on Ali is coming in from an old friend of your dad's. He's feeding me clippings and personal notes from his home office. That's where he's hiding. Says he's got the door barricaded against five screaming kids.'

She pointed to the top of the sheet in Rouge's hand. 'That dateline is from a Stamford newspaper. If you were hoping for a connection to Susan, that story kills it. Ali Cray was in a car wreck in Connecticut. It all jibes with her parents moving out of town that year. Two adults and three other children were killed. The only survivor was the little girl. Satisfied?' She turned to the fax machine, which continued to scroll out paper.

'No,' he said. 'There's more to it than that. There are no names here. You said there were two adults in the car. Not her parents, right?'

'Good guess.' She bent closer to the machine and pushed the reading glasses up her nose. 'The cops always hold back names till they notify next of kin. Now he's sending another news clipping for the following day. According to the local paper, it was a family named Morrison. They lived a quarter of a mile from the accident scene. Only one car in the wreck. Ali was with them when it spun out of control on an icy road.'

'And you believe everything you read in the papers, Mom?'

She wondered if this might be an opportune time to remind him that, in her younger days as a Chicago reporter, she devoured cops like him for breakfast – bones and all. 'What's coming out now is handwritten, personal notes. Hold on – this wasn't in the papers. The little girl was in a coma for two weeks and listed as a Jane Doe for the first forty-eight hours.' She ripped off the sheet and handed it to him, trying not to look smug – aiming for grace and failing, as she always did.

'I'm no doctor, but I think we can read coma for head injury. The scar on her face—'

'Now that's interesting.' Rouge took the curled pages and scanned the lines quickly. 'Five people die a quarter of a mile from home, and Ali's family doesn't hear about the accident for two days. How long did it take for the Morrisons' relatives to claim the bodies?'

'It doesn't say— Wait.' She continued to scan newsprint lines as they rose above the lip of the machine. 'There's an obit here. The family was Jewish Orthodox. They were buried the following day, according to custom. That means there was nothing suspicious about the accident, no autopsy.'

'After all this time, could you locate the Morrisons' next of kin?'

'Sure. Simple trace work – nothing to it. You want me to ask them why the parents didn't—'

'No, Mom. When you talk to the relatives who claimed the bodies, they're probably going to tell you they had no idea who Ali was.'

How was he doing this? 'You think the kid was a runaway?' She was feeling the drag of another night with no sleep and sensed the pressure of a borderline aneurysm in her effort to keep pace with his better brain.

'Don't know, Mom.' Rouge shook his head. 'I just think there's more to it.'

'But the accident is the most likely place for the scar. If she was in a coma, that suggests one hell of a head injury.'

'So the paper didn't mention the scar specifically? And the personal notes didn't mention it either. These are not *facts*, right?'

He had such a talent for throwing her own words back at her. 'Right again. So shoot me. I gave birth to you, but don't let that get in the way. All right – *facts*. We're talking about a little kid here. The cops and the hospital wouldn't release information on a minor until the parents showed up. But two days later, the accident would've been old news.'

'Or the details could've been withheld for other reasons. I think the story behind the scar is a lot more interesting than this.' He pushed the sheets away and bit into his bran muffin.

And to think she had actually considered mixing water and concentrate to make orange juice for his breakfast. 'Okay, there *might* be more to the story. I'll get back on it.' She unplugged the phonejack from the fax machine and hooked it up to her laptop, saying, '*Cops*', as if they were still the bane and chief blight of her existence. And now she had bred one and even fed him a damn bran muffin.

'Thanks, Mom. And get some sleep, okay?'

'Yeah, right, poor old Mom.' She smiled as he kissed the top of her head. He had not done that in a while. How many years? Too long. 'What a good boy you are. When you ship me off to a nursing home, you'll get me a room with a view, won't you, babe?' Her generation had pioneered psychedelic drugs, rock music and free love, but was her son impressed? No, he was yawning as he left the kitchen.

'Damn cops.'

The doorbell rang. Rouge's voice hollered down the hallway, 'I'll get it, Mom.'

Ellen was already deep into the mysteries of making Internet search engines more specific, so they would give her less than a thousand responses to every inquiry. As she was turning the pages of *Internet for Dummies*, she heard a stranger's voice behind her. She turned quickly to see a man standing in the doorway.

'Excuse me, Mrs Kendall?' He smiled an apology. 'Sorry if I— Well, I'm just waiting for Rouge. He's still on the phone. Guess I'm a little early.'

She could tell he was at a loss, trying to make a connection and not finding one. He would be reading the signs of recognition in her own expression, though she only found his eyes familiar – and shocking. Rouge had obviously been expecting this man. He should have warned her.

'Ma'am, have we—'

'No, we've never met. That's quite a shiner.' Between her son's account of the black eye and Julie's more colorful description of an elegant mutt with Los Vegas style, she had no trouble identifying the man in her kitchen. 'Pull up a chair, Special Agent Pyle.'

He sat down at the table, showing no reaction to being called by name and rank, though they had not been introduced. And he offered no explanation for being in her house. The fed must assume she had been told of this appointment. And what else had her son failed to mention? 'Wasn't Rouge supposed to pick you up at your hotel?'

'Yes, ma'am. But I was up early, and it wasn't much of a walk.'

Good guess. Her son must have been surprised when the fed turned up at the door – and displeased. Whatever the boy was planning, he didn't want it leaked to the press, more specifically, to dear old Mom. *Damn cop.* So he had probably asked Pyle to wait in the foyer. But the FBI man had wandered down the hall, perhaps led by the sound of tapping keys – or a second agenda.

Another good guess.

Arnie Pyle was spreading a sheet of paper flat on the table. Penciled across the top in capital letters was tomorrow's headline, THE LADY AND THE SHARKS, followed by a printed synopsis for the political scandal of the year.

Not quite the blackmail story Julian Garret had suggested, it was better – and worse. The opening was a portrait of Marsha Hubble, a strong woman with survival skills handed down from four generations of New York families prominent in political columns and society pages. The lady was born in the arena. With ties of money, politics and blood, she hardly needed blackmail to stave off the top politicians who wanted her resignation. More recently, the lieutenant governor had gained power beyond the state to call out heavy artillery of federal forces, and she had doubled the full-time BCI contingent over any previous case. But she had done all of this through the offices of her enemies, Senator Berman and his pet governor. It begged the question – How?

The lieutenant governor's most devoted staff member had been stressed to breakpoint by the time Ellen got to her. The aide had gone rogue, leaking the story and even providing a direct quote from Mrs Hubble's recent meeting with the senator. The words were underscored on Pyle's copy of the summary sheet: 'Yes, I'll do it, if that's what it takes. Help me find Gwen and Sadie – and then I'll resign.'

Agent Pyle held up a cigarette, asking for permission. Ellen pushed a saucer across the table to use as an ashtray. 'Enjoy.'

'Julie Garret left that bomb at my hotel last night. A little gift, so I could cover my ass with the Bureau.' A plume of smoke twisted up from the side of his mouth. 'You do nice hatchet work, lady.'

'There's nothing like a cup of coffee with a morning cigarette.' She reached back over the edge of the countertop and pulled a mug from the collection on wall hooks. 'I used to smoke myself. Now I live vicariously.' Was the agent running a bluff? Given only what Pyle had in his hand, absent a byline, he should have assumed the article was Julie's work. Ellen filled the mug and set it in front of him. She smiled. The agent didn't smile back.

He knew.

But her own son *didn't* – or he would have been angry with his mother for holding out on him. Someone must have read Pyle the byline off the galley. So the fed had other sources on the same Washington newspaper, probably a night-shift worker. She doubted that Julie was aware of that, but he soon would be.

Ellen glanced down at the penciled headline and shook her head sadly. 'It's a pity Julie didn't give you the story before you got that black eye.' She set down the carafe and picked up a pencil, threatening to make notes. 'Did the lieutenant governor throw a right hook? I like to be accurate.'

'She's left-handed.' He held up the summary sheet. 'Oh,

and this wouldn't have stopped me from going after Marsha Hubble. I know the story is a crock.' He wadded the paper into a ball. 'It was planted. Give me the name of your source, and I'll prove it. Could be embarrassing for you if—'

'Pyle, does that line ever work?'

'On women? No, I never have any luck with women.' One finger pointed to his bruised eye. 'You probably guessed that.' He pocketed the crumpled sheet. 'But it *could* be a deliberate press leak. The lady might have ambitions to run for higher office. Your story's gonna kill the governor's chances for another term. Or maybe Marsha's after the senator's job. Fat chance he'll get re-elected after—'

'Now I *am* impressed, Pyle. You're even more cold-blooded than me.'

'Thank you, ma'am. That's high praise coming from a reporter.'

She understood why Julian Garret liked this man so much, why he spoke of Arnie Pyle with the same tenderness and adjectives usually reserved for his golden retriever. So the agent's night-shift snitch had not known about the tapes. Bless Peter Hubble's paranoid heart and all the electronic bugs in his mansion.

Now where was Pyle going with her son this morning? They were using one car – a trip out of town? If she had pegged this man right, the direct approach would fail. 'You two were wise to get an early start. It's a long drive, isn't it?'

'Not so long, maybe forty minutes. I guess if Rouge does the legal speed limit, it might take us an hour. But I never met a cop that law-abiding.'

As the agent drank his coffee, Ellen did the math for time and distance. The coordinates would best fit one map point along the main highway. A last-minute arrangement? That would explain why Rouge was taking so long to make a phone call. She glanced at the wall clock. The switchboard should be open. Such places did not close on holidays. 'Visiting relatives, Agent Pyle?'

He grinned, taking this for a joke. So their destination was definitely the prison. She wondered if Pyle knew what was in store for him. Probably not.

Rouge was standing in the doorway with his jacket slung over one arm. He was not at all happy with this warm and cozy kitchen tableau. Ellen donned her best maternal attitude and smiled sweetly at her beloved young son, pride of her life. *Gotcha, babe – upstart, rank beginner. Mom is still the master of deception.*

The water was warm, and its current gently lulled Gwen into a deeper sleep as she floated along the river between darkness and light. A small white ghost of a girl was running along the shore, waving her arms. 'Wake up!'

Gwen opened her eyes. Her face was wet, not from the river but the rain. Great dollops of water were falling from the ceiling again, pattering the leaves and dampening her clothes. The flashlight beam darted about as Sadie pulled her up to a stand. Gwen fell back against the rough bark of a tree. The pain in her leg jolted her with sharp surprise. Sadie's arms held her upright as they moved slowly through the darkness and the rain. The flashlight beam picked out the path in front of them as Gwen dragged one useless leg behind her.

'The dog?'

'Don't know,' said Sadie. 'He hasn't moved. No noise either.'

When they entered the area of the mushroom tables, the rain had ceased, but the pumps above the tables continued to spray the air with a cold mist.

'What time is it?'

Sadie opened the door to the white room and flashed the light on the clock. 'Eight-thirty.'

'But, it never rains at night.'

'It's morning, Gwen.'

The air conditioner was blowing on them. Sadie flashed the beam into the drawer of pills. She picked up bottles, read the labels and discarded them. Now she found one that she liked. 'Take off the parka, it's wet.'

Gwen removed the red down jacket they had shared when the temperature began to drop. She spread it on the back of the chair, and then accepted the glass jar and a pill from Sadie's hand.

'This is the only dry place in the cellar, but I can't block off the air conditioner.' Sadie covered Gwen's shoulders with layers of dry towels. 'The vents are too high up. All those plant misters outside are still working, but the dirt under the tables should be dry. We'll—'

'I'm not going into that hole again. I can't. I won't.' Gwen held the flashlight while Sadie changed her bandage. The swelling had not gone down any, and the wound was leaking more of the yellow-green pus. The odor was foul and the skin was darker. She turned her face away from it. The pill was already working on the pain, but the air conditioner was killing the fever warmth. She could feel the cold in all her bones now.

Sadie finished tying off the new bandage and pulled Gwen up from the chair. 'We have to go back to the hole. It's dry under the table.'

'No, I don't—'

'You'll like it better now. Very homey. You'll see.' She circled Gwen's waist with one arm, and they made their way down the aisle to the mushroom table covering the hole. The cart had been pulled back. Sadie shined the flashlight on the grave. It was lined with plastic and magazines for insulation. A pile of batteries lay in one corner on top of the stack of journals.

'See? You can read all you want. It's not so bad now, is it?' Sadie settled her friend into the hole, then climbed in and lay down beside her. Holding out a journal, she said, 'Read to me?'

Gwen trained the flashlight on the book pages. 'This entry was written a long time ago, when Miss Vickers figured out that the trees would never be normal, no matter how much light she gave them. "There is retribution in the world, and justice. I never doubt that anymore. My hands are full of knots, my fingers are misshapen. I have come to resemble my poor trees. This is punishment for the way they twist and bow, stunted in this unnatural world. The advancing arthritis assuages my guilt. Pain is my penance. I am so sorry.'"

Sadie's head lay on the pillow of one arm. Her eyes were closed. She had been tricked into sleep by the false night of failed electricity.

Gwen leaned into the space between table and cart to shine the yellow beam on the oaks, one by one, reaching out to them with this feeble nourishment of light. She felt sorry for the trees, imagining their panic on this first morning when all their artificial suns failed to shine. They could not wring their hands and scream; they could only endure in silent fear and wonder. She clicked off the flashlight and sat in absolute darkness, listening to Sadie's even breathing and endeavoring to be more like the oak trees.

The priest had been surprised when he was told about this interview outside the regular hours. It could only be the police or the FBI. Most visitors over the years had come from these two groups, and all their questions were predictable. But to come on a holiday? It must be related to the missing children.

He sat at the table in his chains, prepared for a quiet hour of no more surprises. As the guard manacled his legs to the chair, two men were being ushered into the room. The man in the suit was engaged in filling out forms as he spoke to another guard at the door.

The younger man who faced him now wore faded blue jeans and an old fleece-lined jacket, not the typical FBI wardrobe. So this must be a police officer, and Paul Marie had no trouble recognizing him, so close was the resemblance to Susan. He also had his father's dark red hair and hazel eyes.

Years ago, the elder Kendall had come to the prison once a week without fail, steadfast as a lover. Susan's father had always seemed gratified to see fresh bruises on the priest's face, a cut lip, or a swollen eye. But there had been a lingering disappointment, an expression to Bradly Kendall's face, which said at each meeting, *What? Not dead yet?*

Only a month-long punishment of solitary confinement had saved the priest. Other prisoners had come out of the isolation cell with aching limbs from lack of exercise, and weak stomachs from the slop that passed for food. Paul Marie had emerged with the idea that he might survive, with the regimen to do it and an enemy with a face.

Over subsequent visits, Bradly Kendall had charted the priest's progress by the expanding muscles of the torso and thickening arms. It must have been difficult for the distraught father of a murdered child to watch his nemesis increasing in size as he grew smaller and weaker. And then Kendall had sickened; his visits ceased.

Paul Marie had felt a profound sense of loss when the publisher stopped coming to the prison. At the time, he had wondered – was it the man's company he missed, or the challenge of slowly destroying the publisher by merely surviving, and then astonishing Bradly Kendall by actually thriving in this place. Years later, the priest had experienced genuine sorrow when he learned of the publisher's death; he had come to understand the true nature of his own loss – the end of his most intense relationship with another human being. His old enemy was the only man he had ever mourned.

Now Paul Marie assessed the younger Kendall, whom he had once known as a choirboy. He sensed great damage in this man. And it was unsettling that Rouge was making his own measurements of the priest, sizing him up with calm hazel eyes as he sat down in one of the empty chairs on the other side of the table.

The second visitor remained with the guard by the door. This slender man had his back turned as he signed forms and took his own paperwork back from the guard. The cover sheet on the man's clipboard carried the familiar crest of the FBI.

So it was to be business as usual. They would ask for his assistance in analyzing the new Monster of Makers Village. He settled back in his chair to await the inevitable questions of—

Now the FBI man was walking toward the table, eyes locked on the face of Paul Marie. Both men were equally shocked and disoriented as each looked into the mirror image of his own eyes.

Only Rouge Kendall seemed unfazed by this striking resemblance between the agent and the priest. Had the younger man set them up for this confrontation? Could Rouge be that convoluted? Oh, yes, certainly. His sister had been a very complex little human being, and they were twins, weren't they?

But whenever Susan had come to him, her small deceits were harmless parts of the game they played together.

The FBI man with the familiar eyes was mute while Rouge was introducing him as Special Agent Arnie Pyle. The agent did not take the third chair at the table, but remained standing. Arnie Pyle had recovered some of his composure, but the shock remained with him. He was listing slightly to one side, as though he had just suffered an injury that threatened to bring him down at any moment.

When the FBI agent spoke, his voice was accusing, 'What kind of contact did you have with Ali Cray?'

This was not the question Paul Marie had anticipated. 'She came to see me a few days ago. She had questions on the murder of Susan Kendall.'

If Rouge found this information interesting, he gave no sign of it. The agent placed both hands flat on the table, perhaps for support. 'Before that – *before* Susan Kendall died. Did you have a thing for Ali?'

And now Rouge Kendall did show some interest in the conversation, but it was fleeting.

'Ali was a little girl when I knew her,' said Paul Marie. 'I've been here for—'

'Same question, you son of a bitch.' Agent Pyle pulled

back. His face was reddening with anger. 'Did you touch her?' He turned his back and walked off a few paces toward the door, only to turn and walk back to the table. Tremendous energy was building in this man, and he seemed to have no way to contain it. His next words had the force and velocity of gunfire. 'You did it, didn't you?' he shouted. 'And Susan Kendall too! You creep, you miserable lowlife! Did you give Ali that scar? Were you the one?'

So this was a friend of Ali's, a close friend, someone who loved her. 'You believe she was attracted to you because of the resemblance to me? You're probably right about that.'

Arnie Pyle flew across the table to put his hands around the priest's neck. Paul Marie was quite capable of breaking this man's back, even given the limited range of movement in his chains, but he did nothing to stop the assault. He only sat there, passive, while Rouge Kendall pried the agent's hands away. Now Rouge and the guard stood on either side of the FBI man and pulled him back, struggling, feet dragging, toward the door at the other end of the room. Only Agent Pyle was facing him when Paul Marie said, 'Maybe she went to you for comfort, for peace and shelter. Did she get it?'

The man seemed shocked anew, and he ceased to struggle. His mouth hung open, and his eyes gave away enormous pain. The two men released him. Pyle's hands rose in a useless, helpless gesture. The guard was at the intercom; the door was opening.

The priest called out, 'Agent Pyle? Ali is still in need of comfort.'

Pyle was pushed out of the room, and Rouge Kendall came strolling back to the table. So the young man had yet another question. The priest sat back, no longer confident of his ability to predict the day's events. 'What can I do for you?'

'My sister had a chain with a small oval of gold. The letters *AIMM* were engraved on it. I know she was in the habit of losing things during choir practice. My mother would like to have this little piece of jewelry back – it's very important to her.

Did you ever find anything like that? Maybe you saw it in the lost-and-found box?'

'No. The silver bracelet was the only thing of Susan's that ever made it into the box. Usually, she'd come back after choir practice to tell me what she lost – always something tiny, hard to find. We'd search the cloakroom and the pews. Once I helped her hunt for a gold bookmark – small, thin as paper and very fine engraving. I remember it well. She said it was your birthday present to her when she was eight. Another time it was a little silver ring you gave her for Christmas. But then, everything she ever lost was something you had given her. This was her way of opening a conversation. Susan would thank me for helping her find it, and then she'd tell me why it was so important – because it came from you. You were always in her mind. That's the way Susan put it.'

And now he had a reaction from Rouge, and he knew he had struck on some old memory that hurt him. Paul Marie continued, 'I think talking about you eased the pain of the separation. But she had no experience with confiding in other people. This game was the only method she could devise. I never saw the necklace you described. I would've remembered it.'

'It wasn't a necklace. It was an ankle chain.'

'Nothing like that either. Tell your mother I'm sorry I can't help. I would if—'

'When did you find the silver bracelet?'

'A few hours after the last choir practice. I found it in the snow near the church steps.'

'Did you expect Susan to come back later and look for it?'

'That was the pattern. Though she always lost things *inside* the church. I thought she'd outgrow this habit eventually. Or maybe you'd come home from military school, and she wouldn't need me anymore. When she didn't return to church that night, I figured the bracelet belonged to one of the other children. So I put it in the lost-and-found box. Was this something that you gave her?'

301

'No, the bracelet was a present from my father.'

'Then it wouldn't have been part of the game. She probably dropped it by accident.'

'It was never in your room? Oz Almo testified that—'

'He lied.'

Did Rouge believe that? There was nothing in the handsome young face to say what judgment he had arrived at. With no goodbye, his young visitor was rising to leave.

There was a rattle from the chains of the leg irons when the priest stood up – as any gracious host would do. The policeman was almost to the door when Paul Marie called out to him. 'Rouge? The ankle chain was from you, wasn't it?'

Rouge said nothing.

'The inscription you mentioned, *AIMM* – always in my mind?'

There was the barest inclination of the young man's head.

Rouge drove the car through the prison gates and turned on to the highway. For the next five miles of road, his passenger carried both sides of their conversation.

'Okay, I screwed up,' said Arnie Pyle. 'Christ, you could've warned me. You gotta admit the connection was reasonable if Ali was seduced as a child. Sometimes the kids gravitate toward the abuser. It's fear – a survival ploy. They want to stay on the bastard's good side. You're not buying any of this, are you?'

Rouge shrugged, eyes wandering to the side of the road, looking for the turnoff. He kept silent for another long stretch of highway and let the other man ramble on.

'So maybe Ali had a crush on the priest when she was a kid,' said Arnie Pyle. 'That could explain it. What about your sister? Her too?'

'No, I don't think so. My sister and I didn't have any friends. We had each other. When I wasn't there for her, she went to Paul Marie – for comfort.' And for confession? Susan could tell a priest how angry she was with their father over the separation, the loss of her twin. 'Arnie, you should've been nicer to the priest. Maybe Ali told *him* how she got the scar.'

'Paul Marie could still be a pervert. That's how some of these freaks work.' Pyle sat up a little straighter, suddenly re-energized. 'Most pedophiles target emotionally vulnerable kids – they flatter them with attention. It's a seduction—'

'The pervert we're looking for doesn't seduce kids, Arnie, he steals them. I think Ali's right. The killer is just a sadistic bastard.'

'Paul Marie could still fit a pattern. What do you know about his early years? Any trouble with the law? If we can find a previous incident like flashing, a Peeping Tom complaint, something like that. The church is a damn magnet for child molesters.'

Rouge shook his head. 'So are schools and summer camps. The priest is clean.'

They were approaching the exit sign for Makers Village. The curve of the side road swung them out of a tight closure of trees and into an open vista. Beyond the lake of sky-blue water were rolling hills marked with broad patches of ever-greens and stripes of brown, dead leaves from a march of trees whose season was done. A mist rolled over the water and softened the edges of every landmark on the far side.

Rouge stopped the car and pointed to the hazy shoreline. 'A man named Oz Almo lives over there. He's an ex-BCI investigator. His house is across the lake from the school and downshore a bit. I need to search that house, Arnie. You could get a warrant.'

'Me? Don't count on it. I don't have much clout on this case, not since Mrs Green killed my ransom note with the purple underwear. Anyway, I thought the cops went through all the lake houses.'

'Oz Almo's an ex-cop. He had rank with the State Police. Oz signed a consent form for a search, but it wouldn't have been hard to sidetrack the troopers. And they were only looking for two little girls.'

'So what are *you* looking for, Rouge?'

'After Susan disappeared, my parents got a ransom demand. Oz Almo delivered the money himself. The rest of the force didn't even know it was going down. He convinced my father he had a foolproof way to track the kidnapper. Afterward, Oz said he lost the guy – gave Dad some story about faulty equipment.' Rouge pointed to the glove compartment. 'In there. Something you might find interesting.'

Pyle opened the compartment and pulled out a sheaf of papers. When he had scanned them, he let out a low whistle. 'Where did you get all this stuff? You'd have to rob a bank to get financial sheets like this.'

Rouge said nothing.

Arnie Pyle nodded his understanding. 'I should have sources like yours. It'd save me a million miles of red tape.'

'See the wire transfers from out-of-state banks? There's a blackmail pattern. That's all you need for a warrant, right? It helps if you know Oz has a silent partner. Every one of those people used his cleaning lady, Rita Anderson.'

'As evidence goes, that's pretty slim, kid. I can't get a search warrant with ripped-off bank records and a cleaning lady.' Arnie was still poring over the financial history. 'This ransom for your sister – how much money are we talking about?'

'Two million in large bills.'

'Jesus Christ.' Arnie flipped through the sheets. 'I don't see any sign of it. You must have missed something here. That kind of cash, even if he was spending it in small—'

'I don't think he spent any of it. That's why he needs the blackmail income. He knew the ransom was marked, and he knew my father had samples. That's all Dad would tell him. He had a lot of faith in Oz, but he didn't completely trust anybody.'

'But a cop would've known how the bills were marked when the police started a trace on the ransom money. That's standard procedure.'

304

Rouge shook his head. 'Oz wanted to do the money trace himself – quietly. He said it would ruin his life if the department found out about the botched ransom drop. When he asked for a sample of the marked bills, Dad refused. I think my father suspected Almo then. I was never sure. Dad might've hired someone to keep an eye on Almo and—'

'*Might have?* So far, you got a lot of supposition, kid, but damn few facts and zero evidence. If nobody knows how the ransom was marked—'

'I helped my father do it.' It had taken two days and a night. 'The ransom note had a specific date. There wasn't time for Dad to mark every bill by himself.'

'Rouge, this guy's had fifteen years to examine the money. He's checked for pinholes, dyes, every damn thing. Now that the currency has changed—'

'You'll be looking for one dot to extend a line of engraving.' Rouge unfolded his wallet and pulled out a hundred-dollar bill with a red arrow pointing to the alteration. 'Printer's ink – almost a perfect match. We used fine-point Rapidographs. You keep that sample, Arnie. I wouldn't like to be accused of planting evidence.'

'Rouge, this guy's an ex-cop. He knows the odds of a marked bill being found, even when it's altered in an obvious way. If he couldn't find your dad's mark, he wouldn't worry about some bank teller picking up on it.' Arnie folded the financial sheets, returned them to the glove compartment and shut the door, as if to say that this matter was closed. He looked down at the hundred dollars in his hand. 'Large bills like this one increase the risk, but after all this time, I think you can kiss the evidence goodbye.' He held the bill out between them.

Rouge shook his head, refusing to take it back. 'Oz didn't spend the money.'

'You assume too much, kid. You don't know—'

'Arnie, who's more paranoid than a cop? And what about

a cop tied to a homicide? Susan's body was found the day after the fake ransom drop.'

'Fake? So now you're assuming—'

'That Oz wrote the ransom note? Yeah, but just go along with me for a minute. So Susan is dead, and now he's made himself part of a little girl's murder. If anybody ties just one of those bills to Oz, his life is over. That's what he's been living with all this time. And he's shrewd but no brain trust. I know he keeps the money in the house – close to him. He's greedy too. So he can't believe there isn't a trace going on for two million dollars. Who lets go of that kind of money? Maybe Oz looks at the bills every night, trying to find the alteration. He's got to know how they were marked before he lets even one of them leave the house. It's been driving him nuts for fifteen years. Oz never spent one dime.'

The beepers in both their pockets went off simultaneously. Arnie Pyle called in with his cell phone. When he had folded it again, he said, 'There's been an accident. They found Buddy Sorrel in the next county. His car was wrapped around a tree.'

It was a bleak flat landscape along this stretch of road. One mile over the county line, there were only three houses in sight, each a great distance from the others, and there were no pine trees to break the monotony of bare branches and boulders. Rouge pulled over to a shoulder of earth curving into an irrigation ditch. The gray morning sky was a stark backdrop for the spinning red lights from more than a dozen vehicles with the markings of local police, county sheriff and state troopers. A tow truck was pulling up to the crashed car. And two men from the medical examiner's office were opening the back doors of a van. A thin straggle of civilians kept their distance behind the blue barricades and the yellow crime-scene tape that stretched across most of the road. A trooper was waving oncoming traffic along the far side of the asphalt.

Officers and techs milled around the wreck. The car was ripped open to reveal the innards of engine parts and shafts through the torn and crumpled skin of blue steel and chrome. A tow truck driver was rigging his chains to pull the car away from the tree, and the medical examiner was bending over the body bag containing the remains of the BCI man, Buddy Sorrel.

Rouge and Arnie Pyle walked through the static of noise from the car radios to join the grim party of men and women. A state trooper was standing next to Captain Costello. She was pointing toward a gray weathered building set far back from the road.

'The guy who owns that farmhouse confirmed it, sir.' The trooper looked down at her notebook. 'The farmer was driving home from a neighbor's party last night. Now the man might've been a little tight – he didn't say – but it would've been hard to miss a thing like this.' She waved at the wreckage of metal and shattered glass extending far into the roadway. 'Even if the guy was plowed, he would've remembered having to drive around a smashed car. I checked with the other people at the party. The farmer was accurate about the time. So the car wasn't here at midnight. But the medical examiner says the victim died maybe five hours before that.'

'Goddamn thing to happen on my watch,' said Captain Costello.

But Rouge saw no emotion in the captain's face, as though this death were a great inconvenience instead of a great loss.

Dr Howard Chainy was probing the corpse and nodding to the other county's medical examiner, the man with jurisdiction and proprietary rights to Buddy Sorrel's body.

Rouge stared at the face of the corpse, the stark white flesh, the open, staring eyes gone cloudy. The coat had been stripped off and the sleeves rolled up to show the massive arms of the ex-marine.

'No defensive wounds on the forearms.' Howard Chainy was shaking his head as he stood up to speak with Costello. 'But I think the accident was staged. There's a trauma at the back of the head that won't fit with the rest of the damage.

307

The local ME's bowing out. My boys will take the body back.'
Chainy was turning to leave.

'Hold on,' said Costello. 'Your guy Hastings says you met
with Sorrel an hour before he knocked off for the day. Wanna
tell me what that was about?'

'Just some damn nonsense. Nothing to do with this.'

Costello was leafing through the pages of a leather notebook and Rouge recognized it as Sorrel's. The captain looked
up at the medical examiner. 'Howard, your name is here as a
scheduled appointment. He didn't just drop by to shoot the
shit. Looks like you saw him last.'

'Well, I certainly didn't kill him. I even liked the son of a
bitch.' Howard Chainy abruptly turned his back on the captain
and strutted over to the van where his crew was awaiting
orders.

'Damn prima donna.' Costello turned to scan the crowd
until he found the face he wanted. 'Hastings,' he yelled. 'Get
your ass over here.'

Dr Chainy's assistant came running. 'Yes, sir?'

'Hastings, were you there the whole time Sorrel was in the
autopsy room? Did you hear the conversation?'

'I was there, but I couldn't hear much from the other side
of the room. Something about another case. I only caught a
word here and there.'

'Another case? Not likely. I had Sorrel working on the kids
and nothing but the kids.'

'Well, maybe I misunderstood. It could've been a private
joke. Yeah, I think Dr Chainy was ribbing him. He asked
Sorrel how he was doing on the great truffle hunt. Now what's
that got to do with missing kids?'

When the man had been dismissed, Costello was facing
Rouge. 'You know what Sorrel's got on his desk right now?'

'A list of dealers in rare mushrooms, importers, customs
material.'

'Any aerial photographs?'

'Those too,' said Rouge. 'But almost everything was

covered. I know he scheduled a team of uniforms to dig up that hazelnut tree in the postman's atrium. I don't know if they started or not.'

Costello was watching the medical examiner in conversation with Ali Cray. 'What's she doing here?' Then he waved one hand in the air to say never mind, it wasn't important. He called out to the three troopers searching the side of the road beyond the wreck. 'Keep looking for that gun.' He turned back to Rouge. 'Go ask that old fool Chainy if he'd mind stepping up to the body again. I wanna get this over with.'

Rouge walked toward the van where Ali was deep in conversation with the medical examiner. As Rouge approached the pair, it was obvious that Ali annoyed Howard Chainy as much as Costello had.

'But you know, don't you?' she asked. 'Myles said you and William went back a long ways.'

'It's no use asking,' said Chainy. 'William Penny doesn't tell me where he spends his damn vacation time. If he won't tell his own brother, why would he tell me?'

Ali touched the sleeve of his coat. 'Please?' She ran her hand up and down the man's arm. 'I wouldn't ask if it wasn't important. My uncle has a heart condition. I really have to find William.'

Rouge stopped some distance from the two and waited. Chainy seemed to be melting. The doctor was a confirmed bachelor, never married. When had he last been touched by a young woman? Ali Cray continued to stroke him. With a subtle shift of her body, a slash of bare leg was showing through the slit in her skirt, and Rouge did not think this was accidental.

'I really don't know where William goes,' said Chainy with some regret. 'But I know it can't be far from Makers Village. Sometimes I see him around town, usually after dark. He's got a high-pressure job, Ali. Probably just needs a little seclusion. I never saw a surgeon so much in demand as William.'

'So he sneaks around town after dark? You don't—'

'Wait now. I saw him in town a day or so ago in broad

daylight – at the tobacco shop. He could be just a few hours from here. You might check that resort up the highway. He's just married to that special blend of pipe tobacco. I could see him making a long drive to restock.'

Rouge stepped closer and tapped the medical examiner on the shoulder. 'Sir, the captain has a few more questions about the body.' He remained behind with Ali as the doctor walked back toward the body bag. 'If the resort comes up dry, check out motels where the cheaters go – married men, women. You can get a short list from some of the village cops – the married ones.' He turned to walk back to the crime scene.

Ali caught up to him. 'But William Penny *isn't* married.'

'Maybe he knows a woman who *is*.' He walked alongside of her for a few more paces, and then she stopped short.

'Wait. Do you know something, Rouge? Is William part of the investigation?'

'No.' But he found her question interesting. 'Only guessing.' He removed his ring to show her a scar encircling one finger. 'You remember this – the skating accident? William Penny did the emergency operation. Up till then, my mother thought he was gay. No one ever saw him with a woman. But he made a pass at Mom when she picked me up at the clinic after the surgery. Maybe he's the type who likes a challenge.'

'If he only chases married women, that would explain a lot. Well, thanks, Rouge.'

So why did she seem disappointed?

He caught her arm as she was moving away from him. 'You might narrow that down to *grateful* married women – the way my mother was grateful after Penny stitched my finger back on.' He waited to see what she would do with that.

Ali's interest was renewed. 'Vulnerable relatives of patients? Wives, mothers – a victim pattern?'

He nodded. But this was only plausible if his mother's incident was not an isolated one. Ali wouldn't make that reach unless she believed the worst of William Penny. And by the slow nod of her head, he could see that she did. In a further stretch, he wondered if Ali might be tying the surgeon to an entirely different pattern with even more vulnerable females. The word *victim* remained with him after they parted company.

When he joined the others at the crime scene, Captain Costello was kneeling on the ground beside the medical examiner and looking down at the wound Howard Chainy was showing him.

'You see this, Leonard?'

'Of course I see—' Costello bit back a few words and nodded. 'Get on with it, okay, Howard?'

'No blood.' Dr Chainy seemed almost pleased as he put a metal probe into a hole in the body's chest. It was not a man any longer; the corpse was evidence.

Rouge wondered if another medical examiner had done this to Susan, probed her small body, her wounds, and then smiled with the same satisfaction. According to the trial transcript, the acting medical examiner had been Dr William Penny.

'A piece of metal punctured the skin on impact. No blood loss. His heart had stopped by then.' Chainy pulled on the shoulder of the corpse. 'Give me a hand here, will you?'

Costello helped him roll the body until Buddy Sorrel's face was in the dirt.

'See this, Leonard?' The medical examiner was pointing to the dark bloody clots of hair and flesh at the back of the head. Dry blood coated the collar of the shirt and the coat. 'Now that's the wound that killed him, the only one he bled from. I'd say it was a quick death, a few minutes tops.'

Costello nodded. 'So he was taken by surprise.'

'I'll say.' Howard Chainy was pointing into the wound, as a large uniformed officer came out of the gully that ran alongside the road. 'Now look here, Leonard, see this?'

The trooper called out, 'Captain?' In one massive hand, pinched between finger and thumb, the trooper was holding up a tiny pair of purple socks. And now Captain Costello covered his eyes.

He had seen enough.

Ali Cray was standing very close to the seat of all power, civilian secretary Marge Jonas. The large woman was leaning over the dispatcher at the radio. 'You need a break, honey. Go get some coffee. I'll watch the board.'

When the trooper had left them, Marge sat down at the switchboard. The radio headset crushed the blond curls of her wig as she opened a line to the village's only police cruiser and the two officers on patrol. 'Hey, guys. . . . Yeah, hold on.' Then she patched in a connection to Chief Croft, who was driving his own car today. 'Charlie? I need to find somebody for Dr Cray. . . . Yeah it has something to do with the kids. . . . Great. Can any of you guys recommend a motel where your wives would go to cheat on you?'

Good-natured obscenities came back across the wires, along with names and locations. The list was not long, only five motels within a few hours' drive. Marge made all the phone calls, passing herself off as a federal agent and warning desk clerks not to approach the suspect, for he might be dangerous. She then described William Penny. 'He's a prissy man with great clothes, dyed hair and a bad nose job. He's in his late fifties, but he doesn't look it. All the wrinkles have been ironed out.'

Within ten minutes, Marge had located such a man at a small motel with a bad reputation for discretion and cash transactions. It was near the county line and only an hour away. Marge was all smiles as she pulled a set of keys from her purse. 'The desk clerk says the guy's a regular. He's been holing up there, same time every year, for nine or ten years. C'mon, hon. We'll take my car.'

If Marge had kept to the speed limit, the forty-five-minute trip on the state highway might have taken a good deal longer. The women pulled into the parking lot as Dr William Penny was being led through the open door of one of the motel units. A village police officer stood on either side of him. Marge turned to Ali. 'That's him?'

'Yes.'

'Go, team,' said Marge, under her breath. She rolled down the window and gave the policemen a round okay sign with thumb and forefinger.

'They're not going to arrest him?'

'Naw, they're only going to question him. He's a suspect, isn't he? It's Charlie Croft's call. He wants to get this over with so he can flush the state cops out of his station house.'

The village officers were escorting Dr William Penny toward the patrol car in the parking lot. He wore handcuffs and a white terry-cloth robe over his perfectly pressed gray pants. A moment later, a woman was led out of the same motel room and taken to Charlie Croft's personal car. Through the woman's flapping winter coat, Ali could see a cheap rayon blouse and polyester pants only minimally buttoned and zipped. The hair was a wild tangle of long henna strands and mouse-brown roots.

Ali looked up when Charlie Croft joined them. He was smiling as he leaned down to the open window of Marge's car.

'I wouldn't want you to get in any trouble over this,' said Ali. Though he was the Makers Village police chief, he was temporarily under the command of Captain Costello. 'You're sure this won't come back on you?'

'Not likely, ma'am. The woman's from Makers Village.' He looked down at the drivers license in his hand. 'Rita Anderson. Her husband's an invalid with a long history of heart trouble. She thinks it might kill him if he finds out she was shacking up with Proper William over there.' He glanced at the other side of the lot where the cruiser was parked with the heart surgeon in the back seat. 'So, if it turns out the doctor isn't our man, I don't think either one of them is gonna say a word about this.'

Now the frightened Mrs Anderson was standing by the chief's car and raising her voice to one of the uniformed officers. 'No! You can't!'

Ali left Marge's car and followed Charlie Croft across the lot. As they drew near the excited woman, the police officer was saying, 'Ma'am, if you answer all the questions, we won't need to file a report. Nothing public, okay?'

'But I don't know anything about missing kids,' she said. 'I'm telling you the truth. I swear it.'

'Sure you are.' Charlie Croft motioned the other officer to put her into the car. The door opened and she was sliding into the passenger seat as the chief took his place behind the wheel. 'Come on, lady. It was big news – national television. You haven't spent all this time on another planet.'

'You don't believe me? You go check that television set. William always does something to the set so it won't work. No newspapers, no radio, nothing. For ten days every year, we might as well be on Mars.'

Chief Croft leaned out the window and spoke to a uniformed officer. 'Go check the TV set. Then look around the room for a newspaper or a radio.' He turned back to the woman. 'Well, Rita, I think we can guess how the time was spent. But you don't stay in the room for the whole—'

'But I do! I'm telling you the truth. I never leave that room. Suppose somebody saw me and told my husband? A thing like this would kill him. And what about my kids? I'd lose his disability checks.'

Ali Cray leaned into the conversation. 'So William is the one who goes out for food, liquor? Things like that?'

'Yeah, and his damn tobacco.'

'Isn't it a little strange,' said Ali, 'a mother not being home with her children on Christmas Day?'

'Lady, I got four strange kids – all teenage boys, and they take after their old man. It's been ten years since my husband noticed I was alive. Believe me, the boys never miss their mother on Christmas Day. Oh, maybe they have to get

314

their own beer from the frig, I'm sure that's a hardship. This vacation is my Christmas present to me.'

Ali had the impression that there was some bitterness in this present, that it was not entirely a joyful experience.

Charlie Croft brought out his notebook. 'Minors? Drinking alcohol?'

'Now don't you get on me about that. Damn kids. Like who can control a teenager, huh? You think their old man is—' She gave up on Charlie Croft and appealed to Ali. 'You won't let them tell my husband, will you, lady? He'll die if he finds out. I mean he'll *really* die.'

'Mrs Anderson,' said Ali, 'I understand you've been doing this for a very long time. Ten years?'

'Yeah. After my husband's first operation, he thought he was gonna have another heart attack if he accidentally saw me naked. I'm still young.' And now she caught sight of her face in the rearview mirror, all those lines in the harsh light of day. 'Well, I'm not old yet.' And once, she had been quite lovely. 'But if my husband ever found out about this—'

'Lady,' said Charlie Croft. 'You've been taking solo vacations all this time, and you don't think your husband has any idea what you've been up to?'

'No. Why should he? We've got all those kids. One of us had to stay home with them, right? That's the damn law! My husband understands that – why don't you?'

Charlie Croft was grinning when he walked away from the car. He motioned Marge and Ali to follow him to the cruiser on the other side of the parking lot.

William Penny was elated to see Ali Cray sliding into the front seat. 'Oh, thank God. Tell these people who I am.'

'I'll see what I can do to straighten this out, William. Can you tell the police anything about Gwen Hubble or Sadie Green? Do you know where they are?'

'How the hell should I know?'

'All right, William. Next question, have you ever been a patient of Uncle Mortimer's?'

'Mortimer is *my* patient, Ali. I cut into his heart, remember? Now does it make sense? You think I could've operated on someone I had that kind of relationship with? Think about it.'

She did think about it; she had never liked William, but was he a sadist? If he was, he would've relished the opportunity of operating on his psychiatrist. What irresistible potential for fear.

But what about Uncle Mortimer? She tried to imagine him willingly going under the knife, knowing all the darkest things about his surgeon. And now she decided that it was not only possible, but even likely. The psychiatrist was so compulsive about his professional ethics. He would not have changed doctors merely because this one was quite capable of killing him. The rigid old man would have made no alteration, no deviation from habit to call attention to a patient relationship. And wasn't he risking death every day with mounting anxiety and guilty knowledge? Mortimer Cray might even welcome a slip of the scalpel, a quick death under the ether. Yes, it fit perfectly with her uncle's character.

The concept of a sadistic surgeon led her down another avenue of thought, the one inspired by Rouge Kendall. She turned back to the other car holding Mrs Anderson, wife of an invalid with heart trouble. 'That woman's husband is your patient.'

William Penny folded his arms in petulant silence, not denying this, nor offering any elaboration. Perhaps he assumed that Mrs Anderson had told her as much.

'William, I know you did his first operation ten years ago,' she lied.

Again, no denial, he seemed only perturbed. 'Is this supposed to be leading us somewhere?' He made a rolling motion with one hand, suggesting that Ali get to the point.

So she was right. 'Did Rita Anderson love her husband? That first time – didn't you take her to bed *before* the operation?'

316

Was he a little frightened now? Oh, yes.

Rouge Kendall's theory only erred because the pass at his mother had occurred *after* a surgery. William was into a much darker form of emotional extortion. He probably took advantage of gratitude at every opportunity, but he preyed on fear.

The exorbitant fees of a top-ranked surgeon would not be covered by a cost-cutting insurance plan. Judging by Rita's low-rent appearance, the woman's husband must have been a *pro bono* patient. Ali slipped into Rita Anderson's state of mind on the eve of her husband's surgery: What would she do when the sexual proposition was put to her? Would she stalk off indignantly, and then seek out a lesser surgeon to cut into her husband's heart? Or would she go quietly to William's bed?

Perhaps the woman loved her husband even now, for Mr Anderson was very ill – and his wife was still in William's bed.

Ali was angry when she leaned forward to kill off Proper William with one final satisfying shot. 'If the other wives come forward— Oh, sorry. I know at least one of them was the mother of a patient. If they all testify, you'll lose your license, won't you?'

Right and right again. So there were others. It was a pattern. And if she was an adept judge of facial expressions and body language, the doctor was about to lose control of his bladder.

And what other patterns might he have?

Proper William, could you murder a little girl?

He had demonstrated sadism, the most necessary element. He also liked a challenge and the element of risk. And he didn't seem troubled by conscience, or ethics. A sadistic opportunist could divide his appetites between children and women. The women could be kept in line.

But the children would have to be killed, wouldn't they?

There had been no reaction when she mentioned the little girls. Could she have misread him? Or was he that cold about murder? Or perhaps he had more confidence in the crime of killing children, since the witnesses never lived to tell about it. What in hell was she dealing with here?

Captain Costello could only watch the flames licking the top of the garden incinerator. He was too late to stop Mortimer Cray. The large metal canister's contents were certainly ashes by now. 'Very thorough, Dr Cray. Why didn't you use one of the fireplaces in the house?'

'Too small for a really good blaze.' The psychiatrist looked at the captain with no hostility, no fear.

'So little time,' said Costello, 'so many files to burn.'

'Yes, there were quite a lot of them. I realize the town codes don't allow outdoor trash incineration anymore. I expect you'll be writing me a ticket for this.'

'I'm not here to trade lines with you, sir. We found some of Sadie Green's clothing in the next county, a tiny little pair of purple socks.'

'But nothing belonging to Gwen Hubble?'

'No. I think the bastard knows we're getting close, and he's trying to lead us away from town. What do you think, Doc?'

'I think a half-bright child might've come to the same conclusion. Do you want to serve me with your search warrant now?'

Costello handed him the document. The doctor only folded it away in his suitcoat pocket without even glancing at it, and this annoyed the captain. It had taken two solid hours of begging before the judge would issue a warrant on thin grounds of probable cause. The district attorney, biggest fool in five counties, had actually argued against it. Only Costello's passionate belief in the imminent danger to a child had finally swayed the judge in his favor.

Uniformed troopers were already at work on the garden, prowling through the plants, and now more of them entered the house. Two dogs from the Canine Corps were inhaling scent from bags containing children's clothing. Men with shovels and men with black bags stood in the yard waiting on a signal. He nodded to them and the digging began. The captain spoke to the two technicians at his side. 'I want every damn print in his private office. You got that?'

'I doubt that they'll find anything,' said Mortimer Cray. 'My housekeeper is meticulous in her dusting and polishing.'

'Okay, boys, you heard that. Check the damn ceiling if you have to. How tall is your housekeeper, Dr Cray?' Costello turned to the flaming incinerator and smiled at an afterthought. 'Oh, and this might be a good time to mention that I only wanted your appointment book. My warrant excluded the patient files.'

When Ali entered the conservatory, she found her uncle amid the debris of overturned giant clay pots. Young fruit trees and evergreens with rounded topiary shapes lay on the floor in the spilled dirt. Delicate orchids with naked roots had been pulled from smaller containers. Other unseated plants were scattered around small mounds of dirt from one end of the long potting table to the other. And a pane in the wall of glass had been broken by a careless searcher. The police had missed few opportunities for destruction, with the sole purpose of pressuring a frail old man with harassment bordering on terrorism.

Ali approved.

Mortimer was standing at the worktable, restoring dirt to a small ceramic pot of bright blue. He seemed in no hurry to rescue his prize plants. He filled the pot with a small measuring spoon, a bit of soil at a time, no hurry at all.

Years ago, as an invisible child, she had walked among these tables of flowering plants, following in the wake of touring houseguests, absorbing adult conversations on the lineage, origin and symbolism of each species. Today, Uncle Mortimer ignored his savaged hybrids of rare and riotous colors. He was concentrating all his efforts on a small plant of common white tea roses, metaphors of silence.

She wondered if this violence on his beloved plants had

unhinged him. Perhaps he was simply slow to cope. 'Can I help you, Uncle Mortimer?'

No response.

Ali picked up another pot and inserted a tender young orchid with torn petals. She scooped soil around the roots, gently, carefully, unmindful of the dirt gathering beneath her fingernails. 'You could have stopped this if you'd given them a name.'

She hadn't really expected a response. Soon she would have to call Charlie Croft and tell him to let William Penny go. There was no solid reason to hold him, no evidence of anything but gross misconduct with the wives of vulnerable patients. And Proper William was going to get away with that. Charlie Croft would never use the information. The chief would want to avoid any trouble over the improper arrest or the search of William's house and clinic.

Ali quickly tamped the dirt down around the stem of the plant and then reached for another one. Her uncle was still fussing over the same blue pot, and seemed not to notice that she worked alongside of him.

'Can't you tell me anything that will keep a child alive? You know he's killed one of them, but what about the other girl?'

'She's already dead.' The blue pot was not yet half full. 'The little princess always dies early on Christmas morning – according to your own research, Ali. I doubt there was ever a variation in that routine.'

Oddly enough, she took this as a positive thing, a sign of communication. He had just confirmed the pattern. She picked up another pot, not wanting to lose control of herself while he was in the talking mode. 'Why does he do it?' Was he even listening to her now? He seemed so distracted. 'Uncle Mortimer? Why is he doing this? What's it about?'

'What is it ever about? A raging, demanding, unrelenting God is always in the details somewhere. The child is only an object, or perhaps a vehicle. He never considers the inside of her, the fear and pain. All the sadism is directed at me. He wants me to suffer, and I do. I was never in control. He was.'

'He's a religious fanatic? Is that what you're—'

'Common people rise, the extraordinary sink, all because of the same incident, Ali.' He had filled the pot now, but kept adding dirt until it overflowed. 'Remember, the priest was once a rather ordinary man. You know that's true — if you haven't colored all your old memories of him. He might've been your soul mate when you were a child, so shy, so soft-spoken, invisible really – just like you. But now? Well, you've seen him.' The spoon scraped the rim of the pot. He jabbed it into the dirt, again and again.

'You're not saying Father Paul—'

'Rather extraordinary now, isn't he, Ali? But it's not just him. Everything is out of balance. It's all up in the air, suspended in cosmic dust.'

'What? Uncle Mortimer, you have to help me out here. I'm still not the smartest—'

'And you're part of it too, Ali. Look at what you've done with your life. Logically—' He held up the measuring spoon and examined it, as though he had never seen one before. Then he drove it into the pot, scraping the ceramic sides with a gritty noise. 'Well, logic has flown, hasn't it? Perhaps it's more a sense of balance, or proportion – an eye for symmetry. He's waiting for the balance to be restored. It's already changing. Rouge Kendall is on the rise, seeking his level. The priest will be diminished soon.'

'And what about me, Uncle Mortimer? Will I disappear again? Blend into some wall, out of sight? Where is all this prophecy coming from? I know you don't believe in psychics, and you're not a religious man.'

He ignored her to stare at the garden beyond the panes of glass. 'And where is the snow, my dear? There has never been a single winter without two feet of snow this late in December. At this altitude, there's— Well, where *is* the snow?'

'Excuse me.'

Ali turned to see Rouge standing at the end of the table.

'I'm sorry to interrupt,' he said. 'I need to speak with you. Alone.'

Had he found out about William Penny's arrest? Not likely. The schism between state and local police had placed Rouge on the other side of Chief Croft's boundary line. William Penny would be secreted in some back room, while the chief made use of his prisoner's house keys. She did not want to keep this from Rouge, but a child was in danger, time was precious, and Chief Croft should not have to pay for empathy with the loss of his job.

Her uncle was still fixated on his snowless garden when she followed Rouge through the side door and into the main house. The foyer was larger than a modest two-story home. The high ceiling, an architect's flight of fancy, was structured around a curving grand staircase. Beyond the wood railing of the upper gallery, men and women in uniforms passed in and out of the doorways of second-floor rooms.

'There's something I want to show you.' Rouge led her to the small door set into the massive structure of the staircase. 'Sorry about the damage. We got all the keys to the house from the valet. But none of them worked on this lock. I asked your uncle for the key, but I don't think he heard me.'

She looked at the scraped and dented metal where it had been forced with tools.

Rouge's hand was on the knob, hesitating. 'The night we met in Dame's Tavern, you told me your uncle was an atheist. Then in the hospital room, you said it again. But you accused him of using the priest as a confessor.'

'The contradiction bothers you? That business with the priest had nothing to do with my uncle's religious beliefs. He could ethically give the burden of knowledge to a priest. It was a ploy for the—'

Rouge opened the door, taking her words and her breath away. Once, this had been a large storage room with shelving, trunks and boxes, and a small ordinary window set into the back wall. Now the clutter had been removed; the window had been enlarged, reshaped with a religious arch, and repaned with stained glass depicting symbols of a mythological creature, Persephone, goddess of spring.

Other symbols in the wall murals came from Christianity – lambs and doves, metaphors of a trinity, and a hundred replications of the cross hung on every bit of clear wall space. But the carved objects on pedestals were images of fawns with flutes and other animals with human characteristics. Her eyes traveled over the fresco on the longest wall; it followed the sweeping curve of the exterior staircase. The mural was amateurish, and she recognized the style. Her uncle had dabbled in art as a younger man. Her father owned several canvases from those early years – but nothing like this.

The entire wall was flooded with Old Testament images. The centerpiece was the depiction of God from the Sistine Chapel, but the face was distorted, enraged. It was a portrait of the old God, Whom Uncle Mortimer had once described as angry and petulant, demanding blood, inflicting sores on the faithful, turning his children to pillars of salt when they displeased him. Moses was among the minions and wearing the horns Michelangelo had given him. Other horned images abounded in and about bright bursts of painted flames. Snatches of imagery from the third panel of Bosch's *Millennium* triptych showed the torments of the damned, the tortures of the flesh. The most hellish scenes were the most recent and as yet unfinished. She could see the pencil marks on the wall, outlines of figures not yet filled in with color, with light and shadow.

The work was not a masterpiece, but very labor-intensive. She knew it must have taken years to do this.

Among the animal objects were small statues of a woman, a gentle goddess of renewal, who shared this space with a deity of destruction. All the pantheistic elements of nature had been overpowered by the work on the walls.

She could smell the stale odors from incense pots. The

many candles about the room had melted down to nubs. There was further evidence of ritual in the cat-o'-nine-tails upon the altar, a tool of self-flagellation.

Rouge Kendall was watching her with great patience, making no sound, nor any movement to hurry her. She picked her words carefully, for she well understood whom she was dealing with, and she would not underestimate him.

'I'd say it began with the aspects of nature, the goddess of spring.' She stood before the stained-glass window. 'It's an elegant gesture, most likely a whim and rather harmless – given his love for plants. This might have been a meditation room, a quiet place to lock out the world and think, or just to find some peace. He's always handled the most bizarre cases. It's not surprising that he would need a retreat.'

She turned to face the massive curving wall. 'And then the Old Testament God moved in and overgrew the space. That's probably when the room became a shrine – the altar, the candles.' She averted her eyes from the whip. 'That made the room dark and violent. No peace anymore.'

'He's insane, isn't he, Ali?'

'It represents a crisis point in his philosophy.' She turned away from Rouge, surprising herself with the calm in her voice. 'It shows the pressure of concealing the murderer. This is what it's done to him. He doesn't see himself as a willing con-spirator, and he can't recognize his own agony as a sign of wrongdoing. In the old Testament, the faithful were punished along with the sinners. I'm sure you recognized the images from—'

She knew he had already analyzed this room with his better brain, and now she wondered if she had done half as well.

'Take it a little farther, Ali. What if he sees the pain as punishment, and not as a test of faith? How does he *really* see himself? Righteous man or sinner?'

'You suspect him of—' She looked at the wall again. What was Rouge finding in the same pictures? 'He sees himself as a very moral man. This is what it cost him to keep a secret, to keep to his own code of ethics.'

Rouge did not seem convinced. He was standing near the altar and staring at the whip of many thongs – ancient method of penance. He was drawing his own conclusions.

She joined him at the altar. 'It would have been easier for him to tell. You can see that, can't you? It's not that he didn't want to. But his personal code is so rigid.'

There was nothing to be read in Rouge's face. Even when they were children in the choir, she had been unable to discern the thoughts of either Kendall twin. In her mind, this survivor of the pair was still one of the strange students of St Ursula's, and she would always be in awe of him.

'Rouge? Will you let me talk to my uncle before you tell the others about this?'

He nodded, saying nothing, probably waiting for a more direct answer to his original question, the one he had posed when they entered the room.

'Yes,' she said. 'He's insane.'

Ali returned to the conservatory to find her uncle working over the same blue pot, churning up the dirt, digging and digging with his measuring spoon.

She touched his shoulder very gently. He only nodded to say he was aware of her. 'Uncle Mortimer? You said *he* wanted you to suffer. Were you talking about a patient, or God?'

He continued to dig in the blue pot, churning up the dirt, directing all of his attention to it, yet unaware of the damage he was doing to the delicate roots.

'Please stop.' She put one hand on his, but the digging went on. 'Uncle Mortimer, we have to talk. I've seen the shrine.'

No reaction, only the gritty noises of the spoon scraping the sides of the pot as he churned up the dirt. She was becoming a small girl again, accustomed to being ignored.

'This is important to me. If you could just give me some

small thing, anything. I believe Gwen Hubble might still be alive.'

He continued to ignore her, finding the dirt in the pot more fascinating. She was becoming Sally again, the invisible child, nothing so grand as anything that grew in Uncle Mortimer's greenhouse. The adults in her memory were walking past her, holding conversations in the air above her head as she became smaller and smaller.

One finger drifted up to touch the scar on her face. Then her hand shot straight out in anger and sent the blue pot crashing to the floor.

Mortimer stared at her with no surprise in his eyes. He seemed only tired when he looked down at the ceramic fragments and the dirt on the stone tiles at his feet.

And now she also looked down at the breakage and saw the glint of gold among the clots of dark-brown soil. She knelt down on the floor beside the debris and spread the dirt with her hands to uncover a tiny ring. She held it up to the light and found the initials she was looking for, S.R.

She whispered, 'Sarah Ryan, ten years old.' Now she uncovered the religious medal. 'Mary Wyatt, ten years old'. Other small things appeared under her probing hands, and she could put a child's name to each one of them. She almost missed the delicate ankle chain attached to an engraved oval of gold. 'AIMM?'

The rain had stopped. They moved under the trees where the plant misters could not reach them with the sprays of water. Gwen held the flashlight while Sadie made a long reach to prod the dog's body with a broomstick. 'I think he's dead.'

'No,' said Gwen. 'You'll know when he's dead.' This was the voice of experience with generations of white mice and hamsters. The first time she found a mouse lying on the floor of his cage, she had known this was not sleep, even though she had never seen death before. There was no mistaking one thing for the other. Death was not a mere lack of animation, but a subtraction from the world.

'This dog is still here, I know he is.' Gwen rolled off the plastic sheet spread beneath the tree. She crept toward the animal on her hands and knees. The last pill was wearing off, and she was feeling more pain now.

'Gwen, no!'

The child stopped and laid her head on her arms, exhausted from this small effort. She knew Sadie was right. If the dog suddenly revived, she would not be able to get out of his way. He was a smart enough animal to play dead, waiting on his advantage.

Her leg ached. It was getting more useless by the hour. She lifted her head again and trained the flashlight on the animal, studying him from this safe distance beyond the reach of his chain. His wound was a small one, only a dark hole and a stream of blood.

The dog moved, and she dropped the flashlight. She picked it up again and shined it on his face. He cried with a human sound. The dog must also be in great pain. 'Maybe we could give him some pills? We could bury them in dog food and—'

'And then maybe bandage him up? I don't think he'll thank us for that, Gwen. Remember the last time I went in there?'

'He's hurting, dying – more afraid than we are.' Fear would be the last thing the dog knew, that and isolation. Gwen could imagine the screaming fear of *alone*. Compared to that, pain was nothing.

Sadie took the flashlight from Gwen's hand and went off down the aisle of mushroom tables. When she came back, she had the light trained on a jar of dog biscuits sodden with water. White pills were dissolving in the mix.

She gave Gwen the flashlight. 'Keep it on the dog.' Sadie was only a vague shape in the dark as she walked into the circle of the dog chain, heading for the prone body in the flashlight beam. The dog cried once more, but couldn't lift his head again.

Gwen's eyes widened as Sadie did the unthinkable. She put her hand into the jar to extract a glob of the soggy mixture and held it to the dog's mouth. The large rough tongue hung out between his jaws as he licked the food from her tiny white fingers. Gwen, who loved all animals, knew she could never have done this thing.

Sadie remained with the dog, petting him and crooning soft nonsense syllables. Gwen saw nothing vicious in the animal anymore. His eyes were all loving sorrow and gratitude. He continued to lick Sadie's fingers long after the food was gone.

And then the dog was dead. Gwen had seen the moment come and pass. All that she was unsure of was whether death had caught him breathing in or breathing out. Now the carcass was more like a picture of a dog, an idea of one. He was no longer in his body. Only the living dwelled in their skins, their soul bags. Had the dog been surprised, or had he sensed it toward the end and even invited death to hollow him out?

Sadie returned to sit beside her in the dirt.

Gwen hugged her knees. 'I'm ready to go back to the hole now.' She shivered under the cloak of towels. Her parka was not yet dry. The mercury in the thermometer outside the white room continued to drop. It was now thirty degrees. When they had settled back into the grave, Gwen asked, 'Do you think the dog has a soul? Maybe he's still here, walking around the cellar like Griffin in *The Invisible Man*.'

'Claude Rains, 1933,' said Sadie. 'Mr Caruthers was wrong when he said you were too literal. You see a lot of things that aren't there.'

And with this pronouncement the dog was altogether gone. *Brave dog*. Gwen looked around at the hole they sat in, more specifically a grave. 'What do you think our parents would say if they could see us now?'

'Well, *my* mother would say I was in my element. She says that every time I die.' Sadie got up and put a piece of the plastic over her head as a makeshift umbrella. The flashlight beam swung back and forth as she walked into the dark trees, saying over one shoulder, 'I'll be back.' The light disappeared around the thick trunk of an oak.

Gwen listened to the patter of rain on the leaves. She believed her pain was easing, but she was only losing the distinction between the black of the cellar and the blackness of eyes closing as she was sinking below the level of consciousness.

When she awoke again, with a stabbing sensation in her leg, the rain had stopped. It was so quiet. Gwen strained to catch a sound, any sound at all. The silence was enormous – bigger than the trees, and suddenly she was overwhelmed by it. Was she alone? The silence loomed over her, it was everything, bigger than the sky. 'Sadie!' she screamed.

Sadie came running back, her shape forming out of the darkness in slices of the darting flashlight beam as she pounded across the floor of the forest. She was covered with dirt.

'What have you been doing?'

'I'll tell you later.'

'You were digging another hole, weren't you?'

'Yeah. It's near the Samuel tree. Very shallow, just the cover of dirt, okay? So we can get out quick. He'll never think to look for us underground. So while he's looking in the back of the cellar, where all the good hiding places are, and the door is propped open, we can—'

'I'm not going to be buried.' Gwen thought of the bugs squirming next to her skin, their antennae twitching, probing, looking for a way to get inside of her. 'I can't do it, Sadie. I can't go back in the ground.'

Sadie climbed into the hole with Gwen and put her arms around her. 'You're in the ground *now*. You just don't have any dirt in your eyes, that's all.'

Gwen shook her head. She didn't want to think of graves. And there was something else that bothered her. 'He had a gun. Why did he just go away like that?'

'The Fly? You saw the dog bite him.'

'But he wasn't even limping.'

'Neither did you, not right away. He probably went off to patch it up. Then he'll come back.'

'But he had a gun, Sadie. He heard you yell the Geronimo command. Why didn't he—'

'Shoot me and get it over with? Think, Gwen. What did he do next? He turned off the lights and the heat, right?' Sadie shined the light on her friend's face. Now she could see that Gwen was not following her. 'That's the biggest part of the game – anticipation. It's the most important part of a good horror movie. Do you get it now?'

Gwen nodded and bowed her head, whispering, 'He's dragging it out, torturing us. Like the dog. The way he—'

'Right. The dog is dead. We're his new dogs.'

Gwen took the flashlight and trained the beam on the animal corpse lying in the dirt. 'The horror movie keeps changing on me.'

'No. It's the same movie, Gwen. The element of surprise is everything.'

'But it hasn't worked so far.'

'A mere technicality.'

'It's Christmas. Miss Vickers will be back tomorrow. She always comes home the day—'

'Gwen, I don't think she's ever coming home.' Sadie took the flashlight and pointed the beam at the stack of journals. She picked up the one for the current year and flipped through the pages to the final entry. 'See the squiggly line that goes off the page? I think this is where Miss Vickers knew she was dying.'

'You don't know that. She was only tired.'

'What about the pills she spilled on the floor in the white room? See anything *else* out of place in that room? And the squiggly line? Tired, huh?' Sadie flipped through all the pages. 'See her getting tired anywhere else?' She picked up another book and opened it to page after page. 'See any other lines like that one?'

And now Sadie was pulling out all the journals and holding

them out to Gwen, one by one, as she ripped through the pages.

'Stop it!'

'She's not coming back, Gwen. If we wait for—'

'Stop! All right – you win. Help is *not* on the way.' She put up both her hands in surrender.

'Finally.' Sadie smiled as a reward for her dullest pupil.

'But I'm not going to be buried in the ground.' She would not be able to stand that. Gwen already had the sense that she was leaving, bit by bit, disappearing from the world. 'Once I go into the ground, I'll never be able to get out again.'

'We'll work on that.'

'You know it's true, Sadie. I won't be going anywhere. But you could make it out of here.'

Sadie upended the flashlight to shine it on her widest grin, apparently amused by this odd idea that she could leave without her best friend.

Gwen drew back from the light, wanting the cover of darkness so nothing could be read into the tears flooding her eyes, the weak tremble of her mouth. Her friend would never know that – given the choice and two good legs to run with – she would have left Sadie behind. Gwen pressed hard on the wound to make it sing and shriek with pain.

CHAPTER 10

Sadie wore a canvas sack around her shoulders to ward off the cold and the damp as she finished changing the bandage, and then rolled down Gwen's tattered pant leg.

'Take my parka,' said Gwen. 'I don't need it. I'm—'

'No, *you* wear it.' She wrapped both feet in cloth tied on with twine at the ankles. It was too cold to go barefoot. Done with this chore, Sadie walked about under the trees, gathering up the debris of the dummy and collecting it in one pile. She sat cross-legged on the ground, took up her blade and stabbed it into the material of the sweater, over and over again.

Gwen leaned back against the trunk of the dead Samuel tree and watched. 'I'm burning up. I don't need the parka.'

'Well, I don't want it.' Sadie returned to the rock wall and the less violent work of honing the blade. 'Remember the tape we played last Saturday – the really hokey axe murders? Joan Crawford made them keep that movie set at fifty-eight degrees. She said it gave her focus.'

'Sadie, you've got to be freezing.'

'Keep it. You have to stay warm. You don't want to get worse, do you?'

Could she get any worse? She unzipped the red parka and wiped the sweat from her face. Her skin was hot to the touch. The sound of the metal grating on stone was relentless. 'Why do you keep doing that?'

'I'm working on plan *B*.' Sadie rubbed the broken garden tool back and forth across an outcrop of irregular rock. 'The blade needs to be sharper. He'll be wearing a coat, so it has to cut through a few layers of heavy cloth. That's one of the worst flaws in the movies – when the knife just slides into the body. It's harder in real life. Hey, Gwen, watch this.' She dropped the knife on the ground, then sank down on her knees. With her legs hidden behind her, Sadie walked forward on her kneecaps. 'Who am I?'

'You're Blizzard, the legless man in *The Penalty*.' Gwen paused for a moment, stuck on the date. 'Is it 1920?'

'Right. Good.' Sadie stood up and clasped her hands behind her back so nothing of her arms could be seen, only the small wings of her shoulder blades. 'Now who am I?'

This one was entirely too easy. 'Alonso the Armless from *The Unknown*, 1927.'

Sadie began to revolve in a very slow turn. When Gwen saw her friend's face come round again, she sucked in her breath. Sadie had a mouthy grin of razor-sharp teeth. But how? Paper – her mouth was full of paper with ink-drawn teeth.

Gwen laughed and applauded. 'You're the vampire in *London After Midnight*, same year. Good one. You scared the shit out of me.'

Sadie pulled the paper from her mouth. 'I'm building up your horror muscles.' She picked up her blade and returned to the dummy's torso and torn limbs.

Gwen stared at the half-moon shape of discarded paper teeth. 'You know what makes a really *good* horror movie?'

Sadie looked up from her stabbing. 'Horror? Sorry – too obvious. I must be getting tired.'

'Well, it's not the monsters, the really ghouly ones. The scariest thing is one shock in an ordinary world – like your paper teeth. No – like blood on Santa's beard.'

'I got it.' Sadie hunkered down in the dirt and trained the flashlight on the lifeless body of her old enemy the dog. She redirected the beam to light up her face and a smile of wholesome innocence. 'We could eat him.'

'That's not funny.' Gwen shook her head, for evidently Sadie had completely misunderstood. 'The dog isn't—' Her words trailed off. She was stunned as she watched Sadie working over the dead body, taking blood from the dog's wound and smearing it on her face. Then Sadie looked up to show her that she *had* understood – perfectly, though this didn't seem the most practical implementation, not quite what Gwen had in mind. 'I don't think he'll be afraid of—'

'I bet he's never had an enemy larger than a little kid. He's a coward.' She said this in anger, an alien tone that took Gwen by surprise. Sadie's voice gentled as she ran one hand across the pelt of the dead animal. 'This dog was more of a man.'

'He's too big, Sadie. He's going to—'

'Think it through. You had the right idea – the blood on Santa's beard. The Fly *is* bigger. All the power is on his side, right? So when *we* go after *him*, he'll be totally weirded out. It'll be the last thing he ever expected.' She dragged one bloody finger down the side of her face in a jagged line. 'He'll pee in his pants. Does this look like a lightning bolt?'

Gwen nodded.

Sadie admired her reflection in the sharpened blade that had once been half of Miss Vickers' garden shears. 'I wish I had my Technicolor blood kit. We can improvise with the real thing, but it's just not the same.'

'Sadie, we can't hurt this man. We tried. If the dog couldn't do it, *we* can't.'

'What about *Freaks*?'

Gwen nodded, conceding the point gracefully, but not with her whole heart. Sadie was alluding to the movie's dwarfs and midgets who had brought down an enemy of adult stature. And then the little people had quite literally cut their opponent down to size. She still had the occasional nightmare about this vintage film, the pride of Sadie's collection.

'You know what Mr Caruthers would say.' Sadie stroked her imagined gray beard and stared into space with a squint. 'It's an interesting problem in logic.' Then she was all Sadie

334

again. 'If we just sit here, he'll come down and kill us.' She sank her blade into the dummy. 'So we're going to kill him first. An hour ago, you were all for it.'

Gwen covered her eyes to block out the beam of light, not wanting to see what the other child was doing with the dog's blood. There was no way to explain this change of heart, not in any way that would make sense to her best friend, the master of terror. Bravery came in moments. Gwen could not sustain it for an entire hour. Perhaps a moment would come again – perhaps not. Though the dead dog lay only a few feet away, the concept of killing was as far from her as the moon.

To kill a *man* – this was unthinkable, impossible.

'It's wrong to take a life.' Gwen knew this was a lame substitute for truth, but plausible. She watched a spider crawling along the ground near her foot. She was terrified of the bugs that lived under the ground. However, this arachnid seemed fairly benign, all eight legs heading in a definite direction, a creature with places to go and things to do. 'Father Domina says life is sacred. All life.'

When Sadie smiled, her dog's-blood lightning bolts jumped. 'You're losing your sense of humor.'

'Do you understand what death really *is*?' Gwen raised her hand high, and though she was weak, she managed to smash it down on the hapless spider. When she turned her hand over, the creature's sticky innards were spread across her palm. 'That's death. You can never undo it. *Never.*'

All the insect legs twitched independently for a while. The girls watched the spider, fascinated, until it jerked one last time and was still.

'Cool,' said Sadie. 'I think you've got the hang of it.'

And it *was* interesting. Gwen shook the bits of the spider's body to the ground. The remainder of the poor innocent little beast was only a smear on her hand.

Well, that wasn't so bad.

'One good shock,' said Sadie. 'That's what we need to work on. He'll lose his mind when he sees this.' She held the flashlight to her face to highlight the blood. 'You get it? Like dogs reverting to wolves.'

'I think he's seen scarier things than that,' said Gwen, appraising the symmetrical rows of jagged streaks on either side of her friend's bloody face. Then her gaze wandered down the rows of mushroom tables, each with its own wooden cart. Why had he dug the graves in the middle of the row? Why not at the end or the beginning? Unless some of the—

'All right,' said Sadie. 'But surprise will still work. We need a distraction – something really gross. So we wait by the door, see? Maybe not *under* the ground, just a little covering of dirt – camouflage. And then when he comes in, he'll see something at the other side of the cellar. When he goes over there to get a better look, we run outside and lock him in. Neat?'

Gwen dropped her head. 'It won't work.' Once buried again, no matter how light the covering dirt, she didn't believe she would ever climb out of her own grave. Buried alive – dying slowly with the dirt in her eyes, the bugs crawling in her ears and her nostrils. And then they would crawl into her mouth when she opened it to scream – unable to fight back against the smallest insect.

Sadie believed she could win against a full-grown man. *Impossible.*

'You know I can't run.'

'Yes, you can,' said Sadie. 'I'll help you.'

'Hiding is better.'

'We can't do that – not if you won't go into the ground.' Sadie pressed on, 'Doing something is better than doing nothing, better than—'

'I know Miss Vickers isn't coming back. But what about our parents? The police? You think they've given up on us, don't you?'

'No, I don't. But it may take a very long time before they find us.' She knelt down beside Gwen and touched her face. 'You're on fire. I have to get you out of here.'

Gwen lay back on the ground, resting her head in Sadie's

lap. It was a fight to keep her eyes open. 'Even if you think I'm dead, don't put me in the ground. Promise me?'

'I promise you're not going to die.' Sadie gently stroked her burning forehead with a cool hand.

Gwen sat up and shined the light on her friend's face. This time she had to know she wasn't being told a comforting lie. 'You won't do that – you won't bury me?'

'I promise. Don't think about death anymore.' Sadie stood up and walked over to the dog's body. She shrouded it with a plastic trash bag, so Gwen would not have to *look* at death, either.

But there was yet another sense of mortality in the stench, for the dog had lost control of his bowels at the end. This smell mingled with the putrid odor of her wound and added a little to her growing store of knowledge about death.

'Take the parka, Sadie.' Gwen struggled to get out of the down jacket, but she was too weak to work her way out of the sleeves. 'You *take* it! You might have to walk a long way before you find help. It makes sense that one of us—'

Sadie pulled the parka back over Gwen's arms and zipped it up, gently scolding, 'You're very sick.'

'Sadie, never mind about me. Run for it when you get the chance.' *Please don't leave me alone.* 'He has a gun. Your knife can't beat a bullet.' *If you leave me, I'll die.* 'You can't fight a grown man. You have to run.' *Don't go.*

One child folded into the other, arms entwining, cheek pressed to cheek, soft as flower petals. So quiet now. Then Sadie whispered, 'How could I leave you behind?'

Arnie Pyle and Rouge Kendall sat on the office couch. Ali Cray was seated on the other side of the desk, facing Captain Costello. Only Marge Jonas remained standing as she stared through the blinds of the second-floor window overlooking Cranberry Street. The sun had been snuffed out by a heavy overcast. Behind her back, Costello was answering Ali's question.

'No, your uncle hasn't told us a damn thing. No confession, no denial, nothing at all.' The captain sat back in his chair. His eyes made a slow roll to the ceiling, as if he could not believe his own words. 'Dr Cray waived his rights to a lawyer, but the DA insisted that we have a doctor present.'

Now he turned to the large woman at the window. 'And Marge? Find out how those local cops just happened to turn up a damned heart specialist in three minutes flat. Sometimes I get the feeling that I'm not in charge anymore.'

'I'll look into it,' said Marge, without turning around. He knew her every expression; she couldn't afford to face him when she lied. The first flakes of snow sifted down from the dark-gray sky. Though it was the noon hour, she would not have been surprised if the thick clouds had parted to show her the moon; it had been that kind of a day.

Three people stopped on the sidewalk. They appeared to be together, yet there were no greetings, no conversation passed between them. And there was no sun to cast their shadows. The strange little trio turned in unison to stare up at the window. Marge took one step back, feeling suddenly naked under the bright light from the office ceiling.

Costello was still talking to Ali Cray. 'So the DA says to me, "Suppose the old guy has a fatal heart attack. We don't want to see a crucifixion on the evening news. Get a doctor." And then two village cops come whipping around the corner with this bastard, this—' He looked down at his paperwork. 'Dr William Penny in a bathrobe. You know this guy, right?'

Marge looked back over her shoulder to see Ali Cray nodding, but volunteering nothing. Apparently, Chief Croft had called it right. William Penny had preferred to keep the details of his improper arrest to himself – along with the facts of his affair.

More people had gathered on the sidewalk below, though not many. A sprinkling of pale faces and dark ones were tilted up to the lighted window. What did they want? Well, nothing dangerous. They had the look of a small band of alien tourists lost on a strange planet and seeking guidance.

Behind her back she could hear Costello tapping his pencil on the desktop – sure sign of an impending storm. He was still addressing Ali. 'Has William Penny always had this bad attitude about cops? You think the guy might've had a prior run-in with the law?'

Marge winced.

'I wouldn't know,' said Ali. 'He's my uncle's doctor. I never heard anything about his personal background. Is Uncle Mortimer all right?'

'Oh, yeah, he's just *fine*. Old Willy boy, the damn heart specialist, sedated your uncle five fucking minutes into the interview. Then this twit heart surgeon smiles at me – pure evil – like he really enjoyed pissing me off. That's when the lawyer showed up. I'm pretty sure Dr Penny called him. So the lawyer pulls all the right strings to have your uncle sent home in the doctor's care.'

'That isn't right!' Rouge Kendall stood up, angry and incredulous. 'I identified that ankle chain. It was my sister's.'

Costello shrugged. 'Unfortunately, that's evidence in a closed case. We're not investigating that death.'

'But they've got to be tied together. All those—'

Costello put up both hands in surrender. 'Hey, Rouge. This is the DA talking – not me. Mortimer Cray visited Paul Marie at the prison. We don't know that the priest wasn't the source of the ankle chain. If we can't prove there wasn't a prior doctor–patient relationship, that visit taints the evidence.'

Marge watched more people gathering outside the building, and others were coming down the sidewalk and from across the road, so silent in their gathering. And the snow continued to fall. Still she had no sense of anything sinister. They seemed helpless. Some were holding hands for courage or comfort in the dark of midday.

'For all we know,' said Costello, 'the shrink collects souvenirs from all his patients. Could be five different perverts contributing to his little stash – that was the lawyer's argument. The only descriptions on the rest of the jewelry are in Ali's case notes. So the fuckwit DA says that's not enough to charge Mortimer Cray with murder, conspiracy or obstruction of justice. Not even if we prove every single trinket is tied to a dead kid.'

Costello cast his eyes down to read from the sheet of paper on his desk. 'This comes from the DA's office. "A psychiatrist cannot be compelled to give evidence against a patient for a crime committed in another state." ' He looked up at Rouge. 'That tears it, kid. Your sister is a closed case. All the other trinkets belong to cases outside the state. True, it's a gray area of law, and the local DA is a moron. He's also pissed off that I challenged him on a warrant, so this paper could be legal bullshit. But he's got jurisdiction. I can't shop around for charges.' The captain pushed his chair back. Turning away from Rouge, he spoke to Ali. 'And both of those kids are dead by now. You *know* that. You were right about everything. Merry freaking Christmas.'

Marge sank down to a chair by the window. She thought Ali Cray was about to say something. Was there still a chance of finding the little girls alive? Apparently not, for Ali's shoulders slumped, and there were other signs of resignation: her eyes were sad, so close to tears, and her hands balled into fists of frustration.

So the children were dead.

Marge stole a glance at Costello in profile. He hadn't shaved this morning – a bad sign. She found worse omens in the clutter on his desk. Fast-food wrappers and take-out containers were breeding on and under the furniture.

She turned back to the window and looked up to the sky. Had the ceiling of cloud cover dropped in these past few minutes? Was it falling as she watched? *Yes, indeed, Chicken Little, the earth and the sky, the night and the day are trading places.*

Oh, and now *more* zombies were gathering on the sidewalk,

escapees from an entirely different story. She counted fifteen people standing beneath the window, all staring upward. Marge looked at the bright fluorescent tubes spanning the office ceiling.

Perhaps the light was attracting them.

'I want a warrant to search Oz Almo's house.' Rouge Kendall was moving toward the door, and he was angry.

'Hold it, Rouge.' Costello's voice was all authority now. 'It's over. All that's missing are the bodies of the kids.'

'Mortimer Cray didn't confess, did he?' Rouge walked back to the desk, planted his hands flat on the wood and stared at Costello. 'And you don't think that old man is the one – do you.' This was not a question, but an accusation. 'I want to search Oz Almo's place. If you want, I'll go to Judge Riley's house myself and get the warrant.'

Marge caught the captain's eye, and now she was nodding, pleading Rouge's case. *Let him do this?*

Costello turned away from her and addressed his rookie investigator. 'No – not today. I'm telling you for the last time, you've got no probable cause for a search warrant. All you've got is an old grudge match, Rouge. I know it and you know it. Nobody goes off spinning their wheels until we find the bodies. I want you to go over everything on Sorrel's desk. But first, stop by the medical examiner's office and try to get something out of him. I still think Chainy's holding out on me.'

Marge could see that Rouge was about to come back at the captain with another argument. Costello also saw it coming and shook his head. 'No warrant – no way. Now get moving.'

Arnie Pyle trailed Rouge out the door. As the two men headed across the squad room toward the stairs, Ali Cray stared after them, looking very much like the leftover child who was not chosen for the baseball team. She drifted out of the office and gently closed the door behind her.

On the sidewalk below the window, the silent crowd had doubled – no, *tripled* in size. Their numbers spilled into the street, and the slow traffic moved around them. Perhaps she should mention this gathering of weird mutes. Ah, but what would she say? *Excuse me, Leonard, but the body-snatching pod people are here.* The captain had seen that movie; he would know how to deal with them.

Marge faced him now. 'So you want me to tell the uniforms to stop digging up the hazelnut tree in the postman's atrium? It's Christmas, they've all got—'

'Yeah, pull them off.'

'And can I tell them *why* they were digging up the postman's tree? Their dick supervisor won't tell them anything. They want—'

'No. You keep that to yourself. That's all I need right now is another damn leak to the press. I just hope they don't find out about the kids' jewelry. There were a lot of troopers there when—'

'You treat every cop in uniform like an idiot.'

'I can't afford a leak!' He slammed the flat of his hand on the blotter, and plastic dinnerware rattled in the take-out boxes at the edge of the desk. 'I've got those bastard reporters on my neck, demanding a dog and pony show for the tabloids. And the people who read that trash are just as bad. The press scum and the public scum – they're all the same.'

'You really don't think the shrink did it. Even with all that evidence? Was Rouge right?'

Costello nodded. 'The kid has real good instincts.'

'Then why couldn't you give him his lousy warrant?'

'Marge, you know what Rouge wants to settle with Oz. From what I've heard, that old bastard really took the Kendall family for a ride. Milked them out of a lot of money when he turned private, and God only knows what else he did to those people before the trial was over.'

He looked up at her, softening now. 'So, pull the boys off the postman's tree, but don't tell them squat about mushrooms or truffles, all right?'

She turned her eyes back to the window. The snowfall had

ended, and the crowd had grown. She saw no more stragglers; they were all assembled now. Of course. It was high noon, the hour of the showdown in Western movie lore.

And now it began.

One person held up a bright candle, and then another and another. Some had cigarette lighters and matches. All the tiny flames shot straight up, unwavering in the dead calm air.

So that was it. Didn't these people know that the candle-light vigil was traditionally held at midnight?

Ah, but the world is upside down today.

Sheets of paper were being pulled out of pockets and purses, and held up to the illumination of the candles. These were Harry Green's posters, portraits of the two little girls. Even from this distance, she had no trouble reading the bold lettering of the simple message, repeated perhaps a hundred times.

To the man behind her she whispered, 'Oh, the public scum you mentioned? They're here.'

He joined her at the window. 'My God.'

Marge looked from the crowd to the slack face of the captain. If only these people had made some noise, chanting for justice or shouting in anger, she knew he could have handled that. But there was no protocol, no department-approved response to this silent begging. Two of the village children were missing, and their people were asking quietly, so politely, could he find the lost girls and bring them home – *please*?

What could the captain do? He closed his eyes.

'Maybe you're giving up on the kids too soon?'

'Marge, don't.' He turned his back on the window, and his voice was husky when he said, 'There's something else you can do for me.' He lowered the blinds over the glass on his office door. 'I'm going to get stinking drunk. If anybody calls, you have no idea how to reach me, okay?'

She nodded and left the office. The door closed behind her, and then she heard the sound of the lock.

It was three o'clock when she looked up from her computer again. She had not been scheduled to work on this holiday. Her only reason for remaining was dead drunk on the other side of a locked door. The captain would have passed out by now, if she was any judge of his capacity for alcohol – and she was. Marge didn't know three women, or even many children, who couldn't drink Costello under the table. She walked over to his office door. Pressing one hand to the wooden frame, she leaned close to the pane of glass and whispered, 'Merry Christmas.'

Then she scribbled a quick note on her yellow pad, a reminder to pick up a few items from the deli on Harmon Street, the only source of groceries on Christmas Day. Oh, and she should stop at the captain's summer house to pick up a clean shirt and his shaving kit. He would need them in the morning. Over the past ten years of their love affair, she had also gained access to his underwear drawer, and now she added socks, underpants and a T-shirt to her list of one quart of milk and a jar of mayonnaise.

Agent Arnie Pyle stood close to the shoreline and away from the company of cops. If they knew what a talented liar he was, they might learn to mistrust him again.

He had located a federal judge at his country home, where the famed slave master was known to keep a cadre of law clerks working on his caseload through every holiday. Over the cell phone, Arnie gave his sworn, generally untruthful statement into the judge's tape-recorder. And then he was left alone on the phone in a living hell of accordion polkas played for the enjoyment of callers on hold.

He covered the receiver with his hand to kill the music, and now he listened to the racket of nature, the slap and receding suck of water on the rocks, the wildlife on the lake. A city dweller all his life, even Arnie knew the ducks should not be here in winter. One bad snowstorm and their little tails would be locked in solid ice. He looked up to see a white bird against the gray clouds, wings spread, soaring – another migratory creature who had missed the last bus to Miami.

He always fell short of poetic ideation, for this required the soul he had peddled too many times, illegally doubling and redoubling the price for something he had not owned in years. He had just sold it again to a gullible judge as payment for a warrant. Every time he did this, he saw his father's pacific blue eyes beholding a disappointing son – a Quaker with a gun *and* a liar. But then Arnie went on to lie again, and worse. Oh, the things he did for truth, justice and ten-year-old girls.

The law clerk was on the line again. Arnie listened for a while, then turned toward Rouge's car, making a thumbs-up gesture as he walked back to the private driveway.

'It's a done deal, kid.' Arnie Pyle closed his cell phone and slid into the passenger seat of the old Volvo. 'You got a trunk warrant – good as paper in the hand. If Almo has a fax machine in there, we can pull the paperwork right off the judge's desk.'

The car's windshield was a spectacular panorama of the large Victorian house, rolling wooded hills, a good portion of the lake and, with a pair of field glasses, a clear view of the boathouse – the crime scene. 'Rouge, if you come up dry, my ass is in a sling, and you lose everything. If I find hard evidence of extortion, we're home free. If I don't, then the search warrant is tainted. No matter what you find in there, you can't use it in court.'

Left of the front door, a window curtain parted to reveal a worried-looking man with a bald scalp and a moon-shaped face. Oz Almo was staring at Rouge's car and the line-up of three more private cars belonging to Makers Village cops. On the other side of the driveway were troopers seated in four more vehicles marked by the State Police logo. All the cherry lights were spinning on the cruisers, and a siren was squealing as one last car screeched to a halt.

Agent Pyle counted fifteen men in the entourage behind them. 'How'd you get the cavalry together so fast?'

'Costello's been locking them out,' said Rouge. 'They're

pissed off and looking for action. All the local cops wanted in, but one of them had to show up for patrol with Chief Croft.'

Arnie put his hand on the passenger door. 'You wanna get this show on the road?'

'No, not yet,' said Rouge. 'Give Oz a few more minutes to sweat.'

'And destroy the ransom?'

'He won't do that. Too greedy. He might move it, though. I'm counting on that. Wait till he leaves the window. Then we'll give him another two minutes of lead time.'

The window curtain closed again, and Arnie watched the second hand of his wristwatch drag itself twice around the dial. 'Time.'

They left the car quickly and took the stairs to the porch two at a time. Rouge tried the knob and found it locked. He pounded on the door. 'Open up, Oz. Police!'

A voice inside the house shouted, 'Just a second, kid. I'm pulling on my pants, okay?'

Apparently this was not okay. Rouge put both hands on the brass knob, forcing it to turn with muscle and a hard twist. The metal gave. The door would not open yet, but now there would only be a bolt to keep them out. The young cop stepped back and kicked the center panel. The door slowly swung inward on its hinge, and Rouge was entering the house, saying, 'That lock's a piece of crap, Oz.'

When they cleared the foyer, they found the man fully dressed and standing at the foot of a staircase. His mouth hung open as the room quickly filled with large men in dark leather jackets, uniforms and guns. Oz Almo wore a sickly smile. 'Hey, guys.' His eyes darted from trooper to village cop, one man to the next, as they fanned out around the room in a living wall between himself and the front door.

There was soot on the man's fingertips, and Arnie wasn't the only one to notice it. Rouge Kendall's eyes met those of another cop. Phil Chapel nodded, saying, 'I counted four chimneys on the roof. We'll check 'em all.'

Arnie Pyle stood in the next room, a small den filled with office furniture, hunting trophies, glass display cabinets of guns and metal cabinets of files. He hovered over the credenza until a fax machine spat out his warrant. Now he walked back to the front room and displayed both his paperwork and his shield to Oz Almo. 'Just a few questions, sir – while we're waiting.'

Oz Almo turned to see two village cops going up the stairs. 'Hey, you guys, where are you—?' He turned to Arnie Pyle. 'What's going on here?'

Arnie made himself at home, sitting down to the old rolltop desk that dominated this room. The slots and small drawers were filled with odds and ends, small bits of junk accumulated in catch-all fashion. The top drawer contained larger unrelated objects of the same species. The more functional desk would be the one in the den where the file cabinets were. So this antique was his first choice for hastily concealed items. He pulled a heavy ledger from a lower drawer. On the cover were telling traces of ash from Oz Almo's dirty fingers; this had not been the suspect's first priority in hidden items. 'Mr Almo, I understand you quit the force right after the little Kendall girl was found dead.'

Oz whirled around to see a state trooper kneeling by the fireplace and poking an iron up the chimney. Another man squatted beside him, saying, 'Light a fire. See if it's blocked with anything.'

He shouted at their backs. 'What the hell are you guys looking for?'

Agent Pyle's voice was calm, even pleasant. 'You left the State Police after Susan's body was found? Is that right, sir?'

Oz was staring at the ceiling now as cops walked over his head with heavy feet.

'Sir?' Arnie prompted. 'About the Kendall kidnapping?'

'Yeah, I quit after we found her.' He watched the agent flipping through the pages of the ledger. 'What do you—?'

'So that was *after* you delivered the ransom money?' This

produced the desired effect, the fear in the man's eyes as he turned to Rouge, pleading, 'I did that as a favor to your old man. He gave me his word of honor—'

'Oh, by the way,' said Pyle. 'There's nothing about that ransom in the police reports. And, of course, no mention of you personally delivering it. You convinced Bradly Kendall that you could only find the girl alive if you worked alone. Later, you told him a planted transmitter failed. Is this an accurate account of your conversation with the dead girl's father?'

'Yeah, yeah. Damn transmitters – they don't work half the time. I lost the bastard.' Oz's eyes were following the search of the closet. 'Now what's going on?'

'Just tying up a few loose ends.' Arnie found a ledger page he particularly liked, and he smiled at Rouge to let him know that the warrant was now bona fide. A lot of the figures matched with Rouge's financial data, but these were in Almo's handwriting. 'I understand the search party never got through all the rooms in this place.' Arnie turned to a trooper standing by the door. 'Isn't that right, Donaldson?'

'Yes, sir,' said the uniformed officer. His partner stood beside him, an older, more experienced cop, but not by many years. 'We only got through a few rooms on this floor, sir.'

Oz seemed to be catching his breath as the sweat trickled down his face. He shifted his weight from leg to leg, all but dancing out the Morse code of a confession. Newspaper was crackling in the fireplace, and he whirled around to watch it burn. 'I didn't want to waste their time. The search party had a lot of ground to cover. Two kids were missing. Time was—'

Rouge stood beside Officer Donaldson. 'Did Oz do any-thing suspicious? Did he deliberately try to steer you away from the search?'

Both men were nodding. 'He stalled us,' said Donaldson. 'Then we caught a radio call and had to leave.'

'But we came back,' his partner was quick to add. 'Same bullshit that time too. And we put that on our log – we never marked this place for a completed search. Finally, one of the dickhead investigators crossed it off the list. He said we wasted *valuable* time on the second trip. Asked us what we used for brains.'

Arnie Pyle was holding the ledger open in his hands as he stood up and walked toward Oz Almo. He was not smiling anymore.

Oz stared at his account book. 'You got no right to look at that. I know the law.'

Arnie Pyle pretended puzzlement as he glanced back at the open desk drawer. 'Oh, you didn't read your warrant, did you, sir? You're probably thinking about the restrictions on the house-to-house search. Captain Costello figured it would be easier to get signed consent if the cops couldn't look in under-wear drawers and read people's mail.' Arnie held the ledger up to tantalize the man. 'Now with a *warrant*, I can look in spaces a kid's body can't fit into. This is an unlimited search for evidence of extortion.'

Oz Almo looked at Rouge. 'And you're part of this? After everything I did for your family, you turn on me like this?'

Arnie Pyle ran one finger down a column of figures and looked up at Almo. 'I know what the out-of-state wire transfers are for. But can you explain these amounts for cash payments? The ones with the letter *D* after each entry?'

One of the uniformed officers kneeling at the fireplace was saying, 'There's a good draw in this chimney, Rouge. Nothing up the flue. We'll check the furnace in the basement.' They were rising, passing through the open doorway to the hall, when a village cop with a very dirty face raced down the stairs. 'I got it! I got it!'

The patrolman opened the soot-caked suitcase, and money spilled over the carpet in a cascade of bound packets and loose bills. 'It was stuffed up a chimney. There's two more bags like this one!' The young officer's eyes were bright jewels in a raccoon's mask of ashes. He was excited; he was pumped, jazzed. They all were. And this was not lost on Oz Almo, who stood alone in a sea of adrenaline – the room reeked of it. Some of the men were focussed on the money, but other pairs of eyes were turning on Oz, staring at him as fresh meat – the next meal. They were gathering around the suspect now, so close, and Arnie wondered if Oz could hear the muscles flexing beneath the leather jackets.

Arnie picked up a magnifying glass from the rolltop desk. He knelt down on the carpet beside the suitcase and picked up a loose bill. He took his time comparing it to the sample Rouge had given him, pretending to match the engraving lines. A documents expert would have to do the real examination with a clean, unmarked bill, but what were the odds that this was not the ransom? He nodded. 'It's a match.'

'You're under arrest.' Rouge nodded to the troopers standing on either side of Oz. They each twisted one of the man's arms behind his back and manacled his wrists. 'The charge is conspiracy to kidnap and murder Susan Kendall.'

'Ah, Rouge? You forgot the extortion.' Arnie turned to watch the prisoner squirm for a few more seconds. 'And I think we can come up with more charges – lots of 'em. Unless of course, the suspect wants to cooperate with the federal government. Mr Almo? Shall we dance?'

Mortimer Cray stood in the doorway to the conservatory. This glass room, full of life, was where he found peace. This was his true church.

Blessed be Dodd, for in his employer's absence, the valet had restored the tender young fruit trees to their pots and rescued the rarest of the orchids. Mortimer was moved by this simple act of kindness, as gardening was not among the servant's regular duties.

The effects of the tranquilizers were wearing off. William Penny had stood over his patient to watch him swallow one more pill, but after the surgeon's departure, Mortimer had spit it out. And now, all too lucid, he surveyed the rows of tables covered with loose soil, plants broken and beyond salvage, and others that might yet be saved. He was pulling on his gardening gloves when Dodd entered the room carrying a telephone.

Mortimer waved the phone away. 'I can't speak with anyone. My lawyer says—'

'Miss Ali has been calling for hours, sir,' said Dodd, cutting off his employer in an uncharacteristic breach of etiquette. 'Dr Penny wouldn't allow me to disturb you. I promised your niece you would make a return call after the doctor was gone.' He held out the phone again. '*Please*, sir?'

Considering the valet's extreme composure and reserve, this was tantamount to an emotional outburst and could not be dismissed. 'Of course.' He dropped his gloves on the table. After the number had been dialed for him, he accepted the telephone and waited for a desk sergeant to connect him to the proper extension. His valet, soul of discretion, was leaving the room.

The psychiatrist had seldom wondered what went on inside of Dodd, the perfect servant, almost an automaton without expression of mood or feeling – at least in Mortimer's view. And now he began to see his valet as a man like any other, easily moved by the desperate plight of small children.

Ali was on the line.

'Dodd asked me to—'

'Uncle Mortimer? How are you feeling?'

'I think we can dispense with the pleasantries, Ali. I know what you did to me, and I mean *all* of it. The consultation on the truffle? You set me up for that, didn't you? You wanted me to be closely involved with the case from the beginning – all that additional pressure. Very neatly done, my dear.'

'Uncle Mortimer.' He heard the tears in Ali's voice as she spoke again. 'I'm begging you. Where is that little girl?'

'It's Christmas, Ali. She's been dead since early morning. You established that pattern yourself, and very—'

'They found some of Sadie Green's clothing at an accident scene this morning. Now that's strange, isn't it? In all these years, he's never shown any interest in items from the Judas child. He was totally, exclusively obsessed with the little princess, the primary target. Gwen Hubble is still alive, and you *know* it.'

'Ali, you're extrapolating—'

'I heard you ask Costello if anything of Gwen's was found. In all the cases I tied together, after he stopped leaving the bodies out on the road, he still left some part of the dead child's clothing where the police or the parents would find it on Christmas morning. That's why he staged that accident. He wasn't trying to cover up Sorrel's cause of death. He wanted someone to find those little purple socks this morning – evidence for *Sadie's* death, not Gwen's. It's a breakdown in the pattern. Something has gone wrong. He hasn't killed Gwen Hubble yet.'

'Ali, you never mentioned that detail to the police, did you? Costello didn't say anything when I—'

'About the clothing? No. Cops hold out information all the time, even from other cops. I thought it could have been one of them. Is it? Will you tell me that much?'

Silence. He would say nothing, but he would not hang up on her.

'You're too close, Uncle Mortimer. You can't see it, can you – your own part in this? Try to understand the break in the old pattern – why he wasn't compelled to leave the bodies for the parents to find on Christmas morning.'

'I thought your own theory was rather good on that point. His fear of exposure – a growing awareness of forensic evidence, what the bodies might tell the police.'

'I was wrong. He doesn't *need* to do it anymore. Think about it, Uncle Mortimer. All those years of therapy. He was getting it all from you – *everything* he needed. You've been feeding the sadist all this time. It must have been so satisfying, delivering those little trinkets to you.'

She waited in silence, perhaps thinking that he would deny his participation, this collaboration with a murderer of children. Mortimer said nothing. Ali went on, 'He didn't need the parents' reactions. He didn't have to settle for watching the mothers crying into television cameras. He had you – right there – in the flesh. Immediate gratification.'

Her voice was breaking, almost unintelligible. She was crying. Then a long silence ensued. And now she must have pulled herself together; he thought her closing shot was comparatively cool. 'All right, one last question. Did he become your patient *after* Susan Kendall died – or was that little girl still alive while he was telling you all the details?'

She didn't wait for a response, but neither did she slam the receiver down in anger, as he might have predicted. If profound despair could be discerned in the simple mechanical click of a disconnected telephone, then he understood her state of mind.

Marge hesitated at the door of the darkened room. The overhead lights had been turned off. In the deep interior gloom, the room's sole occupant, Ali Cray, sat in the island glow of a desk lamp. The agents and investigators had deserted the police station. And there was also a dearth of troopers and cops in the house. She guessed they were all out looking for small children, and with little hope of finding them.

Marge understood.

These men and women could not sit and do nothing, watching the clock, waiting for Christmas to be over and the children to be finally pronounced dead in every mind. So now they were all out spinning their wheels. She imagined a small army of cops on the road, looking for hope, wanting to believe. Some of them, like Leonard Costello, would have lost their faith, and in the private spheres of the automobiles, these people would be in tears.

And then there was Ali Cray.

It was unlikely that this young woman would be spending any part of the holiday with her uncle. Ali was homeless.

'Honey, you can come over to my house,' said Marge. 'I

got a bird all cooked – just needs a little reheating. Got all the trimmings too. Well, *most* of the trimmings. We have to make a deli stop on the way.'

Ali shook her head. She kicked off her high-heeled shoes and folded into herself, arms wrapping around her slender body, legs drawing up. Her bare feet were on the chair cushion now, in the fashion of a child who had not been taught the proper way to sit on furniture. Then one small hand sent a pile of clutter from her desk to the floor in a single angry swipe.

The glossy, full-color portrait of a girl lay at Marge's feet, and she didn't have to be told that this was Rouge Kendall's sister. The resemblance was uncanny. But for the long hair, this might be an old photograph of the surviving sibling.

Marge buttoned her coat against the cold and left Ali Cray in peace – or she hoped as much, for the young woman's head lay on the desk, pillowed by her arms, and her eyes were closing.

On the way out of the station house, Marge stopped near the front desk, temporarily reclaimed by Chief Croft so he could catch up on his paperwork for the Makers Village Police Department. He held a phone to his ear as he screamed for Officer Billy Poor, and then made check marks against a list on his clipboard.

Marge decided to forgo the holiday wishes. For the first time in many years, she would be alone on Christmas night, and she lacked the proper spirit to say the words.

Billy Poor exited the men's room in a hurry, belting his pants as he presented himself at the front desk.

'Hey, Billy,' brayed the chief, as though this young cop were still in the men's room. 'Didn't anybody talk to that old lady's family yet? I got a note here from—' And now Charlie Croft held a sheet of paper closer to his nearsighted eyes. 'Oh, shit. It's from Buddy Sorrel. Must have been here since—'

'What old lady are we talking about, Chief?'

'You know – the *dead* one who lived on the lake.'

'Oh, the *mushroom* lady.'

'Just a minute!' Marge Jonas turned away from the door and walked back toward the young man in the blue uniform.

'Merry Christmas, ma'am.' Billy Poor politely doffed his cap.

'Merry Christmas my ass,' she said, slamming her purse on the desk. 'About the mushroom lady?'

CHAPTER 11

The fever was taking her down and down, slipping into dark water again and floating, gliding along a slow-moving river between the sun and the moon. A small white figure was running along a beach of black sand and calling out to her, but the words were too faint. Gwen looked directly into the face of the sun – the bulb of the flashlight. Sadie shook her again, saying, 'Don't go to sleep.'

'Is that a movie title?'

'If it isn't, it oughta be.' Sadie pulled her up to a sitting position. 'Come on, get up. We have to be near the door when he comes.'

'No use. I can't walk anymore.' Gwen's wound was throbbing, stabbing her with little messages from her nerve endings. But she would not cry, for they were forging a relationship of sorts, the pain and the child. 'It was a good idea, Sadie. It was. But I'd never make it through the door. You know that.'

'I'll carry you. We can do this.'

'*You* can do it – alone.'

Sadie shook her head. 'This can only work if I let the door lock behind me. It's the only way to beat a gun and longer legs.'

'Then take the parka and go. Get out. Get help.'

'And leave you locked in here? With *him*? No way. Get up and do this or we both die.'

'I'm dying anyway, Sadie.'

'Never. I won't let you.'

But this matter of life and death was surely beyond Sadie,

356

not in her bag of tricks. Gwen's wound stank, the swelling bulged over the white line of the gauze bandage. She tried to move her leg and failed; it had grown heavier while she slept. The fever gave way to chills and shaking. Her very bones felt cold, and this growing awareness of her own skeleton was pulling her mind back to the hole in the ground, the grave. 'Don't bury me. Even if you think I'm dead, I might only be asleep, and then—'

'Like Guy Carrell in *The Premature Burial*.'

'Ray Milland, 1962. I couldn't stand that, Sadie.'

'Or the Lady Madeline in *The Fall of the House of Usher*.'

'Marguerite Abel-Gance, 1928. You won't bury me. Promise?'

'I promise. But I don't—'

'I want you to get something for me.' Gwen was totally focussed now. Apparently the axe-wielding Joan Crawford had been right about that connection between shivering and clear thinking. 'There's a bottle in the white room.'

'You want another pill?'

'No, something else. It's in the upper cabinet – green powder.' She clutched Sadie's arm with a weak grip. 'If I could've made that jump from the end of the bedsheet rope to the ground, we'd both be home by now. You *know* that, don't you?'

'Naw, you would've broken your neck. Then I'd be all alone down here.' Sadie hugged her. 'You're in a lot of pain. I'll get you a pill.' She stood up and started off toward the white room.

'No!' Gwen called after her. 'No pills. All I want is that jar of green powder.'

Sadie walked away from the trees, kicking up dead leaves in her flashlight beam. When the child had traveled to the end of the aisle of mushroom tables and passed into the white room, out of sight and beyond hearing, Gwen whispered, 'I *could've* made that jump, Sadie. I'm sorry. I'm so sorry. But I know what to do now.'

*

Chief Croft wore an amiable grin as he ambled across the wide floor and pulled up a chair next to Ali Cray's desk. 'I understand you're interested in mushrooms.'

'And truffles – high-class fungus.' Marge Jonas stood by the open door with her hand on the shoulder of a younger man in uniform. 'Oh, this is Billy Poor.' With a light prod, she propelled him ahead of her as she sailed past empty desks and chairs. 'Sit down, hon.' Obediently, he settled into the chair on the opposite side of the desk. 'Billy's brand-new,' said Marge.

Ali smiled, for the young officer did look freshly minted. He had the chubby, ruddy cheeks of a boy who had recently come in from playing in the snow. His eyes were fresh and clean, and somehow she knew that Billy Poor had never traveled more than fifty miles from his home.

In the same tone she would use to reprimand a puppy, Marge said, 'Tell Dr Cray about the mushroom lady, Billy.'

'She didn't have any *real* mushrooms, ma'am,' said the young officer, removing his cap as he addressed Ali. 'It was just a lot of pictures and books – shelves full of knickknacks, things like that. Oh, and the kitchen clock was shaped like a mushroom.'

'Billy,' said Marge. 'Start at the beginning.'

'We'll be here all day.' Charlie Croft pulled a small notebook from his back pocket and scanned the first page. 'The old woman died a natural death. We searched the house to make sure there was nothing missing. You see, a robbery complicates things, ma'am. And Howard Chainy – that's the medical examiner – he had a damn bug up his butt. 'Scuse me, ma'am. He thought the hired girl might've run off with the old lady's valuables, and maybe that's why she never reported the death.' He closed his notebook and waved one hand to say, *That's it – all done.*

Ali wondered where this was supposed to lead her. The truffle found in the child's jacket did not fit with the old lady's quaint mushroom collection. 'You went through the whole house?'

'Every room – basement to attic.'

'Did the basement have a dirt floor?' She asked this more for the sake of politeness than information. She had lost the threads of the exotic fungus quest, only now recalling that one would need an oak tree in addition to the dirt.

'A dirt floor?' Chief Croft consulted his notebook again. 'One minute, ma'am. We've been through a lot of houses in the past week.' When he had scanned a few pages, he looked up at her again. 'I took the upper rooms. Billy here and Phil Chapel went through the parlor floor and the basement.' He turned to his most junior officer. 'Which one of you searched the basement?'

'I did, sir. I'm pretty sure it had a cement floor. It was just a little laundry room. I remember the washer and dryer.'

Now Charlie Croft turned in his chair to face the younger man. 'Must've been more to it than that.'

'There was a furnace,' said Billy. 'A big one. But there wasn't much room down there for anything else. No boxes, nothing like that. It was real cramped.'

Marge leaned close to Billy's ear, and in the manner of a prompting stage mother, she said. 'So it was a real small house?'

'No, ma'am,' said Billy. 'Big place, maybe fifteen rooms.'

Charlie Croft was nodding in agreement. 'That damn house sprawls out all over creation.' He turned back to Billy. 'And you're telling me the entire basement was a *cramped* laundry room?'

Seconds dragged by as the two men stared at one another, and finally Charlie Croft said, 'Oh shit.'

'I'm just telling you what I saw,' said Billy, sinking in his chair. He stared at the paper plate of cold french fries on the corner of Ali's desk. 'You gonna finish that, ma'am?'

'Help yourself, Billy.' Ali pushed the plate toward him. 'Do you remember seeing a door in the basement?'

'No, ma'am.'

'Did you look for one?' asked Charlie Croft.

'No, sir. We were just making sure the place hadn't been robbed.' Billy had demolished the fries, and now he was appraising a box of doughnuts on the desk next to Ali's. 'I didn't think there could've been anything down there worth taking.'

'That's okay, baby.' Marge ruffled Billy's hair as the young man inhaled a glazed doughnut and reached for another. She handed Ali the list of house-to-house searches in the lake district. 'One of the investigators crossed off the old lady's place.'

'Well, we searched it, didn't we?' Billy had downed two sugar doughnuts at amazing speed, and there was one left in the box – at the moment.

Charlie Croft looked at Ali. 'This is my fault.' He turned back to the junior officer. 'You can go now, Billy. I guess we can handle it from here.'

The young policeman was cramming the last doughnut into his mouth, and he was nearly to the door when Marge called after him. 'Billy? You checked the old lady's refrigerator, didn't you?'

'Yes, ma'am.'

Marge grinned. 'How do I know these things?'

'Nice catch,' said Ali. 'So, Billy – no mushrooms in there, right? Nothing strange looking?'

'No ma'am, nothing at all. Clean as a whistle. I guess the mushroom lady was planning to go on a trip.'

After Billy Poor had left the room, Charlie settled back in his chair and stared at the ceiling. 'Marge, if you promise not to mention this little screwup to Costello, I'll take a run out there now and check the basement.'

'You got it, Boss.' Marge squeezed his arm to assure him that her allegiance lay with the signer of her pay checks and not with the temporary camp of the State Police.

'Mind if I come along?' asked Ali. It was better to be in motion tonight, even if she only moved in circles.

'Glad to have the company.' Charlie was flipping through his notes again. 'I seem to remember one other odd thing about that place, but I can't think what it was.'

It was a pity that Oz Almo's lawyer hadn't spent more money on his toupee. The thatch of young brown hair sat atop graying temples, appearing to have crawled up there of its own volition. Special Agent Arnie Pyle wondered if the attorney had given the hairpiece a name and bought it a flea collar.

Arnie leaned back in the leather chair and lit a cigarette, despite the absence of ashtrays. Almo's attorney waved his hand in the air, batting at smoke that had not yet reached him. This was the man's first physical motion since sitting down to a polite round of plea bargaining. But the lawyer's head never moved. He always remained in profile, and the FBI agent was spellbound by the single round, unblinking eye.

After taking a deep drag on his cigarette to produce the longest possible ash, Arnie smiled at the attorney, whom he had christened Fisheye. 'According to these ledgers—' He paused to open up the heavy volume. 'Oz has income from a lot of different sources, and only two legitimate clients. Interesting? Some of these entries are out-of-state wire transfers. But the one I especially like is probably a local man. His payments are tagged with a *D* after every entry. Always the same cash increments every month. I can backtrack these payments for at least ten years.'

He slammed the book with a loud crack. Fisheye jumped, and Arnie's smile widened. Anything that cracked an attorney's composure was progress. 'Looks like your client is into blackmail.'

'But you don't know that for a fact.'

'I didn't interview the marks, if that's what you're asking. And you don't want me to, Counselor. Once I do that, I have to do the paperwork. You think I'm blowing smoke?' Arnie

361

made a conciliatory shrug. 'Okay, I'll give you a name – Rita Anderson.'

The lawyer turned to his client, who sat at the edge of the couch with his hands cuffed behind him. The look on Oz Almo's face told him the threat was solid. So Rouge had been right about the overpaid cleaning lady.

'Let's say we got your guy on blackmail.' Arnie put his feet up on the soot-crusted bag of ransom money. 'Among other things.'

The point was not lost on Fisheye, but neither did it seem to worry the man that his client was involved in conspiracy charges for the death of Susan Kendall. The lawyer was also aware that two other children might well be dying as they spoke. Yet he retained his composure, showing no angst, no compassion, no hint of any warm blood. Evidently Fisheye's mother had laid her eggs in cold pond water.

'The ransom is old business, Agent Pyle. Unless you have more—'

'Let's see if I can guess where you're going with that. The statute of limitations? It starts rolling on the day of discovery, and that's today.'

'No, I was about to mention the minor detail of the man convicted of murdering Susan Kendall.'

'Right you are. But it looks like the priest didn't act alone. We got Oz nailed for conspiracy.' Arnie absently stroked the cover of the closed ledger. 'I'm interested in the cash entries for the local man.'

The lawyer glanced at the ash on the end of Arnie's cigarette; it had grown. '*Mr* Almo will be happy to assist the police in the current investigation, under certain circumstances.' Fisheye made a polite cough, the nonsmoker's indication that the cigarette should be put out.

Arnie shook his head. 'Sorry, pal. Can I call you pal? No? Well, Counselor, for Oz's sake, I hope the girls don't die while you're jerking me around.' Arnie took another drag, and now the long log of an ash hung out over the arm of the chair, the handwoven rug, but best of all, it threatened the hem of the lawyer's cashmere coat. 'With the interstate wire transfers, the FBI's got your guy on extortion. But with the ransom money, the State Police get dibs on his hide for kidnap and murder – hard time in the pen, even if he weasels out of murder in the first degree. Let's say he wrote the ransom note himself. That would knock down the jail time.'

Fisheye had already framed his rebuttal and would have spoken, but Arnie held up one finger to say he was not done yet. 'This morning we turned up a dead BCI man named Sorrel. He ties in, too. Federal and state – everybody's pissed off.'

The attorney held out an empty nut dish for the agent to use as an ashtray. Arnie ignored this suggestion and let the dish hover in the air between himself and Almo's lawyer. The man's single unblinking eye roved over the cops, who were shifting their weight, tensing their bodies, churning and building the energy in the room.

And then the ash dropped into the dish in Fisheye's hand.

'I'm going to advise my client to cooperate.'

'Very sound advice, Counselor.'

'But I can't advise him to incriminate himself.' Fisheye set the dish on the table with a grimace of distaste. 'Under the circumstances I think immunity from federal prosecution would be a reasonable exchange for full cooperation.'

'You're counting on the pressure of two little girls who don't have much time to live.' Arnie nodded. 'Okay, it's a deal. The government won't pursue federal charges.'

'I'm glad to see we're in accord on this, Agent Pyle, but I need to talk to someone a bit higher up, someone in a *position* to make a deal.'

'There's no way the brass won't support me. You know the drill, Counsellor. This is a one-time-only offer, and time is running out for the kids.'

'So? Use the phone.'

'It's Christmas Day. You—'

'I have the home telephone number for a US Attorney.' Fisheye rummaged through his wallet, withdrawing a business card with a number penned on the back. 'We play golf.'

Charlie Croft was making good time along the deserted Lakeshore Drive, though there were no streetlamps to light the way in the dark evening hour. The beams of the car picked out the trunks of trees and encroaching low branches reaching into the road.

'Like I said, ma'am, this is probably a waste of time.'

'Call me Ali.'

'Billy might've been right about that cramped cellar. As I recall, that old house was added onto quite a bit – but not all at once. It's got a brick wall and a stone one running along the front. The extension in the back of the house is made of wood. Could be the original house only had a small cellar. Buildings on lower ground have crawl spaces, no cellar at all.'

'You were trying to remember something odd about the house. Was it something you saw on the upper floors?'

'Well, no. There were four floors, but not much to see. Looked like the old lady wasn't using the upstairs. All the beds had bare mattresses, and most of the rooms were closed off with weather stripping. She was using the back parlor for her bedroom, so I figured maybe she was trying to save money sealing the rest of— Oh shit.' One hand slapped his forehead. 'That was the one odd thing I couldn't remember – the utility bills. I saw them on her desk when Phil Chapel was going through all the clutter looking for an address book. The electricity charge was a whopper, even for a big place like that one.'

'Maybe electric heating?'

'No, ma'am – Ali. There were radiators in every room – all steam heat. And that water bill was high, too. I run across that combo once before – big water and electric bills. This damn hippie rented a summer house on the lake. He was growing his own weed in the house and selling it to local kids. Now if that old lady hadn't been the only resident, I would've tossed the place looking for seeds or maybe a growing shed near the house. In a slow week, I might've done that anyway.'

They turned off Lakeshore Drive and on to a narrow road with no marker.

Rouge stood by the window overlooking the private driveway. It was almost empty of cops and cars. Only Donaldson and his partner remained behind, waiting for the lawyer to do his backdoor deal with the US Attorney.

When Oz's lawyer had hung up the phone, he turned to the federal agent. 'So we're in agreement? You neglect to pursue an investigation of the interstate wire transfers, and Mr Almo is immune from prosecution on federal charges. Now, about the local charges. The ransom will be turned in by my client as found money.'

'That wasn't part of the deal.'

'It is now, Agent Pyle.'

'All right. Let's get on with it.' In peripheral, Arnie could see Rouge moving toward them. Apparently the young cop did not like the idea of Oz walking away from every charge. Arnie only glanced at him, and with a slight nod, managed to convey that this was a very good deal indeed – for the lives of two small children. So much was riding on Ali's profile of a local man, her belief in the priest's innocence, Oz's proximity to a kidnapping. The slender lead of a local blackmail victim might come to nothing, but this was the only game plan left. The hour was late – children were waiting.

Rouge melted back into the company of the two troopers, who were going over the bags and boxes of collected evidence. He went on with the business of looking for local faces in the photographs of blackmail victims. It was almost a race between the young cop and the lawyer. Who would turn up the local man first?

And now this was also dawning on Fisheye. He turned to his client. 'All right, Oz, give them the name for the *D* entries.'

'I was blackmailing William Penny. He's a local doctor, a heart specialist. I found—'

'That's quite enough,' said the attorney. His glare was fixed on Arnie again. 'I suggest we get on to clearing up the remaining charges. A call to the—'

'Not so fast,' said Arnie Pyle. He was looking at Rouge, and it was very clear that the name meant something to him. Of course – it was the name of Mortimer Cray's heart surgeon. 'I need this in plain English, so I know what we're buying. What exactly was the nature of the blackmail?'

The attorney waved his client to silence. 'That comes afterward. Now I want to talk to the local district attorney. Same immunity on the conspiracy charges. I have his home number. But first, I suggest we begin with a show of good faith. Have them remove my client's handcuffs.' He waved in the general direction of the police officers, clearly minions in his view.

'I don't think so,' said Rouge, without turning away from his task of initialing the paperwork attached to an evidence bag.

Fisheye appeared to be reappraising the young BCI investigator as another source of power in the room. Then he dismissed the idea.

Arnie leaned forward. 'Two little girls are dying, Counselor.'

'All the more reason to close the deal quickly. I want it from the mouth of the district attorney. That's the deal. Take it or leave it.'

'I might just leave it,' said Rouge.

Fisheye turned to face the younger man, who was holding a plastic bag up to the light. The lawyer regarded him with great disdain, admonishing him as a child who was interrupting the conversation of grown-ups. 'You're an investigator with the State Police, right?' The attorney was clearly not impressed.

Arnie spoke softly, almost as an aside. 'He's the brother of

Susan Kendall. You don't think his word pulls weight with the local DA?' He leaned down to rest one hand on the satchel. 'With this money, Oz was supposed to buy Susan's life.'

The attorney waved one hand in the air as though he were shooing this idea away from the conversation. 'You need information – and in a *great* hurry?'

'Hopefully before the kids turn up dead, you miserable—'

Rouge stepped into the space between them and addressed Arnie Pyle. 'I have another witness who might be interested in turning state's evidence.'

Was Rouge thinking of Rita the cleaning woman? Apparently the lawyer thought so, for he was rising from the chair. 'I think we can discuss this further,' said Fisheye.

'Screw it.' Rouge turned his back on the man and missed the sweet sight of an attorney in shock. 'This bastard is only getting away with the extortion, right?'

Arnie nodded. 'But the deal was only good if he cooperated, and he didn't.'

'You asked for a name, Agent Pyle.' The attorney was at their backs, raising his voice for the first time. 'He gave you the name. That was our deal.'

'He might have a point, kid,' said Arnie. 'The US Attorney did a deal for the ledger entry. No conditions that it would take us anywhere.'

'Well, what about this?' Rouge opened the evidence bag and spilled out the charred remains of several magazines on the coffee table. Among the half-burnt scraps of glossy paper with scissor-cut holes were three small squares of letters and words. 'Maybe your lab can match this to the bogus ransom note for Gwen and Sadie.'

'New ball game,' said Arnie, ignoring the lawyer and staring at Oz Almo. 'So, you enterprising, diversified sack of shit – when I go through your books again, am I gonna find any large sums that match ransoms for other kids?'

Rouge turned to the troopers. 'Book him.' To the lawyer, he said, 'Kiss off.'

Fisheye was showing both sides of his face now, and he wore a worried look. He had underestimated the young policeman. Too late, he had learned who was running the game in this room.

As they were walking out the door, Arnie was doing the math on the charges. Oz Almo was not a young man; he would never see the outside world again. When Arnie slid into the passenger seat of the Volvo, Rouge was on the phone, asking for the number of a local judge. He dialed it, and then turned the ignition key. He put the car in gear with one hand, and with the phone in his other hand, he was already scamming the judge for two warrants. 'Yes, sir, I know it's Christmas. . . . Just call the US Attorney. He did the deal. . . . Yes, sir. . . . No problem. I've got his home number.'

Arnie nodded in approval. Rouge was learning the agent's bad habits, and so quickly. The home phone number for the US Attorney was such a nice touch, the judge would probably not bother to call. And the kid's lying was very smooth for an apprentice. There was only one problem – all the evidence was stacked against Oz Almo. William Penny was only a name on a ledger – no substance. But now this young cop was planning to arrest him.

'Rouge, you got nothing on Penny, nothing to say—'

'I'll get it.' By the time they had turned off the access road and on to Lakeshore Drive, Rouge had issued orders for a unit of troopers to search the surgeon's residence.

The FBI agent leaned over with one more reminder. 'You have no probable cause for a search of his—'

Rouge only glanced at him.

'I know,' said Arnie. 'You'll get it.' He was trying to remember the last time he had flown a case by the seat of his pants. His career might go up in a damn bonfire of broken rules and laws and lies, but he did like the feel of the road rushing under the wheels of a car at ninety miles an hour. He would give no more advice to end this sweet chase – not for the whole earth.

'He might be at Mortimer Cray's place,' said Arnie. 'Didn't Costello say the shrink went home in the care of his heart surgeon?'

'That's where we're going right now. I called the trooper watching the house. He says Penny's long gone.'

'So you plan to squeeze the shrink? Good idea. Costello made a big mistake with Dr Cray's interview in the hospital. The good cop, bad cop routine? The captain tried to play both roles by himself. Now with two of us working on the old man, we could do a fast game of—'

'I've got a better game in mind,' said Rouge. 'We're gonna play bad cop and the cop from hell.'

Arnie reached into his coat pocket and pulled out the small gargoyle, a gift from Becca Green so he would not forget her daughter. And against all odds of the child's survival, he found that he could not give up on Sadie. He set her ghoulish toy on the dashboard close to the windshield. Backlit by the headlight beams, the gargoyle made a dark silhouette jumping and bouncing on rubber haunches with every turn of the car. It was alive.

Charlie Croft stopped the police cruiser in the driveway of the old house and picked up the receiver of his car radio. Ali listened to the bad static and the undecipherable words from the dispatcher.

'Must be under a damn power line,' he said. 'Same thing happened the last time I was out here.' Charlie held the receiver to his ear and lifted one finger with each word he recognized. 'We've got to go, Ali. It sounds like they caught the bastard.' Into the radio he said, 'They did?' He turned to Ali. 'They're going to arrest him now.' After another minute of static and garble, he spoke to the radio. 'What about the kids? . . . What? . . . Say it again. . . . Is that what—' He turned back to Ali Cray. 'They need backup.'

'Who is it?'

'No name, just an address. I won't know if I even got that

right till I get clear of the lines or whatever the hell is causing the interference. I'll drop you off on the way.'

'I'd like to stay here, Charlie. I can manage on my own.' She held out hope for Gwen Hubble, but she did not want to be there when they brought in Sadie's body. And though she knew this was rank cowardice, she could not deal with the pain of Becca Green. Ali looked out over the black water of the lake. Darkness, isolation, quiet, these were the things she craved tonight.

'I don't like leaving you out here by yourself,' said Charlie. 'I don't see much point in this now.'

'Just give me the key. I'll be careful.' *I can't face Becca.*

Still he was hesitant.

'You guys caught your man, Charlie. So what are the odds? There isn't room for two monsters in Makers Village.' *And I'm a coward.*

'You got me there, Ali.' He smiled, relenting, or more likely feeling pressure, wanting to be off down the road, part of the chase. 'Okay. You'll find the key over the back door. I left it there for the utility people. You better take this.' He handed her his flashlight. 'I don't know if the electricity is on or off.' He pointed to the wall in his headlight beams. 'That looks like a full cord of firewood. You might need it if the—'

'Right, don't worry about me.' She was out of the car and closing the door.

'I'll swing back later and pick you up.' He put the car in gear. 'Shouldn't be long.'

'Take your time, Charlie.' *The more time, the better.*

'The telephone service is probably cut off. You got a cell phone?'

'No problem.' She pulled the phone from her purse and held it up for him to see.

'Marge is covering for me at the station. You call her if—'

'I'll be fine.'

As his car turned and headed toward the main road, she walked to the house, guided by the beam of Charlie's flashlight. Her fingers explored the ledge at the top of the doorframe. No key. The utility people had probably taken it with them. Well, that was where Charlie had put *his* key. The householder might have had a more imaginative hiding place for a spare.

Now think like an old woman.

Charlie had mentioned arthritic knots in the hands of the corpse, so the hiding place would have been more accessible. She flashed her light on a birdbath of cement. No, too heavy to tip back. On the other side of the door was an old bronze sundial on a pedestal. A frog of a lighter shade was sitting at the edge of the circle. But for the slightly mismatched patinas, it might have been a solid piece. She tipped back the small frog. There was the key.

She entered the house through a modern kitchen. The carved door set into a far wall was somewhat grand for this room; it must have been the original front door before the exterior was added on. She trained the flashlight on a row of copper pots, and then found the mushroom clock Billy Poor had described. Perhaps the chief was right and this was a waste of time.

The house was cold. She flicked on the wall switch, and the ceiling light bathed the kitchen in a warm yellow glow. So only the furnace had been turned off. Odd there was no entrance to the basement off the kitchen, but in this hash of add-ons, she no longer expected to find anything where it was supposed to be. The next room was a dining area, originally the front parlor.

Stashing the flashlight in her pocket, she turned on the lights in all the rooms as she passed through them. Each was filled with a collection of ceramic mushrooms on shelves and tables. Painted mushrooms lined every wall, but there were no signs of any living fungus, no truffles. She opened a door onto a narrow stairwell.

Above her head was a lamp, but the switch failed to turn it on. Pulling out the flashlight again, she descended the stairs and passed through a doorway to the cellar. The yellow beam passed over a washing machine and a dryer. As Billy had said, it was cramped down here. The oversized furnace dominated the space. Only a few steps into the room, she brushed against its cold metal housing as she focussed her light on the tight space between the furnace and the corner walls.

Another door. It was a small one, perhaps only five feet high, and it was ajar. No wonder Billy had missed it. It had probably been more visible and accessible when the house had a furnace of normal proportions.

She flashed the light on the knobs. The button above the catch was set to lock when the door closed. She depressed the button to disable the mechanism. Her eyes followed the flashlight's beam down yet another flight of stairs.

A subcellar? She touched the switch for a wall fixture, but this lightbulb didn't work either. She turned around and washed the beam across the laundry room walls, looking for a fuse box.

Now Mortimer Cray was being haunted by the living as well as the dead. He avoided looking at Agent Pyle's face, for there he saw evidence of possession. Yes, the eyes belonged to Paul Marie. They were chilling, terrifying.

He had seen the priest's eyes in his hospital room. At that time, he had put the delusion down to lapsed medication and his massive anxiety. How to explain it away here and now? He would not even make the attempt. What was the use? Reason had fled; the agent's eyes were proof. In the next moment, the earth might open to disgorge fire and smoke, and he would think nothing of it.

The psychiatrist directed his gaze toward the glass wall and watched as men in uniforms milled around outside in the garden, trampling plants and bushes. Another ghost of past sins was standing among the troopers and policemen in the yard, the only one not in motion – so like his sister. Rouge Kendall opened a cell phone and extended the antenna.

A moment later, Dodd appeared at Mortimer's right hand, carrying a cordless telephone. 'It's a patient, sir. He says it's urgent.

The psychiatrist spoke to the FBI man without looking at him. 'Agent Pyle, this could be serious. I assume you have no objections?'

'Just keep it short and don't promise to make a housecall.' The agent walked off to the far side of the room to oversee the destruction of another row of orchids.

Mortimer held the receiver to his ear. 'Yes, who is this, please?'

'Come closer to the glass, Doctor,' said the familiar voice on the telephone.

Mortimer did as he was told and looked through the panes. 'To your left.'

Mortimer turned to see the young man standing in the garden and speaking into a cell phone.

'Good, I can see your face now,' said Rouge Kendall. 'This makes it a little more personal.'

The FBI man with the priest's eyes was walking back to him, saying, 'Cut it short, Doc. My business takes priority here.'

'I heard that,' said Rouge's lower voice on the telephone. 'Don't listen to the fed. He's only trying to rattle you. You don't have to say anything unless your attorney is present.'

Mortimer turned to the federal agent. 'I have to take this call. I'm exercising my right to remain silent.'

Pyle forcibly turned him around and pushed him back to the wall. 'I don't have time for your rights, Doc. Two kids are dying. I'm flat out of time.'

Rouge's disembodied voice said, 'You have all the time in the world, Dr Cray.'

'We picked up your patient,' said Arnie Pyle, stepping back a pace. 'He's chattering like a magpie.'

'Pyle is lying.' Rouge's tone was all contempt. 'The FBI

has nothing solid, and Dr Penny isn't under arrest. Feds, cops – they're all idiots spinning their wheels.'

The troopers left the garden to enter the main house. Rouge remained to hold him prisoner from the dark side of the glass wall. Yet the young man was as close as a lover when he whispered through the phone connection and into Mortimer's ear, 'You told your niece that I was your patient.'

'I never did.'

Agent Pyle was yelling now. The priest's eyes were furious. 'Your patient is quite a sadist, isn't he, Doc? But you would know all the details better than I would.'

The old man closed his eyes to blot out Arnie Pyle's face – Paul Marie's eyes. Mortimer's hands began to tremble, and he nearly dropped the phone. When he opened his eyes again, the agent was gone, walking away.

Rouge said, 'He's bluffing. Ali gave him the profile of a sadist. That's all he has to work with. And by the way, a sadist was all Dr Penny ever was. But you knew that, didn't you? You told Ali all about me – about us.'

'I never told anyone that—'

'Liar. She was on my case the day she got into town. She knows something. How could she know unless you told her?'

'What could I have told her? This is—'

'Stop lying. Dr Penny promised you'd keep my trinkets safe. But you gave them to the police.'

'That's not true, none of it.' Mortimer watched Rouge pace the garden, one hand rising in a fist.

'I saw you puttering around with that stupid little pot. You did everything but hang a sign on me.'

'I swear I don't know what you're talking about.'

'How stupid do you think I am, old man? You gave the cops my property – mine. I want it all *back*, and I don't care what you have to do to get it. That bastard, Penny. First he only wants to watch, and then he takes my things. He said they'd be safe with you.'

'I never—'

'I was there.' Rouge's voice was rising. 'I saw you and that damn blue pot. You wanted them to find my things – *my* things.'

'No, I swear—'

'You think your hands are clean because you didn't say my name out loud? You *gave* them the evidence. And you *did* tell Ali. I can't let her tell anyone else. She doesn't have your *ethics*. Ali will be Dr Penny's first solo killing. He'll probably botch it. But I can't be everywhere at once, can I?'

'Time's up, Doc.' Arnie Pyle was back and standing very close, too close. 'I need a name, a place, something. I need it now. Get off the damn phone!'

Rouge whispered in his ear, 'Maybe Dr Penny will record Ali's screams. You can play them back at his next session.'

'No, please don't. She's—' Mortimer waved off the FBI agent as the man grabbed at the phone.

'Not a purist, Dr Cray? It's all right to kill other people's little girls, but not your own precious niece?'

It was a penetration of sorts, this voice on the phone, in his head, an invasion, a rape.

'Unlike me,' said Rouge, 'Dr Penny always preferred grown-up victims. He had to make do with little girls. Those were the only murders he had a ticket to watch. But I'd say his first bona fide kill is a sign of real personal growth, wouldn't you? You must be so proud. Do you know how much he really hates women? Of course you do. And he's a doctor. Who knows more about pain? All those sharp instruments—'

'You can't let him do this!'

'Not so loud,' said Rouge, so softly. 'You don't want everyone to know you betrayed a patient. Not after all your sacrifices. Oh, wait – those were other people's sacrifices, weren't they? Well, perhaps what Ali's going through – this is retribution for your sins. I guess you'll have to eat it, won't you?'

'Please, you have to stop Myles before—'

'Myles?' The connection was severed, and the young

policeman in the garden was folding up his cell phone and hiding it away in his pocket.

With only the mention of Myles's name and Rouge's inflection of a question, Mortimer realized, with stunning speed and hellishly clear insight, that he was both betrayer and betrayed.

'Just tell me this,' Arnie Pyle was saying – yelling. 'Did the pervert tell you where he took the girls? Can't you tell me that much? They're only ten years old. You think I can't touch you because of the doctor–patient confidentiality?' said Pyle. 'I might just reinvent the fucking law – all for you, Doc.'

Chief Croft entered the room and walked up to Agent Pyle, trying to get his attention.

The FBI man waved him off and turned on Mortimer again with renewed anger in his eyes – eyes of a priest. 'Oz Almo rolled over on the pervert, Dr Cray. Almo's been blackmailing William Penny. I know what the doctor does with little girls.'

One of the village policemen stepped forward. 'That's not why Oz was blackmailing Dr Penny.'

Arnie Pyle's expression showed real pain. 'Oh Jesus, kid, could you just back off for six seconds?'

'Come on, Billy.' Chief Croft was pulling the officer out of the fray and back toward the wall.

The young man's voice was still clear and carrying to every quarter of the room. 'But Rita Anderson confessed. Cracked wide open. She helped Oz blackmail the doctor. Rita really hates Dr Penny.'

Chief Croft put one arm on the young policeman's shoulder, leading him toward the door. 'Go back to the station and make out a report, okay, boy? It's quieter.'

'When we picked up Dr Penny at the motel,' said the officer, missing his second cue, 'Rita thought we were after *her*. She just broke down, right there in the parking lot. Everybody in screaming distance knows Dr Penny was screwing his patients' wives.' Billy's voice trailed into the garden. 'You should've seen that guy's face while we were cuffing him. Rita was just screaming away and running her mouth like a—'

The FBI man was suffering in silent resignation, staring at some distance point, eyes gone to soft focus.

'It's okay, Arnie.' Rouge Kendall was standing in the doorway. 'We had the wrong Penny brother. It's Myles we want. Dr Cray confirmed it on the telephone.' He turned to the door leading into the main house. 'Hey, Donaldson?' A state trooper stepped into the room. 'Donaldson was listening on the extension – two witnesses.'

Rouge had just shoved his old doctor into the abyss.

With Chief Croft back at his side, the young policeman was directing all the officers in the room. 'Harrison? Call Marge and have her run a license plate for *Myles* Penny. Donaldson? Chief Croft says there's no one at the Penny house, so check the clinic.'

Mortimer stared at his garden beyond the transparent wall, pondering a case of ethics and betrayal. More officers were flooding into the greenhouse. In the dark reflection of the glass, he watched Rouge raise his hand for silence.

'I need all the units on the street. You're looking for Myles Penny's station wagon. Marge Jonas has the plate. She'll be giving out the search coordinates. You're gonna cover all the roads around town. Wherever you find his car, that's where the kids are. Now move.'

The room had been quickly cleared of state troopers and local policemen. Rouge and Charlie Croft stood in conversation at the center of the room. The FBI man was some distance away from them, speaking into his cell phone. And where was Ali? Why wasn't she here in her moment of triumph? The old man walked in halting steps, unsteady as he moved across the stone tiles. Rouge turned around at his approach.

'I need to know,' Mortimer began. 'About Ali—' And then he lowered his head, deciding that he did not want to know if she had planned his destruction. Instead he asked, 'Where is my niece?'

'Ali's checking out a vacant house at the lake.' Charlie Croft glanced at his watch. 'I told her I'd—'

'Checking for what?' Arnie Pyle appeared at the chief's side. 'What's Ali doing out there?'

'She told me she was looking for truffles.'

Ali saw the cellar with more detail now, the film of dust on the appliances, the wadded towels in a wicker basket below the laundry chute, and the dials of the furnace. But no fuse box. Maybe she would find it in the subcellar.

She turned to the top of the stairs leading up to the parlor floor, straining to hear a distant noise. It was the sound of a car engine. So Charlie Croft was back. She debated waiting for him to join her, and then decided to take the second staircase to the subcellar.

The door at the bottom of the stairs opened when she turned the knob. There were no buttons on this lock. And now she saw a shaft of light, interrupted by the trunks of large trees. *Trees in the house – incredible.* Her flashlight followed their branches up into the darkness of a ceiling crossed and recrossed with pipes and lined with a million dark lightbulbs.

How amazing.

She let go of the door and rounded a tree trunk to find the source of the second light. It was another flashlight, trained on a prone figure in a little red jacket and long blond hair. As Ali moved toward the small body, the door slammed shut behind her. She whirled around. Fingers tore at her hair, twigs of a low-hanging branch.

There was no one at the door.

Ali turned back toward the small figure lying beneath a tree at the far side of the little forest. She was running, high heels spiking into the dirt, when she tripped over something that blended well with the dark. Another body. Her flashlight shined on the carcass of a dead dog. She stumbled to her feet again and moved on toward the child with the little red jacket, Gwen Hubble.

Ali sank down on her knees, directing her light to the girl's face. The eyes were closed, as if in sleep. The skin was luminous white against the dark soil and dead leaves. Her golden hair lay across the ground, spread around the small head in a fantastic halo. Ali touched the child's body.

Just like the dog, cold and stiff.

Something green and light as dust trailed from the little girl's clenched hand, and there were traces of it on the breast of the red jacket. Ali wet her finger, dipped it into the green powder and tasted it. Only a few grains burned her tongue at first contact, and she spat it out. Her brain was reeling, trying to make sense of this. Very small children did not commit suicide – not on this planet. This could not be.

The cellar lights came on, bright as day and blinding Ali before her hands could rise to shield her eyes. Her vision was slow to adapt, and she could barely make out the shape of a man standing in the narrow stairway, holding the door open with one hand.

'Charlie?'

She could see more clearly now, but the man's face was averted as he closed the fuse box. It was high on the staircase wall and set into a niche of rock.

'Let there be light,' said the familiar voice. He nudged a block of concrete against the door to prop it open. Ali was seeing afterimages of every object in reverse shadows, nebulae of light. He was coming closer, saying, 'So you found Gwen.'

'Myles?'

He stood over the child's body and nudged it with the toe of his shoe. 'Little bitch.' The prod of the shoe moved the stiffened corpse all of one piece like a statue. 'Stone dead. What a waste.'

Hammerfall.

'You seem surprised, Ali. I gather you didn't backtrack this place through me.'

So William was only a cheap opportunist. Myles was the true sadist in their family, and she had overlooked every one of his signals. 'No, I'm not surprised, Myles.' Not anymore. 'It was the light. It hurt my eyes.'

Now she could see, and she was looking backward, working through the details she had missed. That day in the greenhouse must have thrilled him to orgasm – discussing the autopsy, divulging intimate details of Susan's Kendall's anatomy, setting Uncle Mortimer's hands to trembling, forcing the old man to spill his wine, to lose his mind.

'You didn't know it was me.' His tone was challenging. This was important to him, that Ali could not have guessed.

No, she had never suspected him. 'Remember my first grown-up dinner party, Myles? It was the year I came east for school. I was eighteen years old.' How soon before Charlie Croft returned?

'Yes, I remember that night.' Myles was gloating.

He had probably relived that dinner party a thousand times, for he had been the one who told her about Susan Kendall's death. And so detailed was his description of the crime, Ali had seen that tiny body every single day for years – Susan, lying in the snowbank, so cold, dying.

'That was the first time you heard the story, wasn't it, Ali? Well, I'm not surprised.' He made a halfhearted kick at Gwen Hubble's body. Strands of gold hair moved and shimmered with the illusion of life. 'This is the only one that ever made national television. As I recall, your parents hustled you off to Nebraska that year.'

Ali nodded. Her uncle had convinced her father to accept a Midwest job offer. Uncle Mortimer had even volunteered to sell their house, to take over every chore of settling her parents' affairs so they could move quickly. Ali had been in a hospital for weeks. No one had told her that Susan Kendall had gone missing, that later, she had been found dead.

'Have you figured out why the old man wanted you out of town?'

'Uncle Mortimer thought you were going to kill me.'

'Very good guess, Ali. He probably saw it as the ultimate

test of his ethics, the worst torture I could devise for him – killing his brother's child. Fool – sees himself as a latter-day Job. I swear that muddled old man can't decide if I'm God or the Devil. He must have died when you came east again. Oh, that was a time.' Myles was grinning, clearly enjoying himself. 'The night of that old dinner party?' He seemed almost girlish, giddy now. 'I actually told you details that weren't in the newspapers, things that William didn't even know, and he was the medical examiner.'

Was he waiting to be complimented for taking such a risk? She said nothing. There was no need to goad him. Monsters loved to talk about their work. Where was Charlie Croft?

'That night – did you guess your uncle's part in it? I always wondered.'

'Did I know he was treating a child killer?' Uncle Mortimer's eyes had been so – apologetic. Guilty? Yes, that too. It was the first time she had seen either of those expressions on his face. And that had been the beginning of suspicion, her impression that the old man had heard every gory detail before, perhaps before the corpse had been discovered. 'Yes, I worked it out.'

'But you never caught on to *me*.'

How could I, Myles? I was only eighteen years old. No match for you, not yet. She had missed every sign. 'Eventually I did catch on to you.'

'Liar.'

'But I didn't know then, Myles, not *that* night. It must have been a thrill, talking about the murder so openly – with one of your victims. I don't know why the strain didn't kill the old man years ago. His heart—'

'Now you're wondering – why was I still invited to your uncle's dinner parties?'

'No, not at all.'

Myles didn't like that answer, but she was not lying this time. It made perfect sense. The Penny brothers had always come to dinner once a week. After Susan Kendall's death, that ritual could not be ended or altered, not without calling attention to Myles. William would have thought it odd. There would have been questions to answer, lies to tell. It was so much easier for Uncle Mortimer to have a child killer at his dinner table than to account for the man's absence.

Myles seemed vaguely disappointed in her continuing silence. Was he expecting something more from her, something like food?

At the hospital, during her uncle's interrogation, Myles had fed on the old man – all that fear pouring out of Uncle Mortimer as Costello accused him of harboring a child killer. All the while, the monster was sitting three feet away, listening to every word – feeding. And then he had even baited Mortimer into admitting his patient relationship. Another round of fear, anxiety, more food for the—

The monster?

But just now, she was facing a rather drab creature without fang or claw, unkempt, socially inept, never asked to the party unless by the grace of his more esteemed brother's invitations. She looked down at the child's body. Gwen must have been so repulsed by this man. Of course Myles had to steal the children. What hope did he have of seducing anyone, even a little girl?

'Your uncle wouldn't have given me up if I *had* killed you. But you were such a dull child, Ali. I hardly knew you were alive.'

She smiled, and that irritated him. 'So I didn't even come up to the standards of a child molester?' She slowly stepped out of the high heels that would cripple her in a dead run for the door. 'I suppose that's the ultimate rejection.' Her smile never wavered, and this annoyed him more and more.

'Well, that was *then*, Ali. Things change.'

'Uncle Mortimer betrayed you, Myles.' How would she fare against him in a fight? 'He finally cracked – gave all your little trophies to the police.' Myles was larger, but she was younger, faster. 'They know everything.'

382

'Mortimer didn't even know he had my—'

'He *found* them.' Should she run? 'I was in the greenhouse when he showed them to me.' Could she win in a fight? 'Half the cops in the world were there when he gave you up.' Should she wait for Charlie Croft's return?

'He'd never surrender a patient.'

'Hiding your trophies in Mortimer's greenhouse was so smart.' Did he plant them on the day they met for drinks? She edged off to one side. He no longer blocked her way to the door, leaving her two options now, fight and flight. 'Good move, Myles. You could retrieve your little souvenirs when you felt safe again. But if the police found the stash, they'd never connect it to you. Very smart. Like keeping the children in someone else's house.'

'It'll be my house soon. I made a generous offer to the probate attorney.' He reached into his coat pocket. *For a scalpel, a knife?* She looked at the door, so far away. Her bare feet were cold against the earth, and dead leaves crackled with the shift of her weight.

What?

She stared at the thing in his hand, not quite believing in it. Myles with a gun? This was not the weapon of choice for a sadist. Did it belong to the dead policeman, Sorrel? Would Myles know how to use it? Well, everyone had seen nightly demonstrations on television. Just squeeze the trigger, and the blood flies. So simple. *Where are you, Charlie Croft?*

'Last words, Ali? Something I can tell Mortimer at our next session. This seems so cut and dried.' He pointed the gun at her face. 'Even after I kill you, your uncle still won't give me away.'

'I told you, Myles, he's already done it.'

'No, I don't think so. Mortimer's twice the monster I am. He has a conscience, but he never listens to it.' The gun lowered a few inches. 'Oddly enough, in Mortimer's mind, this passes for nobility. A good man would've sacrificed his reputation and his ethics to save this kid.' He pointed the barrel of the gun toward the body. 'But not a noble man – not Mortimer. His fault that it's dead.'

It?

'I wasn't lying, Myles. Think. How did I know where you kept your trophies?' Why was he smiling?

'You've been living in Boston too long, Ali. You've forgotten about life in a small town. Everybody's heard about the search of Mortimer's greenhouse. I know he didn't give up the jewelry. The cops found it. I *wanted* them to find it.'

He had been playing with her. The sadist's game – he would let no opportunity slide. Strange that she should feel humiliation even now.

'Oh, and you'll love this, Ali. They're over there right now, ripping up the greenhouse *again*. This time, they'll find a medallion.' He looked down at the little corpse. 'Something for its mother to identify. But I don't expect Mortimer to live long enough to stand trial.'

'The police know about this place.'

Myles was close to laughter as he looked around the vast room. 'So where *are* the cops and their shovels? Why are they over at Mortimer's? Why aren't they *here*, digging up all the little graves? Why is the kid's body still here?'

'I called them as soon as—'

'As liars go, you're not much of a challenge, Ali. You're pathetic.'

He was right about that, but even her truths were not believed. 'I thought you wanted to be caught, Myles. Isn't that why you left the purple jacket on the road? The first break in your pattern. You wanted the police to find it – to find you.'

'Pattern? Why go for such a convoluted idea when it's so obvious? I wanted them off my back and searching in the wrong direction. Sometimes life really is that simple.'

She faltered, baffled by his condescending smile. Evidently, she was no better than Myles at discerning truth from lies. *One more try.* 'What about the truffle? The police found it in the jacket lining. That ties the murders back to this place. Isn't that what you wanted? Not to lead them away, but to lead them here? The truffles grow in the ground, so you must have put it—'

'Truffles? Oh, hell no. You're way off. The damn dog was so hungry he was digging them up. There were truffles all over the place before he finished them. So your logic – your second-rate *analysis* won't hold up, Ali.'

'The police know where I am. A cop drove me out here. He might be outside. If he hears the shot—'

'Must I repeat everything twice? The cops are in Mortimer's greenhouse. I doubt if *anybody* knows *exactly* where you are. A hired woman worked in this house for years, and she didn't know about this room. Evy Vickers always gave Rita money to kennel the dog when she went on vacation. But Rita never wanted to spend it. So William – he's humping her – he leaned on me to feed the damn dog and that's—'

'Rita Anderson. Her husband's medical bills are bleeding her dry, aren't they? She *did* know about this room, Myles. She told—'

'First you malign Mortimer, and now Rita.' He shook his head in grinning wonder. 'She's a terrible cleaning woman. Never would've occurred to her to sweep behind a furnace. And if she'd ever found that door, *ever* set eyes on these trees, don't you think everybody in town would know by now? Logic isn't your best thing, is it, Ali? Well, I can see why you didn't make the cut for St Ursula's Academy.'

'So how did I know Rita's medical—'

'Oh, who doesn't know about her medical bills and her husband's heart condition.' He changed his voice to an effeminate falsetto. '*My husband's an invalid.*' He was smiling, voice back in a male's lower register, saying, 'Those were the first words out of her mouth, right? Not even a good try. Poor Ali, still not the brightest kid in town. Ugly *and* slow.'

Her face was burning. Could he see the flush? Was he

loving this? 'Then you know I did meet Rita, and she told me about the door in the—'

'You found this room by accident, just like I did. Well, maybe not the same way. I was kicking a dog into the corner behind the furnace when I happened on that little door. *You* were double-checking the cops – looking for bodies. And that was your only good idea. They didn't spend two seconds in that laundry room upstairs. I should know. I helped them search the house.'

The gun was rising to her face. He was waiting for her to scream in fear, to feed him. 'Chief Croft is on—'

'Oh, give it up.' His irritation was growing. 'You'd never tell the cops you were coming out here to check on their work. It's time, Ali. Wish I could've dragged it out a bit longer.'

Yet he did drag it out. He pointed the gun at her left eye, bringing the muzzle closer. The seconds crawled by while he allowed her to look down the barrel, to imagine what was going to happen to her. There was time enough to know that she was going to die in this place. And finally, he lowered the gun and aimed it at her chest.

Ali heard the explosion of the shot. She looked down in disbelief and saw the red spot spreading from the dark hole in her blouse, in her body, and then she was falling to her knees. There was an absurd moment of surprise, for this was not the television death she had been conditioned to expect; she was not propelled backward by the blast. She toppled forward into the dirt, face down.

The man knelt by the child's body, his head bent low, so close, stale breath blowing across the small white face. He was only inches away when Gwen's eyes snapped open, and she showed him her teeth, curling her lips back, just as the dog had done.

He was surprised. No – better than that, she had frightened him. She snarled, and he never saw her arm rising as he was drawing backward, sucking in his breath. Gwen's hand flashed out, hurling the green fertilizer into his wide and startled eyes. The gun tumbled from his hand. He clawed at his face, fingers probing the burning sockets, and his scream was pure agony. He was on his knees and stumping forward like Blizzard the legless man.

Lon Chaney, 1920.

And now she was certain that he was blind. Again, he screamed in pain. Gwen outshouted him, yelling, 'Geronimo!'

Dry dead leaves went flying as Sadie came out of the earth, sitting bolt upright. The loose covering of soil streamed down her savagely decorated face. Sadie's blood-red lightning bolts were wasted on the blind man, but they gave Gwen a little courage. Sadie held the blade high as the man teetered on his knees, then she plunged the point into his thigh. His face was horribly distorted. He bellowed in his new pain and struck out blindly with a closed fist, hitting Sadie in the side of the head and sending her reeling into the stone wall.

Sadie! No! It was *not* supposed to happen this way.

Sadie was sliding down the rock-faced wall. And the man turned around to look at Gwen.

You can see.

One of his eyes was bloody and bubbling up oozy green, but the other was only bright red and wounded. He was moving toward her, reaching out.

The gun lay only a few feet from her hand. She had heard the noise this weapon made and regarded it as a bomb. Because her leg would not work, would not run with her, she ran away inside herself, and in the dark of her mind she went round and round in screaming terror. To look at her still body, no one would have guessed at the rising hysteria, for she had gone rigid again, eyes screwed shut, mouth sealed and silent.

Only one hand was not a coward.

Her eyes opened. Sadie was struggling to a stand. Gwen felt the muscles loosen in her shoulder as her arm followed the crawling fingers that were inching toward the gun. Would she even be able to lift it? In sidelong vision she saw him hoisting Sadie off the ground. Gwen's hand was closing on the cold metal. Now she could only see Sadie's feet running madly in midair.

Another hand covered Gwen's and the startled child looked into the face of another monster: it was marked with a scar, jagged like the lines Sadie had drawn with dog's blood – but this one was real. The red mouth was twisted, and the teeth were bared. Blood was pouring from a hole in the woman's body, and the face was flooded with terrifying emotion. Gwen had never been this close to hate, never looked into its wide-set eyes. She recoiled as the metal slid out from underneath her smaller hand.

The woman was propped up on her elbows, the gun was rising, taking aim. And then the cellar exploded with another deafening shot.

The man was falling.

Sadie! Where was Sadie?

Gwen's body stiffened again as the man rose up on his forearms and crawled toward her. She was paralyzed. The gun in the woman's hands banged out again, but not so loud this time. How was that possible?

And now the half-deafened child watched the bits of a man's skull, his hair and flesh fly away from the back of his head. Gwen felt oddly detached, hardly noticing the spray of blood from the last bullet.

It was unreal.

'Sadie?'

The whole world had gone utterly silent. With all the strength she had left, Gwen tried to stand, but her body only rolled to one side, and now her face was half buried in the dirt, one eye in darkness and one turned to the light.

Two men were rushing through the door. One had great, sad eyes, and the tails of his long coat flapped like black wings as he ran toward her. The other man, with the brown jacket and dark red hair, was first to reach her side.

She could hear now – a pounding of more feet on the

stairs, and then she saw the pant legs of other people running into the cellar. Their voices and their footsteps blended into the chatter and static of radios; all the sounds seemed to come from a great distance. Though she lay still, Gwen had the sensation of moving away from these people, away from the light, gliding along on black water. She knew this river, but what was its name?

Back to the world again – cold, so cold. Strong arms were rolling her dead weight, and her face was turned out of the dirt and toward the bright lights of the ceiling. The man with the dark red hair was lifting her up from the ground and holding her close, bringing her inside the sheepskin jacket, warming her with his fleece and the heat of his body.

All the while, the other man's voice was crying, 'Ali, Jesus, Ali!'

But what of Sadie?

Gwen knew nothing anymore but the darkness of her passage through delirium and the lightness of floating on the black river. As the current gently rocked her in a warm fleece-lined boat upon the water, she slowly turned to face the other child, small and solemn, left behind on the receding shore – left *behind*.

CHAPTER 12

li Cray had lost her paper slippers, and the belt on her
hospital robe came undone as she ran barefoot down
the corridor of the pediatric wing, racing toward the
room of the screaming child.

The doctors had encouraged her to walk on the day after
surgery, but now, more than two weeks later, the short run
down the hall had exhausted her. She leaned against the doorframe, catching her breath as she watched the spectacle of two
adults terrorizing a little girl who could not even walk yet.
Half of Ali's sympathy went to the terrorists, for the parents
meant well.

Marsha Hubble was hovering over her child. 'We talked
about this, Gwen. I know you—'

'Don't say it!' Gwen put her hands over her ears, yelling,
'No! Don't you say it *again*!'

'Oh, honey, please,' her father was begging. And now they
both fluttered around the little girl, trying to calm her with
soft words and helpless gestures, reaching out to touch her.
Gwen batted their hands away, then covered her ears again,
screaming to block out their words. The parents would seem
like monsters to this ten-year-old; their speech would be the
ramblings of lunatics. Even as the Hubbles were professing
their love, they were trying to stab the child in the heart
with their own vision of what had happened in that cellar.

And now the Hubbles had noticed Ali. The moment might
have been comic if the child were not so distressed. The parents
froze in position, then their hands slowly dropped as they

backed away from the child's bed. Did they look a little sheepish? Yes they did. *Good.* Healing was a long process. A young body recovered quickly; the mind must take its own time.

'This is not what we agreed on.' Ali waved in the general direction of the door to say that the parents must leave the room, and right now. 'I'll speak to you in a few minutes.' *After I clean up the damage.*

Marsha Hubble made no protest, for Ali had fought her and beaten her down. The woman quietly followed her husband into the corridor. Ali closed the door, shutting them out to protect Gwen from any more assaults by good intention, from pain in a child's best interests.

'Hello, baby.' Ali pulled a chair up to the bed and smiled at the dazed little girl. 'I came to say goodbye. I'm going home today. Another doctor will be stopping by to see you this afternoon. I think you'll like her.' But the parents would not. The child psychiatrist Ali had selected was known for siding with children against parents.

The girl's small hand curled around her own. 'Before you go—'

'I'll talk to them, Gwen.' The concept of a child's autonomy was always a difficult sell. Eventually, the parents would come to understand the child's right to own her faith in Sadie Green. 'They make mistakes sometimes, but they love you, Gwen – more than anything in the world.'

'I know. But they want me to change so I can see it their way. My way is better.'

'I think so too.' And Ali believed this, though it shattered the fundamentals of her profession. She sat back for a moment and regarded this young girl who lent credence to the rumor that all of St Ursula's children were a bit strange. There was certainly more to Gwen than her parents supposed. They had defined her as perpetually frightened, but Ali strongly disagreed. Reading psyche was an art, and with an artist's eye, she had come to admire Gwen. The child had more presence in the world than most adults – and the courage of conviction.

'Now I'm going to go out in the hall and yell at your parents. I'll get them back in line, all right?'

Gwen nodded, but she would not let go of Ali's hand. 'You were there. You know what happened. You saw.'

'No, baby, I wish I had.' Her own eyes had been fixed on the monster – or as Sadie would say, The Fly, the insect. Over all the long days of healing, Ali had also learned a lot from the late Sadie Green, and she agreed with that valiant child's estimation of Myles Penny: he had been less of a man than the poor brutalized dog lying under the oak trees.

Ali had not seen the miracle in the cellar, yet she could not shake the images that Gwen had put into her mind. The pictures were so vivid that, as years passed by, Ali would become less clear about the events of that Christmas night.

There was not much to pack, for this space had always been austere, without photographs or any personal objects to humanize it. The guard stood behind him, waiting to take the priest to the warden's office to sign more papers before the final walk through the prison gates. A white-haired trustee in prison garb was dunking a mop in the soapy water of a bucket, appearing anxious to get on with the job of cleaning out Paul Marie's cell.

The iron doors in this older section of the prison were not automated. They opened and closed with conventional locks. The guard was idly swinging this one on its hinges. 'You should've sued the bastards.'

The old trustee nodded in agreement with the guard as he pushed the mop around the stone floor.

Paul Marie shook his head. He would rather be freed this morning than wait a year for a new trial. That had been the deal he agreed to, bad as it was: a governor's full pardon for a promise not to litigate the matter of fifteen years' false imprisonment. Over his head they hung old charges of assaults on other prisoners – no matter that each bit of violence had been in self-defense.

The guard opened the iron door and beckoned the priest to follow him. When they were both standing in the corridor, the door slammed shut behind them with the authority of a loud clang, but then it swung open again. 'Well, that never happened before,' said the guard, opening the door wide to better examine the hinge and the lock. He closed it once more to complete a solid wall of bars.

The trustee in the cell was done mopping the floors. He had quickly stripped the sheets from the bed and was about to turn the mattress over. In an accidental, inadvertent test of faith, Paul Marie glanced back through the bars as the mattress was raised. Now he could see through the bed's iron frame-work to the floor below.

His old companion was gone – no shadow, only soap and water and morning light.

An hour later, when he left the prison's main building, he was dressed in a priest's cassock and the same shoes he had worn fifteen years ago. He did not raise his eyes until he was beyond the tall gates. He had long anticipated the first glimpse of sky that was not bounded by walls and covered with nets of woven metal. When he did look up, instead of being over-whelmed by infinite space, he saw low cloud cover and pearl-gray light. This fell far short of his imagined scenario of freedom.

Father Domina was there to greet him with a gentle smile, as though the younger priest had only been gone for a few hours of a single day. Paul Marie's body became lighter and lighter. At each step in his old shoes, he felt the bulk of his muscles falling away from him as he walked toward the elderly man, the faithful keeper of his old life and ordinary destiny.

The old man recited a litany of attendant chores and parish calls – the small details of a simple cleric's life as they rolled toward the village in a hired car. The prison receded to a small gray dot on a flat landscape of vast open fields. The overcast heavens had disappointed him, but the earth did not – so much space, an endless horizon.

But something was missing, something was lost.

Father Domina patted his hand and smiled, taking the younger man's silence for unspeakable joy, missing all the signs of a broken mind – the idiot's grin, the fixed and staring eyes, the rolling tears.

Paul Marie slowly shook his head, dismissing the idea that the shadow beneath his bed had been killed by the light. He decided that it had gone elsewhere while the cell door was open.

Arnie Pyle entered the hospital room before she had finished dressing. He smiled, hoping that Ali would turn around to catch him eyeing her like a peep-show client. And she did. Her blouse hung open, revealing the dark thickened flesh of a crooked suture line. It was not the neatest embroidery job ever done on human skin, but considering the large caliber of the gun and the close range of the shot, he had seen worse. She wasn't angry to find him staring at her breast, and she did nothing to hide the new scar.

He whistled the traditional three notes of appreciation for half-dressed women with bullet wounds. 'Well, that's fascinating, Ali. From now on, only wear low cleavage. Advertise it.'

'Degenerate.' She lowered her face to the work of buttoning her blouse and covering the wound. 'Ugly, isn't it?'

'The bullet hole? No, Ali. That's chump change compared to your face.'

Perverse woman – she laughed; he knew she would laugh.

'I love your face.' He caressed her cheek on the damaged side. 'It's not symmetrical, but you can't have everything.'

'Still curious about it, Arnie?'

'Always.' He touched her twisted mouth with the tips of his fingers. 'If you're smart you'll never tell me how it happened. Just keep me enslaved for the rest of my life, going quietly nuts.'

She didn't pull back or brush his hand away this time. Finally, he was teaching her to trust him again. One day, he would get the right words out, perhaps today. Within his circle of intimates, she was one of the few who didn't know how much he cared for her. There were lamp posts and bartenders from coast to coast who knew of his capacity for the love of Ali Cray.

She was finishing the last few buttons on her blouse, and in a perplexing sense of embarrassment, or inexplicable chivalry, he turned to the window to give her privacy from his eyes. 'So, how's the Hubble kid doing? She's got her leg in one piece?'

'Yes. She's going home in another week. No complications with her surgery.'

'But?' He knew Ali well enough to fill in the words she left out. He turned to find her sitting on the edge of the hospital bed, high heels dangling a foot off the floor. What sorrowful eyes. 'So the kid is still totally nuts, right?'

'She only needs some time to heal.' Ali made a game attempt at a smile. 'Have you seen Rouge Kendall yet?'

'Yeah, he picked me up at the airport. He's waiting in the hospital coffee shop with an armload of roses – long stems, all for you. Must be at least two dozen.'

'I wish he hadn't done that.'

'So do I. It makes me look bad.' But with all that recovered ransom money, Rouge could afford mutant roses with even longer stems. 'Want me to get him?'

'Not yet. I'm going to tell you how my face was scarred.'

'You don't have to do that.' And why, after all this time, did he suddenly not wish to know?

Her smile was wry. 'You think you've guessed, right?'

'How could I—'

'I always know when you're lying, even before you open

your mouth.' She patted the mattress as an invitation to sit down beside her. 'My own parents don't know this story.'

So now he would have the secret, but some instinct made him worry that it might cost him the lady. It was the tone of her voice he was reading, that touch of trepidation. And then he realized that they shared this same fear. He sat on the edge of the high hospital bed, his legs swinging free, feet pacing on thin air.

'I was the invisible child,' she began. 'You have to know that before you can understand how it happened. My parents dropped me off at the church on their way to the airport. They were going out to the Midwest for a few days. Dad had a job interview in Nebraska. I was told to go to Uncle Mortimer's house after choir practice. But the Dodds – my uncle's housekeeper and valet – they didn't know I was expected. My uncle forgot to mention me, or maybe he thought it wasn't necessary.

'Uncle Mortimer came home late that night, after the Dodds had gone to bed. The next day, he left early for an appointment in the city. I suppose he assumed the Dodds were taking care of me – or he just never gave me a thought. He stayed at his club in Manhattan that night, and the following afternoon he got a call from his valet. My parents were at the house to collect me, and where was I? Well, my uncle had no idea. And where would you even *begin* to look for an invisible child?'

'You're serious? They all *misplaced* you for two days?'

'I never made it to the church door. A bag was pulled over my head. There was this smell – something sweet, probably ether, and then I blacked out. When I woke up, I was lying on the floor of a speeding car. There was the monster in the driver's seat. A black ski mask covered his head, all of it. But I always remembered him with long sharp teeth. Isn't that strange?'

Arnie was thinking of the mask recovered from the cellar – the white stitches over the felt mouth – fangs of thread.

*

Sometimes Myles Penny had resorted to taunts of, 'The strain will kill you if you don't tell.' Not once had Dr Mortimer Cray considered this as evidence that his patient wanted to be stopped, for he would not have known what to do with that information, so rigid was the psychiatrist in the keeping of his own commandments.

Mortimer looked up to the sky beyond the transparent ceiling. Tardy winter had come rushing down upon his glass house, flinging the season everywhere with careless cold winds to rattle the panes, and snow to kill the leaves of every tree and plant outside the protection of his conservatory.

He thought to ring for Dodd when he felt the first pain in his chest, but his hand trembled over the intercom button as he envisioned a stark white hospital bed, tubes of fluid running in and out of his body, machines humming and clicking, mechanizing his demise.

He shuffled to a chair and slowly sat down. Turning his head stiffly, he scanned this domain of delicate orchids and rare violets. The shapely yew tree was tall as a goddess and green with new shoots extending beyond the careful pruning of her rounded shape. On the near tables, young plants pushed up through the soil of shallow beds. Within the shelter of his greenhouse and outside of the proper season, he had forced new life into the world in a heresy of pantheism, though Persephone was the deity he loved best.

It was not the sky growing dim; he knew that. The yew tree was less distinct in form and darker now. The world under glass was an assembly of vague black silhouettes, and one of these shadows was moving toward him. Gentleman that he was, he stood up to receive his anticipated guest, his goddess, the bride of Death.

His heart beat in an erratic rhythm. The pain began in earnest, spreading outward from his breast. He fell quickly, not folding gracefully into soft arms, but slamming into the stone floor, as though he had been struck down with a force of great anger.

*

Though the hospital coffee shop was full, busy and noisy with a multitude of separate conversations and patrons walking to and fro, Arnie Pyle easily spotted Rouge Kendall near the window. The surface of his corner table was covered with a profusion of blooms in bright florist wrapping.

On the other side of the room, a young waitress stood by the cash register. She ignored the other customers to stare at the handsome policeman in blue jeans. Rouge was deep into the sports section of a newspaper and oblivious to the teenager falling in love with him. At Arnie's approach, the younger man looked up from his paper with an easygoing smile. 'How's Ali doing?'

'Not great.' Arnie pulled out a chair and sat down at the table. 'She looks a little shaky to me. But they're letting her go home anyway.'

The wide window gave him a view down a rolling hill to the streets and houses below. Snow was flying over the roof-tops, and he could see smoke rising from almost every chimney. Ant-sized youngsters were dragging sleds uphill, and some were already screaming their way down on swift running blades. One rider in a pink snowsuit was actually aiming her sled at a helpless little boy on foot. But Arnie still wanted children.

Over the past ten days in Washington, he had missed this little town. He hadn't realized how much until now. He watched as the law-abiding driver of the only car on the main road stopped for the only traffic light in Makers Village.

Rouge lifted his cup as an invitation. Arnie waved it off. 'Nothing for me, thanks. Well, now that you're rich, I guess you can leave this place.'

'I don't think so, Arnie. I just bought a baseball field.'

'No shit.'

'Don't get excited,' said Rouge. 'It's a vacant lot next to the station house. If you come back in the spring, I might let you pull a few weeds on the pitcher's mound.'

'You got a deal.' He glanced at the waitress, so lovely with

398

her long blond braid. This might be Gwen Hubble in a few more years, glowing with health and merely boy-crazy, coloring her lips bright red in the chrome reflection of a cash register. He rarely thought of Sadie Green. He had sent her to the back of his mind to keep company with all the other children who had not come home alive.

'Got all your answers, Arnie?'

'Yeah, Ali cleared up some loose ends.'

'Not too many of those left. We identified the last of the bodies from the cellar. Penny must've been using the Vickers place for years.' Rouge finished his coffee and signaled the girl for his check. 'Now we're looking at all the summer houses with dirt cellars. Maybe we'll find the rest of the kids on Ali's list.'

The young waitress strode boldly across the room, faking more confidence than she could possibly possess. This was almost painful to watch, for her mouth was freshly painted, and her bright eyes were set on Rouge. She presented herself at the table, small breasts thrust out as far as a training bra would allow, an offering to the handsome cop. But he only laid a few dollar bills across the check in her hand, then turned his full attention to the chore of folding a newspaper.

The girl stood there, very still and tightly clutching the money. Her cheeks were a deep crimson flush, as though she were suddenly naked in public. And she was.

So exposed – nowhere to hide.

Arnie extracted one long-stemmed rose from Rouge's bouquet and handed this tribute to the pretty teenager. She smiled, only a little disappointed that it had come from the hand of the wrong man, for a conquest was a conquest.

And a rose is a rose. Well, not always. Arnie believed that more experienced females used flowers to divine the most embarrassing things about men – their true intentions toward women. But this girl was too young to suspect him of kindness, and he got away with it.

'Ali has something to tell you.' He sat back in his chair,

watching the waitress walk away. He was unwilling to meet Rouge's eyes. 'I know it's going to be hard on her, so—'

'It isn't necessary.' Rouge gathered up his bouquet. 'I know.'

'No, I don't think so, kid. You might have guessed right about the scar, but there's more to it.'

Rouge set the roses down again. 'The only thing I don't know is whether he threw Ali in that ditch *before* or *after* the Morrison family crashed their car.'

Oh, sweet Jesus, he did know. 'It was before the accident and after he cut her,' said Arnie. 'If the Morrisons hadn't crashed, no one would've found Ali in time. The kid lost that much blood.' Penny had intended a slow death and a lonely one. 'But now she—'

'Ali was only ten years old,' said Rouge. 'She doesn't have anything to apologize for.'

And how did he put that together?

The young policeman leaned forward to make his next point very clear. There should be no misunderstanding between them. 'My mother is starting a new life in Washington. I don't want this following her around. It's over.'

Arnie put up his hands. 'Understood. Nothing in writing, okay? Just tell me how you worked it out. And you can skip all the billboards and neon signs – like why Ali devoted her life to tracking pedophiles.'

Rouge shrugged to say that this was really very simple. 'She was tying my sister into her pattern.' He was apparently crediting Arnie with the intelligence to know that this required a second little girl. But Susan Kendall had died alone – just the one small body bag.

'Another odd thing,' said Rouge. 'Most people see pedophiles as *little* men.'

Arnie nodded. All his experience backed up that profile on so many levels.

Rouge continued, 'But Ali – an expert in the field – she always called this one a monster. Not a technical term, is it?

Not very accurate, either. I had to wonder about that. Maybe the last time she saw him, he was monster size.'

'He was a grown-up,' said Arnie. 'And she was only ten years old.'

'Right. And then there's *kids* and *guilt*. If she met up with this man, why didn't she tell somebody?'

'She was ashamed.' Arnie stared at his hands, following the reasoning now. According to Ali's case notes, the Judas child was never sexually molested. So Rouge would know that wasn't the reason. She was ashamed of what she had done to Susan Kendall. *Oh, Ali.* Every time he had badgered her about that scar—

'It's all child's play for you, isn't it?' Emotions under control, Arnie looked up to meet the younger man's calm hazel eyes. Would Rouge be so understanding if he knew *how* Ali had called his sister out? Or did he know already? The young cop had everything he needed to work it out. The Judas child was always a best friend to the true target, the little princess. But the Kendall twins had no close friends, only one another. Susan would never have come out at the invitation of Ali Cray – the invisible child who had blended into every wall she leaned against.

Rouge might only be missing a few details in the lie told to Susan, that her brother had run away from military school, that he was waiting for her at the church. This had been Ali's work. Oh, the things a little girl would do – just to make a grown man stop whittling on her face with a knife, to end the blood flow, the pain and the panic.

'Ali wants to see you. She has to—'

'No, she doesn't. Here, take my car.' Rouge pushed the keys to his Volvo across the table. 'I've got a police cruiser picking me up in a few minutes.'

'You have to see her. She needs to tell you.'

'No, that's what she *wants*, and it's not going to happen. Give her what she needs, Arnie.' Rouge put the roses into his arms. 'Give her these, and tell her they're from me.'

Arnie stared at the flowers. They meant something to him, some forgotten thing. He couldn't recall the words of the sentiment, though his favorite poetry revolved around roses. Their scent was intoxicating; his favorite adjectives revolved around alcohol.

'I got her a cactus.'

'Interesting. But I'm sure Ali knew you were lying.' Rouge smiled. Apparently, he also understood the dangers of plants talking to women.

When Arnie left the coffee shop, he took the stairs because the elevator was too fast. Climbing step by slow step, he tried to recall the text for these roses. Every florist had a cheat sheet for clueless men, a list of the correct blooms and the right colors to say to the fair sex, 'Let me back into the house.' For other occasions there were flowers to say, 'Hello', and with a change of color, 'Goodbye.' Because Ali was a psychologist, he had always given her a mixed bouquet to confuse her.

Arnie paused on the landing. A single bloom from Rouge's bouquet could stand for 'I am jealous', but that didn't fit. 'I wish you joy' was another line. No, not that one. Rouge was anything but cliché. Arnie opened the stairwell door, still determined to divine their meaning before he carried the flowers to Ali. If there was something subversive in the bouquet, he would dump it.

When he entered the sterile corridor on Ali's floor, he dragged his feet all the way toward the door at the end. 'Let us be friends' was the last thing he could think of in his floral lexicon. It was a harmless sentiment that would at least not cause her any pain. But now he recalled that only men read the instructions for flowers. Women knew how to operate them without manuals.

The door to her room was open, and she was still sitting on the edge of the high bed, feet dangling like a child perched on grown-up furniture. The child in stiletto heels slipped down to the floor and walked toward him, looking

402

over his shoulder to the hallway beyond, slow to understand that Rouge was not coming.

Arnie had botched her errand, the only thing she had ever asked of him. What could he say to ease her disappointment? He held out the bouquet, old reliable mainstay of men in deep trouble with women. 'These are from Rouge.'

Ali accepted the roses and carried them to the better light of the window. He followed close behind, prepared to fling himself on her if she tried to jump from the third-floor balcony – or if she cried. 'Rouge said to thank you for the flowers you left on Susan's grave. A hyacinth and a peony?'

This startled Ali. Had he screwed up? Had he missed another meaning?

Cradling the bouquet in one arm, she tore away the wrapping, the better to study the individual blooms, as if each one were the separate word of a very important message.

Women and their dark art of reading flowers.

And now the forgotten thing was remembered – the text in the roses, the last line from the cheat sheet, 'Let us forget.' Arnie leaned his head against the cool window glass and called himself a fool.

Of course she had no use for his own fumbling attempts at comfort. She had wanted pain, and lots of it, for this was the stuff of atonement. And it could only come from Rouge Kendall, survivor of the pair that had been ruined, killed by half. But instead of hurting her, Rouge had given Ali something fine and good. Now her arms were flooded with the color of morning sun born out of darkness, symbols of purification by its fire – yellow roses of forgiveness.

She was smiling, healed and whole. Of course, she still had the scar and a twisted mouth – Rouge was good, but not that good. Yet somehow the prescient young cop had known exactly what Ali needed and precisely when she would be ready to receive it.

As the locals were fond of saying – all of St Ursula's children were strange.

EPILOGUE

Winter was late again this year. Perhaps order had not been completely restored to Makers Village; the dust had not yet settled in all the chimneys. He had paced through the month of December, waiting on some event he could not name.

This Christmas morning was another anniversary of Susan Kendall's death. Her oldest friend laid a bouquet of snow-white flowers on her grave. Next, Paul Marie stopped by Father Domina's simple stone marker. The old priest had lingered only long enough to hand over the stewardship of his parish, never doubting that Father Marie would accept.

The church had been filled on his first Sunday behind the pulpit – a record attendance. One year later, they still came in great numbers, and this mystified him. Surely by now they had found him out as a fraud, one who went through the motions with no feeling or faith. He looked down at the tattoos on the backs of his hands. Perhaps it was only novelty that so intrigued his parishioners. He toyed with the idea of emblazoning his vestment with an elaborate *C* for convict.

He said a ritual prayer over Father Domina's grave. It was only a small spate of words that meant very little to him, and so his mind wandered even as he spoke. What would the old man think if he knew his acolyte had ambitiously evolved into a hypocrite, an agnostic *and* a heretic. In closing the prayer, Father Marie addressed the Lord, Who *might* exist, in the too familiar form of 'You Bastard'. He alternately referred to God as the Great Baby Killer in the sky.

As he walked away from the old priest's grave, he still held one bright cluster of flowers. Their colors reminded him of a child's paint box. He held them up for Sadie's mother to see from the distance of the gravel path.

'Aw, they're beautiful,' said Becca Green as he came closer. She sat on a stone bench, holding her own bizarre bouquet, a loose arrangement of dead blooms, their large heads impaled on wire stems. She clutched them tightly, not yet ready to commit them to the ground.

'An odd color for sunflowers.' He smiled as he knelt by the brass vase at the base of Sadie's stone.

'Gwen gave them to me last Mother's Day – filling in for Sadie. She couldn't find anything purple at the florist shop, so she got these. She thought Sadie would've bought me sunflowers – so bright and cheerful. Of course, that was before Gwen painted them.' Becca looked down on the dead flowers encased in thick globs of dark purple. 'I thought that was so great. I laughed – Harry cried.' And now one stalk dropped to the ground and went unnoticed. 'Ah, Gwen, what a practical kid. I thought Sadie might appreciate the joke more than Harry did.'

Though Gwen Hubble never came near the cemetery, he had seen the child in church every Sunday. She walked without a cane these days, and the bruised look in her eyes was passing off. He had taken this for a sign of healing.

He remained at Becca's feet beside the monument, a low piece of slanted marble with a violet cast, engraved with letters of a simple elegant script. He finished arranging his flowers in the brass container and looked up at her. 'David Shore doesn't come anymore?'

Becca shook her head. 'He has a new girlfriend. Sadie had a big heart – when she was alive. I don't think she would have minded.'

Over the past year, the priest and Becca Green had wandered into a strange friendship over the graves of children. He had heard all the best Sadie stories. But this was the first time the mother had alluded to death. All their previous talks had centered on the exploits of a very lively child. And Becca had never brought flowers before; that was a service one performed for the dead, and it would have interfered with her deep denial.

In the months following Sadie's funeral, there had been so many flowers heaped on this plot of earth, the engraved marble had been hidden from sight. One family had driven a hundred miles to lay a wreath on the grave. And now and then, the priest would encounter policemen walking through the cemetery, their large meaty hands awkwardly clutching small sprays of delicate violets.

Today the stone was exposed. Becca could read the dates of life and death – if she chose to. But she only stared at her hands, plump and white, folded around the painted flowers. 'Gwen came by the house yesterday.'

'Is she done with the therapist?'

'Not yet. She still has a lot of strange ideas.'

'Does it upset you when she visits?'

'No, I love having her around the house. Oh, I almost forgot.' She rooted deep in her coat pocket and pulled out an envelope. 'Harry's latest batch of baby pictures. Gwen says the kid looks just like Sadie.'

He sat down on the cold stone bench beside Becca and looked at each photo with great care. Yes, the likeness was there in the large brown eyes and the wide generous mouth of the infant. The mother also bore a resemblance to her many wallet photographs of Sadie.

When he turned to Becca, she wore a puzzled expression and held the purple sunflowers closer to her breast. 'I wish I knew what happened in that cellar.'

So Gwen had been at her again, attempting to heal her best friend's mother, driving Becca insane to make her well.

'The kid does have a good argument.' Becca said this tentatively, as though testing the words in her mouth. 'Yesterday, Gwen said—' And now the rest of the dark flowers fell to the ground at her feet. 'She said – only Sadie could have known what commands the dog would respond to. I keep thinking about that dummy they found in the cellar, the one Gwen used to train the dog. It all happened just the way she said it did. The holes in the ground, the dead dog – everything. And that bastard was attacked by the dog, wasn't he? And his knife wound – that was real. Gwen could never—'

'Becca, let it go.' This woman was in deep trouble, and he was ill equipped to help her. In the church-approved role of *advocatus diaboli*, he might point out that the mushroom lady's journals were a more likely source for the dog's commands, though no such mention was made in any of the newspaper excerpts.

'Listen!' She grabbed his hand and squeezed it hard. 'There's more. Only Sadie could have told her I was pregnant. I didn't know for sure myself until that afternoon. Just before Sadie left the house, my doctor called to confirm the test. I didn't tell Harry until after the funeral. But Gwen knew about the baby before my own husband did – and Marsha Hubble backs that up.'

Or perhaps at some earlier date, Becca had given away her secret by keeping Sadie waiting on a sidewalk, lingering awhile in front of a store window decorated with cribs and baby clothes. And there was another possibility. 'Gwen might have talked to Sadie before she died.'

Becca shook her head. 'Gwen says Sadie wasn't conscious in the boathouse. That medical examiner, Chainy, he told me she was dead by then. He showed me the report. The blow that knocked her out was the one that killed her. Sadie died the day that freak stole her from me – over a week before they found Gwen.'

'*If* Dr Chainy was right.' He had no great faith in either realm, supernatural or scientific.

She squeezed his hand again. 'So what happened in that cellar?' The wind whipped up around them, collecting the painted flowers and driving them toward the grave. 'Where do

I put my faith? In a little girl's crazy story – or a pathologist's report?'

'Both things could be true,' he said, raising his voice with this lie, so the wind wouldn't take it. 'Gwen didn't believe she could survive all alone. So her best friend came back for her. Does it matter *where* Sadie came from – Gwen's own mind or that shallow grave?' He lifted Becca's face to his and winced at the mad hope in the woman's eyes.

No – call it faith. Becca needed to believe that Sadie was an ongoing little force of nature before she could let go of her child. Gwen had understood that. Why hadn't he?

'It doesn't matter, Becca. They were so bound to one another, one child couldn't leave the other behind—' He began to revise his deception, hunting for better words. He had spun so many tales for the parish, this should have been so easy. It was not.

And Becca Green was not comforted. Bright woman, she knew the sound of lies. Her eyes were decomposing now, giving him a view of the grave and its attendants, things that writhed and slithered, worms of the mind. He had failed her by planting doubt in a child's ghost story.

Her face was a work of agony: her mouth opened and closed, as though gasping for air, making strangled sounds. His arms enfolded her, and he held her for a very long time. It had begun to snow, and a hard wind was driving the flakes into his skin, stinging him as he rocked Becca, gently stroking her hair until the ground at his feet was shrouded in swirling white and he had read the words on Sadie's monument for the hundredth time: 'Beloved child'. Snowflakes filled in the graven letters, and he closed his eyes.

'Sadie can't be dead.' Her voice was muffled against his coat. She shivered. He held her closer, believing she was only cold. The snow had ceased, but the wind was rising and roaring all around them. The woman in his arms began to shake and thrash in a full-blown seizure. She screamed, and he came undone in his panic. This was his fault; he had brought this upon her. Her pain was cruel, and it was coming all at once – too fast. She could not stand it, and he could think of nothing to ease it or slow it. Her body was quaking so violently he feared that she would fly apart.

Then the wind ceased abruptly, and she lay exhausted against his chest, a spent storm of a woman. The world was utterly quiet and still as she lifted her wet face from the folds of his coat.

'How could Sadie be dead?' Louder now, she said, 'Tell me how!' One hand formed into a claw and raked through her hair as she moved away from him. 'I wake up every *single* morning, hoping it was all a lying dream. *Praying* that it never happened – that this damned piece of granite didn't even *exist*!'

She thrust out one angry fist toward the carved stone and then fell silent. Stunned, she slowly turned her head to stare at the surrounding grounds. Her eyes came back to Sadie's grave.

The sheltering windbreak of their own bodies had allowed a light cover of snow to accumulate over this one plot of earth, while all the rest had been swept clean – as if the snow had fallen on Sadie's grave and no other. The priest knew it for a hoax, only an illusion of the elements. The rational explanation was there for anyone to see. Yet Becca's eyes were shining, entranced and enchanted.

Paul Marie bowed his head, but not to pray. The woman beside him was smiling now, and he was the one in deep pain. So there they were, two people of radically different faiths, for hers was great and his was small.

He knew she was finding more ghosts in the weather, as though this fragile white covering of snowflakes might be a grand gesture of sorts – to erase the grave from her sight, hiding solid proof of Sadie's death, allowing a mother to keep her child alive for one more day – a present for Becca.

Paul Marie stared at her radiant face, and there he found peace. He would not be the one to say that she was deluded.

Maybe there was a God. And perhaps the Almighty had learned a bit of humility, for the priest now saw this unnatural act of deceit by snow as almost human in the frailty of a lie.